Sing a Song of Murder

KD Ryder

This book is a work of fiction. Any resemblance to any actual persons, living or dead, is purely coincidental.

First publication March 2012 as The Elements of a Murder

ISBN-10: **0615609090**
ISBN-13: **978-0615609096**

DEDICATION

This book is dedicated to my father, who is also an author, who line edited the first draft and helped me see things about my writing that I never noticed. Thanks, Dad

SING A SONG OF MURDER

PROLOGUE

It wasn't supposed to work this way.

It was the last thought the boy had before slipping into unconsciousness. His mouth gaped vainly for air; his eyes bugged out of his reddening face, staring up at the dark-haired man who had pinned him to the ground. The man's fingers encircled the boy's neck, thumbs pressing against his larynx, squeezing the life out of him.

A horse danced and snorted at the end of the reins that were looped around the boy's left wrist, tugging the boy's arm uselessly to the side as the horse tried to pull away from the life-and-death struggle going on at his feet.

A moment later, the terror left the boy's face, the body relaxed, and he lay still, his eyes staring unseeing at the storm clouds building overhead. Slowly, warily, the man relaxed his grip on the boy's throat and straightened up.

The man straddled the body, breathing hard, his left knee pinning down the boy's right arm, his right foot flat on the ground next to the boy's chest, ready to propel himself away from the horse if necessary.

He glanced at the animal and lurched unsteadily to his feet, shaking from the adrenaline. The horse started to move away, dragging the boy with him, so the man untangled the reins from the boy's wrist and led the horse away from the body. He leaned against a tree, holding the reins, trembling, while he caught his breath and looked back at what he had done.

He reflected that the horse had actually helped by keeping the boy's left arm outstretched to the side, unable to hit or scratch. Probably made the difference between getting the man's DNA under the kid's fingernails or not. One less thing to worry about, not that anyone could ever trace the kid to him anyway. This was the first time they'd ever met.

He glared over at the other man, the blond man who had witnessed the whole thing in stunned silence and was still standing there staring at the kid's face. The dark-haired man scowled. It was all *his* fault. *He* was the one who had picked the kid out. *He* should have known the boy was lying about who he was. Shit. Idiot kid should have known better than to try the stunt he had pulled, hiding in the bushes with a camera like that. He should have just done what he was told to do and shut up about it.

But he hadn't. At least it was over now, and they had his camera and tape recorder.

There was exactly one person who could connect him to the boy, and his very presence at the boy's death would forever ensure his silence. Thanks to the felony murder law, the blond man legally was as responsible for the boy's death as if he had strangled him himself. The look on his face said as clearly as words that he knew that, too.

The dark-haired man flinched when the crack of a distant gunshot reverberated through the trees, reminding him that they were not alone in these woods. The body needed to be moved, quickly, away from there before any hunters happened by. The body would likely be found one day, but as long as it wasn't found where he was killed, there would be no way to connect the kid's death to any trace evidence that could prove either man had been there.

It was time for the blond man to do his part now. The dark-haired man shoved away from the tree and led the horse over to the other man. He tossed him the reins and nodded toward the body. "Get rid of it."

Part I
October 16 – November 2, 1993
The Accident

CHAPTER 1

IT WAS HARLEY WATSON'S First Commandment, and Jim Harrison knew he must obey it: Thou shalt not give the press the time of day without permission.

The Second Commandment was like it: Thou shalt not give the press the *correct* time of day, even with permission.

It was a game he had learned to play in the three months since coming to work for the sheriff of the small county located about thirty miles from Denver. Sheriff Harley Watson wanted things done his way, and Detective Jim Harrison had to go along to get along. Giving the press the runaround was a minor compromise compared to some of the things he'd been expected to go along with while working in the big city.

He'd refused to go along with his previous bosses. Refused and found himself ostracized from one department; refused and found himself quitting another department to avoid the inevitable. His father's old fishing buddy, Sheriff Harley Watson, had hired him after his last unplanned deviation from his chosen career path. Somehow, he had to make this job work – or give up being a cop for good.

Compared to Jim's previous bosses, Harley Watson was a pussycat – a bit gruff on the outside, a bit of a redneck, a bit of a chauvinist, a bit controlling, but basically a decent, hard-working, law-abiding guy. He was a lot like Jim's late father had been.

Jim didn't really mind playing Harley's "beat the press" game. He wasn't all that fond of the news media, either.

But sometimes it wasn't that easy to obey Harley's Rules.

On this cold mid-October Saturday, Jim had driven up the mountain to the parking lot where he expected to rendezvous with a helicopter who would take him to the scene of a hunting accident. He wasn't thinking about Harley's Rules while he opened the car door and took a deep breath of the crisp, pine-scented air and glanced at the ominous gray clouds overhead. He was thinking about the weather. The ground was already lightly frosted with the leavings of a brief snow flurry that had come and gone a couple hours previously and he hoped the expected snow storm would hold off long enough to get the helicopter to the injured man.

He also hoped the injured man would live long enough to make the effort successful.

The initial call to 911 had reported a riding accident involving a deer hunter. The victim was lying with his head on a rock, unconscious, and bleeding from a wound on the forehead.

Jim had surveyed the parking lot as he drove in, noting as a matter of habit the vehicles present. On opposite sides of the parking lot, two Ford four-wheel-drive pickup trucks with horse trailers were parked. Both were lightly coated with snow crystals and had local license plates and he jotted down the license numbers after he stopped. One of the trailers bore on its sides the identification "Mike Griffith Packing and Outfitting" and a saddled buckskin gelding with orange ribbons tied to his tail and mane was tied to that trailer. The horse paced at the end of its tie rope, alternately pawing the ground and whinnying toward the forest, blasting a cloud of white vapor with every frantic call. There were no people present in the parking lot.

Jim had called Dispatch after he arrived and was told that additional information had been received. The caller now speculated the man may have fallen off his horse and been kicked. If that were true, Jim surmised, this horse was probably the perpetrator. In any event, the man had been unconscious for at least two hours at this point, and the injuries suggested the likelihood of brain damage. This was one rider who would not be able to get right back on again after a fall. The connection was breaking up when the dispatcher relayed some final information, the name of the victim and the name of the person reporting the injury, but Jim couldn't make out either name. Knowing he could get all that information at the scene, he didn't ask for a repeat.

He glanced at the clouds gathering overhead and hoped the helicopter could get in and out before snow would turn the rescue from a quick airlift into a time-consuming carry-out. Four miles is a long way to hike carrying an accident victim through a snowstorm, and if they had to abort the helicopter, it would take another hour and a half just to get rescuers to the victim.

The silence was shattered by another shrill whinny, and the horse pawed the ground again. Jim climbed out of the Blazer and walked over to the animal. "Easy, boy," he said as he approached. The horse pricked his ears at Jim, then tossed his head and whinnied again.

Jim slid a hand along the horse's neck and grasped the butt of a rifle sticking out of the scabbard on the horse's right side. He pulled the gun out and stepped away from the horse. Unloading the rifle with experienced ease, he wiped it down with a rag and put it in the back of the Blazer for safekeeping. Apart from the risk of some unauthorized person gaining access to a loaded weapon, it looked like a nice rifle and Jim didn't want it to get damaged by exposure to snow.

The helicopter was on the way, and would pick Jim up in the parking lot of the trail head for the Mount Evans wilderness area, located in the Rocky Mountains about forty miles from Denver. Permission had been obtained to land the helicopter in the legally protected wilderness. The rescuers would stabilize the victim and carry him to the helicopter before hiking out on foot. There would be no room in the chopper for passengers once the patient was aboard.

Jim had already changed into hiking boots and was just pulling a wool-lined cap over his short brown hair, covering his ears against the cold, when another car pulled into the parking lot and skidded to a halt about ten feet away.

Glancing quickly at the driver, he saw a young woman with curly red hair and a determined look on her face. For a moment, he wondered if she could be a relative of the victim, then he noticed the police scanner on the dashboard and groaned, exhaling a cloud of vapor into the cold October air. Not a reporter already. He looked up. Where was that damn helicopter? Grabbing his heavy jacket from the seat, he pulled it on quickly over the long-sleeved shirt he wore, covering up the handgun he carried in a shoulder holster. He checked the pockets of the jacket to make sure his gloves were there, then reached between the seats for his clipboard and shut the door of the Blazer.

"Excuse me," the woman called, climbing out of the white Subaru wagon. "Are you with the sheriff's office?"

He glanced at the county insignia on the side of the Blazer. He might have brushed her off without a word in accordance with Harley's First Commandment, but wearing plain clothes doesn't help conceal the identity of someone who has just climbed out of a marked car. Besides, Jim's mother had taught him better than to be rude to anyone, reporter or not, Harley's Rules notwithstanding. Reluctantly, Jim turned back to her. Mentally, he noted her physical description as if he were filling out a report. Female Caucasian, age approximately thirty, about five foot five, curly red hair, green eyes, average build. Little makeup in evidence. Wearing a bulky white ski jacket, black stretch pants, hiking boots, black knit cap, and tan deerskin gloves. She was attractive, but there was no space on any of his report forms for that attribute, so he didn't consciously note it.

He'd never met her before but suspected she was the reporter Billy Williams had warned him about. Jim's now-retired predecessor had laughed about how determined she was to get a story and how determined Sheriff Watson was not to cooperate with her in any way. Billy Williams had elevated the following of Harley's Rules to a fine art form in his dealings with the ambitious young woman. Jim had managed to avoid most encounters with the press so far, but now that he was the only detective on the squad, he supposed he would have to get used to it. Billy's last day had been almost three weeks ago. Jim was now the keeper of Harley's commandments, but that didn't mean he had to be rude. "I'm Detective Jim Harrison," he admitted. "What can I do for you?"

"Detective? You must have taken Billy's place. Nice to meet you." She thrust out her hand. "I'm Sheila Fernelli. *Rocky Mountain Chronicle*. I understand you've got a medical rescue going on."

He shook her hand briefly. Her grip was strong and assertive. Her gaze was steady and bold. "That's correct, and I have no comment to make. I just got here."

"Do you know if he's expected to live?" she persisted.

Jim heard the helicopter and looked up without answering. He waved at the pilot, then turned and locked up the county Blazer.

Ignoring the reporter, he walked over toward the wide spot in the road where the chopper was landing. Dust and snow swirled in the downdraft from the rotor as the chopper settled lightly to the ground. He glanced back at the horse, who was wide-eyed with fright, pulling against the rope he was tied with, but the rope held and Jim turned back to the helicopter.

Sheila followed him. "Detective Harrison, this is really big news. Can I ride in with you in the helicopter?"

Jim turned on his heel to face her with a frown. "What big news? A hunting accident? As far as I know, he's not even dead. Since when is that newsworthy?" At six-foot two, he towered over the reporter, noting that the top of her head came about to his chin.

Sheila stopped short, looking up at the broad-shouldered detective without flinching. "Don't you know who it is? It's Ryan North." She met Jim's blank stare. "The singer," she added urgently. "You know, the one who lived in Denver until a couple years ago. International celebrity. So, yes, it is very newsworthy. This will be all over the country within hours and I'm the first reporter on the scene."

"How do you know who it is?" he demanded. "I just heard the name myself a few minutes ago, but the transmission was garbled." He shot a glance at her police scanner. That couldn't have been it; that transmission had been made less than five minutes previously. She must have known before she started up the mountain, or why was she here at all? "Who told you? Are you eavesdropping on cell phone calls now?"

"Of course not," she retorted. "That's illegal. I can't reveal my sources. Please. Let me go in with you. It's really important."

"Not a chance, Miss," Jim replied, abruptly turning back to the chopper. "Not a chance." He climbed in with the rescue workers and the aircraft lifted into the sky, leaving Sheila Fernelli standing in another swirl of dust and snow. He glanced down once as the craft ascended, feeling the slightest twinge of guilt. She was just doing her job. But Rules were Rules, and following them was now *his* job.

Less than ten minutes later, the helicopter set down in a clearing a few hundred yards from the victim. Jim and the rescue volunteers climbed out and made their way downhill over the rough, rocky terrain to the injured man, carrying the Stokes litter. As reported, he was lying on his back, his head on a rock. A trickle of dried blood ran from a wound on his forehead down the side of his head, where it matted his dark brown hair. A pink rain slicker, a saddle blanket, and a red plaid jacket with a bright orange vest still held in place by the jacket sleeves covered the man's body from neck to feet. A bearded blond man wearing an orange hunting cap and a green polo shirt knelt at his side, holding the victim's hand, oblivious to the dusting of snow still clinging to the hair on his own bare arms. Relief mixed with anxiety on his face as he stepped back to let the rescuers work. A pair of binoculars and another orange hunting cap lay on the ground by the victim's head.

Standing on the other side of the victim were a middle-aged man holding a cell phone and a teenage girl, both dressed for hunting, also wearing orange caps and vests. The girl looked like she was about to cry. They moved away as the rescue team reached the victim.

Three horses were tied to trees. One was unsaddled, her back damp from melted snow. A saddle was lying on the ground. All three horses were festooned with bright orange ribbons on their heads and tails, and the two that were still saddled sported hunting rifles sticking up from scabbards on the off sides and binoculars hanging from the saddle horns.

Jim took in the scene without comment as he approached, mentally noting who was where, what they were doing, how they were dressed, and their emotional state. He rapidly jotted notes on his clipboard. He paused by the victim for a minute, looking briefly at his injuries. The dispatcher had told him this was a riding accident, but the injuries did not seem to bear that out. The paramedic handed him a wallet and Jim removed the driver's license, confirmed that the victim's name was indeed Ryan North, replaced it, then handed the wallet back to the paramedic who slipped it inside the victim's jacket. After seeing for himself what there was to see, Jim finally approached the middle-aged man.

"I'm Detective Harrison," he said. "You called in the report?"

"No, but I found him. I'm Howard Vincent. That man actually made the first call on his cell phone." He nodded toward the blond man still crouched anxiously by the victim. "I have the phone now so I could tell the chopper where we were. He didn't want to leave his side after we got here."

"What can you tell me about what happened?"

"Not much, I'm afraid." Howard Vincent quickly explained that they had been looking for deer when his daughter Cindy had spotted the man through binoculars. He had left Cindy to try to keep the victim warm while he went for help. He had seen nobody until about thirty minutes later, when he had encountered the blond man. "His name is Doug something. He said he was looking for his hunting companion. Said his horse had returned without him. Soon as I described the man, he knew it was his friend. Luckily he had a cell phone with him, so we didn't have to ride all the way back out to call for help. After we got back here, he gave me the phone and I stayed on the line until you landed. That's really all I know. He's lying exactly where we found him. It's Ryan North, you know. Cindy recognized him right off."

Jim took Vincent's name and address, then walked back over to the victim and addressed the blond, bearded man kneeling by his feet. "Excuse me," he said. "I understand you know the victim?"

Ever since help had arrived, the blond man had been crouched on the ground at Ryan North's feet, staying out of the way of the rescuers but watching every move they made. He had put his jacket back on when the rescuers tossed it aside with the slicker and horse blanket. He glanced up at the detective, stared a moment at the clipboard Jim held, then got to his feet.

"May I have your name, please?" Jim asked.

"Just a minute. Who are you? A reporter?"

"Detective Harrison. Sheriff's office." He moved the tail of his jacket aside so the man could see the badge that hung from his belt.

The blond man's eyes narrowed. "Why'd they send a cop? There's been no crime committed here. I said it was a riding accident. All I wanted was medical assistance."

"Sheriff's department is responsible for all rescue activity, and I'll decide if there's been a crime committed or not," Jim replied firmly. "This looks like an assault case to me. Now, please tell me your name and relationship to Mr. North."

With a scowl, the man replied, "Doug Norton. I'm his business partner. We were hunting together."

"Mr. Vincent said he met up with you alone on the trail, after he found Mr. North."

"We came up here together, but we split up around eight o'clock."

"So he was alone when the accident happened?"

"As far as I know." He gestured at Howard Vincent. "He said he was alone when they found him."

"When did you first realize he was missing?"

"We were supposed to meet at a trail crossing at noon. I was late getting there, so I figured he'd gone on to the parking lot. When I got there, I found his horse so I came back to look for him." He sighed. "I told him he shouldn't have ridden that horse," he muttered, half to himself.

Jim glanced up at him. "What do you mean?"

"That horse of his is half-trained, young, and spirited. He's never been hunting before but my stubborn … buddy … insisted on using him." He sighed again. "This wouldn't have happened if he'd listened to me."

Jim detected a slight catch in Norton's voice and took note of the caring concern reflected in Norton's last comment, a sharp contrast to his open hostility of only a few moments before. "Anything noteworthy about the horse when you found him? Broken reins? Scrapes?"

"No."

"I take it this is the buckskin I saw in the parking lot?"

"Yes."

"I put the rifle in my car for safekeeping."

"Oh. Guess I forgot about it."

"What did you do after you tied up the horse?"

"I thought the horse had pulled away from him and left him on foot. I wasn't too worried, because we both know this area like the backs of our hands from when we were teenagers. Figured I'd find him walking out. I was maybe twenty, thirty minutes in when I ran into that man and he told me he'd found him." He nodded toward Howard Vincent.

"How late were you getting to the trail crossing?"

"What difference does that make?"

Jim looked up from his clipboard to meet Doug Norton's defiant gaze. The hostility was back just as suddenly as it had left. "Just answer the question, please. I'm trying to figure out when he might have fallen."

Doug glared back at him for several seconds before answering, "I don't know. Maybe a half hour."

Jim glanced at his watch and made a note. "The little girl said she recognized him as the singer. Is that correct? Not someone else with the same name?"

Doug glanced over at Cindy Vincent and sighed. "Yes. I was hoping to keep that quiet, but I guess it doesn't matter."

Jim realized that the switchboard to the tiny sheriff's office was about to be swamped over the next few hours with demands for information that would not be forthcoming. Harley Watson hated the media, but he especially hated the tabloid reporters who tended to follow celebrities wherever they went. Jim surmised he would probably write a third commandment after this incident, something like, Thou shalt deny any rumors that a celebrity has been seen in the county, especially if one has been. A fourth might quickly follow: Thou shalt get all injured celebrities out of the county by the quickest means possible and let the media uproar be in someone else's jurisdiction.

Jim finished by getting Norton's address in Denver. He suspected Doug Norton wasn't any fonder of the media than Harley was.

The rescuers had Ryan North strapped onto the litter and stood up, ready to take him to the helicopter. Doug Norton started to follow, but Jim stopped him with a firm hand on his arm. "Sorry, Mr. Norton, you can't go with them."

"I have to go with him," Doug argued, angrily shrugging off Jim's restraining hand.

"Regulations. I'm sorry. Please don't make this difficult, Mr. Norton. I know you're concerned, but I can't let you go in the chopper.

They're taking him to Lakewood General. I could ask Wayne to take your horses back home for you and someone could give you a ride to the hospital if you want."

"Never mind," Doug answered, "I don't need any favors from you." He looked back at the trail, where his horse stood tied to a tree. He retrieved his cell phone from Howard Vincent and called Mike Griffith, the owner of the ranch where the horses were kept. After arranging for Griffith to bring another truck to pick up the horses and trailer, he had a quick discussion with Howard Vincent, then mounted his horse and rode back down the trail as quickly as the rocky terrain would allow.

From years of experience working homicide investigations, Jim was quite familiar with the appearance of different kinds of injuries. The two-inch long bleeding gash over his left eye could not have been caused by the rock he had landed on, but any sign of a possible scuffle which would have suggested another person had caused the injury had been obliterated by the half inch accumulation of snow covering the ground. And it didn't look like the kind of damage he would have expected if the horse had kicked or stepped on him after he fell.

He walked back to Howard Vincent. "When you got here, had it already been snowing?"

"No."

Cindy spoke up. "It started a while after my dad left to go for help. I tried to keep it off him," she added in a whisper.

"Did you notice the ground while you were waiting?" Jim asked the girl gently. "Did you see any footprints near him before the snow started?"

"I didn't notice. I don't think so. I put my rain slicker on him. I didn't know what else to do." She turned her face into her father's chest and started to sob. Jim looked at her curiously, wondering why she was so upset. Didn't she know she had probably saved the man's life?

"I don't think there were any," Howard Vincent said, holding his daughter and patting her back. "Anyway, I didn't see anything but hoof prints."

"Well, I don't understand how he got hurt like that, then," Jim said. "It looks like he was hit on the forehead with a two-by-four."

Howard Vincent looked around uneasily. "Never thought about that. I sure wouldn't have left Cindy alone with him if I'd thought there was someone else out here."

Cindy had stood back, wide-eyed, while men had worked quickly over the singer she idolized. "I hope he doesn't die," she had whispered over and over, tears trickling down her face while her father stood behind her, holding her by the shoulders, murmuring, "He'll be okay. You did fine." Now she sobbed openly into her father's chest while the men talked.

Jim surveyed the area, hoping to spot a broken branch that might have been used as a club, but found nothing in the vicinity. Then he looked up at the trees. The wind-whipped Bristlecone pines sported solid, heavy branches that stuck out perpendicular to the stark white trunks. On a hunch, he climbed on Vincent's horse and examined a solid bare branch sticking out from a tree at face level about ten feet behind where the injured man had lain.

"Blood," he declared, finding a fine red spray on the stark white branch. "Looks like his horse ran him into a branch." He dismounted and made a few notes on his clipboard. Unless the man died, there was nothing else for him to do. For all his unwarranted hostility, Doug Norton had been right. No crime had been committed that Jim could see. It wasn't an assault after all.

Jim tied the horse and walked back over to the Vincents, picking up the rain slicker from the ground where the paramedics had tossed it. He folded it and handed it to Cindy. "Thanks for taking care of him until we could get help here," he said.

"Will he be all right?" she asked, wiping her face with a handkerchief her father had handed her. "I tried so hard to keep him warm. I didn't think about putting the horse blanket on him until later. There was so much snow I couldn't keep it all off him. Why didn't I think of it sooner? What if he dies now? It will be all my fault. Dad told me to keep him warm."

Jim saw her lip quiver and he touched her chin gently as the tears started to flow again, finally understanding why she was so distraught. "No, it won't, Miss Vincent. It was clever of you to think of the horse

15

blanket at all. I don't think I would have. You did all you could; now the doctors will take care of him. Remember, if you hadn't found him, he wouldn't have had any chance at all. You understand that?"

She nodded, unable to speak. Her father patted her shoulder, then picked up the saddle blanket and began saddling her horse. Up the hill, the helicopter's engines reached a high whine as the craft lifted gently from the ground and turned east, carrying Ryan North to safety.

Howard and Cindy Vincent mounted their horses and said good-bye to Jim Harrison. Howard had promised to keep an eye on Ryan and Doug's horses until the outfitter came to retrieve them, and they followed Doug's trail toward the trailhead. Jim Harrison and the rescue workers began the long hike out on foot.

Harley Watson, the county sheriff, was still waiting in the parking lot for Jim Harrison to hike out with the rescue workers an hour later. He had come out personally to control the reporters who had driven up the mountain as soon as the name of the victim was broadcast over the radio. There had been six reporters at one point but most of them had driven off toward town as soon as the helicopter passed overhead on its way to the hospital. He had allowed none of them to try to hike in to the scene.

Only Sheila Fernelli from the *Rocky Mountain Chronicle* remained to interview the rescuers. Doug Norton ignored both the burly, graying sheriff and the petite redheaded reporter, refusing comment on Ryan North's condition while he quickly tied his horse to the trailer next to the buckskin gelding who finally quieted now that his buddy had returned. Doug took a moment to lock his rifle in the horse trailer, then blocked the wheels with a rock, unhitched the trailer, got in the truck and drove down the road toward Lakewood.

Sheila watched in frustration as he drove away, then she turned her attention to interviewing Howard Vincent and his daughter when they emerged from the trailhead about ten minutes after the pickup truck disappeared around a bend. She knew Sheriff Harley "no relation to the motorcycle, thank God" Watson would never allow her to ask his detective any questions even if she waited for him to emerge from the woods. She already had learned the names of the rescue workers from their own dispatcher so she could contact them later, knowing from past experience that the sheriff wouldn't let any of them talk to her at the scene either. The sheriff's department was in charge of all rescue operations in the county, and none of the volunteers had ever talked to her in Harley's presence, although some of them would do telephone interviews. The Vincents were her only hope for any information, and she spent several minutes talking to both of them while Howard Vincent unsaddled and brushed his own horses before turning his attention to Ryan and Doug's horses. After learning all she could from them including Doug Norton's name, she got in her Subaru and drove to Lakewood, hoping to interview the elusive business partner at the hospital.

Jim Harrison and two of the rescue volunteers came into view of the parking lot just as Sheila turned onto the road leading back to Idaho Springs. He was surprised she had stayed around that long. The helicopter had left over an hour before.

He noticed Doug Norton had already left, and Howard Vincent had unsaddled the horses and was giving them all water while waiting for Mike Griffith to come get them. He had suspected from Norton's anxiety and agitation at the scene that he was much closer to Ryan North than he had let on and was sorry he couldn't have let Norton go with him in the helicopter, despite the man's apparent hostility toward Jim himself. But rules were rules. Even North's next of kin wouldn't have been allowed in the helicopter.

For now it didn't look like there was much of a case left. The rescue had been a success. The victim had lived long enough to get on the helicopter and on the way to the hospital. Jim would check with the hospital later to find out if North was expected to survive or not, but other than that he had nothing left to do but paperwork.

And, with Sheila Fernelli already driving down the mountain, he'd even managed to duck the press on this one.

Harley Watson would be pleased.

Jim felt a twinge of regret as he watched her drive away. Harley might be pleased she was gone, but Jim wasn't so sure *he* was.

He walked over to the sheriff's car to fill him in on the rescue.

A quarter mile from the place where Ryan North had lain unconscious on a rock, a fallen tree creaked as moisture trapped within its trunk froze, fracturing wood fibers and cracking bark due to the expansion of the ice crystals. The roots, torn from the earth as the tree fell earlier in the year, stretched skyward, clumps of earth still clinging in spots. In the hole vacated by the base of the tree, the dead body of a teenage boy was giving up the last of its heat to the frigid alpine air. Sightless eyes stared through the scant pile of branches that covered the body.

A rabbit, trying to reach its burrow under the boy's body, nudged against one of the branches, dislodging it from its position. The boy's hand, held in place by the branch, slowly flexed outward, finally flopping against another branch, sticking out through the pile, the hand drooping down.

The rabbit squeezed behind the boy's back and into its burrow.

The clouds overhead finally released their burden. It started to snow.

CHAPTER 2

"Forget Ryan North," Sheila Fernelli's editor insisted the following Friday morning. "I told you Dennis would handle the follow-ups. It's not even news any more now that he's out of the coma. Go cover the mayor's race in Silver Plume."

Frustrated, Sheila took her notepad and walked back to her own desk. Mayor's race. Some mayor's race. Two brothers were running against each other in a tiny town just west of Georgetown. Did anybody really care whether the race was won by Tweedledum or Tweedledee?

Grumbling under her breath, she reluctantly gathered up her purse and walked out to her car. She had tried to convince her boss to let her stay on the Ryan North case but the man had insisted this pathetic bit of small town politics was more newsworthy than trying to be the first to answer the question of whether Denver's darling, Ryan North, would ever sing again.

Prior to getting a job at the *Rocky Mountain Chronicle*, Sheila had spent two years working for a national tabloid, something she wasn't particularly proud of, but she had learned one thing in those two years: celebrity sells. A story about Ryan North, any story, would sell more newspapers, and hence more of their advertisers' products, than any story about any mayor's race in Silver Plume.

It would also bring much more attention and prestige to the reporter whose name was on the story.

She had been lucky to break the news about the accident. Dennis had been off that weekend, and Sheila had a source in the sheriff's dispatch office – an old friend who occasionally would call her with a tip if something happened to break in Clear Creek County. It was sheer luck that her friend found himself alone and unobserved in the dispatch room a few minutes after the call came in about the injured hunter. He quickly called her and let her know where to go, then managed to call her back

19

on her cell phone a few minutes later as she drove up to the trail head with the news that the injured hunter was none other than Ryan North.

Sources were everything in this business, but Sheila had to be careful not to take too great advantage of her friend. If Sheriff Harley Watson ever found out one of his people was leaking tips to a reporter, especially a female reporter, her friend's job would be in jeopardy. She knew she could never get any real inside information from him. The risk of being found out was too great. At best, her friend could give her a few minutes' head start on other reporters. It was better than nothing.

Since the accident, it had snowed for five solid days. Every morning and afternoon, Sheila Fernelli called the hospital and was told the same thing: No change in the condition of Ryan North.

Her editor would not let her go to the hospital and wait. Another reporter who lived in the area made a daily trip to the hospital to try to get an interview with Ryan North's business partner, who was believed to be staying in his room day and night.

Sheila wanted the story so badly she could taste it. She'd spent two years working for the tabloid, in large part fabricating marginally libelous stories about celebrities – most of whom she'd never been within a hundred yards of. Now she had a real story in her lap and her editor wouldn't even let her try to pursue it. It was officially assigned to the reporter who lived in Lakewood, Dennis Ingram.

The accident had happened on Saturday. She had spent Saturday evening in the lobby of the hospital waiting for any news, any chance to interview the partner. Surrounded by five other journalists on the same mission, Sheila had the slim advantage of having seen, however briefly, the man the Vincents later told her was Doug Norton, Ryan North's partner, while he tied his horse to the trailer before unhitching it and driving away. He had ignored her completely, not even snapping, "No comment," for which she had braced herself, when she asked if he would talk to her for a moment.

But she had known his name and what he looked like, and when he came to the lobby in search of a pay phone that evening, she had been the one who led the assault. He had been surrounded with microphones and cameras and had reluctantly told the crowd of reporters that Ryan

North had come through a surgical procedure to relieve pressure building up in his head several hours before but had not awakened from the anesthesia. He had a fractured skull. He was in a coma. The prognosis was uncertain. He could live or die. He could live and recover fully or survive with severe impairment. Nobody knew. And no, he didn't know how the accident had happened. He believed Ryan had fallen from his horse. And he would answer no other questions. Anything else would have to come from hospital administrators, who had been given permission to issue press releases if there was any change in Ryan North's condition.

Sheila had the slimmest advantage. She had talked to Howard and Cindy Vincent and learned that after Doug Norton left the scene, Detective Harrison had discovered that Ryan's horse had run him under the solid bare branch of an ancient Bristlecone pine. This had knocked him from the horse onto the rock, causing the head injury that now had his life hanging in the balance.

She didn't share that information with the other reporters. She called in her story, and she alone had that information. The other news agencies didn't have that information until a day later. Her moment in the sun had been just that – a moment. While pleased to have any exclusive information, the editor felt the story was not a story until something else happened, and that was up to Ryan North, not Sheila Fernelli.

So she continued to call, knowing it was now Dennis's story, but unable to let go.

In the midst of this vigil, another celebrity story broke. Colorado State Senator Gene Walker returned home from a convention to find his sixteen-year-old son was missing. For a few days, news of the disappearance bumped Ryan North's plight from the headlines. Again, Sheila was denied the opportunity to follow the story. The missing boy lived near Lakewood. Dennis could cover that story, too.

It was the day the snow finally stopped that Ryan North came out of the coma.

Unfortunately, her editor, although pleased that she had been first on the scene, nearly beating the sheriff's detective there, had been unmoved by her pleas to stay on the story. Not if it meant having her drive to the hospital every day, hoping to catch sight of North's business partner or to find a way to sneak in to Ryan's room. No, Dennis Ingram lived in Lakewood, not far from the hospital. It would be much easier for him to do the follow-up stories – especially now that Dennis was also working the story about the Senator's son who had run away from home the day of North's accident.

It was another celebrity story Sheila would have to read about. When would she get her chance at some real news?

She turned her car west on Interstate 70, heading for Silver Plume and an interview with Randy Jackson, the younger of the two candidates, regarding his views on law enforcement. Tomorrow she would get his brother Tom's opinion of the crime wave sweeping through their town. She had already done her homework. Illegal parking was up thirty percent over last year. Fifteen percent more loose dogs had been impounded. Two teachers had been caught driving under the influence of marijuana. And the sheriff's department had no leads regarding who had been shooting out streetlights with a BB gun. What plans did the Jackson brothers have to stop this terrible trend? Did they plan to call on the sheriff's department for increased patrols? Perhaps organize neighborhood block watches?

Oh, all right, so burglaries were also up and half the kids in town were smoking pot and using cocaine in a shack near the old silver mine behind the park every day. It still didn't qualify as a crime wave.

Probably the story would run on the want ad page, between the obituaries and the personal ads. With any luck, nobody would ever see it. Sheila would rather nobody knew how low she was having to stoop just to be able to say she was still a working journalist.

Oh, for one little scoop about something important. Or someone important. Something on her turf, where her editor would have to let her do the follow-up stories, instead of breaking the news then handing it off to someone else. To some man.

Later that afternoon she had just left Silver Plume to drive back toward the newspaper office in Idaho Springs to write up the interview with Randy Jackson when her stomach growled audibly and she realized she hadn't eaten anything since breakfast. Not wanting to wait the fifteen minutes to get back to town, she pulled off at Georgetown and parked in front of the tiny diner near the county courthouse. She was partial to their chicken and avocado sandwiches anyway.

The sheriff's department was housed in the east end of the courthouse building. She had been in there the morning after Ryan North's accident, trying to get some information about Detective Jim Harrison. Harrison was relatively new to the county and she was curious to know more of his background. She had known his predecessor, Billy Williams, rather well and thought him a chauvinistic pig like his boss Harley Watson. She had hoped Jim Harrison would prove to be different, but he had brushed her aside at their first meeting.

Unfortunately, Harley had shown her the door within two minutes of her arrival, explaining sarcastically that Jim Harrison's background was none of her business. He was fully qualified to do his job and she didn't need to know any more than that.

Later that day, she had called her friend in Dispatch at home and learned only that Jim had come from Denver Police in July after working homicide for several years. His personnel information, along with everyone else's, was locked up in Harley's office.

If Jim Harrison was the county's only detective, she knew their paths would cross again. Since it appeared Jim was going to be her new adversary, she wished she knew more about him. She glanced across the street at the row of windows on the south side of the building. The second window from the left was his. The one next to it was Harley's. She wondered briefly if Jim Harrison himself would consent to be interviewed for a human interest story about the big-city cop turned small-town sheriff's deputy, but before the thought finished forming in her mind, she dismissed it.

Harley Watson would never allow it anyway. And from what she'd already seen of Jim Harrison, he wouldn't be interested either. She sighed and walked into the restaurant to order her chicken sandwich to go.

Across the street, Jim Harrison happened to be looking out his window when the white Subaru pulled up to the diner and parked. He saw the red-haired reporter step out of the car and walk inside after glancing briefly in his direction. Was there some news to be found in the diner, or was she just hungry?

He had read her story about the rescue. While Harley had loudly denounced her writing style, her choice of sources, and her breast size all in the same tirade, Jim had been pleased with her treatment of the subject. She had given credit to the Alpine Rescue Team for their quick action in stabilizing and transporting the victim up the rocky slope to the waiting helicopter, and even given Jim himself a compliment by describing his discovery of the blood-spattered tree limb that was now blamed for knocking North from the horse.

He surmised she had done a good job interviewing Howard Vincent to get that much detail. The information about the tree limb had not made it to the first official press release, and even the second release did not describe the details of how Jim had reached that conclusion.

Jim was secretly happy with the story. It was the first time his name had appeared in the paper since his arrival at Clear Creek County and she had made him look good. But he had to keep his thoughts to himself on the matter. It was clear Harley had no use for reporters, and if Jim was going to make this new job work, he had better keep that in mind. He couldn't afford to get Harley upset with him already by trying to take sides in Harley's war with the media.

But Jim knew their paths would cross again someday and he was surprised to find himself looking forward to it. He wondered if she lived nearby, or ate at that diner very often. He had lunch there himself several times a week.

He was still staring out the window, hoping to catch sight of Sheila again, when Harley walked into his office, shut the door, then settled his ample frame into one of the visitor chairs in Jim's office. "You busy?" he asked gruffly.

Guiltily, Jim looked down at the report he had been writing before being distracted by the arrival of Sheila Fernelli across the street. "Busy but not on a deadline," he replied. "What's up?"

"Your ninety-day probation period was up last week. Never did the review. Thought this might be a good time for it."

Jim flushed. Fine time to be caught staring out the window. "Sure, no problem. Here or in your office?"

"Here's fine," Harley replied. He looked down at a paper in his hand. "This won't take long." He hesitated. "Good news is you're doing fine and I'm pleased with your work. I was just talking about you to Jeff Martenson in Gilpin County the other day. He was wondering how I managed to land a seven-year homicide veteran from Denver after taking that last round of budget cuts."

"What did you tell him?"

"I told him I was wondering the same thing myself and for him to stay the hell away from you. Last thing I need is someone bribing you away from here behind my back." He chuckled.

Jim smiled, relieved. Things were a little tough financially but he felt the job change had been worth it. "I appreciate that, Harley. So what's the bad news?"

"The bad news is that much as I'd like to, I can't give you more than a three percent raise until next year at least. I know when I hired you I said I'd try to get more money after ninety days but the Board says this is all they can do, especially since they approved my request for another patrolman."

Jim shrugged. "It's okay. I'm getting by all right. Thanks for trying."

"Well, keep up the good work, and stay away from Jeff Martenson, okay?"

"Sure, Harley. So that's the review?"

"That's the review. I figure if something ain't broke, don't fix it. You're no rookie. You know what you're doing. Keep doing it."

"Thanks. I appreciate that."

"Anything you'd like to say to me? Any problems I should know about?"

"Everything's fine, Harley."

"Things are a little slow right now, so take advantage of it. Learn all you can now while you have time."

"I've already figured out things are different out here. I've been reading through some of the old unsolved cases and realizing this is the other side of the missing persons coin."

"How do you mean?"

"In Denver, we work a lot of cases involving missing persons who are never found. Looks like out here you get a lot of unidentified bodies in the mountains. They're obviously missing from somewhere."

Harley nodded. "Yeah, I guess this is the other side of the coin, isn't it. Half the people who get murdered during the snow season around here seem to end up in the mountains somewhere. The bodies don't get found until after the spring thaw, sometimes not until years later. We've had our share, plus an occasional lost hiker or hunter that nobody knew was up here until the body is found. Billy got to work a case once where a mountain lion decided to make a snack out of the victim before anyone found the body. He got to search all over the mountain for body parts, plus try to help the coroner figure out if it was a homicide or accidental death."

Jim grunted. "I read the report. They decided it was a homicide, but looks like he never developed any likely suspects. At least that's one thing we didn't get much of in Denver. Usually the bodies were found where they were killed or the parts weren't much farther than the bottom of the nearest freezer. The suspects usually weren't too far away, either."

"Yeah, I know," Harley replied, rising to his feet. "When Denver's killers want to get away with murder, this is where they dump the bodies. Some of your old buddies in Denver are probably chasing their tails on a missing person report right now, and all the time the victim is out there somewhere, preserved like a frozen turkey under six feet of snow. Most of them will never be found. I guess given our budget, I should be glad about that. Imagine what your caseload would be if all the bodies out there ever were found."

As Harley left the office, Jim decided he didn't want to think about it too much. He already had five old cases to work on, plus a couple dozen new cases in three months. For a one-man department, that was definitely more than enough.

He glanced at a pile of missing-persons reports on the corner of his desk, glad they weren't from his jurisdiction. He had enough to do. He needed to file them somewhere, but hadn't finished moving Billy Williams' files out of the office yet. The latest was a teenage boy from Denver, a runaway. His father was a Colorado state senator. Funny the kid hadn't come home yet. Most runaways were back within seventy-two hours. He wondered idly if the boy was into drugs, like those kids in Silver Plume. One had recently OD'd at a party and nearly died.

He looked out the window again just in time to see the Subaru pull away from the curb and drive past the sheriff's office toward the freeway. He quickly noted the license plate number and typed it into the computer, thinking to get her address. Then, with a flash of shame, he hit the escape key before the information came up. What was the matter with him? He knew better than to use that computer for personal searches. Besides, she was a reporter, someone on the other side, his adversary. Harley had made that abundantly clear the first week Jim was in the department. Thou shalt not give the press the time of day, Jim reminded himself.

Jim didn't have to be told that becoming friendly with the spunky red-haired reporter was strictly out of the question. So it was none of his business where she lived.

* * *

While Sheila Fernelli ordered a chicken and avocado sandwich in Georgetown, Ryan North returned to surgery in Lakewood for removal of the drain in his head. With nothing to do until Ryan returned, Doug Norton went out on the fire escape for a cigarette, then he wandered down to the cafeteria for a cup of coffee. It was almost as cold in the cafeteria as it had been on the fire escape.

He had spent the entire week since the accident at Ryan's side, leaving only briefly to smoke a cigarette on the fire escape and occasionally to visit the cafeteria for coffee. The nursing staff had conspired to help him, providing a cot for him to sleep on and even running his clothes through the laundry since he refused to go home even once to pack a bag. Meals were sent up from the kitchen if he felt like eating. He knew he wasn't supposed to be there around the clock, but the hospital was unused to having a celebrity for a patient and with Doug there constantly they did not need to have a guard outside the door to keep out the more persistent reporters, so they allowed it.

Now he sat by a window, wearing his jacket, staring out at the snow-covered grounds, holding his cell phone in his hand. A couple of nurses he knew walked in and greeted him. He nodded back and resumed staring out the window. Every few minutes, he would start to call a number on his phone, but snapped it shut before he finished dialing. The battery had died the day of the accident after he spent a few hours notifying Ryan's manager and other associates about the situation but the night nurse had since lent him a compatible charger and he kept the phone with him constantly. But although it rang with a quiet musical tone occasionally, nobody had ever seen him answer it. He would always look anxiously at the display, then mute the tone and return it to his pocket, later listening to the messages left on voice mail, but nobody ever saw him return any calls the entire time Ryan was in the coma.

Nobody knew whose call he was hoping for … or avoiding.

After awhile, he slipped the phone back into his pocket and got up to get another cup of coffee. He glanced briefly at another man who had just entered the cafeteria. "Looks like we shopped in the same store," the man said, gesturing at Doug's plaid jacket. He had a similar jacket draped over his arm.

Doug glanced at it without much interest. "Sale at REI?"

"No, I got mine at Sears." He looked closer and said, "Guess they're not exactly the same, are they?"

"Guess not." Doug filled his coffee cup and returned to his seat.

The other man followed him. Doug ignored him and resumed staring out the window, sipping his coffee.

"So how's Ryan North doing?" the man finally asked.

"Why are you asking me?"

"Heard he was out of the coma."

"I heard that, too."

"How'd it happen, anyway?"

Doug shot him a glare. "What did the papers say?"

"Papers say he doesn't remember how it happened."

"Well, there you are then." He turned back to the window.

The man sipped his coffee. "I met him once."

"Good for you."

"He did an interview for a TV station I used to work for here in Denver. Ran into him in the hallway. He said hi."

"How thrilling for both of you, I'm sure," Doug muttered.

"I also know you from somewhere," the stranger said.

Doug pulled his gaze from the window again and looked at the other man. He was about forty, heavy build, with short blond hair and a beard. "I doubt it."

"I think so." The man took another sip of coffee. "I think I saw you last week. Tuesday night."

Doug's face reddened slightly in front of his ears. "I think you've confused me with someone else."

The man eyed Doug across his coffee cup. "I don't think so." His gaze held Doug's for a long moment. "I know who you are."

"And who do you think I am?"

"You're his partner."

"Whose partner?"

"Ryan North's."

Doug turned back to the window. "Anyone here could have told you that."

"Someone here did," the man admitted with a shrug. "Last Tuesday you were somebody else, though, weren't you?"

"I think you should go see the doctors on the seventh floor," Doug snapped. "You need a reality check."

The other man laughed. "You probably think I'm some snoopy reporter trying to trick you into an interview or something, don't you?"

"Or something."

"Look, your secret is safe with me. I'm not trying to start any trouble. I just saw you in here and recognized you and thought maybe you'd like some company."

"I don't even know you."

"Well, I know you, though, don't I?"

"I have no idea what you're talking about. I'm sure we've never met before and I'm starting to wish it had stayed that way." Abruptly, Doug stood, leaving his coffee on the table. He walked out of the cafeteria.

"Oh, hi, Mr. Norton," he heard from behind him. He turned around to find one of the nurse's aides pushing a meal cart.

"Hi, Rita," he replied.

"Did that guy find you?"

"What guy?"

"Some blond guy was looking for you. I told him you were in the cafeteria."

"He found me. Who is he, anyway? I never did get his name."

"You didn't know him? He said you were expecting him. I saw him here earlier this week. I thought maybe he was a relative of yours. He looks a little like you."

"He's no relative of mine. He's probably a reporter."

"I'm really sorry, Mr. Norton. I never would have sent him in there if I'd known that."

"Don't worry about it, Rita. No harm done. I expect this sort of thing. It happens all the time. But if he asks for me or Ryan again, call security. And be on your guard. Now that Ryan is out of the coma, we'll probably have a lot more reporters hanging around here."

CHAPTER 3

SATURDAY MORNING RYAN received his first visitors. Howard Vincent had finally gotten a message through the hospital's bureaucracy to Doug, who had left strict orders to take no messages from anyone. Vincent had persisted until he finally reached the nurse's station and pleaded his case until the nurse in charge agreed to give Doug the message. Now that Ryan North had regained consciousness, Howard needed to do something about his daughter. "I know it's a lot to ask right now," he explained when Doug returned his call, "but if she sees for herself that he didn't die, maybe she'll stop waking up at night crying." Seven days of nightmares were taking a toll on both father and daughter.

Doug explained it to Ryan for the fifth time that morning. "She's the one who found you, Ryan. If she hadn't seen you, you'd probably be dead now. She doesn't believe you lived. She thinks the newspapers are lying about your recovery. She's been dreaming you died."

"Oh," Ryan replied for the fifth time. "Then I'll see her. I don't want one of my fans thinking I'm dead."

An hour later, Doug had to go through it one more time. Ryan was awake, but in addition to not remembering several weeks before the accident, he could not remember things that happened thirty minutes ago.

Fifteen minutes later, Cindy Vincent entered the room with her father and Ryan turned to her, confused. "Who is this, Doug?" he asked, having already forgotten that a visitor was expected.

"This is the girl who saved your life, Ryan."

For the first time that morning, Ryan didn't ask for an explanation. "Oh. Right. Hi," he said to her. "What's your name?"

"Cindy Vincent," she replied. "Are you all right?" She stared at the bandages covering his head, then looked back at his face.

He smiled. "No, but they say I will be soon. Thank you for finding me, Cindy." He held his hand out to her and she stepped to the bed and took it. He squeezed her hand gently.

She smiled, relieved. "He's all right, Daddy," she said, turning to her father. "He's really all right!"

Howard Vincent smiled back. "Thank you for seeing her, Mr. North. I hated to impose like this, knowing you've only been out of the coma a couple days, but she's been so worried about you."

Cindy clutched Ryan's hand tightly. "I was afraid I didn't keep you warm enough that day. I keep having this nightmare that you died and everyone blamed me because I couldn't keep the snow off you."

Tears came to Ryan's eyes and he pulled the girl toward him, hugging her as well as he could around the IV tube. "I'm sorry you were so worried, Cindy. I really am. You saved my life. Nobody can blame you for anything. I owe you a lot."

"I do, too," Doug said. He pulled out his wallet and handed Howard Vincent a card. "If there's ever anything we can do for you, please say the word. Maybe when Ryan is feeling better Cindy can come see him again. That's the number of Ryan's office in Los Angeles. Cindy is welcome to visit any time. At least, any time after he gets better. It's going to be quite awhile before he can go back to work."

"Do you mean it?" Cindy asked. "I can see him again sometime?"

"Yes," Ryan replied. "After I get back on my feet. Just call. And give Doug your address and phone number. It may be a long time, but my next concert in Denver, you've got all the front row seats you and your friends can fill up. Backstage passes, too. Okay?"

"Wow! Thanks!"

"I think we'd better go now, honey," Howard said. "Mr. North needs to rest so he can get better. Thanks again, gentlemen. Maybe my little girl will be able to get some sleep now."

Doug walked them out. "Thank you both, for everything. Ryan isn't remembering much right now, but I'll make sure he remembers who saved his life. Give me your phone number and address so we can get in touch with you later."

Howard handed him a business card, and Doug slipped it into his shirt pocket with his cigarettes. He was wearing a yellow polo shirt with a skunk over the pocket. Cindy smiled when she saw it. "That's cute."

Doug glanced down and smiled back. "One of the nurses gave it to me yesterday. It's sort of my trademark to wear polo shirts with little animals on the front. Like Ryan and his corny ties. That's his trademark."

Cindy nodded knowledgeably. "Ryan North has fifty-seven ties in his tie collection," she reported. "I read that in a magazine. Maybe he'll let me see them someday. They hardly ever show pictures of them up close."

Doug smiled and winked at her father. "You'll have to wait until you're over eighteen to see most of them, Cindy. Very few of them have cute, innocent little animals on them like my shirts do."

He returned to the room after the visitors left and found tears running down his brother's cheeks. "I could have died, Doug. I don't think I really understood that until now. I could have died. If that one little girl hadn't seen me when she did, I could be out there, right now, maybe still buried in the snow, dead."

An hour later, Doug said, "I'll bet Cindy Vincent doesn't wash her hand for a week after today. She's a big fan. She even knows how many ties you own."

"Who's Cindy Vincent?" Ryan asked.

Doug just shook his head. "Never mind, Ryan. I'll tell you later."

CHAPTER 4

MONDAY MORNING JIM Harrison called Lakewood General Hospital to confirm the reports he had read in the paper over the weekend. *The Rocky Mountain Chronicle* had reported that Ryan North had come out of the coma Thursday. By Sunday's edition, a follow-up story reported he had had his first visitors, Howard and Cindy Vincent. Jim spoke to North's doctor, who confirmed that Ryan North was considered out of danger and expected to eventually recover from the accident, although possibly with some impairment yet to be determined. He discouraged any attempt to question North about the accident, saying that North still did not remember what happened.

Jim sat at the computer and quickly entered a report on his conversation with the doctor and figured there wasn't much else to do on the case. Had North died, additional work would have been necessary before the file could be closed, but with the doctor's declaration of expected recovery, Jim's involvement was essentially over.

He saved the file, printed a copy, and filed it in the top drawer of the file cabinet he had emptied out after Billy Williams had left. He had boxed up all of Williams' copies of his closed cases, leaving only the dozen or so ongoing investigations Jim had inherited. Those cases resided in the top drawer of the cabinet with the files of new cases opened since Williams' departure. As each was cleared, it would move to the second drawer.

Jim wondered how long it would take until that drawer was crammed full and he started on the third and fourth drawers.

He remembered the room that housed the files of the detective squad at his old precinct in Denver. His former co-workers would no doubt find it amusing that Jim's new caseload could be contained in one drawer of a single file cabinet.

He walked into Harley's office.

34

Harley was leaning back in his chair, reading a fishing magazine when Jim walked in. "There's an update on the Ryan North case if you're interested," Jim informed him when Harley glanced up.

"Let's see," Harley said, turning to the computer screen. He quickly located the report and scanned it. "He's going to live, huh?"

"Doctor says so. Of course, I heard it first from the *Chronicle*. Guess the hospital forgot I asked to be notified whenever his condition was upgraded or downgraded. They told me about the upgrade from critical to serious last Sunday, but I never heard anything after that."

"Typical." Harley read through the brief report and glanced up. "This wraps it up then?"

"No, I haven't talked to North yet, just the doctor. The doctor suggested I wait awhile to talk to North," Jim replied.

"I'm sure the doctor knows what he's talking about. What else could North add anyway?"

"What happened. There were no witnesses to the accident, remember, and I'm still a little bothered by the attitude of his business partner. The doctor told me North has some amnesia and still doesn't remember the accident yet. I thought I should hold the file open for a while, wait to see if he remembers anything."

Harley waved the idea aside. "Nah, don't waste your time." He clicked the mouse, restoring the main menu to the computer screen. "Close it out. You've got enough to do without hand-holding some celebrity who can't ride a horse."

"You're sure?" Jim asked doubtfully. "I'd rather get some kind of statement directly from the victim, even if it's just to get on record that he doesn't know what happened."

"Forget it. The reporters finally quit calling every day for information about him. You talk to him now, and it will start all over again. Consider it closed."

Jim decided to let it go. "You're the boss," was all he said.

"So, anything interesting going on this week?"

"Still trying to find out where those kids in Silver Plume are getting their cocaine from. I found the marijuana patch last week but someone's dealing and I can't figure out who yet. CBI is trying to get someone to go inside. Soon as they find an agent they can pass off as a seventeen-year-old we might get some information."

"Reason I'm asking is I just hired another patrol officer. Clayton Burns. Fresh from the academy. Take him with you if you get any accidents to investigate or need any help with something in the next few weeks. He's supposed to be a good photographer and does pretty fair crime scene drawings. I want him exposed to as much as possible his first month. After that, he'll be on patrol all the time."

"Haven't met him yet. When did he start?"

"This morning. He's spending the morning in dispatch, learning protocol. Black kid, about twenty-two, skinny, big grin. You'll like him. He wants to be a detective someday."

"Make sure you don't call him black to his face. They want to be called African-Americans now," Jim corrected with a grin. "My last partner was black and female. I had to learn to be politically correct in a hurry."

"They stuck you with a chick? Who'd you piss off to get that assignment?"

"She was a good cop, Harley," Jim replied firmly. "And a good friend. And she preferred to be called a woman – not girl, not lady, and certainly not chick. Is Clayton from around here?"

"Nope. City kid. Moved here from Phoenix a few years ago, went through the academy, then applied to every law enforcement agency up and down the Rockies. Guess he likes to climb and wanted to live in the mountains. Tried to get on the Alpine Rescue Team a couple years ago but he couldn't handle the high altitude. They told him to get some more climbing experience, get used to the altitude then come back. Instead he went to the academy and became a cop."

"I'll try to meet him today. Anything else?"

"Not at the moment." Harley turned back to his fishing magazine. "Let me know if anything interesting comes of that drug case."

"Sure thing."

Two hours later, Jim walked across the street with the new deputy, Clayton Burns, to have lunch with him in the diner. After being seated in

Jim's usual booth with the view of the county building, the two men ordered and sat back with their drinks. Jim added sugar to his coffee and stirred it slowly while Clayton finished telling him about his abortive effort to join the Alpine Rescue Team two years previously. "Sheriff Watson said you used to work for them, Detective Harrison," he finished. "Did you enjoy it?"

"Call me Jim, please. I was with them for three years, while I was going to college. Yes, I guess I'd say I enjoyed it, to the extent that I get a lot of satisfaction out of helping people. It's a lot of hard work. I enjoyed the searches most. I got pretty good at tracking."

"Why did you leave?" Clayton squeezed lemon into his iced tea and stirred it.

"Went to the academy. I was still living at home with my dad while I was going to college. Majored in Criminal Justice with a minor in Psychology. After I got my degree, I went straight to the academy."

"How long you been a cop then?"

"Guess I was twenty-three, so that makes twelve years. Got a job right out of the academy with Denver P.D., working over on the east side of town. Married, divorced three years later. Made detective a couple years after that. Then Dad got sick and I wanted to move back in to help him so I transferred to the west side. That was two years ago. Dad died a year later."

"Why did you leave the department? County pay more?" Clayton took a drink of his tea.

Jim gave a short laugh. "Hardly. Things just didn't work out there. I'd rather not talk about it."

Clayton arched an eyebrow over his iced tea but said nothing.

"What about you?" Jim continued. "Why did you decide to become a cop?"

"All little boys want to be cops. Guess I never grew up." He grinned at Jim. "Can't wait for my first shootout."

Jim snorted. "Rookie. Wait till you've been in one. You'll change your mind quick enough. Although, I've known a few cops who seemed to live for them."

"You been in one?"

"Yes. Believe me, the lucky ones are the ones who get to retire without having to kill anyone."

"You killed someone?"

"Yeah. In front of his kid, too."

"Who? What happened? If you don't mind my asking," Clayton amended.

"I don't mind," Jim assured him. "It was a domestic violence case when I was a patrolman. Guy was holed up in the house with a thirty-eight and his three-year-old son. The wife escaped and called the cops. She was beaten pretty bad, black eyes, broken arm, bleeding from her nose and mouth where he'd slammed her face onto the table."

"Nice guy. You shot him?"

"Yeah. We were waiting for the hostage negotiator to arrive when he broke out the front window of the house, stood the kid on the window sill and said if we didn't back off, he was going to kill the kid. He had the gun pointed right at the kid's head, the kid was crying and screaming for his mother."

"What happened?"

Jim shrugged. "We got lucky. The kid slipped. Fell outside the window. The second he dropped, the guy panicked, he fired at us, and three of us returned fire. Two of us hit him."

"You were one of them."

"Yes."

"Kid okay?"

"Split his lip when he hit the ground. Some bruises. Probably a lifetime of nightmares. He must be a teenager now. Probably still needs therapy."

"You said he fired at you? Were any of the officers hit?"

Jim gave him a wry grin. "Just me. Grazed my left arm." He took a sip of his coffee. "Would you believe I didn't even know I'd been hit until someone told me I was bleeding?"

The waitress brought their sandwiches then and the two men ate in silence for a few minutes. Then Clayton said, "Maybe I can wait awhile for my first shootout. Shooting a guy in front of his kid can't be much fun, even if it was to save the kid's life. Sounds like maybe my fantasy is better than the reality."

Jim laughed. "Glad to hear you say that. Not likely to have much shooting out here anyway. Things are pretty quiet in Clear Creek. Maybe you'll get to be one of the lucky ones."

"What do you consider to be quiet?" Clayton asked, grinning. "Sheriff Watson says you're pretty busy already."

"By quiet I mean no homicides," Jim replied soberly. "I've seen plenty of them in my former life. I was with Homicide in Denver for seven years. A few of those cases I still have nightmares about. Completely senseless, brutal killings. The worst are when kids are involved, at either end of the weapon. Mostly out here I deal with drugs and burglaries."

"Sheriff Watson says you're pretty good at what you do."

"He said that to you?"

Clayton nodded.

"I suppose by now I probably am," Jim said with a shrug. "Nothing special about it, though. I try to be thorough and don't rule out any possibilities until I have all the facts. Some cops get sidetracked by prejudices or stereotypes or focus too quickly on one scenario to the point where they ignore alternatives. I try to learn all I can about the victim and suspects, look for motives. I play devil's advocate with myself constantly. As soon as I think I know the answer, I play defense attorney and try to shoot holes in the theory. When I come up with the theory I can't shoot holes in, that's the one I go for."

"Is it really true that if a case will be solved, you'll have a suspect within twenty-four hours?"

"That's often the case, but not always true. There are certain elements of a murder that go beyond the motive, means, and opportunity that you hear talked about on TV crime dramas. There's the victim himself, of course, assuming he has been correctly identified, and he may have secrets his family and friends know nothing about. Then you have the witnesses and their prejudices and motivations and bad memories, and then there are clues which often are red herrings, but which sometimes lead to suspects. Sometimes that happens quickly, because there was an obvious relationship between victim and killer."

"And that's usually the case, isn't it? I remember learning that totally stranger-on-stranger murders are actually fairly rare."

"That's true, Clayton, but if a victim had secrets it can take awhile to find the relationship. But the ultimate element of a murder is the killer himself. And it's generally a good idea to keep an open mind when questioning everyone because it often happens that your killer is going to turn out to be someone you originally interviewed as a witness early on. And frankly, Clayton," he said with a smile, "luck is the final element of a murder. Sometimes that's the only thing that makes or breaks a case. I've been fortunate enough to have had my share of luck in solving cases."

"Somehow, Detective Harrison," Clayton said respectfully, "I have a feeling there's a lot more to it than you give yourself credit for. I hope I get to work with you on something. I hope to be a detective someday, and to hear Sheriff Watson talk about you, I could do a lot worse for a mentor."

Jim flushed, pleased but embarrassed to hear Harley's second-hand comments about him. "I'll see if I can get you involved if something interesting comes up, Clayton. I've heard some good things about you, too."

CHAPTER 5

THE FOLLOWING SUNDAY night nurse's aide Rita McConnell was collecting dirty dinner trays for return to the kitchen. After collecting trays from the regular ward, she stepped into the isolation area where Ryan North's private room was located so she could pick up his tray as well. She left the security door blocked open with her cart, glanced into Ryan's room and saw that Ryan was asleep and his ever-present partner, Doug Norton, was gone. She picked up Ryan's tray, put it on her cart, then left the cart where it was and stepped out on the fire escape for a quick smoke with Doug.

The nurse's station was unattended. With Ryan out of the coma and ambulatory, and Doug staying with him around the clock, his call button had been routed to the regular nurse's station outside the secured area and the isolation ward was now left unstaffed after the day shift ended.

There had been several times in the past two weeks when Rita had used the excuse of a smoke to spend a few minutes with Ryan North's taciturn partner. She knew the quiet, good-looking, stocky blond man with the somber gray eyes under the heavy eyebrows lived in Denver. She also knew he had had no visitors and had never left the hospital since the accident. While she never had the nerve to ask, she surmised that he was not married, nor involved in a relationship.

In their quiet moments alone on the fire escape, he was sometimes willing to chat and had shown that he had a sense of humor lying beneath the somber exterior. As Ryan's condition improved, so had Doug's mood, and Rita had occasionally been rewarded with a flash of his wide grin and the sound of his laughter. While knowing nearly nothing about each other, they had become friends. Rita had fallen into the habit of flirting with him, ever so slightly, and he took her teasing with good-natured humor, sometimes teasing her back.

This evening would be their last, since Rita knew the doctor planned to release Ryan to a rehabilitation center the next morning. If she was ever going to let Doug know of her interest in him, it was now or never.

She slipped out onto the fire escape where she found Doug halfway through a cigarette. "Hi, Handsome," she said.

Doug smiled. "Hi, Rita." He pulled out his cigarette pack and offered her a cigarette.

"Thanks." She took it and placed it between her lips, expectantly. Doug flashed his lighter and held the flame to the tip. Rita took a deep breath and cupped her hand around his to steady it. Her eyes met his momentarily over the flickering flame, then he withdrew his hand and snapped the lighter shut. She dropped her hand to her side.

She exhaled the smoke through her nose. The first few inhalations were always the best, and she savored one more drag before facing him. He leaned back against the wall, staring out at the city lights visible across the roof of the adjacent three-story parking garage, pulling on the last of his own cigarette.

"Tomorrow's the day, isn't it," she said.

"That's what they say."

"You'll be leaving here."

"That's right. I guess I have to go back home. The rehab center won't let me stay with him. I doubt I'll miss that cot much, though. And I'll be glad to get home and shave this off," he added, stroking his beard. "I've decided I don't like it after all but didn't have my shaving stuff here to get rid of it."

"I'll bet you're really handsome without it," she said sincerely. "I'm going to miss you, you know." She swallowed hard. "Anyone waiting for you at home?"

Doug shot her a glance then turned back to the distant lights. "No. Nobody."

She nervously drew on the cigarette as if she would somehow gain strength from it. At twenty-five years old, she shouldn't be this nervous but she was and it bothered her. She exhaled another cloud of smoke and shivered a little. "It's colder tonight," she said, realizing how trite it was to talk about the weather.

Doug crushed out his cigarette in the coffee can full of sand they kept there for that purpose. "Want my jacket?" he offered. "I'm going to go get some coffee while Ryan's asleep."

She stepped closer to him, dropping her half-smoked cigarette into the can. "Not your jacket." She was facing him now, looking up at him. "You. Don't go. Please." She reached to touch him on the shoulder, laid her hand there and left it, then raised her other hand and placed it on his other shoulder, clutching slightly at the red plaid jacket he always wore. She looked up at him.

He looked down, suddenly understanding. He smiled slightly, then took her hands in his and pulled them off his shoulders. "I'm sorry, Rita."

She blushed and started to turn away, but he held her, forcing her to look back at him. "This is embarrassing," she murmured. "You must think I'm an idiot."

"I don't think anything of the kind," he pulled her to his side and held her with an arm around her shoulders. "I'm flattered. And your friendship has meant a lot to me these past two weeks, but I'm sorry if I've given you the impression I was looking for a relationship."

"I'm sorry, Doug. I know you've got a lot on your mind with Ryan and all." She glanced up at him. "Can't blame a girl for trying, can you?"

He laughed. "Believe me, this is good for my ego. Usually Ryan is the one the women all go for. Nice to know someone prefers me for a change. Even with this beard."

Rita laughed, the tension broken. It felt good having Doug's arm around her, even if it was just as a friend. "If you change your mind, you know where to find me," she said.

"I'll remember that," he answered. "I'd better go now. You coming in? Or do you want another smoke?"

He left her there, smoking another cigarette, while he went inside.

Five minutes later, she followed. She turned the corner at the end of the hallway in time to see a flash of the familiar red plaid jacket entering Ryan's room.

Still slightly embarrassed about having come on to him, she quietly pushed her cart back through the door and parked it in front of the elevator while she stepped into the restroom.

She stepped out just as the elevator opened on that floor to pick up a passenger she could barely see on the other side of her cart. She started to call out for the rider to hold the elevator for her, then noticed the blond hair and plaid jacket and decided to wait for the next one. She wasn't ready to be alone with Doug in an elevator - not after what just happened on the fire escape.

Normally, she would have tried to join him for a cup of coffee after dropping off the cart full of dinner trays, but she decided she'd made a big enough fool of herself for one night. Maybe she'd come back up while Doug was downstairs and say good-bye to Ryan if he was awake. She wondered if Doug had told Ryan she had come on to him.

She returned thirty minutes later to find a crowd of people around Ryan's room, including a doctor and a security guard.

"What happened?" she asked an orderly.

"He got the wrong medication, apparently," the man replied. "Luckily he didn't take it. The doctor said if he had, it might have caused seizures or even killed him."

"Oh, my God! Who mixed it up?"

"Don't know. In fact, according to his chart, he shouldn't have any more medication tonight. He said he fell asleep after dinner after taking his usual medication with his meal. When he woke up, there was another cup with some pills on his tray, but he noticed they weren't the same kind of pills he's been getting. Luckily, he was smart enough to call the nurse to find out what they were before he took them. Nobody knows where they came from. The medication nurse says she never even went into his room."

"Where was Doug? Did he see anyone come into the room?"

"Doug went out for a smoke when Ryan fell asleep, then went right downstairs to the cafeteria for some coffee so he wouldn't wake Ryan up. He said the pills weren't there when he went out for the cigarette, so whoever left them did it within the last forty-five minutes or so."

"They weren't there when I picked up his dinner tray. I had a cigarette with Doug after that. Were they there when he went in the room after he had his cigarette?"

"What are you talking about? He didn't go back into the room until a few minutes ago after we paged him. We'd already called for a doctor at that point."

"But I saw him – " She broke off at the sound of a voice behind her.

It was the security guard. "Saw who?"

CHAPTER 6

J IM HARRISON WAS TRYING to decide where to file the bulletin on the missing teenager that had landed in his basket the next morning. Denver Police were dropping the investigation into Daryl Walker's disappearance, believing the boy had simply run away as he had threatened. They couldn't justify tying up resources trying to find a kid who didn't want to be found.

Not even the son of the senator? Then Jim remembered the long-standing animosity that existed between the senator and the Denver police commissioner. No, the son of that particular senator wouldn't be getting any special treatment from the Denver Police Department. No leads plus no evidence equals no case. And the detective squad was already up to their eyeballs in crimes to solve.

He shrugged and finally decided to put it with the original missing person report and file them both in the "closed case" drawer. It wasn't his jurisdiction anyway, and if Denver had closed the file, there was no reason for him to keep it open. He had enough of his own work to do.

He had closed the file drawer and returned to his desk when his phone rang. It was a Detective Jack Curry in Lakewood. He was investigating a possible attempt on the life of Ryan North that had occurred the previous evening. He told Jim that North woke from a nap to find some pills in their usual place on his tray. Luckily, he realized they weren't the same pills he'd been receiving every day and asked a nurse what they were. Had he taken them, he might have died from a drug interaction with other medication he was taking.

"None of the nurses will admit leaving them there, so naturally we have to wonder if his accident really was an accident," Jack concluded. "What do you think?"

Jim leaned back in his chair, remembering the nagging doubts he'd had about the situation. He had wondered about foul play at the time, but there was no evidence at the scene. "There was a branch, Jack, at the height of my own forehead from the back of a horse, with blood on it, a few feet behind where he fell. I don't see any explanation fitting his injuries other than that his horse ran under the branch, it knocked him on the forehead, and then he slipped to the ground, landing on a rock. There were no suspicious injuries that I know of. I did do a follow-up inquiry the next day. They stitched his forehead. He had a skull fracture from the rock and they had to drill. Other than a couple of black eyes from the blow to the forehead and some minor bruising to his elbows and hip from hitting the ground, there wasn't anything else."

"Jim, if you were riding toward a branch at face level, wouldn't you duck?"

"Sure, if I had time and saw it coming. According to North's buddy, the horse he was on wasn't much more than green-broke. He could have spooked, reared, bolted, spun around."

"What if someone deliberately spooked the horse?"

"Not very likely. How could he know the horse would run under an appropriate branch? I've got a horse of my own and when he spooks, I never know which way he's going to jump to get away from whatever scared him. Besides," he continued, "if someone was trying to kill Ryan North by spooking his horse, they risked having North pull out his hunting rifle and defend himself if the horse had missed the tree branch. The rifle was still in the scabbard when I saw the horse."

"Well, I thought it might be a long shot, Jim, but I wanted to bounce it off you anyway. Seems odd enough that a popular, well-liked guy like Ryan North would have someone trying to kill him in the first place, but having him incapacitated in the hospital from a freak accident at the time seemed a little too convenient to be coincidence."

"Then I'd look to his friends and relatives, Jack. Who else would have a motive? The accident may have given someone an opportunity they wouldn't have otherwise had."

"Well, there is some indication his brother might have been involved, but we have no real evidence. That's why we were wondering if you'd seen anything out of line. I understand the brother was hunting with him."

"There was no brother there that I know of. He was hunting with his business partner."

"That's his brother. I did a little checking. His name used to be Victor Robert North. He changed it to Doug Norton a few years back to try to avoid publicity. He was pretty upset when I found out. I assured him we wouldn't tip the media unless we found reason to actually arrest him for something. He probably didn't want to tell you he was his brother if there were any witnesses hanging around."

Jim tried to remember the scene of the rescue. "There were several rescue volunteers within earshot when he told me he was North's partner. I never checked him out because there was no sign of foul play. I still don't think there was any foul play, and Doug Norton certainly didn't act like he wanted Ryan North dead. He was worried to death about him. Not," he added, "that that's necessarily proof of anything. My initial impression was that they might have been lovers. Guess I was wrong about that."

Jack Curry gave a nasty chuckle. "Well, you never know about celebrities these days. As I said, we have no evidence he was the one, but an eyewitness said she saw him go into the room at a time when Norton says he was down in the cafeteria. She didn't see his face, and nobody saw him in the cafeteria until after the window of opportunity was past. He could have done it, but my eyewitness can't swear it was him at all. All she really saw was his jacket. She didn't even want to admit that much. I think there might have been something going on between them, although they both denied it."

"Any obvious motives?"

"Not that we've found. The brother is his sole heir, but he also already owns a good chunk of North Star Productions and gets a hefty percentage of North's income. Seems like Ryan North is worth a lot more to Doug Norton alive than dead. Of course, that doesn't rule out family-based motivations. The other thing is that if Doug Norton wanted his brother dead, he probably could have made sure it happened while North was still in the coma. This incident almost feels more like a threat than an actual attempted murder. Sort of proving the perp could have killed him if he wanted to."

"Maybe it's a set up for some kind of extortion. If it is, North will be hearing from someone about it soon enough."

"Could be. Well, if you think of anything that might help, call me. There's one other possibility, and that's that the nurse made a mistake and is afraid to admit it. Maybe nobody was trying to kill him at all."

"Hopefully that's all it was." Jim hung up the phone. Could he be slipping? Had there been evidence there that day that he had overlooked? No, not overlooked, he reminded himself. It had already been snowing. Any evidence that might have been there would have been covered with snow.

"Oh, well," he muttered to himself. "He's still alive anyway. No harm done. But maybe I better go have a chat with him anyway." Harley Watson might consider the case closed, but Jim Harrison wasn't so sure anymore.

"No, Sheila," her editor said. "Dennis will handle it. It happened in Lakewood, not here. You're assigned to the elections right now. When we get an ongoing story based here in the county, you can handle that. Fair enough?"

"I guess it is," she replied glumly, heading out to interview a candidate for the county Board of Selectmen. Should be an exciting race, she thought darkly. The man was running unopposed.

* * *

"Mr. North?" Jim Harrison hesitated at the door to Ryan North's hospital room. Doug Norton, standing by the bed, his back to the door, whirled around at the sound of the voice. "Sorry," Jim said, "I didn't mean to startle you. I'm Detective Harrison, Clear Creek County Sheriff's department. I need to speak to Mr. North."

Doug gave the detective a searching look, then said, "I know who you are. He's asleep. Is something wrong?"

"Just need to ask him a few questions now that he's out of the coma. Finish up the paperwork."

"Oh. Well, as I said, he's asleep."

"Sorry," Jim said, "I know we've met but I've forgotten who you are." Jim had forgotten nothing, but he was curious to know how Doug would introduce himself without any witnesses within earshot.

"Doug Norton. I'm his business partner."

Jim arched an eyebrow. "His brother Victor, too, I think. Is that right?"

Doug flushed. "How'd you find that out?"

"Well, it wasn't from you, now, was it?" Jim replied pointedly. "You've had two chances now to tell me. Why did you lie to me?"

Doug turned away and walked around the bed to adjust the blinds at the window. "I didn't lie. I know better than that. I am his partner. You never asked if I was a relative."

"Normally people volunteer things like that."

"Well, I don't." Doug turned around to face the detective. "I changed my name so people wouldn't know I was his brother. I certainly don't go blabbing it around in front of strangers. Too damn many reporters everywhere he goes. And police reports get leaked to them all the time."

"Not my reports, Mr. Norton, and I still need to talk to him, but I do have some questions for you, too, since you're here. Is there somewhere we can go to talk?"

"If you insist." Doug picked up his cigarette pack from a table. "I need a smoke anyway. We can go out on the fire escape." He led the way through the door, down the hall to the exit door. He stepped out onto the landing and shoved the brick against the doorjamb to keep the door from closing.

Jim followed, wondering what was the cause of Norton's continuing irritation. He decided to ask him. "Mr. Norton," he started as Doug lit a cigarette and snapped the lighter shut, "I can't help noticing you seem upset by my arrival. Why?"

Doug leaned on the rail and stared out across the parking lot below, declining to look at Jim Harrison. "No big thing," he replied with a shrug. "Nobody told me you were coming. I was surprised, that's all. There was supposed to be a guard out there. Are you here about what happened last night?"

"I heard about that but no, I'm here about the accident." He pulled a notebook out of his pocket. "I just need to check a few details. Now, the day of the accident, what time did you get to the trail head?"

"Before dawn. Seven or so, maybe. I don't really remember."

"How long did you ride together before you split up?"

"Maybe an hour. We rode around one area for awhile, then came back to a trail crossing and split up there, agreeing to meet back there at noon."

"Why did you split up?"

Doug didn't answer right away, drawing thoughtfully on the cigarette, then exhaling slowly. He straightened up and glanced sideways at the detective. "Am I under suspicion for some reason? I mean, it was an accident, wasn't it? That's what you told the Vincents that day. Because if I am under suspicion for something, I'd like to know why I haven't been read my rights."

Jim didn't visibly react, but he recognized the cold hostility in Doug Norton's technically polite response and wondered about its source. Innocent people generally don't worry about their rights, but guilty ones usually don't remind cops about them, either. "As far as I know, Mr. Norton, it was an accident. I'm just trying to put it in a context. Is there some reason you feel answering that question would be incriminating?"

"I know how cops work." He propped one foot on the lower bar and leaned back over the top rail of the balcony. "They can always find something to hassle you about."

Jim ignored the comment and continued, undaunted. "Did you have a fight? Is that why you decided to ride alone?"

Doug studied the tip of his cigarette. "It wasn't a fight. Just some childish argument."

"What did you argue about?"

"He wants me to come work for him, be his manager."

"You fought about that? Why? Aren't you already his partner?"

Doug shook his head in frustration. "You don't understand. We have a song writing partnership. I'm his lyricist. That's fine. I live here, he lives in L.A., we talk on the phone, kick around ideas, I send him a song, he writes music for it, records it, goes on tour, makes a bunch of money, sends me my share, I stick it in the bank and ignore it. But I stay in Denver. He tried to get me to move to L.A. a couple years ago when he moved there, but I refused. To be his manager I'd have to leave Denver, go to L.A., and run his life for him – while he simultaneously runs mine."

"So tell him no."

Doug gave a short laugh. "I tell him no all the time. It doesn't matter. What he wants, he always gets. It's just the way things are between us. He'll get his way this time, too. Assuming he recovers." He flicked another ash off the balcony. "The thing is, I actually wouldn't mind doing it all that much. I'm kind of burned out at my day job anyway. I was mostly pissed because of the way he asked. Not like he was asking, more like he was telling me what he'd decided I should do."

"So you argued about this and you decided to go hunt by yourself, is that it?"

"I told him to go piss up a rope. He said fine, meet you back here at noon, you bring the rope. I rode off. Got back about twelve-thirty, he wasn't there. Back at the trailer I found his horse running around loose. I rode back to try to find him. I think you heard the rest from Howard Vincent."

"When you left him, was he angry?"

"He never gets angry. He lets me get angry. He knows he'll get what he wants eventually. When I left him, he waved good-bye. I flipped him off. He laughed." He shook his head.

"At the scene of the accident, Mr. Norton, you didn't seem angry with him anymore."

"No, I got over it a few minutes after I rode off. I'm not angry with him now, either." Doug took another drag off the cigarette and flicked the ash again. "I told you it was just a childish squabble to begin with, and it's hard to be angry with someone you think is going to die. He's my brother, after all. We squabble all the time. It's no big deal. But he's the only family I have left. Besides that, I was already blaming myself."

"For what? The argument?"

"For the accident. I knew he was riding a half-broke horse. I should have stayed with him. Maybe if there'd been another horse with him, his crazy horse wouldn't have freaked out."

"You think the horse freaked out?"

"You said yourself he ran him under a branch. Probably spooked at a rabbit or something. Ryan doesn't ride much any more and probably lost control of him. If my horse had been there with him, his horse would have been calmer, maybe I could have warned him about something. If nothing else, I had the phone with me and could have gotten help to him a lot faster. So, yeah, I blamed myself. Still do, for that matter. I shouldn't have left him alone."

"Did he tell you the horse spooked at a rabbit?"

"He doesn't remember the accident. He doesn't even remember going hunting. In fact, I'm sure when he wakes up he won't even remember what he had for breakfast this morning. His head's still all fucked up. The doctor said it will be weeks, maybe months before he remembers everything, if at all. Tomorrow he's going to rehab for at least a month. He doesn't even remember how to feed himself, Detective. I have to help him in the bathroom. He can't dress himself. And yeah, it's my fault and I blame myself. Myself and his crazy horse. Make of that what you will."

"When you got back to the trailer and found the horse, Mr. Norton, you said you figured the horse had pulled away from Mr. North and he was walking out, right?"

"That's what I said. Didn't you write it down the first time?"

"So you tied up the buckskin and rode back to look for your brother."

"That's right. What's your point?"

"If your first assumption was that he was probably walking out, why didn't you take his horse with you, so he'd have something to ride back?" Jim looked at Doug's face for a reaction.

Doug didn't even look over at him. "I told you the horse was crazy. I didn't need to be dragging some flighty half-broke horse through the woods at the end of a rope. If I'd found Ryan walking, he could have ridden back with me, or walked out if it wasn't too far." He glanced sideways at Jim. "Why? What are you trying to suggest?"

"That you already knew he wasn't going to be able to ride out. That you already knew he was hurt."

Doug took one final pull at the cigarette, then crushed it out in the coffee can full of sand in the corner of the landing. He turned to glare at Jim Harrison. "Well, you're wrong. And by the way, I didn't give him those pills the other day either. No matter what anybody says. I was in the cafeteria. Any more questions?"

"Just one. Why are you being so hostile?" He looked straight into Doug Norton's eyes.

Doug met his gaze levelly for a long moment then turned to pull the door open. "You're a cop. And if you have any more insinuations to make about me, you'll be making them through my attorney. This interview is over." He walked through the door and strode to the elevator, leaving Jim Harrison alone on the balcony.

After Doug Norton's angry departure, Jim Harrison returned to Ryan North's room where he found the famous singer awake – and much more cordial than the brother had been. Ryan North quickly confirmed what Doug had said about his not remembering the accident and explained that the last thing he remembered was Doug picking him up at the airport the Wednesday before the accident. It was an improvement over his first waking memory, when he thought he was in Albuquerque. At least now he remembered that he had come to Denver for a week when part of his concert tour was canceled due to a fire in the Tulsa concert hall where he was booked for five nights. But he didn't remember anything else until a few days after he came out of the coma. "And some of that, I only know because Doug has told me about it over and over again," he added. "Like seeing the little girl who found me. Doug said she was here two days after I came out of the coma. She was having nightmares that I died, so he let her come see me. He says that I talked to her, held her hand, gave her a hug, promised her tickets to my next show, invited her to visit again when I get better. Which I hope she will do. I owe her a lot and I'd like to meet her again. But I don't remember her being here at all. The best I can do is remember that Doug said she was here."

"I'm sorry to hear that. Must be pretty difficult for you."

Ryan North sighed. "You don't know the half of it. I try to be optimistic, Detective. I get a little depressed sometimes, then Doug kids me out of it and I'm all right for a while. I don't know what I'd do without him. Right now I'm feeling pretty good. I wish I could help you."

"Not a problem. If you don't remember, you don't remember."

"Maybe I will someday. The doc says I'm getting better. I'm gradually remembering a little more each day of what happened before the accident but I'm still shaky about everything that happened after I woke up. Doug said when I first came out, I couldn't remember things right after they happened. Now it takes me a few hours to forget them. If I'm lucky, I'll still remember this conversation when I go to sleep tonight, but chances are I won't remember it in the morning. In fact," he added with a sheepish smile, "I've already forgotten your name. Nothing personal, you understand. It's just the way things are right now."

"I understand." Jim stood to leave. "Here's my card, but I guess there's no point in my expecting you to remember to call me if you ever get your memory back," he said with a smile.

Ryan picked up the card and laughed. "No, Jim Harrison," he read, "but I'll try to remember to mention it to Doug when he gets back. He can remind me if it ever happens."

Jim grinned wryly. "I doubt he would. I don't think he likes me very well." He hesitated a moment. "You have any idea what he has against cops?"

Ryan sobered. "No. He's never told me. I didn't even know it until I asked him to help me with a benefit for a Denver police officer earlier this year. I'm sure you heard about him. Shot in the spine, left a paraplegic. I don't remember his name. I was stunned when Doug flat refused to help. Absolutely stunned. Something must have happened somewhere along the way that I never heard about, but he refused to tell me what. As far as I know, he's never been arrested. Several speeding tickets, but he always goes to court and fights them. I think he's beaten all of them so far. I'm really sorry if he gave you a hard time. You're just doing your job. Do you want me to talk to him about it? Assuming I remember to do it," he amended.

"No, Mr. North, you just try to remember to get better. I don't need to be liked in order to do my job, and I can't say he was actually uncooperative. He did answer all my questions, and I have no reason to believe he didn't tell me the truth. But it is a little unusual to get this kind of animosity from a relative of someone whose life has just been saved. Usually the folks who act this way have handcuffs on at the time or are getting a ticket they think they didn't deserve."

"Again, Detective Harrison, I'm really sorry. He's really a great guy. He's hardly left my side since I got here, and I know the nurses all like him a lot. Several have commented to me about how much they've enjoyed having him here these last two weeks. He's normally friendly, although a little shy around women, great sense of humor, practical joker, very creative. He's an accomplished guitarist and writes the lyrics to all my songs, and there have been over a hundred so far. He's also a good cook, which was nice when we were living together in college."

"Sounds like a great guy," Jim agreed. "Maybe I'll get to meet him someday. So far all I've met is his pal, Chip."

Ryan looked puzzled.

"The nasty little guy who lives on his shoulder," Jim explained, and was rewarded with a laugh from Ryan North. Jim grinned back and put away his notebook. "I think we'll consider this case closed. As far as I can tell, it was an accident." He shook Ryan North's hand. "Good luck in your recovery. I know there are a lot of fans out there waiting for you to get back on that stage again. I think I just became one of them."

"Thanks. Now if I could just remember how to play the cello again."

Jim did a double take. "Cello? I thought you played piano." Then Ryan winked and Jim knew the singer was joking. Jim laughed. "I see your sense of humor survived intact. Take care, Mr. North." As he walked out, he contrasted the injured singer's friendliness and sense of humor with his brother's open hostility and anger.

He decided he liked Ryan North. He seemed to be a really nice guy, and Jim could understand why his fans, including the Vincent girl, were so devastated by his accident. The brother was another story. Jim knew enough about human nature to know that anger and hostility often masked fear. What was Doug Norton afraid of?

He walked across the parking lot to the Blazer and slid into the driver's seat, tossing his clipboard to the side. Everyone has a skeleton in their closet somewhere. What was Doug Norton's secret? Somehow, he had a feeling their paths would cross again

CHAPTER 7

"AND OVER HERE is the recreation room," the middle aged, gray-haired woman said, gesturing to a room where Ryan could see couches, chairs, a TV set, tables with chess pieces, and a piano. Doug maneuvered the wheelchair through the door and stopped.

Several people stopped their activities and turned to stare at the newcomer, some pointing and whispering. Ryan felt his face flush. "Get me out of here," he muttered, and Doug pivoted the chair back through the doors.

"I'm sorry about that," the woman said. "Word got around this morning that you would be coming here for rehabilitation. Once they get used to the idea of having a celebrity in their midst, they'll ignore you. We did ask them all not to bother you, but some of them won't remember. Keep in mind, they're all here for the same reason you are."

"I know," Ryan said. "It's not the other patients that will bother me, though, it's their visitors. I hope this doesn't turn into a big mob scene on visiting day."

"We have an open visitation policy, Mr. North. Visitors are welcome any time between eight in the morning and nine at night. Most people only have visitors on the weekend, though. You may want to keep to your room on Saturday and Sunday afternoons if you want to avoid most of the visitors."

"I'll be here every day," Doug said, pushing the wheelchair down the hall, away from the rec room. "All day."

It was a week after Ryan woke from the coma and he had just checked in to a brain injury rehabilitation center in Denver. His physical injuries were healing well, but he had forgotten how to make his body do things like holding a fork and tying his shoes. Even walking was difficult, but the doctor felt he would make a quick recovery once he started therapy.

They continued down a hallway, stopping in front of room 27. "This will be your room, Mr. North. As requested, it is a private room. Most of our residents share a room, but we understand your circumstances and will do whatever we can to maintain your privacy. There will be no reporters allowed here. The door locks only from the inside and only the staff has keys. Please don't keep personal items of value here, though. Clothes and toiletries and books are usually okay, but we've had a few minor thefts of watches and rings that were left unattended, so we discourage items like that."

Ryan looked around the room that would be his home for at least a month while he regained lost motor skills. There were two beds in the room but only one was made up. There was a dresser, a desk with a phone, a lamp, and a window overlooking the grassy courtyard. Just inside the door was a bathroom. On the wall was a small television. The whole arrangement reminded him of the hospital.

"Tomorrow you will start your therapy, Mr. North. We start with basic self-care skills and the first days focus on the two essentials of feeding yourself and using the bathroom. Later you will learn to dress yourself, tie shoes, things like that."

Ryan looked at Doug, who had crossed the room to open the blinds wider. "I feel like a baby," he said.

The woman laughed. "You'll feel that way for a few days, Mr. North. All our residents say that at first, but you'll be surprised how quickly it all comes back. You'll have several therapy sessions a day at first, working with a specialist. Later you'll take charge of your own therapy, practicing on your own the skills that are important to you."

"Like the piano?"

"Like the piano. Feel free to use it whenever you want. Actually, it's probably terribly out of tune. I don't think it's been played in months."

She left the two men alone then, promising to return in a couple hours with Ryan's dinner, which Doug would feed him for the last time. Starting tomorrow, she promised, Ryan would feed himself.

Doug closed the door behind her and locked it. "You okay?" he asked Ryan, who was struggling to turn the wheelchair on his own.

"I hate this, Doug. I hate being helpless. I hate not knowing if I'm going to be all right. I hate being in a fish bowl, with people I don't know staring at me, pitying me."

"They're not pitying you, Ryan. They're commiserating. They know what you're going through. You'll be all right. The doctor told you that you were very, very lucky. There's no reason to think you won't make a full recovery."

"Full recovery, my ass. I still don't even remember what happened."

"Well, at least you remember that you're not in Albuquerque."

"I still don't remember going hunting. And I don't even remember waking up from the coma any more." He shook his head in frustration, then regretted it when his head throbbed. He put his hands to his head. The bandages were gone and a fine covering of hair was starting to mask the bald area where they had shaved his head for surgery. "You know, I understand about amnesia, and I understand why I may never remember the accident, but I don't understand why I have trouble remembering things that happened after I woke from the coma."

"Don't try to understand it, Ryan. You'll make yourself nuts. It's normal for brain injury patients to have memory lapses after the fact. The doctor said it may happen for months. Just like your hand needs to relearn how to hold a toothbrush, your brain needs to relearn how to move short term memories to long term storage. Or how to retrieve the memories after it stores them."

"Oh. You explained that to me this morning, didn't you."

"Twice. See? You're making progress already." He helped Ryan out of the wheelchair and onto the bed. "Don't worry about it, Ryan. Do what they tell you and you'll be all right."

"Who knows I'm here?"

"Probably the world knows by now. I told only Tony." He paused. "Tony DiMartino. Your manager."

"I remember who Tony is."

Doug glanced around. "Is there anything you want me to bring you? I still have your suitcase and stuff at my house, I'll bring them tomorrow. You want any books or anything?"

"No, thanks. I'm not here to read. I'm here to get better. As soon as they give me those exercises, I'll be working every minute. I have to get back to my life, Doug."

"I know. Just don't expect too much, too soon. And I'll be here to help you, every day. I promise."

"What about your job at the ad agency? You've been at my side for two weeks now. Not that I don't appreciate it, but don't you have to get back to work?"

"Screw the job. I took a three-month leave of absence, and I'll quit if you need me longer than that. It's not like I need the money, you know. I had to tell the personnel director I was your brother, though. She promised to keep it quiet."

Ryan lay back on the bed, suddenly tired. Although he had been in the wheelchair most of the time, this was the longest he had been out of bed since the accident. "Thanks, Doug. I'm really glad you're here. I think I should rest awhile before dinner, though."

"You want me to close the blinds?"

"No. It's nice to have something to look at beside the sky. I probably won't sleep anyway."

"I'll go have a cigarette, then."

"Those things will kill you, you know."

"Your horse is just as dangerous."

"Stop ragging on me about the horse. It was an accident."

"Ryan," Doug said as he turned the lock to let himself out, "you have no idea what that horse may have done. I hope someday you do remember the accident. Maybe then you'll admit I was right about him."

Ryan lay on his side and looked out the window into the tree-lined grassy courtyard. The huge elm trees cast shade from the mid-afternoon sun over several benches. The courtyard was surrounded on three sides by resident rooms and on the fourth side by the parking lot. A large hedge screened his view of the parking lot. The trees were changing colors, and a scattering of yellow and red leaves littered the grounds.

Ryan sighed, enjoying the view. His room faced the west, and in the distance he could see the snow-capped peaks of the Rocky Mountains. Somewhere out there, he had fallen from his horse. He wondered if he would ever remember it. He'd have to have Doug take him back to the place after he was better. Maybe if he saw the location, he would remember the accident.

And maybe it would be better if he didn't remember it, he mused. As long as he didn't remember it, he couldn't have nightmares about it.

Doug walked into view and took a seat on one of the benches under a tree. Ryan watched his brother take a cigarette pack out of his shirt pocket. The shirt was red. He tried to remember if the creature over the pocket had been a fox or an elephant. Doug had at least two red shirts, but it had already been at least three minutes since he had seen this one and he no longer remembered what was on it. He sighed when Doug lit the cigarette. Smoking had killed their mother, of that Ryan was certain. Why had Doug started after her death?

He'd started a lot of things after her death. Including pushing Ryan away from him, he recalled.

He saw Doug pull his cell phone from the holster on his hip and dial a number. Idly, Ryan watched as Doug talked, occasionally gesturing in the air with the cigarette, sometimes shaking his head. Then he was silent for a long time, puffing on the cigarette before Ryan saw his lips move again. He was shaking his head again.

Then he punched a button on the phone and set it down on the bench next to him. He finished the cigarette, crushed it out on the bottom of his shoe, and expertly flicked the butt into a nearby trash can.

Ryan continued watching, starting to feel a little drowsy, and noticed a reflection shining off his brother's cheek. Puzzled, he saw the reflection move, then Doug raised his hand to his face and wiped. Could it be a tear? Ryan wondered if Doug knew something about Ryan's condition that Ryan didn't know.

Doug put the phone back in the holster and stood, pulling a handkerchief out of his hip pocket. He wiped his eyes with the cloth, blew his nose, then stuffed the handkerchief back in his pocket and walked across the lawn toward the parking lot.

Ryan fell asleep.

Two hours later, Doug returned with Ryan's dinner. Ryan woke, confused. "Where am I?" he asked.

"The rehab center. Remember? You checked in a few hours ago."

"Oh. I forgot."

"That's okay, Ryan. You'll remember eventually."

Doug left the center shortly after nine that evening, promising to return in the morning to help Ryan start learning to feed himself again.

Alone for the first night in more than two weeks, Ryan turned the television on to ease the total silence and fell asleep just before the news came on. An hour later, the timer he had set clicked the television off and Ryan started to toss and moan in his sleep.

He was riding down a hill when a flash of movement between the trees caught his eye and he turned in that direction. A tail swished from behind a bush – a long, black, horse's tail, the horse itself not visible behind the bush. The tail swished back and forth, back and forth, then another movement got his attention and he looked again.

A green unicorn stood by the bush, the sun reflecting off its long horn, and a trace of snow clinging to its beard as it tossed its head, shaking its long green mane.

The unicorn's muzzle lowered to the ground, picked up a long branch, and dropped it into a hole. It picked up another branch, adding it to the pile, then another.

From the back of his horse, Ryan watched with a mounting sensation of dread washing over him. The unicorn picked up a red cap – a beret – from the ground, and threw it into the hole with the branches. Then it reached in and took the cap back, tossing it to the side.

A loud, shuddering scream split the air!

Suddenly the unicorn swung its head around. Heart pounding, Ryan snatched his horse's reins and turned him sharply, trying to leave the scene before the unicorn saw him.

"Go!" he moaned, his legs twitching as he urged the horse on. But he wasn't moving. His legs twitched harder, to no avail. His horse was gone from under him.

Darkness descended. "Don't go over there! Don't go for help!" he shouted into the blackness.

He stilled as he became aware of a distant buzzing sound. A voice echoed in his head: "We'll go in here." The buzzing grew louder, buzzing over and over.

He looked for his horse, but saw only the green unicorn. It stood over Ryan and said: "Duck! Do it!"

Ryan answered, "I think it sucks!"

The unicorn turned to leave. "Don't leave me!" Ryan shouted as it galloped away.

A blinding white light blocked his view of the unicorn, growing brighter as it drew nearer. He started falling, and threw his hands over his eyes to ward off the blinding light. He continued falling, down, down, into the hole. "No!" he screamed just before he hit the ground.

Part II
May 7-22, 1994
The Murder Victim

CHAPTER 8

SUNLIGHT DAPPLED THE small clearing in the Colorado Rockies, dazzling off the patches of snow near a large fallen pine tree. The uprooted tree had torn a great hole in the earth, a hole well-shaded by the bare roots that still reached skyward from the base of the trunk, a hole now filled with snow ... and something else.

A coyote sniffed the ground under the tree, scratching briefly under the trunk, his nostrils filled with the scent of squirrel and something unfamiliar. Intrigued by the new scent, he moved to the base of the tree and nosed around a pile of branches. It was a warm day in May, and water dripped onto his fur from melting snow that still clung to some of the branches.

Excited by his new discovery, he began digging and pawing in earnest, sending snow flying in all directions, until he finally reached the source of the tantalizing odor. He tugged earnestly at his quarry, growling slightly, trying to dislodge it from its hiding place. Suddenly he paused, head raised, listening, the strange taste lingering on his tongue.

Sounds approached, growing louder and more disturbing. With one last sniff at his treasure, the coyote reluctantly loped into the forest.

The coyote gone, a squirrel emerged from its hiding place in the pile of branches and ran along the trunk, pausing to listen to the sounds its sharp ears detected. Its bushy tail twitched nervously while the sleek, furry rodent listened to the human voices singing in the distance. As the voices drew nearer, it raced off the end of the log and scurried up a pine tree, chattering a warning to its fellow forest creatures.

"Forty-nine bottles of beer on the wall, forty-nine bottles of beer. If one of those bottles should happen to fall, forty-eight bottles of beer on the wall!" the scout troop sang with lagging enthusiasm as it tramped higher up the mountain.

"Forty-eight bottles of beer on the wall …" the singing continued, punctuated by the huffing and puffing of the young singers as the climb began to take its toll.

"Company, halt!" Scoutmaster Gary Nixon interrupted the singing with an upraised hand and a smile.

The marching and singing stopped abruptly and the five boys caught up to their leader. They turned around and waited patiently for the father of one of the boys to catch up. "I'm here, I'm here," the man panted. "You don't have to stop for me."

"That's not why I stopped, Herb," the scoutmaster replied with a grin. "I don't think I can handle any more 'beer on the wall.' Let's take a short break here. I knew I shouldn't have had that second cup of coffee this morning, and that song isn't helping my bladder any."

A cheer from the tired young boys split the air. They had stopped next to a fallen tree in a small clearing, and the boys quickly sat on it and opened canteens for a drink of water while their leader stepped out of sight behind some bushes.

Although it was May, there was still snow on the ground in the shady areas, and it didn't take long for a snowball fight to break out.

Nixon reappeared a few moments later, good-naturedly dodging a snowball that one boy carelessly threw in his direction. Ruefully reflecting that the energetic young boys were making him feel older than his thirty-seven years, he stopped at the base of the fallen tree and picked up a broken branch to use as a walking stick. Tapping the stick against another branch to shake the snow from it, he noted the paw prints the coyote had left in the snow a few minutes before.

Suddenly he stiffened, blanched, and stared through the pile of dead pine branches heaped over a hole at the base of the tree. He prodded gingerly with the branch he held before dropping it back on the ground as if it were hot.

"Come on, men," Nixon said, quickly walking back toward the trail. "Haven't I gotten you too tired for such shenanigans yet? This is far enough for me, so let's head on back down the hill. By the time we get out of here, you'll be ready for lunch. Let's go." He whispered something to the other man, who glanced back apprehensively at the fallen tree before falling into step with the leader.

"Hey, Dad," one of the boys called as they started to leave the area. "Do you smell something funny?"

"Yeah, your armpit!" another boy answered, giving the first boy a shove.

"Cut it out! I'm serious!"

The man didn't turn around. "Probably a dead animal," he called back to the boys. "And no, we're not going to look for it. I'm not going to have you all describing to your mothers in graphic detail what some maggot-infested carcass looks like. Come on, let's hike!"

* * *

Having been tipped off by her source at the sheriff's office, reporter Sheila Fernelli was waiting alone at the trail head when the Alpine Rescue Team emerged from the forest shadows carrying a body bag, followed by the coroner and sheriff's detective, both also on foot.

While the men prevented her from asking questions until the body was loaded into the ambulance, Sheila recognized the coroner and some of the rescue workers and wrote down their names so she could interview them later.

It was the detective who would have the most information, and she sighed when she realized the investigation was being headed by Jim Harrison. Her previous encounter the year before with Jim and his chauvinistic boss, Sheriff Harley Watson, had been less than satisfactory. She knew it would be a battle to get information from either of them.

Jim had been fairly new to the department back then. It was now seven months later. Harley had had plenty of opportunity to create Jim in his own image. By now, he might be as surly and uncooperative as his predecessor had been. Still, her friend in dispatch had told her that Harrison was a pretty nice guy, so maybe he had been immune to Harley Watson's brainwashing. Maybe if she treated him as if she expected him to be nice, he would be.

She hadn't seen Jim Harrison since the day of Ryan North's accident. Her editor had kept her on local political issues, covering town council and school board meetings. There had been no major crimes in the county all winter, and the few crime stories her editor had allowed her to write had been recitations of crime statistics of the "police blotter" variety. But Dennis Ingram, the other staff reporter, was on vacation this week. This story, whatever it turned out to be, was hers.

She stood back and observed the action without interfering, hoping to get a few words with the detective before he climbed in the Blazer and left.

Finally, with the body on its way down the mountain in the back of the rescue ambulance, she was left alone with Jim Harrison and a large duffle bag lying on the ground by his county vehicle.

He nodded at her and opened the rear gate of the Blazer.

"Sheila Fernelli," she said with a confident smile. "*Rocky Mountain Chronicle.* You're Jim Harrison, right? We met last year on the Ryan North case. I don't know if you remember me. I'm afraid we didn't get much chance to talk then."

"I remember you. You wanted to ride up there in the helicopter. Nothing personal," Jim continued, "but we prefer not having the press around while paramedics are working. I imagine Mr. North was glad to get to the hospital without having to stop for an interview first." He picked up the duffle bag and set it on the tailgate.

Sheila flinched, and any illusions she might have had about this being a friendly interview evaporated. "I had no intention of interfering with the paramedics, Detective. And an interview with a coma victim is a pretty one-sided conversation at best." She paused. "So what do we have this time?" she asked boldly. "My source only told me you were bringing a body out. Do you know who it is?"

"No." Jim opened the bag and rummaged through its contents, pulling out his clipboard. "No identification on the body."

"Man or woman?" Sheila persisted, pen poised over her notebook.

"Teenaged boy," Jim replied, zipping the bag shut again.

"Race?"

"Caucasian."

"Who found it?"

"A Lakewood scoutmaster, Gary Nixon, who was up here hiking with some kids this morning. He showed us where the body was, but he left before we bagged it. He was in a black Bronco. Didn't you see him?"

"I got here just as he was pulling out in his car," Sheila explained. "I'll talk to him later, if you'll give me his phone number."

Abruptly, Jim answered, "You'll have to ask the sheriff about that." He tossed the duffle bag in the back of the Blazer, then sat down on the tailgate and sighed. "You know how he is," he said finally, glancing sideways at the woman. "I can't help you there."

Sheila wondered if she could be imagining the sudden shift in his attitude. "Detective?" she said tentatively.

"What?"

"Will you tell me off the record what this is? I know the sheriff has a low opinion of the press, but if you'd give me some information, I'll know what questions to ask the other witnesses. I won't use you as a source."

Jim sighed again, studying her face for a moment before answering, "That's all right. There's no point in trying to keep it under wraps anyway. I'm sorry I was curt with you. I'm just tired from the hike out, and not looking forward to this investigation much. I worked a lot of homicides in Denver, but one thing I really hate is when a kid is involved."

Sheila looked at the tall, broad-shouldered detective, and wondered if she'd misjudged him. Maybe Harley's attitude hadn't rubbed off on his new detective as thoroughly as he would have liked. "It's okay. I understand," she answered. "This is a murder, then? I assume you will be in charge of the case?"

"Murder," Jim affirmed, nodding. "The body was hidden in a hole, covered by branches. It obviously didn't crawl in there by itself."

"How did he die?"

"This is not for publication, but the coroner said it was probably strangulation. Don't quote me on that, though. That has to come from him after the autopsy Monday."

"When does he think it happened? If he's guessing strangulation that quickly, it must not have been very decomposed, right? That would suggest a recent death."

"There's still a lot of snow up there and the body was buried in it. It may not be as recent as you think. You'll have to wait for the coroner's report to be sure."

"Can I use you as a source to write that the scoutmaster found a body hidden under some branches, buried in the snow, that there was no identification but it was a teenaged boy, unknown time of death, unknown cause or motive, and that you are investigating this as a homicide?" Sheila asked.

"That's about all you can write, because that's about all we know so far." Jim stood up abruptly and closed the rear gate.

Sheila closed her notebook. "Thanks for the interview. I'd better get to my desk and write it up before your boss issues a press release and I lose my advantage. Can you call me when the body is identified?"

"Sorry, I probably said too much to you already. You know how Harley is about the press, and I have to admit I sort of agree with him. I gave you what I did because I knew you could get that info from Mr. Nixon anyway and I'd rather give you some facts than have you print speculation. But you need to go through channels for the rest of the information, okay?"

"I understand." She shook his hand. "I'm sorry you feel that way, though. We really are on the same side, you know."

"I'm not so sure. Too many investigations have been hurt by reporters inadvertently tipping off suspects before the police can get to them."

"You're saying we're going to remain adversaries, then," Sheila said sadly. "I was hoping we could cooperate."

Jim shook his head. "That's not how Harley does business. You know that."

"And he knows how I do business. If there's something to report, I'm going to report it, no matter whom it might hurt. I won't protect the guilty," she said firmly as the detective stepped in behind the wheel, tossing his clipboard on the passenger seat.

"It's not the guilty we're worried about," he replied as he put the car in gear and backed out. "You don't protect the innocent, either."

As he pulled away from her, he glanced back in the rearview mirror with mixed emotions. He had rather enjoyed sparring with her. She had stood her ground, despite his initial brusqueness. Harley Watson had a deep-rooted dislike of the press, especially tabloid reporters, and he knew that Sheila Fernelli would have gotten little information from Harley directly. Harley was fond of replying to reporters' inquiries with the line, "Sorry, it's a police matter and I can't discuss it."

To the extent he could answer questions without compromising his investigation, Jim was somewhat more forthcoming, but he couldn't help enjoying playing with the press, too. It was the sort of thing Harley would want him to do.

Then he remembered his last meeting with Sheila Fernelli, and the story she had written about the rescue. She had done a good job, and had mentioned Jim by name in a favorable light. Being new to the area, he had been pleased that the first publicity he received in his new job had been so favorable. Most of the press coverage of police action in Denver had focused on what cops did wrong.

He'd forgotten about that article in the intervening months. He sighed, glancing back in the mirror again, wishing they'd parted on a better note – not because she might now feel like making him look bad, but simply because she deserved better treatment than that. He'd been around Harley too long.

He decided he deserved the sharp twinge of guilt he felt as he drove away. "Be what you are, Harrison," he muttered to himself. "Don't turn into another Arlo."

CHAPTER 9

MARTY HENDRICKS WIPED his brow on his sleeve and straightened up. Peeling off his surgical gloves, he switched off the tape recorder and sighed. *It's hard enough to embalm dead children,* he thought, *cutting them up like this is worse.* In cases like this, cold, professional detachment carried him only so far.

He picked up the clipboard holding a partially filled out coroner's report form. He read over what he had written before the state pathologist and the sheriff's detective had arrived for the autopsy.

Male Caucasian, age approximately fifteen to eighteen, height sixty-nine inches, weight one-thirty-two, brown hair, light brown eyes. He glanced at the naked body on the table. Nothing about whether the victim liked skiing or sunsets or girls or chocolate ice cream or life in general. Just cold, bare facts, describing the cold, bare remains of what had once been a handsome young man with his entire life ahead of him.

He carried the clipboard to a desk and sat down to write. Estimated time of death, unknown. Probably one to six months ago, possibly longer. Probable cause of death, strangulation. *Homicide.*

Restlessly, he stood up again and walked over to the coffeepot. There was a scant half-cup of coffee left in the pot, and he poured it into a cracked ceramic cup and flipped off the heating element. He glanced at the clock over the door. It was already five-thirty in the evening. The pathologist had left with his tissue samples an hour before, leaving Marty to sew up the body cavity and begin filling out the preliminary reports. Jim Harrison had taken his own notes during the autopsy and left shortly after the pathologist.

He walked back over to the desk and sat down again. Lab results would not be in for several days, but they had seen none of the typical and more obvious signs of drug abuse, such as needle tracks or irritated nasal membranes. But samples had been taken of a fine white powder

74

that had been discovered clinging to the treads of his right gym shoe. Further examination had revealed traces of the powder inside his right pant leg as well.

The three men had discussed this finding at length, speculating that he might have stepped on a packet of the powder, causing it to puff upward into his clothing. Had he been at a drug party of some kind? Had he threatened to call the police when the drugs came out? Had he tried to destroy someone's drugs? Was that why he had been killed? Then how had his body come to lie in a remote section of wilderness area?

And why in the world was he wearing pantyhose under his jeans?

Lividity, the discoloration indicating the settling of blood into the surrounding tissue after death, showed on both the front and back sides of the body, indicating he had been moved after he had died; it was most pronounced in the area of the head, hands, and feet. For some period of time, he had lain face-down, possibly draped over something, with head, arms, and feet dangling. Then he had been placed on his back in the hole at the base of the uprooted tree and covered with pine branches. An outstretched arm protruding between the branches had apparently caught the attention of a coyote who dug snow away from the hand then tried to make a meal of it before being scared away by a noisy scout troop. The bite marks had been fresh.

The boy was not wearing gloves, but they found no microscopic rolls of skin under his fingernails, which they would have expected if he had fought and scratched his attacker. There was bruising on his shoulder blades, bruising on his right forearm, a reddened area on his left wrist and a round red mark about the size of a quarter on the front of the throat where the attacker had crushed his larynx with some object. Some older bruising and abrasions were found on the insides of each knee and on the seat bones, suggesting a lengthy horseback ride several days before his death.

The bruising on his back suggested he had been strangled while pinned to the ground, possibly with the killer kneeling on the right forearm. Why the boy had not fought back with his left hand was still a mystery. Based on the red mark on his wrist, they surmised he had been tied down, preventing any defensive action.

They had puzzled over the mark on his throat for some time. With strangulation, they would have expected to see marks of the attacker's thumbs there. The only conclusion they could reach was that the boy had been wearing a medallion and the killer had gotten it under his thumb as he choked the boy to death. But the medallion, if that's what it had been, was missing. *It's too bad*, Marty thought. *It would have been a big help when a suspect was arrested.*

IF a suspect was arrested, he corrected himself. They didn't know who the victim was yet, or even when he had died. The body had been found buried under the snow and very well-preserved. From the lack of decomposition, the coroner was certain the boy had been covered with snow within hours of his death. Since there had been snow in the area all winter, and the last heavy snowfall had been only a month before, there was a six-month window of time during which the homicide could have taken place.

First they needed to learn who the boy was. Marty already knew there had been no unresolved missing persons reports filed for that general mountain area all winter, and if the boy had been "last seen" anywhere else, it could take weeks to identify him. There had been no identification on the body. Fingerprints and a general description were being sent to the Colorado Bureau of Investigation, CBI as it was called, but Marty knew that prints of missing children were not always available.

He hoped he would soon be able to remove the name "John Doe" from the records and replace it with the kid's real name.

Marty rewound the tape recorder and began to play back the observations made during the autopsy. He turned to the computer terminal on the desk and began to type.

An hour later, Marty put the printouts in a folder and stood. He walked over to the table to gather his instruments, pausing to pull a sheet over the boy's body. Coarse black thread closed the incisions made earlier when they had examined the internal organs. He stared again at the boy's face before pulling the sheet over it. Why did it seem so familiar?

"You should be begging your dad to borrow the car tonight, Son, not lying here on a slab in a mortuary, cut up by an autopsy knife."

With so little evidence found with the body, there was nothing to tie the boy to his killer. He might as well have strangled himself for all the clues the body had yielded. Perhaps after he was identified, some critical witness would be found who might have a clue of what had happened and, ultimately, who had killed him and why.

Why any such witness had not already reported the crime was a question the sheriff would have to ask, assuming a witness was ever found. Marty had little experience with homicide investigations but it was enough for him to be amazed at the variety of reasons offered by witnesses who chose not to come forth until forced to do so.

Of course, based on where the body was found, it was entirely possible that there simply were no witnesses and this homicide might never be solved. Considering how little effort the killer had put in to concealing the body, he probably wasn't worried about witnesses at all.

Hopefully he would be in for an unpleasant surprise someday.

With a sigh, Marty dropped the knives, needles, and bone saw into the sterilizer, pushed the table with the boy's body into the cold room, locked up, and went home.

CHAPTER 10

IT HAD BEEN FOUR DAYS since the boy's body had been discovered in the mountains, and they still hadn't identified the victim, which Sheriff Harley Watson found very odd considering that this was probably the first time in years they'd actually had a complete body with virtually no decomposition found in the mountains. Identification should have been a breeze. The state bureau of investigation had come up dry on the fingerprints, and had sent him pictures of every unprinted kid in their files that had disappeared in the past year, but so far, unless the kid for some reason just didn't resemble his photo, there had been no match. The coyote had destroyed the only fingerprint that might have been easily matched – the index fingerprint required to get a driver's license – assuming of course, that the boy had a driver's license and was from Colorado in the first place.

He wasn't ready to run a photo on television yet. That was no way for some grieving parents to learn that their missing son was never coming home again. They'd have to keep working at it.

With a sigh, Harley picked up the stack of photos they had received since the body was found. As soon as the wire services picked up the story of the body's discovery, photos had come in from all over the country, from government agencies and parents of missing children, as well as from private investigators. Most had arrived within hours of the news reports. There were more than fifty in all, but many were duplicates, having been sent from more than one source. Harley, Jim, and Marty had all looked through them twice each already and concluded the dead boy's photo simply wasn't in the pile. But it wouldn't hurt to try again. With the picture of the John Doe propped on his desk, he began to look through the photos again. Perhaps the hair color had changed, a beard been shaved? How much of a beard did a boy this age have, anyway?

He decided to study the written descriptions, comparing them, one at a time, to the picture on his desk. Occasionally, he would turn the photo over and compare it more closely before laying it aside with the rest. He was halfway through the pile when suddenly he stopped, puzzled, and turned one photo back over. While the description on the back matched the brown-haired victim, the photo was of a very blond boy who looked nothing like either the victim or the description on the back of the photo. He set it aside and continued through the pile. By the time he reached the bottom, he had found three photos of the same boy. He looked again, perplexed, at the reports on the backs of the photos. How could there be three pictures of the same kid with different descriptions? Only one photo resembled the description on the back.

"Damn!" he grumbled. "Maybe one of these kids is the one we've got." He read the written descriptions on the fact sheets and realized that both of the other two boys fit the John Doe's general description. One was listed as a runaway, the other as a possible parental abduction. He started to reach for the phone when he recognized the name on one of the sheets. Daryl Walker. Son of State Senator Gene Walker, a sixteen-year-old listed as a runaway the previous fall. He looked thoughtfully at the autopsy photo on the desk as he picked up the phone and dialed the agency who had sent the pictures.

"Hello," he said when the phone was answered, "this is Sheriff Harley Watson over at Clear Creek. I'm the one who has that teenaged John Doe we're trying to ID."

"Oh, yes, I remember you," said the girl on the other end. "This is Mary. I took the information from you originally."

"Yes." Inwardly he groaned. *The airhead*, he recalled. "Uh, the reason I'm calling is there seems to be some sort of a mix-up. I have three photos of the same boy here, but with different fact sheets. They came from your office. Only one of the fact sheets matches its picture."

"Oh, dear, I was afraid of that. When I was putting the files away, I had two folders with photos but no fact sheets and one folder with three fact sheets. I wondered how that had happened." She giggled nervously.

Watson held his tongue, resisting the urge to tell the incompetent bimbo that she was filing people's missing children, not old invoices, and she should be more careful.

Instead he gave her the names of the two boys and asked her to please wire new photos, correctly identified this time, thank you very much, yes, I'll have a nice day.

Exasperated, he hung up the phone. Those photos had all come in the second day of the investigation. No one had given them another glance at the time because the blond boy in the photos clearly didn't resemble the John Doe. Only by looking at the fact sheets instead of the photos could anyone have noticed that there was a mismatch.

"Oh, well, there's nothing you can do about it now. Just hope the ding-a-ling wires the right pictures this time. And hope that boy doesn't turn out to be Daryl Walker." He walked into the dispatch room to tell the dispatcher to let him know the minute the photos came in over the wire.

While he waited, Harley looked at the information on the missing person report that had been attached to the photo. The senator had reported his son missing just a week after the boy had stated he was going to run away. The investigation had been dropped after a couple of weeks, the police believing he had simply made good on his threat.

Harley wondered what politics had been involved in that decision. Could it be that the senator didn't have any influence over Denver's police force? Senator Walker had a reputation as a crusader and often stepped on toes in the process. Once he espoused a cause, he carried it through to the finish. Early last year he had launched an attack against a chemical plant that had two toxic spills within three months. The senator had succeeded in shutting down the plant, to the delight of several environmental groups. Other groups were not so delighted, including the union whose workers lost their jobs due to the shutdown. The company had lost millions between fines and lost revenues and eventually filed bankruptcy. Harley had heard that the police commissioner's brother-in-law was one of the workers who lost their job. He had also heard that the commissioner's wife had most of her personal savings invested in stock in that company.

Several years earlier, Walker had been an eyewitness to the near-fatal beating of a young gay man at the hands of a gang. That incident, and the police officer's callous handling of the victim, had repulsed him so much he had begun a one-man crusade for gay rights and increased sentences for a number of hate crimes, helping several area cities pass several new ordinances as he pressed unsuccessfully for similar state legislation.

Later, when an anti-gay-rights state amendment was proposed, which had the effect of overturning the new laws he had rallied into existence, he fought hard against its passage but the measure was passed by voters – a victory publicly praised by the Denver police commissioner. The amendment was currently on hold pending review by the U.S. Supreme Court but the subject remained a touchy one for many residents and Senator Walker continued his fight.

Had the crusading senator been so powerless that he had really had to give up on his own son after only two weeks? Harley was glad he would not be the one to break to him the news of his son's death. That was the coroner's job.

Harley jumped when the dispatcher buzzed the intercom to tell him the photos had come in. "Bingo," he said to himself as he compared the photo identified as Daryl Walker to the one of the homicide victim. While the coroner would make the official identification, Harley knew there was no doubt that the boy found dead in the mountains several days earlier was, indeed, Daryl Walker. But who had killed him? And why? And when? He pressed the intercom to summon Jim Harrison into his office. With the senator already at odds with the Denver police, there would be no mistakes made finding the boy's killer. This was one investigation that would be handled carefully, thoroughly, and strictly by the book.

"Yes, Harley?" Jim Harrison said upon entering the office.

"We have a tentative I.D.," Harley replied. "Look at these photos." He pushed the photos across the desk.

Jim pulled up a chair and studied them. "Looks like a match, all right. Who is it?"

"Senator Walker's kid, Daryl. Ran away last October sixteenth, or at least that's what they thought." He handed the bio to Jim, who quickly scanned it.

"Apparently they were wrong, or else the kid didn't get far," Jim mused. "I assume we got all the wire reports at the time. I'll look them up. Wonder what he was doing in the woods before he died."

"If he died in the woods," Harley amended. "Of course, being a wilderness area, it's not likely the body was hauled in from somewhere else."

"No, he would have been thrown into a mine shaft near a road if he were killed somewhere else." Jim leaned back in the chair, thoughtfully. "October, huh? That would tie in with the snow. He must have been killed just before the first big snowfall up there."

Harley thumbed through the back of his desk calendar, looking at the previous year. "That was the second weekend of deer season, remember, Jim?" Harley said. "That hunting party got trapped over on the Evergreen side on Sunday because they drove off the main roads and got snowed in."

"I remember that one. The rescue squad got them out, but they had to wait for a snow plow and a tow truck to get their car out of there a week later after it finally stopped snowing."

"In fact," Harley continued, digging in his bottom drawer for a battered notebook, "we had a pretty busy time that weekend. I think that was also the weekend that singer had the riding accident up in that area." He thumbed through the book, stopping on a cluttered page. "Yes, here it is. A call to send a rescue helicopter up on Goliath to pick up an injured hunter October sixteenth. You took the call because Patrol was tied up on a couple accidents. It wasn't until you got up there that you found out you were rescuing a celebrity."

"I remember. I remember being informed by a news reporter who almost got there ahead of me. The same one, incidentally, who met me at the trailhead when we carried the body out Saturday. She must carry a police band radio wherever she goes."

Harley grunted. "Sheila Fernelli, queen of the tabloid press. Stay away from her, Jim. She's nothing but trouble."

Jim shrugged. "She's not so bad, Harley. A little enthusiastic maybe. She gave us a nice write up on that rescue last year."

Harley arched an eyebrow. "She's a pain in the ass, Jim. Stay away from her."

Jim flushed slightly, coughed once, then said, "Anyway, with all the people we had up in the woods that day, maybe we can find someone who saw Walker or his killer."

Harley snapped the notebook shut and tossed it back in the drawer. "Let's hope so. Start with the rescue workers, and the hunters that found the singer. Leave the celebrity out of it as long as you can. Don't even comment that he was there that day, except to people who already know it, like the rescue squad. You know how the press is. You talk to Ryan North about a homicide and it will be front page news on every damn tabloid in the country thanks to idiots like that Fernelli woman. I want to keep this investigation low-key if possible. Nothing but the facts. You know how Senator Walker gets when he's crossed, and he already has it in for the Denver police over the kid's disappearance in the first place. Let's see if we can handle this with a minimum of interference from the press." He added firmly, "And keep that pantyhose business quiet. We're not going to embarrass his father with that sort of thing, at least not until we find out what was going on. If his kid was a tinkerbell, I don't want him reading about it in the paper. Understand?"

"Yes, sir," Jim replied.

"Now," Harley went on, "this is our jurisdiction and I don't want anyone interfering with your investigation. I'm sure you'll enjoy a chance to show up Denver PD, especially since they were the ones who gave up on finding the kid last year. I'm sure they think we're nothing but hicks out here. We'll ask for help from CBI when we need it but I think the clues are going to be found in those mountains and that's where your expertise lies. I doubt anyone else in the state is better qualified to handle this thing, you know? Between your rescue and tracking background and those years you spent working Homicide in Denver, this should be right up your alley. So you're in charge of the investigation but keep me posted every step of the way."

It was the nearest thing to a compliment the gruff sheriff had given him to his face in months and Jim didn't know how to respond so he said nothing.

"In the meantime," Harley continued, not noticing Jim's discomfiture, "get this photo over to Marty. He'll have to confirm the I.D. but I have no doubt this is the right kid."

"No problem. I'll get right on it." Jim stood up, took the picture, and walked to the door. He hesitated, turned, and said, "I really appreciate your support, Harley. This means a lot to me. Thanks."

Harley dismissed him with a wave of his hand. "Yeah, yeah, yeah. Now cut the touchy-feely crap and get to work."

CHAPTER 11

THANKS TO HER FRIEND in the county dispatch room, Sheila Fernelli had been the only reporter on the scene when the boy's body was carried out of the woods the previous weekend. Her story of the discovery had given her newspaper, the tiny *Rocky Mountain Chronicle*, a moment of glory, as she was able to file on deadline and the sheriff's press release wasn't issued until after the *Denver Post* went to bed. Her editor was quite pleased.

She had experienced a flash of irritation when she read the sidebar in the *Post* about the Alpine Rescue team who carried the body out. It mentioned some other rescues they had done in that part of the mountains, including the Ryan North rescue the year before. It still rankled her that she had not been allowed to do the follow-ups on that story, and the sidebar about the rescue group only reminded her of it. But at least her editor was letting her do the follow-ups on the discovery of the boy's body.

Now, thanks to her source, she had learned the names of the boys whose pictures were mixed up, and been told that one of these boys was, in fact, the murder victim. But the sheriff refused to say which until the coroner confirmed it, and he was holding up any press release on the subject until he had a positive ID and the family had been notified.

She had already written two stories, one for each boy, and only awaited the official statement from the coroner before inserting the correct story in the next edition of the *Rocky Mountain Chronicle*. Her editor had already approved both stories for publication as written and a spot was being held open on the front page in anticipation of the announcement that was expected to come any minute.

The word came about twenty minutes before press time and the presses were held until the story could be typeset. *Body Found in Mountains Identified as Senator's Son* was the headline. "Film at ten," Sheila said to herself, wryly making a mental note to watch all the news that night to see if any of the media reporters revealed any information she didn't already have.

Sheila didn't just want to report the investigation. She was determined to be a part of it. For two years, she had choked back her integrity while writing for a tabloid just to get the writing experience. She had been relieved to finally land a position where she could do some real reporting for a small but respectable newspaper in Clear Creek County, but found that her past haunted her in dealings with the police. Jim Harrison and his chauvinistic boss Harley Watson hadn't been the first to brush her aside – just the most recent.

Unfortunately, she knew she needed cooperation from the police. Sheila wasn't interested in investigating grocery store meat handling practices or automotive repair rip-offs or political conspiracies, which is where most investigative journalists seemed to end up; Sheila wanted to solve this murder. Maybe then she could get some respect. Her editor had given her permission to stay on this story – her first assignment of any importance since she had started working there – mostly because the senior reporter, Dennis Ingram, was busy with a series of stories on water contamination from certain mining operations. It was her first big opportunity, and she was determined to do a thorough job of it.

She turned back to the notes she had used for the story that was running through the presses. It would be on the streets by four o'clock that afternoon. She had a lot to do before it came out if she was to beat other reporters to possible witnesses.

Daryl Eugene Walker had been sixteen when he disappeared, a Junior at Lakewood High School. She noted from one of the original articles that he had worked on the school newspaper as a reporter on the various clubs on the campus. His column had been titled the "DEW Point," using his initials in the title.

He worked at King Soopers, the new grocery store that had recently opened up a few blocks from his home. He had worked there for less than two months before his disappearance, working a couple hours at night three times a week unloading boxes of meat from the delivery trucks, and a few hours on Sundays restocking the meat case first thing in the morning.

His parents had told reporters the boy had been acting strangely for several weeks and had threatened to leave home after his driving privileges had been revoked for two weeks following a violation of his curfew the Saturday before he disappeared. They had not taken him seriously at the time, but when he disappeared the next weekend while they were gone they assumed he had made good on his threat.

His parents had been out of town October sixteenth through eighteenth, and Daryl had said he would stay at a friend's house that weekend. The friend said that Daryl had mentioned coming over, but when he didn't show up that Saturday night, the boy concluded Daryl had decided to stay at his own house instead.

It wasn't until the parents arrived home on the eighteenth that anyone realized Daryl was missing. His supervisor said he had not been scheduled to work on Saturday, but had not shown up for his shift on Sunday. The phone was unanswered when his supervisor called his home to find out where he was.

Sheila read through the notes she had borrowed from Dennis Ingram, the reporter who had written the original stories the previous fall. Police had talked to Daryl's two "best buddies," but neither boy had heard from Daryl nor had any idea where he might have gone.

Both boys said Daryl had acted distant and distracted for several weeks, and had not been hanging around with them as much as he usually did. They felt it was because his new job at the grocery store kept him too busy.

Police had made some routine inquiries, concluded that the boy most likely had run away as he had threatened, and closed the case several days later, despite his father's growing insistence that the boy had not been serious and certainly would have returned by then if he had run away. They had restored his driving privileges so he could take care of himself while they were gone; why would he leave after his punishment had ended?

The senator was sure something had happened to his son, even though there had been no evidence of foul play. A neighbor had seen him apparently willingly climb into a dark-blue pickup truck on Saturday. Since it appeared he was not abducted, and the neighbor was unable to describe the driver, the case was closed with little investigation.

Sheila frowned at the police commissioner's quotation the reporter had jotted down with the words "off the record" written after it and underlined. "I know he's the senator's kid, but to us, he's just another runaway who doesn't want to be found. I can't justify tying up detectives on this case any longer when there's no indication of foul play. I'm sure the kid will come home when he's ready. If Senator Walker wants to pursue this, he'll have to hire his own detectives."

"Wonder how he got Dennis to put that off the record *after* he already had it written down," she mused. "I'm not sure I would have been that nice, but I suppose maybe Dennis was trying to maintain a working relationship with the man." The idea was relatively foreign to Sheila Fernelli. She wondered what it would be like to have a working relationship with the police, instead of having to fight for every crumb they threw her.

She shrugged and picked up the phone. One item on her list was to get into the school and try to talk to some of the people Daryl had known. Since Daryl had worked on the school paper, it gave her a way in without anyone knowing she was investigating his disappearance. She was sure his school would jump at the chance to have a real live reporter talk to the journalism students about careers in investigative reporting.

* * *

"Mrs. Moore?" Sheila Fernelli stood at the doorway of the office, waiting to see the faculty sponsor of the school newspaper at Daryl Walker's high school.

"Come in," the woman replied, standing up to shake hands. Evelyn Moore was a tall woman, about fifty-five, with dark hair pulled up on top of her head.

"I'm Sheila Fernelli," Sheila said. "I called about giving a talk to some of your budding journalists."

"Yes," Evelyn Moore replied. Her own journalistic instincts told her that Sheila Fernelli had not been *quite* frank when she had called with her offer a few hours before. In the fifteen years that Evelyn had been faculty sponsor for the newspaper, she had never before had a professional journalist *ask* to give a talk to her students. It was always the other way around, and such talks were normally set up through a newspaper's public relations department, not one-on-one with a reporter. And the timing was just a little too much of a coincidence. "Have a seat, Miss Fernelli, or should that be Ms?"

"Please call me Sheila."

"Fine, Sheila. Now, tell me why you want to talk to my students."

Sheila launched into her prepared story about remembering her own days on the school paper and wanting to share some of her experiences with other students to help them decide if investigative journalism was for them.

Evelyn listened to the fabrication without interrupting, then asked, "Why did you choose our school, Sheila? Were you ever a student here?"

"No, I wasn't. I – I just chose Lakewood at random. My editor wanted me to get some experience speaking before groups, and I thought this would be a good way to do it."

Evelyn Moore leaned across the desk and looked into Sheila's eyes. "Why are you really here, Sheila?"

Sheila fidgeted uncomfortably. "What do you mean? I told you why I'm here. If you don't want me to speak to the students, I'll go somewhere else."

Evelyn leaned back and shook her head. "Sheila, I was a practicing professional journalist while you were still in diapers. I learned to read body language while you were learning to read *The Cat in the Hat*. You're not telling me the truth. What's going on?"

Sheila's shoulders slumped. "Okay, I'm really here to investigate the disappearance of Daryl Walker. I know he worked on the paper and I was hoping to talk to some of the students who knew him."

"That's better, Sheila. Now maybe we can work together. I knew Daryl very well. What did you want to know?"

"I'm not sure. I guess you should know that they've found his body in the mountains. It'll be in the papers this afternoon."

"I heard it on the radio an hour ago. I had a feeling that's why you were here. He was a good boy. A good student, too, at least until the last month or so before he disappeared. He had a regular column on the paper, and he never missed a deadline. And he liked the idea of investigative reporting. He always wanted assignments where he could work under cover in some way." She smiled sadly as she remembered the boy. "Not," she added, "that there was much undercover work to be done on a high school campus."

"Was there any particular area he showed interest in?" Sheila asked. "Like trying to expose graft and corruption in the cafeteria, or anything like that?"

Evelyn laughed. "No, not really. He investigated rumors that the student body election was fixed, and he once staked out the locker area to try to find out who was pouring a substance called 'Slime' through the vent slots in the locker doors. But he never found anything in either investigation."

"What was he working on before he disappeared?"

"His weekly column reported on the various clubs on campus, their activities, members, accomplishments. Not much cloak-and-dagger work there."

"Did he have any notebooks or anything that was left behind?"

"He had a desk that had some papers and things in it. I offered them to his parents after he was gone, but they didn't want them. Actually, I still have them. We kept hoping he'd come back someday. You know the police thought he had run away. I suppose now that he's dead, the police will be asking for them. I'm kind of surprised they never talked to any of his teachers last year when he disappeared. The senator hired an investigator a week later, but all he wanted to know was if Daryl had ever told anyone where he would go if he did run away. He didn't seem to believe it was anything but a runaway case either."

"I probably should talk to that investigator, too. Do you remember his name?"

"No, you'd have to ask Senator Walker about that. He talked to me for about two minutes."

"May I see the papers Daryl left?" Sheila asked.

"No harm in that." Evelyn stood up and walked to a file cabinet. She extracted a folder from the bottom drawer and handed it to Sheila.

"Thank you." Sheila looked through the notes, puzzled. Most of the pages had doodling in the margins, and some of the pages had homework assignments mixed in with random notes about names, dates, and places for various club meetings. Some were abbreviated. It wasn't much to go on.

"May I make photocopies of these?"

"If you want. I never could figure out if there was anything important on them or not. It all looked like the typical teenaged clutter."

"Mrs. Moore, I'd still like to talk to any students who may have known him. Would that be all right with you?"

"I think, now that you're finally being honest with me, we can arrange something. We often have guest speakers, and sometimes professionals come and actually work with our different departments for a day. The students really enjoy that."

"Whom have you had?" Sheila asked. "Maybe this is something my paper would like to be a regular part of."

"Well, last month the *Post* sent someone to talk to the students who run the press, and he talked about how different paper needs different handling in the press, and how to judge the quality of inks, and how printing in color is accomplished. An editor from the *Tribune* comes every spring to talk about ethics in journalism. And every fall, we ask someone to come over from one of the ad agencies to talk about how ads are written. We even had a celebrity once, when Ryan North worked at an ad agency, but that was a few years back, before he was really famous. He hadn't quit his day job yet." She chuckled.

"Really? I didn't know he worked for an ad agency. I did a story on him last year when he was found unconscious in the mountains. I got a tip and managed to get to the trailhead just as the rescue helicopter arrived to take the deputy up to the accident site."

"I remember that. We reported it ourselves in the school paper that week. We also sent him a get-well card in the hospital. The ad man who talked to us last fall used to work with Ryan North. He was at the hospital the day my students visited to get an update on Ryan's condition after he came out of the coma. As I recall, they were excited to get a hard quote from someone who actually knew Ryan personally. I think they felt important to know someone who knew someone famous."

"It would have been a highlight in my life when I was their age," Sheila agreed. "Anyway, nobody from my paper has been here before, I take it?"

"No. And we're a little short on investigative reporters, so I'm sure the students will give you their undivided attention."

"If it goes well, I'll talk to my editor about coming back next semester," Sheila promised. "But for now, when would be a good time?"

"Can you come back tomorrow at three o'clock? The club meets then and we have nothing special on the agenda. School's nearly out so it's pretty quiet now."

"That would be great, Mrs. Moore. And thank you. I think I've learned something from you today."

"Well, that's what I'm here for," Evelyn said with a laugh. "The copy machine is right outside. Go ahead and copy those papers. I have a few phone calls to return now."

Sheila copied the pages, returned the folder, and left the school. She was somewhat chagrined at having been found out so quickly, but relieved that she could ask questions freely. She just hoped the students wouldn't realize they were being pumped for information when she casually brought up Daryl's name.

* * *

Howard Vincent shook his head sadly. "The senator's kid? That's who that was?"

Jim Harrison had gone to the busy accounting office where Howard Vincent worked to talk to him about the Walker homicide investigation. He was perched uncomfortably in a hard plastic chair at the edge of Vincent's cubicle.

"Yes," he replied. "There's no doubt now. The coroner confirmed it this morning. I'm trying to interview possible witnesses, and we know you were in the area the day he likely was buried."

"What day was that, Detective? I was up there at least three times, hunting. Finally had to give up because of snow. Never did get a shot off." Howard ignored his ringing telephone.

"We believe it was Saturday, the sixteenth, the same day you found that unconscious singer."

"Oh, that day," Howard said, nodding. "Yes, I was up there with my daughter Cindy that day." He indicated a photograph on the corner of his desk. "She's actually the one who found him. Maybe you should talk to her." The phone stopped ringing when a secretary took the call.

Jim dismissed the comment with a wave of his hand. "That's all right, Mr. Vincent," he said. "We're not interested in Ryan North, we're hoping you saw someone else in the woods, or a vehicle on the road, or a loose horse, or the kid himself." He showed Howard a picture of Daryl Walker.

"Sorry, Detective," Howard replied, shaking his head. "I can't really help you. Cindy and I got there late that morning. We were almost ready to leave when I saw the trailer had a flat tire. Had to take it into town to get it fixed, then go back and get the horses. When we finally got to the mountain, it was nearly noon already so we unloaded the horses in the parking lot and started right up the trail. The only vehicle there was Ryan and Doug's truck and trailer. We didn't see anyone else, and had only been riding about an hour when she spotted Mr. North down the side of the hill."

"So you rode for help."

"Yes. Ran into his hunting buddy, what's his name? The blond guy. His business partner."

"Doug Norton?"

"Yeah, that's the one," he affirmed, nodding. "We saw him again later, in the hospital, when they let Cindy in to see Mr. North."

"So you didn't see anyone until you saw Mr. Norton?"

"That's right. He tried to call for help on his cell phone but didn't get a signal until we were almost back to his friend. I guess the cell coverage up there is pretty spotty." Jim nodded agreement. "Later there were a whole lot of people that came up there, but I'm sure you know about all of them. Paramedics and rescue workers. And you. Later at the trailhead there was the sheriff and a reporter. I talked to her for a while. Oh – and Mike Griffith came up with a truck to collect Mr. North's horses and trailer. And a car came to collect the rescue team about then. No other hunters, though. Of course, there are two other ways into that area. I know someone was out there because I heard a gunshot once. But I remember hearing that nobody took a deer or elk in that section after that day. Probably spooked the hell out of them with that chopper. Supposed to be a wilderness area and all – they're not used to that kind of ruckus." He winked, grinning, at Jim.

Jim smiled back. "Well, sir, we were trying to save a man's life. In fact, we succeeded. Better luck in next year's hunt."

"Ah, I'm just giving you a hard time. We were glad to help. My little girl has had stars in her eyes ever since over being able to meet Ryan North in person, so I guess a few spooked deer are a small price to pay." He chuckled. "We'll get one next season."

CHAPTER 12

THE FOUR-WHEEL DRIVE county Blazer bumped and lurched over the ruts in the dirt road leading to the ranch house. A calf darted across the road, and Jim Harrison swerved to miss it, grinning at the defiant buck the little creature gave as soon as he reached the other side.

Several minutes later he stopped in front of a run-down ranch house. The grizzled rancher came out to meet him.

"Hey, Wilson, how you doing?" Jim greeted him, stepping out of the cab to shake hands. He grabbed the binoculars before following the rancher across the yard. Wilson Shaw was not a man to waste time jawin'.

"Fair, Jim, just fair," Wilson answered, walking briskly toward the barn. "Beef prices not what they used to be, you know." The old rancher's face was lined and creased from years in the sun and wind, his hands gnarled with age. But despite the obvious signs of age, his step was sprightly as he led Jim around to the back of his barn. "We wouldn't get by without the little bit we get from the gov'ment, you know."

He stopped at the gate to a muddy corral. "This is where I was standing the first time I saw it, Jim," Wilson said, pointing up to a spot on the side of Mount Goliath. Mount Evans towered in the background, above the timberline.

"Tell me what you saw, Wilson. Harley didn't give me many details."

"I'd been fixin' that fence there," he answered, pointing at a couple of relatively new boards along the top of an otherwise dilapidated corral. "I heard the sound – you know, that thump-thump-thump sound they make and I looked up the mountain. That's when I saw it land up there on the hill."

Jim squinted against the sun in his eyes. "When was this?"

"Waall, the fust time, it was the second Saturday in October. I remember because I used part of my Social Security check to buy them boards there. But I didn't nail 'em up till the next weekend 'cause the wife made me take her to Colorado Springs that same week to visit her sister a spell. Wanted to spend some time with her before snow fell. Such a couple of old busy-bodies those two are, Jim. If I'd a known what I was lettin' myself in fer, I'd a left her there and come back after she'd got it out of her system. All day long, just talk, talk, talk about Mabel's hair this and Della's dress that, and who Myrtle Corning was going to marry next now that Henry up and died."

Jim smiled, only half listening, scrutinizing the side of the hill, trying to get his bearings before looking through the binoculars.

"Anyway, they 'bout drove me to distraction with all that yammerin'. Three whole days' worth, it was, and me with nothing to do but play checkers and watch Janie's husband Abe settin' there, grinning, with his hearing aid turned off. Never again, I tell you. She wants to see her sister, next time I'll take her into Idaho Springs and let her take the bus from there."

"I don't blame you," Jim replied. "Wilson, take a look through these and see if you can tell where it landed." He handed over the binoculars.

Wilson adjusted the glasses to his eyes and peered at the mountainside. "There's a little bit of a clearing, Jim. It's straight up from that lightning-struck tree over on the right side of the slope."

Jim took the glasses back and located the spot. "I think I see it," he said. "Did it land in the same spot both times?"

"There was three times, not two. The second time was in that same spot 'bout a week later. Maybe nine, ten in the morning it was. Landed, then took off about twenty minutes later. Then I saw another one later that same day, after lunch time it was. Only I didn't see it land. It showed up and acted like it was going to land, but it dropped down around the other side of the slope, where I couldn't see it. I figured it found another place to land that was better. But it wasn't the same one I saw the other two times. I figured they was just the rescue boys until I saw the third one. It had a red cross on it. When I saw that, I remembered the other two had been just plain black. That's why I called the sheriff when I saw the news story the other day. Figured something wasn't quite right. Nobody's allowed to land in the wilderness 'cept for medical emergencies, I know'd that much."

Wilson paused to pat his big yellow dog that sauntered up, tail wagging lazily, tongue lolling. "Hey, Buck, where you been keepin' yourself today? Out chasin' a rabbit, no doubt." He straightened up and continued his story while Jim studied the mountainside, trying to figure out the relationship of the clearing to any of the roads in the vicinity. "That one took off again 'bout a half hour later, headed east. Funny thing, though. The very first one I saw was only on the ground two, three minutes before it left. I figgered it was the rescue boys at first, but it really warn't on the ground long enough to get a stretcher out. But the first one I saw the next week was there a long time. If it warn't a rescue, I wonder what they wuz doin'."

"You seen anyone up there since then?" Jim asked, lowering the binoculars.

"Nope. I only saw that second one that day because I was out here bringin' the cows in before a snowstorm hit. And it were a humdinger, too. Warn't much more 'n an hour after I saw that thing take off from the other side of that hill that all hell broke loose and it snowed for five days after that." Wilson picked up a shovel that was leaning against the corral and turned again toward the barn. "Burning daylight, Jim. Gotta go clean some stalls now. Wouldn'a bothered you with such a thing, but the TV news said you were interested in anything unusual going on up in the mountains last fall, so I thought I oughta mention it."

CHAPTER 13

"SOMETIMES YOU HAVE witnesses who contradict each other," Sheila said to the group of seven young journalists. She had spent over forty minutes explaining the investigative process to them and was about to wrap it up. "When that happens, you have to decide who is more credible. Sometimes a journalist guesses wrong. That's why you should never report anything unless you have some kind of corroboration for what you've been told. You have to keep in mind that people will lie to you even if they aren't guilty of anything. But sometimes even the lies can help you get to the truth. So, you see," she concluded, "successful investigative reporting is always a combination of luck and skill, being in the right place at the right time, as well as being able to figure out whether you're being told the truth or not."

She took a deep breath before continuing. "There's a case in the papers right now that some of you are probably following that could use a little luck." Heads were nodding with recognition. "I'm talking about Daryl Walker's murder. Did some of you know him?" All the students nodded soberly.

A thin black boy spoke up. "Daryl wanted to be an investigative reporter, Ms Fernelli. He worked on the paper with us."

"How would you begin an investigation into his death?" Sheila asked, looking to Mrs. Moore for reassurance that she was not overstepping her bounds with the question. Mrs. Moore nodded.

A hand went up. Sheila pointed to the girl. "Yes? What ideas do you have?"

"Ms Fernelli," she blurted, "I think Daryl was hiding something before he disappeared. There were a couple of times when I asked him what he was working on and he said it was a secret project and it would be in the paper when he was through with it."

Mrs. Moore's face changed. "Kimberly," she said, "the only thing I knew Daryl was working on was his column on the clubs, the *DEW Point*. Did he lead you to think he was working on something else?"

Kimberly flushed. "No, I don't think so. He kept saying he had some meeting to go to on Tuesdays sometimes. He never told me what club it was though. And he was always talking to himself in that tape recorder he had but always made sure nobody was listening when he did it."

Sheila's heart pounded at the clue she had been handed. "That's a good example of what I mean by luck. Sometimes the hardest part is finding that one certain person who heard something, or saw something, and maybe didn't realize it was important."

A heavy-set boy in the back raised his hand. "Is what Kimberly said that important? You think he was killed because of something going on with one of the clubs?" A buzz of conversation swept through the room.

"Not necessarily," Sheila said hastily. "But that piece of information is what we call a 'lead.' It's something that might lead to something else. Perhaps someone in that club, whatever it was, might have heard him mention something or someone else, and if you follow the clues you eventually find out why he was killed." She turned to Mrs. Moore. "Does anyone know what happened to his tape recorder?"

"I have no idea. If he didn't have it with him, I would imagine it would have been at his home, in his book bag. But I'm sure his parents would have listened to the tape already in case there had been information about where he would have gone." Mrs. Moore stood up. "Let's think about what the next step would be, students. We have a clue. What do we do next?"

"Find out what clubs meet on Tuesday," Kimberly said, jumping to her feet. "There's a club schedule on the bulletin board outside." She ran into the hall and returned in a moment with a slightly torn piece of blue paper. "First and third Tuesdays of the month are the Biology club. Second Tuesday is the French club. Second and fourth are the Astronomy club. The Lesbian and Gay Society meets every Tuesday." She stopped as some of the students snickered loudly. "And the Chess club meets every Tuesday."

"Very good, Kimberly," Mrs. Moore said, joining Sheila at the podium. "Now, let's assume you're going to visit these clubs. What sorts of questions would you ask to find out information about Daryl?"

Sheila left the school an hour later, her head spinning with the information she had gained. The students had really gotten into the game, and by the time they had to end the discussion, several other students had remembered things about Daryl that might be useful to the investigation. Mrs. Moore asked them to write down what they remembered, and she promised to give the information to the police.

But Sheila had the information now, and couldn't wait to act on it.

CHAPTER 14

I T WAS A LONG, STEEP CLIMB, but Jim Harrison and Clayton Burns finally reached the clearing on the side of the mountain. A perfect landing site for a helicopter, level and clear, an anomaly in that part of the forest; nevertheless, Wilson Shaw had obviously seen what he said he had seen. They stopped well away from the clearing and Jim dropped his pack frame and evidence kit to the ground. He pulled out a roll of yellow plastic tape. "Stay here, Clay," he said. "I want to get the lay of things before we start searching."

"Okay, Jim," the young deputy replied, lowering his own pack to the ground. Jim had brought him along to take notes and make any needed sketches, since Clay was the better artist and was eager to put his skill to use for something other than accident investigations. He was also the photographer, and he began taking photographs of the clearing while he waited. It was the first time he'd gotten to work with Jim Harrison on a case and he intended to do a good job.

Watching the ground carefully for evidence before he stepped, Jim slowly made his way into the center of the clearing, where two parallel ruts in the now-dried mud showed where the helicopter's skids had rested when the machine landed. Although he searched the ground around this area carefully, he found no footprints or other evidence. He returned to Clayton.

"Okay, Clay, we're going to mark out an area with the tape that includes the entire clearing. Then we'll search for clues like you were taught at the academy, one of us zig zagging north and south, the other crossing east and west. That way if I miss something, you might see it, and vice versa."

"Any idea what we're looking for, Jim?" the younger man asked. "I've never done this before, you know."

"I know," Jim replied. "And I have no idea what we're looking for. Could be something as innocuous as a hunter's cap, if all they did was drop off some hunters illegally, or there could be evidence of drug activity. Or, it's remotely possible this might have something to do with that homicide investigation I'm working on."

After draping the yellow tape around the clearing to mark the search area, the two men began searching the ground for any clues that would explain why a helicopter was up in this wilderness area the previous fall.

"Jim!" Clayton called out from behind a bush. "I've got something here. Pop can and candy wrapper. Dr Pepper and Baby Ruth."

"Take some photos but leave them where they are for now. I'll pick them up in a few minutes. Better to have just one of us handle the evidence," Jim replied.

Clayton photographed the items and continued the search. It wasn't a minute later that he called out again. "Jim, there's also some horse manure here. Two piles. What do we do about that?"

Jim straightened up from peering at the ground. "Same thing. I'll take samples later. We can't tie it back to the horse that left it, but the lab can tell if it was left by the same horse on the same day by analyzing the feed content. We found some manure near the body, so it would be good to know if it was the same horse."

It was Jim who made the next discovery. A wooden box, about eighteen inches long and twelve inches high and deep, was concealed under a bush on the other side of the clearing from where Clayton had found the other evidence. The box had been painted green and gray camouflage, and could not be seen from a distance of ten feet away.

"Someone sure didn't want this found, Clay," Jim commented while Clayton snapped pictures of the box from all angles before they carefully pulled it out and checked the ground underneath it. "This smacks of a drug drop. They had an operation like this up by Rocky Mountain Park last year. Helicopters dropped drugs off in some remote area, then later someone rode up on horseback to retrieve them. Made it damn difficult to catch anyone, since no one knew when the chopper would come, or when the horse would arrive, or from what direction. And they covered their tracks further by using several different sites. Each site was used only once or twice. They never were caught. This is probably the same gang."

They continued searching, but found no more evidence, so they placed the box in a large bag, gathered the other evidence, placing each item in individual, pre-numbered paper bags. While Jim made notes describing the search and the results, Clayton made a detailed sketch of the area, showing exactly where the items were found. Then, mindful of the time needed to get back, they packed the items on the pack frames and left.

"Jim," Clayton said as he labored down the hill after the detective, "why would anyone do this? Aren't there easier ways of moving drugs around?"

"There are. They also carry some risk of getting caught. Think about it. Bad guy number one in the helicopter gets the stuff God knows where. Probably did a reverse of this kind of drop for him to pick them up. If he never personally saw anyone at the other end, there's no tracing him to the source. So he drops the stuff here. Someone comes in on horseback after he's gone and picks the stuff up. The rider never sees bad guy number one. So nobody knows who the pilot is. If they try to bust the organization at the source end, they can't touch the pilot unless they actually catch him in the act of picking the stuff up, right?"

"Right."

"And if we try to bust it at this end, all we can get our hands on is the rider, right?"

"Right."

"The guy in the helicopter is untouchable. Nobody can ever place him with the drugs, and nobody can catch the helicopter because who knows where it came from or where it's going. By the time anyone could get up here to find out what he was doing, he's long gone because the drop took place so far from any roads. You'd have to chase him with another chopper, and there aren't many around here."

"It still seems like a lot of unnecessary precautions."

"Well, in your typical drug deal, you have a face to face at some point. Somewhere along the way, someone hands over money and gets drugs. Cops infiltrate those deals all the time, making phony buys, or even phony sales. Usually once you have one guy on the hot seat, he'll name names up the line to save his own butt."

"I still don't see why they went to this trouble."

"Let's say we bust someone, maybe one of those kids over in Silver Plume that we know is dealing. He knows who his source is because he exchanges money for drugs. So we get that source. Maybe that source gets it from the rider. So we get the rider. Who's the rider going to give us?"

"Didn't bad guy number one hire the rider?"

"Maybe it was bad guy number two. He pays the rider either in drugs or cash to pick up the stuff and stash it somewhere else."

"So the rider names him."

"And he denies it. Remember, the rider never saw bad guy number two with the stuff either. So far, only the rider has laid hands on it. He stashed it somewhere, and some local dealer picked it up after he was gone."

"How does bad guy number one get paid?"

"Who knows? Maybe he gets a money gram from Western Union. Maybe cash is left at another drop site by another rider hired by bad guy number two. As long as the cash and the dope are never together, it's tough to make a case for who's buying and who's selling."

"So where does your homicide fit in to all this?"

"Maybe Daryl Walker was the rider. Or maybe he was up here for some perfectly innocent reason of his own and happened to stumble over the drop site. Or maybe he caught a poacher who killed him, and he had nothing whatsoever to do with this drug drop. Until I learn more about this, I have to stay open to both possibilities – the possibility that there's a connection, and the possibility that there isn't."

"What's your gut feeling? Connected or not? What's your intuition telling you?"

"Intuition is for women, Clay," Jim said with a grin. "Detectives work from facts. I'll sometimes let my gut tell me when someone's lying to me, but I don't let it tell me what the solution to a case might be. I let the evidence tell me that."

"Always keep an open mind, right?"

"Right. Things are so seldom what they seem at first glance, it's a waste of time to let yourself focus too hard on what appears to be the obvious answer."

CHAPTER 15

THE NEXT DAY, JIM finished his morning coffee and called his old precinct to request copies of the reports from the boy's disappearance before driving to the ranch of Mike Griffith. Griffith ran a packing and outfitting operation located near the wilderness area. He made his living renting horses and mules for use by hunters and others who wished to explore the wilderness area but didn't want to do it on foot. He also boarded a few horses in a large pasture and did some training.

Jim drove across a cattle grate into the ranch and honked the horn once to get the attention of Griffith, who was already up and working a horse about a hundred yards away in the middle of a field.

Griffith waved, recognizing the county Blazer, and trotted over to the fence. "Howdy, Jim," he said, dismounting and tying the horse to the fence post. "The wife said you'd be coming by this morning." He shook hands with the detective, then pulled out a package of chewing tobacco and stuffed a wad into his cheek.

"Glad I finally caught you in, Mike. Tried to see you yesterday, but Kate said you were out guiding a church group."

"Boy, was that a mistake," Griffith chuckled. "Baptists. It was the choir. Six of them. Halfway up the mountain, they started singing. Damn near spooked the horses. Guess those church organs must cover up a lot of off-key singing. Or maybe this bunch is just really, really bad. At least it wasn't an overnighter, but four hours was bad enough. And me agreeing before we left that there would be no alcohol or tobacco on the trip. I would have killed for a bottle of whiskey by the time I got back. Even a set of earplugs would have been nice." He chewed earnestly for a few moments. "Couldn't even chew while we were out. What a disaster. Had to watch my language, too. Shit."

Jim roared with laughter at the thought of hard-riding, hard-drinking, cussing and spitting Mike Griffith being forced to behave like a proper gentleman for four whole hours. "Must be some kind of penance, Mike. You been a bad boy lately?"

Mike spat tobacco juice on the ground. "No more than usual. What's this about, anyway?"

"Long shot, Mike. Remember last fall when that singer fell off his horse?"

"Sure do. What about it?"

"Well, you also know we found a dead body last week."

"Senator's kid, is that right?"

"Yes, that's the one. Well, anyway, we have reason to believe he was killed the same day as Ryan North's accident. His body wasn't very far from where North fell. I'm talking to everyone we know was there that day to see if anyone saw anybody else that day. I know you drove up there to pick up the horses after the accident. We had already left by the time you would have gotten there. Did you see anybody while you were there, maybe someone coming out of the woods?"

Griffith spat again. "Nope. Nobody except the folks who found Ryan. They were waiting with the horses. Little girl was crying her eyes out, worried he was going to die, poor kid. Her daddy told me she was a really big fan."

"I remember her. Her dad told me they let her see him in the hospital since she was so worried. Well, as I said, it was a long shot. Oh, one other thing. We're also looking into possible drug activity up there, someone using a helicopter to drop drugs and a rider on horseback coming to pick them up. There were a couple of helicopter sightings last October. Did you see anything unusual?"

"I saw a chopper once, about a week before Ryan's accident, but assumed it was a rescue. Sometimes when I'm up there with a group, we'll run into people on horseback or on foot, but I usually don't pay much attention to them, other than to thank them for moving off the trail so we can pass with the horses."

"You ever see Daryl Walker in the woods?" Jim held out a picture of the boy.

Mike studied the picture. "You know, it's hard to tell. But I might have. I do remember one thing. When he disappeared last year, I remember seeing him on TV because I was watching the news really close to see if they said how Ryan was doing. I remember saying to Kate that he looked familiar and I wondered if he was the same kid I'd seen in the woods recently. I know I didn't see him the day of Ryan's accident, but the week before the accident I had some hunters up in that area. In fact, I think that was the same day I saw that helicopter. One of the hunters started to take aim at what he thought was a deer, then realized it was a horse. It shook me up a little, so I caught up to the horse and it was being ridden by a teenaged boy. I warned him that it was hunting season and gave him some orange ribbon to put on his horse's tail and bridle. I didn't really look at him that well, but when I saw the picture on TV, I thought maybe it might be the same kid. I never said anything to police because it was a week later when he disappeared so I knew he wasn't still up in the woods."

"Little did you know," Jim said thoughtfully. "Any idea what he was doing?"

"He was just riding up the mountain. No gun, so he wasn't hunting. But he had saddlebags and it didn't appear there was anything in them. I noticed that."

"Where did he go after you talked to him?"

"He didn't. I left him tying the orange ribbon to his horse and we continued on the trail. I never saw him again, but there are trails intersecting the one we were on so he could have gone anywhere. He might even have gone back down the hill. He seemed pretty upset when I told him he'd almost been shot at."

"Understandable. Anything else you can recall that might have been unusual?"

"Not that I can think of."

"Well, I guess that's it. You have any idea how I can get hold of Ryan North's friend Doug Norton? The phone number I had on him last year has been disconnected. Any idea where he moved to? I need to talk to him, too."

"You're just a little late, Jim. He was gone to L.A. with Ryan after the accident but came back the end of December. He's been in Denver ever since, used to come around about once a month and check on the horse for Ryan. But he called Monday morning, said he was going out of town for a while and had arranged for North's horse to be shipped to L.A. the next day. A horse transporter picked up the horse Tuesday morning."

"He tell you where he was going, or give you a number?"

"Not for Doug, and I don't even know where exactly they took the horse. The hauler gave me a receipt for him but when Doug called Tuesday to make sure the guy had shown up, he told me to mail it to Ryan's office in Los Angeles so I did. I sent it to the same address where I sent the board bill every month. I can give you that address if you want. Might have the phone number somewhere, too. They oughta know where Doug went. He's Ryan's partner, you know. I suppose they have to have an address to send him his checks, wouldn't you think? You want to wait while I go to the house and look for it?"

"Just call it in to the office when you get a chance. And if you happen to hear from him again try to find out where he is and call me. Don't ask him to call me, though. He doesn't like cops."

"Sure thing, Jim."

"Thanks, Mike." Jim shook hands with the old rancher and left.

* * *

Eighteen-year-old Jeremy Dominick worked as a checkout helper at the King Soopers where Daryl had worked. He had agreed to meet Sheila Fernelli Friday during his lunch break.

At the appointed time, she pulled her car into the parking lot of the grocery store and parked. Inside the store, she found a tall, thin boy with short black hair and an earring standing near the time clock at the front of the store, waiting.

"Jeremy?" she said, noticing his name tag. "I'm Sheila Fernelli. Are you off work now?"

"Yes. I can go now." Jeremy led the way to the far end of the parking lot, where the employees were required to park. He leaned against his car, a battered blue Toyota, and lit a cigarette.

"So," Sheila started. "How long did you know Daryl Walker?"

Jeremy blew a smoke ring. "Not long. He only worked here a month or so before he disappeared. I didn't know him that well, but sometimes we'd be in the break room at the same time and we'd talk a little."

"Did he ever give any indication that anything was wrong, or that he was worried about anything?"

"He used to talk about his job on the paper once in awhile. He reminded me of a little kid sometimes, playing cops and robbers. He said he was onto this investigation that could get somebody into trouble. He was always making notes to himself in this little tape recorder he carried around."

"So I heard. But what do you think he meant? Legal trouble? Or was he talking about getting some kid in trouble for cheating or something?"

"No, something more serious than that. But he never said what it was. He just said he was working undercover to try to catch the guy at it. That's how he put it. He was going to catch the guy. But there was something else going on, too."

"Why do you say that?" Sheila asked, making notes on her notepad.

Jeremy took another drag off his cigarette before he continued. "He got this phone call one day. We're not supposed to get phone calls unless it's an emergency, but he got paged to the phone one day when we were just about to go on break. He took it in the office next to the break room, and I could hear him through the wall."

"What did you hear?"

"I don't know if I remember it right or not, but I think he said something like, he couldn't do it again. Then he said, 'Why don't you just leave me alone?' and his voice sounded like he was scared, or maybe was going to cry or something. I didn't even want to listen anymore after that. It was embarrassing, you know?"

"I understand. But did you hear anything else?"

"Yeah. He was quiet for a long time, then I heard him say that he guessed he didn't have a choice. And he sounded real subdued, like all the fight was out of him."

"Did you say anything to him about it?"

"No, I didn't think he'd appreciate knowing I had been able to hear him, but he came into the break room and kicked the pop machine and swore. Then he said something about, that's what you get when you open your big mouth to the wrong people. And then he said, 'And it's not even true, anyway.'"

"You didn't ask him what he meant?"

"I said, 'Hey, what's the matter, Daryl?' But he said it didn't matter and walked out. Later on I saw him talking to that tape recorder again but I didn't hear what he was saying. He was always real careful that nobody heard him when he was doing that."

Sheila scribbled furiously to take down the words. "Is there anything else you can tell me?"

"Well, I don't know if this means anything or not, but the day he got that phone call I noticed he was limping a little. Well, not quite limping," he corrected himself, "just walking funny. Like he was stiff. I asked him about it and he said he had spent several hours riding that Saturday and was pretty sore."

"Riding a horse?" Sheila asked.

"Yeah, a horse. Said he wasn't that used to riding but he'd spent about four hours on a horse that weekend."

"Did he say where, or why?"

"Didn't seem to want to talk about it, but he did say he almost got shot at by a hunter. I told him he better wear something red if he was going to go riding around in the woods during hunting season."

"Well, that's interesting," Sheila remarked. "Anything else that might be helpful? Did he have any other friends here I could talk to?"

"Daryl kept to himself here. He'd talk to me, I think because I was a little older and didn't go to his school. But there was someone I saw him talking to the day after he got that phone call."

"Who was that?"

"Don't know. Some skinny kid with brown hair dropped him off for work one evening, and they stood on the sidewalk talking for a few minutes. It looked like the other kid was trying to talk Daryl into something, and Daryl shook his head like he was saying no. I don't know who he was, but he drives an old yellow Volkswagen bug."

Sheila made a note. "Did Daryl say anything to you when he saw you?"

"No, but he acted a little flustered when he realized I had seen them. I had been in my car smoking one last cigarette before I went inside. I got out of the car just as their conversation ended and the other boy walked back to his car. I'm not surprised Daryl was embarrassed that I saw them."

"Why is that?"

"I'm pretty sure the other kid was a fag."

Sheila bit her tongue to avoid lecturing Jeremy about his choice of words and said instead, "He was gay? How do you know?"

"Something about the way he walked, I guess. And the way he waved goodbye to Daryl before he drove off. Sissy-like, you know? But the clincher was the Gay Pride bumper sticker." He snorted derisively.

"Is there anything else you can remember?" she asked, feeling that this had been one of her more productive interviews and not wanting it to end.

"That's about it," Jeremy replied, crushing his cigarette under his foot. "Except I don't think it will be that hard to find that fag if you want to talk to him. I see that Volkswagen around here all the time. I think he lives nearby. You might ask at that gas station," he said, pointing across the street. "Most of the kids buy their gas there." He unlocked his car door and climbed in. "Gotta go get a burger now. Is that all?"

"Yes, thanks for your help," Sheila said, stepping out of the way so Jeremy could back out.

"No big deal," he replied with a wave. "Just spell my name right."

After talking to Jeremy, the information she obtained from the journalism students gained importance. Particularly, the information provided by Lincoln Hart occupied Sheila's thoughts that evening. Lincoln was the editor of the school paper, and had remembered that Daryl was upset the Friday before his disappearance because Lincoln had insisted on cutting a few lines from Daryl's column because they had nothing to do with the story he had written.

After searching around through several boxes of diskettes, he found Daryl's original submission in its entirety and printed it out. It was the only file on the disk.

The article itself was a report on the Astronomy club's sighting of a comet. At the end of the article, Daryl had wanted to plant a teaser about a future column he was working on.

It was only three sentences:

There's an investigation under way right now that is getting close to a conclusion and you'll read all about it right here. I'm bashing away at the truth already! Watch this column for breaking news that will rock this school to its core!

Sheila couldn't help smiling at his enthusiasm. As a young writer, she, too, had the tendency to exaggerate, and she was sure Daryl's investigation would have produced results somewhat less than earth-shattering in importance. But a stink bomb in the chemistry lab was on a par with a nuclear attack for a high school newspaper, so his excitement about his story was understandable.

But what was he working on? And did it have anything to do with his death? It was a slim chance, but if he really was working on something of serious importance, could he have stepped on someone's toes? She knew the substance found on his clothing had been identified as cocaine. What if he was trying to bust a drug operation?

Then she got a mental picture of the conservative, clean-cut boy and knew he wouldn't have gotten anywhere near a drug operation. He just didn't look the part. The coroner's speculation was probably more accurate, that he had been at a party and stepped on a dropped packet of cocaine. The traces could have lingered on his clothing for some time.

Well, she needed to focus on what she knew for now. She picked up the phone and called Evelyn Moore. "Evelyn? Sheila Fernelli."

"Hello, Sheila. What can I do for you today?"

"Do you have the names of the faculty sponsors for those clubs meeting on Tuesdays? I'd like to get membership lists so I can talk to the students on the phone at least."

"Sure. Got a pencil?"

Evelyn read off the list of names and numbers. When she was finished, Sheila said, "There should be one more, shouldn't there? The Lesbian and Gay club?"

"We don't have an actual sponsor for that club. There's someone at the college who coordinates it, I believe, but I don't have the name."

"Oh, well, it's probably not that important. I can't see him investigating that group. What would he be doing? Trying to 'out' someone? His father would never approve, we all know that for sure."

"You're right about that, Sheila, and I'm pretty sure Daryl shared his father's views on that point. I'll never forget the day — last spring I think it was — that one of the black students used the word 'fag' in front of Daryl and I thought he was going to sock the kid. He told him the word was 'gay' and saying 'fag' was as bad as calling a black person the 'N' word. To the other kid's credit, he apologized to Daryl and there were no other incidents."

"Sounds like Daryl was a chip off the old block," Sheila mused.

"Well, you'd never know it to hear him talk about his problems with his father, but I guess all teens go through that battle. It's part of growing up."

"I know. Well, thanks for your time. I guess this is all I need." She hung up the phone and returned to her notes.

There was one other lead the students had provided that she wanted badly to follow up but had no idea where to start.

The tip had come from a girl named Brenda. During the discussion of which club Daryl might have been investigating, she remembered that the last Tuesday before he disappeared, she had been walking out to the parking lot to meet her ride home when she saw Daryl get in a car with two men. She didn't know who the men were. The driver was dark, the other man blond. The car was a dark Volvo. Daryl had greeted the men with a smile, climbed in the back seat, and they had driven off.

Brenda recalled the incident because she had spent a minute or two trying to remember who the blond man reminded her of. She was never able to recall if he was someone she'd seen before, or if he just reminded her of somebody, maybe an actor she might have seen.

It had been a vague, *deja vu* type of incident. She mulled it over for a while, decided to ask Daryl who the man was, then forgot about it.

She knew it was Tuesday because the girl she normally rode home with had an Astronomy club meeting that afternoon, so Brenda had called her brother to come pick her up that afternoon.

Unfortunately, she could provide no other information. Sheila knew that Daryl had lost his car privileges so it made sense he might be depending on others for rides.

But a ride to where? And who was the man who seemed so familiar to Brenda? Sheila felt certain if she could find those two men, a lot of questions might be answered.

* * *

After leaving Mike Griffith, Jim dropped by his old precinct near the west edge of Denver and picked up the files on the Walker disappearance from the year before. It had been a bit awkward seeing his former partner, Pepper, but it happened that her group had been in charge of the brief investigation. He deliberately timed his arrival for the middle of the shift to avoid seeing his other former co-workers, got what he needed, and quickly left, managing to avoid his former captain, Arlo, entirely.

Then Jim dropped off at the CBI crime lab downtown the evidence he and Clay had found the day before in the mountains, then drove up to Rocky Mountain National Park and talked to the rangers who had investigated the drug activity up there. He came away with little information. It was the same M.O. but they had nothing else to add. A few camouflaged boxes had been found at some of the reported landing sites. There were no suspects, no witnesses, and no other evidence. The helicopter had last been seen in September of the previous year, about a month before Wilson Shaw's first sighting.

He returned to his home near Idaho Springs, the three bedroom house on three acres where he had grown up. He had inherited the house, along with his father's old white 1962 model Chevy pickup, his twelve-year-old paint horse, Patch, and a battered horse trailer a year previously. It was another reason he was grateful to Harley Watson for his job, as it made it possible for him to keep his boyhood home and the horse. He had already started applying for work out of state when he decided to talk to his dad's former friend about a job. Harley had gotten to know Jim years before, when Jim was a member of the Alpine Rescue Team that served Clear Creek County. He had hired Jim on the spot, without requiring any explanation for why Jim had left Denver P.D. before he had another job lined up. Billy Williams had given notice of his plan to retire October first, and Jim knew Harley had been faced with the choice of promoting a patrol officer with little detective experience, or hiring from outside the area and having to invest a lot more time in training.

Jim had been very lucky. The timing had been perfect for both of them.

He watched the sun set over the Rockies while he fed Patch and cleaned his stall before going inside. He ate a can of soup and spent the rest of the evening alone at his mother's old kitchen table, poring over the file Pepper had given him.

He was amazed at how little had actually been done to investigate the boy's disappearance. Over the course of three days, a single detective from his old squad had questioned the parents, their neighbors, Daryl's boss at work, and two of Daryl's friends. All they had learned was that a neighbor had seen the boy get into a truck that Saturday morning, and that Daryl had not told anyone he was going to run away, other than the threat he had delivered up to his parents when they took away his car privileges. His grades had slipped a little in the weeks before his disappearance, and he was said to have been secretive and preoccupied. Furthermore, the threat to run away had been made a week before he disappeared, and the parents reported that he had calmed down in the meantime.

Nobody had forced him to get into that truck. Nobody had paid any attention to the driver or the license plate. Nobody had seen him since. He had contacted nobody after disappearing.

Two weeks after the disappearance, the file was closed.

Jim sighed. He wondered what he would have done differently if he had been in charge of the investigation. With no evidence of foul play, the questions he was asking now would not have occurred to him. A disappearance in Denver would not suggest that ranchers and hunters near Mount Evans should be questioned.

But if the boy hadn't actually threatened to run away, if he had been on good terms with his parents when he disappeared, would it have been different?

Jim realized that the only way additional leads could have been developed at the time would have been by keeping the issue alive with the public ... and that required the cooperation of the media. After all, it had been the news report asking people to come forth with information about unusual activities in the mountains that had brought Wilson Shaw's helicopter sighting to light. And that really was their only lead so far.

If it turned out the boy was not connected to the drug drop, they were back to square one.

The mistake that was made, he realized, was that the investigator had accepted the runaway scenario as being correct. He had tried to investigate where the boy might have gone, instead of investigating whether the boy had actually run away at all.

Jim had always prided himself on keeping an open mind, not jumping to conclusions, and being sure the facts fit any theories he came up with.

Well, that had not happened when the boy disappeared. He would make very sure that he did not make that kind of mistake now.

CHAPTER 16

SATURDAY HAD PROVEN TO be a huge waste of time for Sheila. She had spent it calling one student after another to talk about Daryl Walker. The four Tuesday clubs included a total of thirty members and she had reached twenty-seven of them by the time she gave up Sunday evening.

She reviewed her notes that evening, having given up trying to reach the remaining three students at home. While several of the students knew Daryl from classes, none remembered him visiting any of the clubs for at least two weeks before his disappearance. He had been a member of the chess club at the start of the semester, but, according to the faculty sponsor, he hadn't been there for a couple of weeks and the sponsor assumed he had simply dropped the club due to his job.

Even the news he reported about the comet sighting, she learned, had not been obtained at the regular meeting. One of the members was in Daryl's Chemistry class, told him about the comet, and Daryl had dictated a comment into his tape recorder. The other information Daryl had printed about the sighting he had obtained in a ten-minute interview with the faculty sponsor.

So what had the boy been doing every Tuesday?

Sheila took a deep breath and called Daryl's mother.

"Mrs. Walker?"

"Yes?"

"This is Sheila Fernelli, reporter for the *Rocky Mountain Chronicle*," she plunged in without giving the woman a chance to protest, "and I just have two small questions I hope you won't mind answering for me. I'm trying to clarify some information I received. Do you know what happened to Daryl's tape recorder? Everyone tells me he used to make notes in a tape recorder all the time. Did you find it with his schoolbooks after he disappeared?"

"I don't know anything about any tape recorder," she replied. "We never found one and if he had one I didn't know about it. Are you sure it didn't belong to the school?"

"I have no idea, Mrs. Walker. I just heard from a few people that he had one. I assumed it was his and that you would have found it."

"Well, we didn't. Is that all you wanted?"

"No, I had one more question," Sheila said quickly. "Was Daryl a member of any clubs at school? Other than journalism, I mean. I know about that one."

There was a long pause. "He also belonged to the chess club."

"Did he attend the meetings regularly?"

"Yes, every Tuesday. He went to the meeting, then he usually worked at the store after the meeting. I was usually in bed when he got home, so we never really talked about it much. I guess they just played chess for an hour and a half every week."

"Mrs. Walker, according to the faculty sponsor for that club, he had not been to any of the meetings for several weeks. Do you remember why he stopped going?"

"What do you mean, he hadn't been there? He went *somewhere* every Tuesday. He said it was the chess club. The week before he … disappeared … he lost his car privileges but he still went to that meeting. He just stayed on campus after school and said he'd get a ride to work after the meeting. I guess he walked home after work that night. It's only three blocks."

"I'm sorry, Mrs. Walker. This must be terribly hard for you. But if he wasn't where you thought he was, there might be some connection to his … uh, to what happened to him. Mrs. Walker," she continued quickly, "just one more question. Do you know anyone who drives a dark colored Volvo who might have picked Daryl up from school the week he lost his car privileges?"

"Look, I'm sure we know lots of people who drive Volvos. In fact, we have one ourselves. I don't know of anyone who would have given Daryl a ride. I know neither of us did. And I don't think I want to talk about this anymore. This conversation is very upsetting to me. Please don't call me again. Good-bye."

The phone went dead and Sheila reluctantly replaced the receiver in the cradle. Maybe Daryl's investigation had nothing to do with the clubs at all. Perhaps he was using Tuesdays to do his investigating so he wouldn't have to explain to his parents where he was going.

But Kimberly said he had a "meeting" to go to on Tuesdays. What was left? The Lesbian and Gay group? She sighed. It made no sense, but she supposed she would have to check it out. She would have to wait until the next morning to call the college and try to track down the coordinator.

* * *

"Well, what have you found so far?" Harley asked Jim during their Monday morning briefing. "And has Sheila Fernelli been getting in your way?"

Jim ignored the second question. "Talked to Mike Griffith Friday. He may have seen the boy in the woods the previous weekend, but isn't sure. He saw nothing the weekend we are interested in, though. Oh, and it sounds like he saw the first helicopter that Wilson saw. He just assumed it was the rescue squad."

"That's probably what anyone would think."

"Anyway, we should be hearing from the lab today on that pop can I dropped off the other day. I told them to test for fingerprints and saliva but I'm not very optimistic they'll find anything at this point."

"You think there might be a connection between the drug activity and the boy's murder."

"Could be a coincidence. If that pop wasn't drunk by Daryl Walker, then we have nothing connecting him to it at all."

"Did you talk to Denver P.D.? How did that go?"

Jim shifted uncomfortably. He had never told anyone, including Harley, why he had left Denver, but he knew Harley would know that there must have been some awkwardness in visiting his old precinct. "Went okay. My former partner will help me with anything else I need from them. It'll be all right."

"Did you talk to the parents yet?"

"Not to interview them. Just expressed condolences and told them I was handling the investigation. Asked them a few general questions but didn't get anything helpful. Mostly they seemed relieved it wasn't going to be handled by the same people who called off the investigation last year without finding out what happened."

"I'm not surprised. I got a call from CBI yesterday. Senator Walker specifically requested that Denver P.D. be kept out of the case as much as possible. You must have impressed him when you were there, because he said he wanted us to handle it."

"I just hope he doesn't turn out to be my prime suspect, Harley. Although, if there is a connection to this drug activity, we may end up quickly with no suspects at all. I'm going to go to the high school and see what any of his friends can tell me today. Looks like Denver PD didn't talk to many people at the school or the store where he worked last year. They just talked to two of his best friends and his immediate boss. And I need to talk to the PI the parents hired, to see what he picked up on that the PD missed. If anything, " he amended. "Doesn't sound like he did any better job than the cops."

"Probably a waste of time anyway, Jim. Before you do that, I want you to follow up with the lab on the stuff you picked up with Clay. And see if the blow ups are ready of the pictures he took. Whether that helicopter has anything to do with Daryl Walker or not, we've got to find out what we can. Then we'll turn that over to CBI. Since it appears to be part of a major operation, we'll let them handle it. Then you can get back to this homicide."

Jim felt a slight flash of irritation. "Harley, I need to stay on this thing. The trail isn't getting any warmer while I chase down drug dealers and I already spent two days in the mountains that should have been spent interviewing witnesses. Clay can follow up with the lab. I really want to get to the students as quickly as possible."

Harley was unconcerned. "I want to get this helicopter thing out of our jurisdiction if possible. The sooner we rule it out as a factor in the Walker homicide, the sooner we can forget about it. You can get to the students tomorrow."

Jim walked back to his office, torn between the need to do things the right way and the need to keep his job. The last time he had quit his job as a matter of principle, he had felt fortunate to be hired by Harley Watson.

He quickly realized that while Harley respected Jim's ability, Harley had a need to be in control. He did not take criticism, and did not take no for an answer.

Somehow, he needed to learn to accept Harley's control without taking it personally. He sighed, picked up the phone, and called the lab.

As he had been told to do.

CHAPTER 17

J IM HARRISON SHOOK HIS HEAD with surprise and annoyance. "Sheila Fernelli had no business questioning the students," he said firmly. "This is a police matter. Why would you let her do that, Mrs. Moore?"

Evelyn Moore smiled contentedly, knowing full well that he knew that *she* knew there was no legal reason for keeping Sheila out. "Because they're journalists, Detective Harrison. This was a tremendous learning experience for them, as well as providing them the opportunity to feel that they could do something for Daryl Walker. Sheila Fernelli just happened to call me before you did. Almost a whole week before you did, as a matter of fact," she added pointedly.

Jim exhaled explosively, annoyed that the helicopter investigation had taken him from the Walker homicide long enough to allow Sheila Fernelli to beat him there. "Sheriff Watson thinks Sheila Fernelli has a lot of wild theories, Mrs. Moore. She hasn't always been very objective in some of her reporting. I hope she didn't plant a lot of crazy ideas in the heads of potential witnesses."

"Well, why don't you judge for yourself, Detective?" Evelyn handed him the statements the students had written after the discussion with Sheila earlier in the week. "Read these, and then you can decide if she planted any crazy ideas in their heads. In my opinion, she conducted the meeting quite professionally. She never once led the students – she asked, and they answered."

Jim reluctantly took the papers and sat at a desk to read them, wishing he had gotten there before Sheila. After Harley's insistence that he follow up immediately with the lab, the fingerprint test on the pop can had been inconclusive anyway and the photos Harley wanted blown up didn't show Jim anything he hadn't already seen the day they were taken. A single partial thumb print was on the indentation on the bottom of the can. Daryl Walker was "not excluded" but the lab could not positively state it was his print. He still had no idea whether the investigation of the helicopter sightings was going to help him solve the homicide or had just wasted two days of his time.

He had been reading for an hour, grudgingly impressed by the objectivity demonstrated in the statements, when a young woman came by and offered him a soft drink. "Thanks," he said. "Are you one of the journalism students?"

"I'm Kimberly," she said shyly. "That's my statement you just finished reading."

Jim took a long drink from the Pepsi can and studied the girl. Tall, thin, wearing glasses that seemed too big for her face, she seemed to be a serious young woman, a little insecure in the presence of the man with the badge, but apparently anxious to talk to him. He put the can down and picked up her statement.

"It would appear from these statements that Daryl gave you some information he didn't give anyone else," he began. "Have you remembered anything else since you wrote this?"

She flushed slightly. "No, and Mrs. Moore told us not to do any investigating since it was a police matter, but someone told me something and I thought you should know."

"What was that, Kimberly?" Jim prodded gently.

"Daryl told me he was working on a secret project – something to do with one of the clubs on Tuesdays."

"Yes, that's in your statement."

"A friend of mine is a volunteer at the hospital, and when I told her about the reporter who was investigating the murder, she told me that about two weeks before he disappeared Daryl had visited someone in the hospital."

"Did your friend think this was unusual for some reason?"

"She said the boy he visited didn't go to school here and she didn't remember his name but he had been beaten up by a grown man. After Daryl visited the boy, he came out of the room and told my friend that after he broke the case his dad was going to be really proud of him."

"Broke what case?"

"That's just it, we don't know," Kimberly said sadly. "But Sheila Fernelli said things like that are leads so I thought I should tell you."

"Thank you, Kimberly. May I have your friend's name? I should talk to her, too."

After Kimberly wrote down the name of her friend, she left Jim Harrison alone. He drank the last of the Pepsi and sat quietly for several minutes, thinking about what she had said.

So Daryl was working on something that would make his dad proud of him? He already knew that Daryl Walker and his father had not been particularly close for about a year before Daryl disappeared. Sources close to the Walker family said it was the typical teenager problems, neither side understanding the other. It was complicated further because Senator Walker was kept pretty busy with his pet political projects and didn't have the time or patience for his son's problems.

The day before, he had confirmed, quietly of course, the senator's alibi for the weekend Daryl had disappeared. The senator and his wife had, in fact, been away at a convention, and neither of them could have returned to Denver without being missed. So Jim had ruled out both of them as suspects. No other family members lived in Colorado.

Daryl was an only child; he had no siblings who could have done him in while the parents were gone. No, whatever the reason for his murder, it had nothing to do with his family.

But the strain between boy and father was well known. Daryl had proclaimed his frustration to his friends, Mike and Josh, many times, complaining that nothing he ever did to try to get his father's approval was ever "important" enough. All his dad cared about were his three pet political projects – the environment, the homeless problem, and gay rights.

But Daryl had told – Jim looked at the name – Robin Melville that Senator Walker was going to be proud of him when he "broke the case." A case involving a mugging victim? What sort of investigation was the boy conducting?

Jim gathered up the papers and slipped them into the envelope Evelyn Moore had given him. Perhaps all that had happened was that a young boy had gotten carried away with some teenaged fantasy about being an investigator and had seen or heard something he shouldn't have.

Jim stopped by the records office to get the address and phone number of Robin Melville before he left the campus to drive to the hospital. *Better find out whom he visited,* he thought to himself as he drove out of the parking lot, *before you read about it in the Rocky Mountain Chronicle.*

"We get dozens of emergency patients in every day, and you can't be more specific than 'sometime last October'?" Nurse Friedman, the middle-aged triage nurse at the hospital emergency room shook her head. "How do you expect me to give you a name if that's all the information you have?"

Jim shrugged, trying to hide his relief that Sheila Fernelli had not beaten him there. "That's all I've got. It was a teenaged boy who was beaten up. That can't be a very common occurrence, can it? I mean, to land the kid in a hospital? I doubt we're talking about a schoolyard slugfest here."

"Have you checked with the police? If he was mugged, as you say, it should have been reported."

"First I have to have a list of potential names and dates, then we'll run them through the computer to see if an assault was reported. There's a good chance it may not have been reported, though, depending on the circumstances."

The nurse sighed. "I'll see what I can do. It may take some time, though. Check back with me in a couple of hours. I'll see what Gwen in Records can find for me."

"Thank you, ma'am," Jim said with a smile. "I'll be back later this afternoon."

When Jim returned for the information, Nurse Friedman was waiting eagerly for him. "Detective, I discovered something very interesting here. I don't know if it has anything to do with your case, but I found it curious."

"What is that?" Jim asked, surprised by her sudden enthusiasm for the project.

"Gwen made a list of all mugging and assault victims that came through ER in October of last year. There were quite a few, but most were never admitted, just treated and released. I then looked for the teenagers – there were four – and read the case histories. All four came in between eight o'clock Tuesday night and noon Wednesday – but the assaults all took place on Tuesday nights. So I had her go back and look at the September records, too. Detective Harrison, we had a teenaged assault victim every Tuesday night in those two months!"

Jim's brow furrowed. "That's quite interesting, but I don't think it has anything to do with my case. But let me have the names anyway, in case some other connection turns up."

The nurse handed him the list and pointed out the names of the boys who were treated during October. All four had been hurt badly enough to be admitted and stayed from one to three days. "Richard Farrell, Lowell Smith, Felipe Gomez, James Garcia," he read. "Thanks. Now I just have to find out which one my homicide victim knew."

CHAPTER 18

I T TOOK SHEILA FIVE DAYS to locate Jeremy's "fag." She finally traced him through his brother's friend who worked at the gas station Jeremy had mentioned. But getting him to agree to talk to her had been another matter.

She had reached him by phone Wednesday morning. After insisting three times that he didn't know Daryl Walker, he finally agreed to meet her when she told him she had an eyewitness who had seen them together. She also had to promise to pay him for the information and to keep his name out of the paper, two things she knew her editor was not going to like to hear. Nevertheless, she was about to meet the boy, alone, in a park, that same afternoon.

For this sensitive interview, Sheila had left her notebook in the car, but a tape recorder was running in her jacket pocket. She had thought of Daryl's missing tape recorder when she turned it on, wondering if it would ever be found, and if it held any answers. She knew she'd be lost without hers. Would Daryl have left home without his? She sighed as she tucked it into her pocket. Chances were the killer had taken it. She knew it had not been found on the body.

She walked toward the designated park bench and the young man who waited for her there.

Richard Farrell, known as Ricky to his friends and Fairy to his enemies, was a very obviously gay young man of about eighteen. Sheila didn't remember ever seeing anyone who so completely fit the gay stereotype before. The boy was slender as Jeremy had described, and sat with his legs crossed in an almost feminine pose, twisting his hands together nervously. While Jeremy had described him as having brown hair, it was now bleached a bright blond. But she could also see he was clearly ill at ease, glancing nervously around as he waited. She smiled and held out her hand to try to show him he could trust her.

"Hello, Richard. I'm Sheila," she said warmly. He was her best lead so far, and she did not want to spook him.

"Hi," the boy replied nervously, shaking her hand with a weak grip. "Call me Ricky." His voice was slightly high-pitched and she realized it would easily pass for a woman's voice. Sheila couldn't help feeling sorry for the boy. A quirk of biology had obviously dictated a difficult and confusing childhood for this young man.

"So, Ricky, I heard you might have known Daryl Walker. Is that true?"

"I knew him as Danny."

"Danny?"

"I didn't even know he was the senator's kid until they showed his picture on TV after they found his body. Then when that detective came around last night asking if I knew him, I was scared so I said I didn't."

"What detective? Jim Harrison?"

"I don't know his name. I – uh – I was beaten up last fall, and the detective wanted to know if Daryl Walker visited me in the hospital. I told him no. Then he wanted to know who beat me up, you know? And why? And I remembered my rights and told him I wasn't going to answer any questions. Police don't care about gay bashers. Nobody cares. That's why we had to hire Jeff."

"Who was Jeff?"

"Our own private detective. He told us his name was Jeff, but I don't think that was his real name since he was undercover. He tried to help us, since we knew the police wouldn't. It's okay that I lied to that detective, isn't it? I wasn't under oath. He would have just made a lot of trouble for everyone, and since the beatings stopped last January, what difference did it make, anyway?" He ended this speech on a pleading note that made Sheila feel sorry for him. Obviously he was feeling a lot of anxiety about the Daryl Walker murder. Probably some guilt, too, and that was why he had agreed to talk to her after brushing off the detective.

"Back to Daryl Walker," she said. "Why do you suppose he said his name was Danny?"

"We – uh – usually don't give our real names. I met him at a Lesbian and Gay meeting over at the college, you know?"

"Daryl was gay?"

"I don't think he really knew for sure, you know?" Ricky was fidgeting. "I mean, sometimes a guy thinks he is because he's having trouble with girls or something, and he comes around to the meetings a little, but the first time someone tries to pick him up, he panics, you know? Like he suddenly realizes he's not that way, really, and he's scared to go through with it. You can understand that, can't you? But Danny – Daryl – was really nice to me. He was really interested in how I got beat up and said he wished he could do something about it."

"I see," Sheila said thoughtfully. This was something new. Of all the people she had spoken to about Daryl, no one had ever mentioned that the boy had thought he was gay. She wondered what the implications were. "You said at the college? Why doesn't the club meet at the high school? It would probably be safer that way, wouldn't it?"

"It's not a high school club. Some of the high schools allow us to list the meetings. We had to fight pretty hard for that one. One of the faculty members helped us get that through the school board. We wanted a support group for teenagers who were starting to face their sexual identities for the first time. It's … not easy coming out, you know? Of course, I'm so stereotype I've sort-of been out most of my life, but I just couldn't admit it to anyone until a couple years ago. I've been beaten up seven times, starting when I was nine. Daryl was so nervous about it he always wore a disguise to the meetings, which is why we never knew he was the senator's kid when he first disappeared. As far as I know, I was the only one from the group who ever saw him without his dark glasses and fake mustache, and that was just once because I gave him a ride to work after the meeting. I guess they must have shown his picture on the news when he disappeared but I don't watch much TV so I never saw it. Hearing on the radio that the senator's kid was missing meant nothing to me because I didn't know who he really was. That's why I had no idea he was missing, I just thought he figured out he really was straight. I didn't go to his school, so I never heard anything."

"So when was the last time you saw Daryl?"

"It was last fall sometime. Let me think. I know now that he disappeared in October. I got out of the hospital on the seventh and saw him again at the meeting the following Tuesday. After the meeting, he had to go to work and that was the day I gave him a ride because he didn't have a car that day. Oh – I remember. He was really sore from riding a horse that weekend. I tried to talk him into going out the next weekend, but he was real nervous-like, and said he couldn't because he had something he had to do."

"He had something to do on the weekend? Which day?"

"It was Saturday. I asked him if he wanted to go up to Rocky Mountain National Park with me to do a little hiking if he wasn't still too sore."

"But he said he couldn't go because he had something to do."

"Right."

"But you don't know what it was?"

"He said he had to go ride for Peter again. Then he got all upset and said for me to forget he said that." Ricky smiled, wanly, for the first time. "I suppose that's the only reason I remembered it, because he told me to forget it."

"You're sure he said Peter?"

"Oh, yes. I thought he meant one of the men at the meeting, who calls himself Peter Knight, but he said, no, it wasn't him. I mean, I asked him because if he and Peter were having a thing, I didn't want to intrude on it, you know?"

"I see. You have no idea who this other Peter is, then."

"No. It's been a long time, lady; you're lucky I still remember the conversation."

"Ricky, did Daryl ever talk to you about being on the school paper?"

Ricky shifted uncomfortably. "Sometimes. He said he had some information about someone but couldn't prove it yet but it was going to be a big scandal when he broke the story. He spent a lot of time asking Jeff questions about investigating, I think. He said he knew some big secret about someone. He said it would be a big scandal because this guy was related to someone everybody knows."

"Someone everybody knows? You mean like someone famous, like a politician or an actor or a football star?"

"It could have been anyone, for all I know. He was real secretive about the whole thing. Maybe you should try to find Jeff. He probably knows. Except I haven't seen him in months and have no idea what his real name is." Ricky looked anxiously at his watch. "Look, can I go now? I think I said enough."

"Yes, of course you can go. Thanks so much for talking to me. If you think of anything else, I'd really appreciate a call." Sheila handed the boy her card and a folded bill.

"You're not going to use my name in the paper, right?" Ricky said, pocketing the money.

"No name. And thanks again."

So Daryl Walker had been trying to get someone in trouble. One could assume that "someone" would take steps to prevent him from succeeding in his mission. But who could it have been? Sheila returned to the office after the meeting with Ricky Farrell with the intention of reviewing her notes.

Her information on Daryl Walker was starting to make a large pile on her desk, so she decided to try to weed out casual information from the actual clues.

In the pile were copies of newspapers that held the stories of his disappearance the previous fall. The *Chronicle* articles were all available on her computer, but she had also printed off microfilm entire pages from back issues of the *Denver Post* to help in her research and the pile was taking up a lot of room. Maybe she should clip out those articles and get rid of the rest of the papers. She got out her scissors and picked up the first page, from Tuesday the nineteenth. Its headline proclaimed: *Senator Walker's Son Still Missing.*

Sheila clipped the story on the front page, then turned to page five for the rest of the story. As her scissors worked, she glanced at two other articles sharing the page with a large ad for a furniture store. *Beating Victim Found in Alley* was the head over one article describing the finding of an unconscious young man early that morning. The man was identified as Felipe Gomez and he had regained consciousness en route to the hospital. Police had no clues to the assailant and Gomez said he did not remember what happened. Sheila read it again. "That's right down the street from the college," she observed, making a mental note to stay away from that area at night.

The other article on the page was just two paragraphs, headed: *Ryan North's Condition Improves*. It was a statement released by North's doctor, and only mentioned that Ryan North had been upgraded from guarded to stable condition but remained in a coma. Doctors were optimistic that the singer would soon wake up for good.

Sheila's scissors halted when she recalled something Ricky Farrell had said. "Someone everybody knows," he had said.

She grabbed her area map and noted the location of the trail on which Daryl Walker's body had been found. Then she slid her index finger from that site to the trail near which Ryan North had been found.

"You idiot!" she scolded herself. "You knew it was the same day! Why didn't you think of this before?"

She turned to her computer and did a search for the name Ryan North in the database. As references scrolled up her monitor, she clicked the Print key at each article relating to the accident, as well as a few articles run during the years prior to the accident, when Ryan North had been a Denver resident.

She walked over to the printer and waited while the pages came out. "So much for weeding out the pile," she commented wryly as she added them to the stack on her desk.

Thirty minutes later, she had finished reading them, and, with a satisfied look on her face, she picked up the phone. She had an idea, but was going to need some help to prove her suspicions.

CHAPTER 19

THIRTEEN-YEAR-OLD CINDY Vincent poured milk on her bowl of corn flakes and carried it to the table. She waited patiently for her father to finish reading the comics and turn to the news sections of the *Rocky Mountain Chronicle*. Without being asked, he handed her the section she wanted and she settled down to eat and read, as she did every morning.

The silence in the small kitchen was broken only by the rustling of pages being turned, the clank of coffee cup on tabletop, and alternating suppressed slurping and crunching as Cindy ate her cereal, quickly before it got soggy.

Cindy's father, Howard, cleared his throat once and she looked up.

"Looks like they're not making much progress on solving the murder of that boy they found up on Mount Goliath," he commented casually.

"Oh, really?" Cindy really wasn't very interested in dead bodies on Mount Goliath. She had other things on her mind, like a trip to Disneyland the next week.

"You know it was Senator Walker's son Daryl. He disappeared last year and they thought he had run away." He sipped his coffee. "Did I tell you the other day that the sheriff's detective came out to ask me if I'd seen anyone up there when we were hunting? He said the body was found in the same area where you and I found that singer, Ryan North, last fall."

She perked up at the mention of her idol's name.

"It was?"

"Yes. You didn't see anyone else up there that day, did you?"

"Just a blond guy. Daddy – "

Howard cut her off, distracted. "They already know about him. I didn't think you'd seen anyone else."

Cindy didn't want to talk about the murder, now that her favorite subject had come up. "Daddy," she said insistently, "you never said if we were going to be able to go visit Ryan North like he invited us to when we saw him in the hospital. He must be feeling better by now, and he said we could come see him after he was better. Disneyland's not that far from where he lives. We could go see him when we're over there."

"Honey, I'm sure he's far too busy for us to be bothering him. He was probably just being polite when he said that. People say that all the time – about dropping by if you're ever in town – and they secretly hope that you won't take them up on it."

"But Daddy," she pleaded, "I think he really meant it. He's not a Hollywood snob like some of those actors out there. He's from Denver and he knows what it's like to be an ordinary person. He wouldn't say it if he didn't mean it. Why would his partner have given us their phone number if they didn't mean it?" She ended her speech with a rush of words, afraid her father didn't understand how important this was to her. This was the third time she had brought up the subject since her father said he would take her to Disneyland when he went to California for a business conference the following weekend.

Howard pushed his chair back from the table and stood up. He gave his anxious daughter a tolerant smile and said, "Tell you what, Honey. You make the long-distance call to that number and ask. If they say it's all right for you to see him, I'll drive you up there. I guess if I'd had some celebrity's phone number when I was your age I wouldn't have wanted my old fuddy-duddy dad telling me I couldn't even try to cash in on it." He planted a kiss on the top of her head and carried his coffee cup to the kitchen sink. "But don't be too disappointed if they tell you he's too busy."

"Thanks, Dad. And I promise I won't stay on the phone too long."

After her father had left for work, she washed up the few breakfast dishes and walked outside to wait for her ride to school. She knew it was only six-thirty in California. She would have to wait until after school to place the call.

She could only hope and pray that he would not be too busy to see her.

* * *

Wayne Elliot turned in the saddle to face Sheila and said, "You know, I may not be able to find it from the ground. I came in on the helicopter when we carried Ryan North out and didn't pay all that much attention when we were hiking back out."

Sheila reined her horse around a large rock in the middle of the trail. "I know. I'm grateful you're even trying. The sheriff refused to send his detective up here on what he called a guided tour, and suggested I invest fifty cents in a trail map. But I knew I couldn't find the actual location without the help of someone who had been there. Other than Jim Harrison, you're the only person I know of who was at both scenes." She swatted at a large fly on her horse's neck. "And trail maps are now four dollars. Harley probably gets them for free."

Wayne laughed. "Well, I don't mind helping out. When are you going to tell me what theory you're working on?" Wayne nudged his horse to the right to avoid an overhanging pine bough.

"When I find out if I'm right or not. I don't want to make too big a fool of myself over this. I'm curious about something, but it may be just a coincidence."

She was reluctant to say anything until she was sure. Her map showed her that Daryl Walker and Ryan North were within a quarter mile of each other on October sixteenth, the day Walker was believed to have been buried.

That afternoon, the first major snowstorm of the season hit the area. The ground at that elevation would have been covered with snow, preserving the body, she knew, from that moment until the spring thaw and a curious coyote worked together to finally expose the protruding hand.

She always hated it when women relied on "intuition" instead of facts, but in this case she had a hunch she wanted to play out. Much to her irritation, the sheriff had not been even slightly interested in her theory and had refused to send his detective to investigate.

While she was sorry the boy had died, she felt lucky it had turned out that the victim was Daryl Walker instead of one of the boys missing from another part of the state. Her editor would not have let her pursue the investigation of a case that was not close to home. He would have sent another reporter, one with more experience, *and testicles*, she thought bitterly, if the investigation had led out of the immediate area.

Wayne pulled up his horse and looked around before extracting a map from his pocket and studying it.

"That's what I thought," he said with a self-satisfied grunt. "Sheila, this is the bend in the trail I was looking for, which means the clearing where we landed should be right over that rise." He pointed to a shrub-covered mound about a hundred yards away. Without waiting for her to answer, he kicked his horse into a trot and quickly reached the top of the little hill.

Sheila appeared at his elbow a moment later. On the other side of the rise was, indeed, a small clearing, about fifty yards in diameter. It was just big enough to safely land a helicopter. "Okay, Wayne. Good work. Now, do you remember which way it was from here?" She shifted uncomfortably on the hard saddle. It had been years since she'd been on a horse and she knew she'd be blistered by the time they got back.

Wayne rode thoughtfully into the clearing and looked around. It had been many months since the last time he had been there, and there had been more snow on the ground under the surrounding trees. He thought hard, trying to remember which direction the chopper had been facing when it landed. If he could remember that, he would know which way to go from there.

He turned around slowly, looking at the landmarks. In one direction lay a solid thicket of young pine trees; to the left, some massive bristlecone pines reflected the sun off their stark white trunks; to the right, more bristlecones, mixed in with some other conifers. Then he spied a long, slender tree trunk on the ground and he remembered that he had tripped over it as he climbed out of the chopper.

"Come on, Sheila," he called. "I know where I am now."

Sheila followed as he rode away from the clearing, down the slope in the opposite direction from where they had come.

She was straining to see to the east as she rode, and didn't see that Wayne had stopped short until her own horse stopped suddenly with his nose jammed firmly into the other horse's tail. Wayne's horse stamped a hind foot menacingly. "Oops, sorry, Wayne. I wasn't paying attention." She pulled her horse away. "Why did you stop? Is this the place?"

Wayne pointed to a large rock deeply embedded in the ground near a bristlecone pine tree. "That's where he was."

Sheila climbed off her horse and handed the reins to Wayne. She walked over to the rock and looked at it, then reached down and brushed some pine needles away, wondering if the dark area on the rock was blood. Lying nearby, half buried by forest litter, was a weathered piece of paper. She pulled it out and could barely make out the words "Red Cross Sterile Gauze." *Okay, this is the place. Now see if you're right.*

She walked to her horse, pulled a pair of binoculars out of her saddlebag, then walked back to the rock. Standing on it for added height, she slowly looked around.

To her left, she looked up at the clearing where Wayne said he had landed in the helicopter.

Slowly, she turned to the right. Her view was immediately blocked by a thicket of small pine trees about fifty yards away. She rotated further to the right and it was the same story. Trees blocked her view in every direction except toward the clearing. She lowered the glasses, letting them hang from their strap around her neck.

Disappointment showed on her face as she walked back to her horse.

Wayne could contain his curiosity no longer. "Well? Did you find what you thought you would find?"

She took her reins and remounted before answering. "No, I'm afraid this was a waste of time. You can't see anything but that clearing from here. So he couldn't have seen anything."

Wayne started to turn his horse back the way they had come, then stopped. "But Sheila, he wasn't on foot. He was on a horse, like we are. What can you see from your horse?"

Sheila's face lit up. "I forgot about that." She rode her horse over past the rock, ducking under a low-hanging branch on the tree. She raised the glasses to her eyes and to her delight saw that she could now see right over the small pine trees that had blocked her view.

Slowly, she panned the area. A broad smile split her face. "All right!" she almost shouted. "My hunch paid off. Put that in your pipe and smoke it, Harley Watson." She lowered the glasses and turned to face Wayne.

"Watch that branch," he cautioned.

She looked at the branch just above her head, then down at the rock. She ducked and rode up to Wayne.

"That must be the branch that knocked North off his horse onto that rock," she said, half to herself. "Well, we can head back now. I'm going to go pay a visit to that sheriff."

"You said you'd tell me if you were right. What did we just prove?"

"There's a lot of ifs, Wayne, but if I'm right about this, there's a good chance Ryan North knows something about that boy's murder he's not telling."

* * *

The desk was now completely covered with piles of the various pieces of information Sheila had gathered since returning from the ride with Wayne. Through news articles and information from electronic news databases, Sheila had searched for a link between Ryan North's accident and Daryl Walker's murder. While it was likely he was only a witness, at best, Sheila was intrigued with the notion that he might have had something to do with the boy's death.

But Ryan Edward North's background was as unmarred by crime and violence as an altar boy's. Even his ex-wife had nothing bad to say about him other than that his work had taken him away from home more than she liked.

Sheila had spent all afternoon reading the stories, and many bore the markings from her yellow highlighter pen where she had marked names of people who might be potential interviews. She also pulled up a biography on the database that gave a brief family history.

His parents had divorced when he was a boy. His mother had died three years ago. He had a brother, Christopher John, who was killed by a drunk driver at the age of twenty-one. Another brother, Victor Robert, was probably still alive, although a database search turned up no recent information on him.

She made a note to try to find Victor. If North were connected to the murder, a reaction quote from his only brother might make a good lead for a story.

North had divorced his wife, Linda, the year before his mother died and had not remarried. There had been no children. There was no indication of where Linda might be living now, or if she had remarried. The tabloids did not report any new love interest for Ryan either, not since his breakup with a woman named Lisa several months before his accident.

One article reported that he had been released from a brain injury rehabilitation center in December and was recuperating at home in the Los Angeles area. There was nothing else until a small item appeared in the entertainment section of the Denver Post dated the day after the boy's body was found. It was very brief, and only mentioned that he had just begun work in a studio in Hollywood on a television special to air in July. Apparently he had recovered from the accident and gone back to work. It was followed a few days later with a small item mentioning that the studio he was using had been vandalized over the weekend. That was the most recent story with his name in it.

Any link between Ryan North and Daryl Walker was elusive.

In one article, Sheila discovered Ryan had once met Senator Walker at a fund raiser for a local conservation society. She reread that article slowly. It was the only place she had seen Ryan's name mentioned in the same article as the senator's. All it said was that Ryan had recorded a song for the Wilderness Society. Senator Walker was chairman of the fundraising committee and had presented Ryan with a plaque of appreciation.

Sheila sighed. Ryan had known the senator, but did that mean he knew the son?

Another story said Ryan had worked for the Marvin Bryce Ad Agency before his first hit. She looked up the phone number and made a note of it.

Maybe North wasn't really hunting? Could this have been some sort of rendezvous? Maybe the boy was blackmailing North? Sheila shook her head and sighed. With what? That he saw North with a woman? That he saw him with a man? Or what if he was blackmailing him because of information he had about some relative of North's? Ricky had said the target of Daryl's investigation was related to someone everybody knows. Was Ryan trying to protect someone?

But what the hell were they doing in the woods? You don't ride five miles from nowhere to blackmail someone.

There was another problem. Horsehair on the boy's clothing indicated he had been on a horse, but had it been his own horse, or Ryan's? If the boy had been on a horse by himself, *where was the horse?* She had checked with Animal Control. There had been no reports of stray horses found in the mountains last year.

Sighing, she put away the files. She had a lot of work to do before she wrote the big story she hoped to get on the front page. Hopefully she could get the sheriff interested in what she had learned. Maybe Jim Harrison could find the connection.

* * *

"It's ringing!" Cindy Vincent bounced on the bed with excitement. Her friend Gloria hugged herself, excited for Cindy, but very, very jealous. For *years* (or so it seemed) they had dreamed of meeting Ryan North, and Cindy, the lucky stiff, had not only *met* him, she had gotten to stay with him for almost *two whole hours* while her father went for help and had gotten to visit him in the hospital too. Now, Gloria thought wistfully, the lucky duck might get to visit him in Hollywood. It was almost too, too, much to bear. She sighed, but then she met Cindy's eyes and she quickly hugged her friend. She smiled and showed Cindy that her fingers were crossed for her for luck.

"Hello?" Cindy said eagerly. "Is this Ryan North's office?"

Gloria pulled the receiver away from Cindy's ear so she could hear what was being said.

"Yes, it is," came the magical voice from Beverly Hills. A woman. Probably his gorgeous secretary, Gloria thought with another twang of jealousy. "This is Wanda. May I help you?"

Cindy had been holding her breath, and it came out in a rush. "My name is Cindy Vincent, and Mr. Norton gave me this number last year and said if I was ever in the area to call, and, and, – "

"Just a minute," the woman said with a gentle chuckle. "Who did you say you were?"

Cindy took a deep breath. "I'm Cindy Vincent. Last year, when Ryan North had his accident, my father and I found him in the woods. I hope he wasn't just being polite, like my dad said he was, but he did invite me to come see him if I could, and we're coming to Disneyland next weekend, and my dad said I could call and see if it was okay to come and he'd drive me up there and – " Cindy stopped, out of breath, having delivered the last sentence in another rush of words.

Wanda was laughing aloud now. "Slow down, Honey, so I can understand you. I'm not going to hang up on you. You don't need to talk so fast."

Gloria pulled the phone away from a suddenly tongue-tied Cindy.

"Hi, I'm Cindy's friend Gloria, and Cindy's a little weirded out right now. Look, they really did find Ryan North last year. It was in all the papers. What she's trying to say, if she could get her head put on right, is that Ryan North told her when she saw him in the hospital that if she ever got over there to call this number and she might be able to see him again."

"Oh, I see. And is she coming our way soon? Is that what this is about?"

"Yes. Her dad's taking her to Disneyland next weekend and Cindy's hoping that she could see Ryan North. If he's not too busy, that is."

"Well, actually," Wanda began slowly, "Mr. North is very busy right now, making a television special. I don't know what his schedule is right now. When will Cindy be coming over?"

Cindy pulled the phone back. "We're flying over next Friday night and we'll be there until the following Tuesday morning. Oh, please say it's okay for me to see him. I'll just *die* if I can't."

"Cindy, give me your phone number. I know Mr. North is very grateful to you and your dad, and if he can arrange it, I'm sure he'll try to see you, even if it's only for a few minutes. I'll just have to ask."

"My phone number? Uh, it's, uh," Cindy turned pleadingly to Gloria, who took the phone again.

"She's so excited she doesn't even know her phone number." Gloria quickly read the number off the phone to make sure she got it right.

"Okay, girls, I'll see what I can do. This isn't a very good time for me to ask him, so it may take a few days before I'll know. Try to calm down in the meantime, Cindy. I'll call you back for sure by Thursday night, no matter what he says. Okay?"

In unison, Cindy and Gloria both answered, "Okay." Cindy added breathlessly, "Thanks a lot." She hung up the phone and gave a shriek. "Ooh, Gloria, I can't stand this! What if he says no? I'll *die!*"

CHAPTER 20

THE NEXT MORNING, SHEILA leaned determinedly across the desk and looked Harley Watson in the eyes. "I can't believe you won't send anyone out to check on what I told you. I should think you'd show a little more interest in what I discovered, Sheriff. You know I could be right."

Harley Watson gazed right back into her green eyes and said mildly, "Miss Fernelli, what you brought me is hardly what I would call evidence. Coincidence, maybe. Figment of your imagination, most likely. Evidence? I don't think so. What you're suggesting is preposterous. I thought you quit that tabloid you used to write for. What does your editor think of these crazy ideas of yours? Or have you had the nerve to tell him how you've been wasting your time lately? But you're not wasting my time, little lady, or my detective's. So go waste someone else's time, okay?"

Sheila set her lips in a firm line at his condescending tone. "I should've known you'd react like this. How are you going to feel when this all comes out in the paper and you have to admit you weren't even interested enough to come see for yourself? And what are you going to say to the senator when he asks if you've followed every lead to find his son's killer?"

Watson's patience was beginning to wear thin. First, the ding-a-ling over at the bureau sent him the wrong photos, now this pushy female reporter was trying to tell him how to run a homicide investigation. He had just about had enough of women this month.

"Miss Fernelli," he began, his voice rising with impatience, "I should warn you that if you run these crazy allegations of yours in the newspaper without proof, you will be setting yourself and your paper up for a huge libel suit. Do you really think you can accuse a man like Ryan North of murder strictly on the basis that he happened to have an accident in the same part of the woods where a body was buried? How about motive? Means? That kid was strangled by a fairly strong man. Ryan North is a pianist, for Pete's sake, not a wrestler! And if he wanted to kill someone why the hell would he risk damaging his hands when he had a loaded gun with him at the time? You go ahead with that crazy story and you're going to get yourself in trouble. Big trouble."

"Truth is an absolute defense against libel suits, Sheriff. You know that." She was not about to be bullied by this man. "All I'm asking is that you let me take your detective up there and seek the truth. When he sees what I saw, he'll want to talk to Ryan North. I'm sure of it."

"Miss Fernelli, you can leave right now. If our investigation indicates that questioning Mr. North is necessary, we will take care of it ourselves. In the meantime, you'd better hold onto your so-called story until there's some proof that a story exists."

She opened her mouth to protest, but he cut her off curtly. "That will be all, Miss Fernelli. Good day."

Sheila stalked out of the office, angry. "Damn small-town cops anyway," she muttered as she got in her car and slammed the door. "Bunch of chauvinist pigs. Never want to hear what a woman thinks." Then a smile played at the corners of her lips. "But maybe he'll listen to another man."

Harley Watson shook his head as he watched through the window while the stubborn young woman drove away. He supposed she was just being over-zealous. After all, it would make a great story if the famous singer were linked to this homicide, and quite a feather in her cap if she could say she broke the case.

But her allegations were not worth wasting a day of his detective's time to go back up to the scene on a horse and look for evidence that probably wasn't there.

* * *

"Well, this is a coincidence, Jim," Wayne said later that morning, shaking Jim Harrison's hand. "I was just getting ready to call you."

"About what, Wayne?" Jim Harrison replied. "Did Jack tell you about my meeting with the rescue boys?"

"No, but the wife said he called while I was out yesterday. I got home too late to call him back. Why don't you go first, Jim? Maybe we're both sniffing the same trail already."

Jim entered Wayne's living room and seated himself on the sofa, clipboard in hand. "I'm trying to talk to people who were in the woods the day the Walker boy was buried. As it happens, that was the day we were all up there carrying out that singer that hit his head, so I was hoping one of you might have seen something while you were there. Maybe other horsemen or hunters, vehicles parked by the road. I know we went in together, but some of you hiked out after I did and might have encountered someone I didn't see, or seen something from the helicopter that I couldn't see from where I was sitting."

"Sorry, Jim," Wayne said, sitting down in his armchair, "but we can't see much through the trees up there, and we were looking for a landing site. As far as cars, the only new cars we saw after we walked out that weren't there already when we picked you up was a reporter's car just leaving the parking lot, and the sheriff had arrived in his car and was still there. There were four horses present, but they're all accounted for. Oh, and the outfitter showed up to get the horse trailer and our car came to pick us up. That was all I ever saw."

"What about any other time you were in that area last fall, prior to the North rescue? We're also looking into helicopter landings in the wilderness area. We think it was a drug drop, with a rider going in later to get the stuff. Do you recall anything unusual you might have seen on any other rescue?"

"I wasn't up there much last fall. We had some rescues in the summer, but the whole month of September I was on vacation. The Ryan North rescue was my first one after I got back."

"Well, Wayne, that answers my questions," Jim said, putting his pencil down. "So what were you going to call me about? I already made a donation to your fund raiser."

"It's a related matter, Jim, and probably you've already figured this out, so stop me if you're way ahead of me, okay?"

"Sure, Wayne."

"Jim, did you know that Ryan North had a view of the murder scene from where he had his accident?"

"He did? I didn't realize he was that close. He was clear over on the Goliath trail, wasn't he? The body was over on Resthouse."

"I know, Jim, but I was out there yesterday and those two scenes are right across the draw from each other, almost at eye level. It takes binoculars, but you can see your yellow Police Line tape quite clearly from where North fell."

"You know, Wayne, we're trying to leave Ryan North out of this if we can. I've already got a reporter dogging my trail as it is. If Sheila Fernelli gets wind that North might be a witness, she'll have it all over the paper in no time. You're real sure of what you saw? You're sure you were at the right location?"

"I'm sure, Jim," Wayne answered. He paused a moment before continuing, "And Jim?"

"Yes?"

"If you're worried about publicity, you'd better get up there and find out the truth pronto."

"Why is that?"

"Because your reporter already knows. She's the one who tipped me off. In fact, Jim," he confessed, "I took her up there myself. She told me the sheriff wouldn't listen to her, so I told her I'd talk to you about it. Jim, it's a heck of a coincidence, you know, that both events took place so close together physically, and on the same day. It might be there's a connection somewhere."

"She talked to Harley? Funny he didn't mention it." Jim sighed. "I guess I'd better get up there, if for no other reason than to prove her wrong. I can't question Ryan North without some evidence linking him to the scene, or the press will try to make him into a suspect, which he is not." He stood up. "Sheila Fernelli is a pretty good reporter, Wayne, but she's like a dog with a bone sometimes. If she has it in her head that Ryan North is an eyewitness, she won't rest until the rest of the world thinks he is, too."

Wayne walked Jim to the door. "I hope I didn't do anything wrong taking her up there, Jim. I'd hate to think I got something started here."

"Don't worry about it, Wayne. She'd have found her way there eventually. At least with you there, we know she didn't try to plant any evidence, or destroy anything, right?"

"Right. She didn't touch a thing. Just looked through her binoculars to see what she could see."

"You looked through them yourself?"

"Yes. That's why I thought I should let you know. If you go up there, you'll want to go on a horse. You can't see it from the ground, even as tall as you are. I can let you use one of mine if you want."

"Thanks, but I've got a horse of my own who can probably use the exercise. If Sheila calls you again, do me a favor and tell her to talk to me instead. She's doing her own investigating, and she's already beaten me to a couple of witnesses." With a wave, Jim walked out to his truck. With a glance at his watch, he decided he would just have time to make it up the mountain before it got too dark to verify what he had just been told.

* * *

"What you're calling information, Jim, I call nothing but speculation," Harley Watson said, shaking his head. "And I thought I told you to stay away from her anyway." He glared across the desk at his detective.

"Who?"

"Sheila Fernelli. Isn't she the one who sent you out on that wild goose chase?"

Jim flushed. "No, not exactly. I talked to Wayne Elliot. He's the one who told me that you could see the crime scene from the accident site."

"It figures. She must have asked him to talk to you after she struck out with me." Harley rocked back in his chair. "Okay, so now that you've been out there, what did you find?"

Jim Harrison flipped open his notebook. "I rode up there and found the accident scene. Of course, it was a long time ago, and there are no tracks left to indicate what direction North took to reach that spot. But I found the rock he landed on and the branch he hit. Then I looked through the binoculars and saw, across the gully, the yellow tape we had put up around the crime scene to keep people away from the grave until we finished. I could see it quite clearly through the binoculars from the back of the horse. So I tied a red handkerchief to a tree branch and rode, in a more or less direct line, over to where the body was found."

"How far away was it?"

"Maybe five hundred yards, but over rough, rocky ground with a lot of trees and shrubs. Then I tried to see the accident scene from there. I couldn't find it. Too many trees."

"So North had a view of the crime scene, but it didn't work the other way around."

"Right. As I rode over, I watched the ground closely, but I didn't see any sign that anyone had ever passed that way before. There were a few hoof prints pointing in a direct line toward the murder site, but they ended in some bushes about fifteen feet from where North was found, then turned and went off toward the trail. Other than that, I didn't find anything. And those tracks could have been left by anyone, North, the Vincents, other hunters."

"So what does this all mean?"

"That if North was the killer, and had his accident while fleeing the scene of the crime, he didn't follow the path I took, which was the most direct way of getting there. It wouldn't even make any sense to make a getaway like that," Jim continued. "The body was near an established trail already. Riding down one hill and up another would not be a very efficient way to get the hell out of there. Even if he wanted to alibi himself by coming out on a totally different trail, he would have taken a terrible risk of being seen in the immediate vicinity. His best bet would have been to continue up or down the Resthouse Meadows trail and put as much distance as possible between himself and the body. It took me nearly twenty minutes to get from one site to the other, and remember, he would have been in sight from the crime scene nearly the entire time he was escaping."

"Do you think he would have known that?"

"I checked my notes from last year. There was a statement made by his companion, Doug Norton, that they were pretty familiar with it. Spent a lot of time in that area as teenagers."

"So you're satisfied that there's no real evidence linking him with the crime."

"Right."

"So much for Sheila Fernelli's information," Harley snorted. "I knew it would be a waste of time. That's why I didn't say anything when she came to see me the other day."

Jim thought briefly about challenging Harley on that point. Harley wasn't investigating, and shouldn't try to second-guess the validity of potential evidence. But it was water under the bridge at this point, so Jim decided to let it go. Instead he argued, "Even though I don't think he was *at* the crime scene, he still may have seen it. For instance, the horse that walked into those bushes and stopped would have had a lovely view of the scene."

"Provided, of course," Harley said sarcastically, "that he just happened to be looking that way at the exact moment in time that the killer was dumping the body. A time span of probably, what, five minutes, tops? Jim, don't you agree that if Ryan North had seen something, he would have mentioned it to someone?"

"That is the puzzler, Harley. But you have to remember, he is a big celebrity. Who knows how his mind might work? He may not have wanted to get involved because of the publicity. Or he may have seen something, but didn't realize what he saw. Like maybe he saw the murderer after the body was already buried. Or maybe, with his own head injury, he thought he dreamed it. I mean, we just found the body recently. If he'd been asked right after the accident, who knows what he might have told us. Come to think of it," he added, "there was that possible attempt made on his life. Maybe the killer thinks he saw something, too. I really should talk to him. Maybe he didn't say anything because he was afraid next time the guy would succeed."

Harley was unconvinced. "Jim, this could get awfully damned embarrassing if you go interrogating him and it turns out he never saw anything. You know the press will make it look like we're accusing him, and I'm convinced he had nothing to do with it. We've got to proceed carefully with this case. I don't want any false publicity with the senator watching us so carefully. We've got enough problems without following up Sheila Fernelli's so-called evidence. I don't need a pack of tabloid reporters on my doorstep."

"But Harley, if he did see something, it could give us a lead to follow."

Harley shook his head. "Now you sound like that idiot woman. Do some checking first. If by some remote, improbable chance he *did* have something to do with it, we better know it before we question him. Otherwise, we'll just put him on his guard. Convince yourself of his innocence before you think about questioning him."

"Okay, Harley," Jim agreed reluctantly. "I'll go slowly with him. And I'll see what I can do to get Sheila Fernelli to hold on to her story until we know if there even is a story."

"Just stay away from her, Jim," Harley said firmly. "I'm seriously thinking of getting a restraining order against her if she doesn't stop undermining your investigation."

CHAPTER 21

J IM DIDN'T ALWAYS DO WHAT he was told to do.
Jim Harrison and Sheila Fernelli were about to have their first face-
to-face meeting since the day the body was found. They had each
been aware almost constantly of what leads the other was following, but
they had never sat down and talked about it. Jim had asked her to meet
him on the neutral turf of a booth in a coffee shop in Idaho Springs. She
had eagerly agreed.

Jim was a little irritated by a phone call he had received from
Senator Walker that morning. He wasn't sure how to do it, but somehow
he had to convince Sheila to talk to him first before she wrote any more
stories or talked to any more witnesses. Sheila, on the other hand, hoped
that she could get Jim to cooperate by giving her exclusive information
in exchange for her helping him with the legwork.

It did not promise to be a fruitful discussion. A waitress brought
coffee for Jim and iced tea for Sheila, and left them alone to talk.

"Sheila," Jim said earnestly, "Harley's been talking about getting a
restraining order against you. He's serious. He does not want you
investigating ahead of me. Frankly, I don't appreciate it either. I had a
very uncomfortable conversation with Senator Walker this morning. He
wanted to know why a reporter thought to ask about his PI and I didn't.
He didn't know I already had the guy's name from Denver PD. Then he
started asking about Ryan North."

"I'm sorry, Jim, I thought we understood each other on that point.
It's not like I haven't been trying to help you, but Harley won't listen to
any of my evidence."

"Harley doesn't consider what you tell him to be evidence," Jim
pointed out firmly. "You've brought us rumors and hearsay and
speculation, not facts. Who is Peter? You don't know. What was Daryl

investigating? You don't know. Was he riding a horse that day? You don't know. You've brought us a lot of questions, but no answers. And in the process, you've beaten me to a number of witnesses. As far as Harley is concerned, he doesn't need the kind of help you offer."

"That's Harley's opinion, Jim," Sheila said, looking into Jim's brown eyes. "What's your opinion?"

Jim hesitated, torn between his loyalty to his boss and his deep-down belief that Harley Watson carried male chauvinism a little too far sometimes. Finally, he admitted, "I think you make some pretty good guesses sometimes, but, Sheila, you should leave the police work to people who are trained in it. I'll get to the truth eventually. Harley deliberately doesn't want to bring in a bunch of detectives from CBI because he wants to restrict any possible leaks. I can't be everywhere at once, though, and when you talk to witnesses before I do, you can put them on their guard."

"That's not quite what happened with Ricky Farrell, now, is it?" Sheila expected no answer, and got none. "He didn't give you the time of day. I got names and dates from him. You got lies."

Jim flushed. "You got lucky."

Sheila pressed her advantage. "What else have you done with the information you got from the school? What did you learn from Jeremy? Or did you even talk to him?"

"Yes, I talked to him, Sheila. He told me the same thing he told you." How had she managed to get him on the defensive so soon, Jim wondered.

"Two days before," Sheila said pointedly. "And did you ever figure out that the 'fag' he saw Daryl with was the same Ricky Farrell you had already interviewed? And another thing, Jim. I found out there were blond horse hairs found on the body. Do you know that Ryan North's horse is a buckskin?"

"So what's your point?" Jim exploded. "You think we should put you on the squad just because this is the only case you have and I've got other duties as well? I don't need your help. I've investigated more homicides than you've ever written about. And did it ever occur to you, Sheila, that one of these days one of your witnesses might turn out to be the killer, and he might not appreciate your questions? That he might decide you know too much and kill you too?"

Sheila glanced at Jim sharply. "Why, Jim Harrison," she said coyly, "if I didn't know better I might think you cared! You don't, do you?"

"I just don't need another homicide investigation right now," he protested, blushing furiously. He tried to meet her gaze, then wavered, looked away, and pretended to be very busy adding sugar to his coffee.

Sheila became thoughtfully silent. At length, she said, "I'm sorry, Jim. I suppose I have been taking some risks, haven't I? I never thought of it that way."

"Well, you should," Jim grunted, looking back into the spunky redhead's green eyes. "I wouldn't enjoy finding your body under a pile of branches somewhere."

"But, Jim, think how happy it would make Harley," she replied lightly.

He looked at her for a moment, then started to laugh, joined by Sheila. Other diners glanced their way, wondering what the joke was. Jim reached across the table and touched Sheila's hand. "I think maybe that was the first thing we ever agreed on."

Sheila looked down at his strong, masculine hand, lying protectively over her small, feminine one and felt a tingle run through her body.

Jim patted her hand once, then withdrew his own, lifting his coffee to his lips.

Sheila took a drink of her iced tea and regained her slipping composure. Why did she feel such a need to compete with men? Why couldn't she be like other women, instead of insisting she could do anything a man could do, and better? She sighed. Cinderella she would never be.

"Jim," she said at last, "I promise to be careful, but we need to reach some agreement here. We both have a job to do. I think we can help each other. I know you can't give me any official standing in your investigation, but can't we cooperate somehow?"

"Sheila, I can't, as an officer of the law, give my permission to a civilian to involve herself in a homicide investigation."

"Okay, Jim, let me ask you this. Do you consider Ryan North a suspect in this case?"

"Certainly not," Jim answered, perhaps a little too huffily. "He might be a witness, but I haven't talked to him yet."

"Then if I investigate the Ryan North angle, I really wouldn't be involved in your murder investigation, right?" she pressed.

"No, he's a public figure. You can investigate him all you want – *as long as you do not in any way suggest that what you're doing is part of this homicide investigation.* If you find evidence, I expect you to bring it to me, first, before you take it to your editor."

"I can't work that way, Jim. I will agree to tell you before any story runs, however."

"Before it's written, Sheila. If you expect me to keep Harley off your back, I need to have a chance to confirm it before you write the story. And stay out of his office. All you do irritate him, then he takes it out on me. I've been walking a fine line with him as it is. You think you've found something, tell me, not him."

"And if I agree, Jim? Will you give me exclusive access to the facts you uncover in your part of the investigation?"

"Sheila, as you know, right now we are working on the theory that there may have been drugs involved. If you promise to keep your hands off that part of the investigation totally, then I'll let you know what I can before any press releases are issued. And stop calling the senator with your ideas. I don't need him thinking I can't do my job without a reporter's help. Okay?"

"Fair enough. Now, will you promise me something?"

"What?"

"That if I find a connection, you'll really listen to my evidence with an open mind, regardless of what you think Harley might think?"

"I promise to listen. I don't promise to take a report, nor do I promise to act. I will listen. If you have some tangible proof, and I can confirm it myself, then it might become part of the investigation." He finished his coffee and pulled a couple of bills from his wallet. "I trust you'll allow me to pay for this?"

"I have an expense account – " Sheila started to protest, then caught the look in his eyes and said, "Yes, Jim. Thank you."

* * *

"Sheila Fernelli caught something else, Harley," Jim informed the sheriff later that day.

"A good case of exotic flu, I hope," Harley growled, glaring up at Jim over the report he had been reading. "And I thought I told you to stay away from her, Harrison."

Jim didn't respond. Harley grunted. "Hmph. So what did she catch that we didn't already know?"

"Somehow she found out the horse hair found on the body is the same color as Ryan North's horse. The coroner's report mentioned that the hair found was a light gold or beige color, and I do remember that North's horse was a buckskin. I had known all that, but didn't have any reason to compare the color of the hairs with anyone's horse. But she noticed it, and it will probably be in a story at some point."

"Have you confirmed it's the same animal?"

"No, but that hasn't stopped her from speculating all the same. It would be nice to be able to prove it's not the same horse, but the horse isn't here anymore. He was shipped to Los Angeles and I don't know exactly where he is now so I can't send anyone to collect hair samples from him. Hair typing with animals isn't an exact science anyway."

"Lots of buckskin horses in the world. In fact, are we even sure it was horse hair that was found? Maybe it was from a deer."

"It's horse, all right. We confirmed that a long time ago. And you're right, there are a lot of buckskin horses, and a lot of palominos, pintos, roans, and Appaloosas that could also have had golden hair. Even my horse, Patch, has blond hair on his belly."

"Watch it, Jim. You'll become her number one suspect. Sheila Fernelli will report anything," Harley grunted. "She used to work for a tabloid."

"I know." Jim looked thoughtful. "I guess that would explain why she's so determined to link a celebrity to this homicide." He ignored the little pang of guilt he felt. He was so used to agreeing with Harley's sarcastic comments about Sheila Fernelli it was a hard habit to break. He was also relieved that Harley had dropped the subject of why Jim was talking to Sheila in the first place.

"So what do you want to do next, Jim? Somehow I have a feeling you want to pursue this Ryan North angle, no matter how unlikely it seems."

"All the solid information we have leads in a different direction," Jim replied. "The drug angle, for instance. Ryan North is supposed to be really straight-laced. I can't see him involved if the drug courier theory turns out to be correct."

"But?"

"But you're right, I think I'd like to talk to Ryan North. Not as a suspect, but as a witness. He might have seen someone or something out there that day and never thought another thing about it. Maybe a loose horse, maybe he saw the kid before the murder, maybe there was a car parked on the road. We've checked with the wildlife department. No deer or elk were taken in that area that day, so we have no record of who else might have been hunting there that day. Nobody else has come forth with any clues since Shaw told us about the helicopters. Ryan North, his brother, and Howard Vincent are the only ones we *know* were there that day. Vincent didn't see anything. I can't find the brother. We should ask North."

"You sound like you're trying to convince yourself," Harley observed.

"Maybe I am. Hopefully North will be able to tell us where his brother is, too. I'd like to at least rule them both out. Even the senator called me about it. Apparently Sheila talked to him, too. She called him a week ago to get the name of the investigator he hired last year, then yesterday morning she called him back with another question about it and just casually mentioned that she felt Ryan North may have been involved in some way."

"I'll bet she just 'casually' mentioned it," Harley growled with disgust. "She was probably reading from a script to make sure she didn't leave anything out."

"Well, it was slightly embarrassing, anyway, Harley. The reason he called me was to find out why I hadn't asked him for the name of the investigator yet. He seemed surprised that a reporter had asked him first. He didn't know I already had the information. But unfortunately, he seemed very interested in the Ryan North angle."

"You know you can't do a telephone interview of a witness in a homicide case. And I can't afford to send you to Los Angeles on what is sure to be a wild goose chase."

"Harley, we've got another witness to interview over there already. I didn't tell you this yet, because I just found out last night, but the Walkers' next-door neighbors moved to Santa Barbara three months ago. They're the ones who saw the vehicle that may have picked up Daryl the last time he was seen alive."

The sheriff sighed. "Well, Jim, I guess Sheila Fernelli is going to win this round. Get out to California and see them both. And as long as you're out there, try to find the horse, too. Let's rule him out as a suspect as well. Maybe that will shut up Sheila Fernelli once and for all. Although how you're going to get an appointment with Ryan North without a warrant is beyond me. I doubt he's in the phone book."

"I'll find a way. Thanks, Harley. I'll leave in the morning."

Part III
May 12-22, 1994
The Suspect

CHAPTER 22

DOUG NORTON SAW the news report of the boy's death while packing to go back to Los Angeles the day after the body was identified. Ryan North had gone back to work, over the objections of his doctor, trying to make the television special he had been planning before the accident. Doug knew his brother well enough to know all along that the doctor's admonishment to work no more than eight hours a day would be ignored within a week – as soon as Ryan decided things weren't going quite the way he wanted. He knew Ryan would work longer and longer hours, trying to keep to the unrealistic timetable he had no doubt set for himself, until he landed back in the hospital.

And Doug had been right, and Ryan had asked him to come back, and he was going. At Ryan's request, he had just sent Ryan's horse to California and had arranged for stabling in a nearby equestrian center in the care of a trainer until Ryan was ready to start riding again.

The horse was Ryan's only other tie to Colorado, and Doug was sure that Ryan would renew his campaign to get Doug to move back to Los Angeles permanently.

Ryan had spent just over a month in the rehab center, and Doug had returned to Los Angeles with him when he was released. Just after Christmas, they had invited Ryan's band and crew over for dinner where they had discussed the plans for the television special and agreed to go ahead with it a few months later, as long as Ryan was up for it. Doug had hoped it wouldn't be necessary, but he knew he would come back and help if he was needed.

Now it was five months later, and rehearsals had just begun, and Ryan was already running behind schedule. So Doug was reluctantly on his way back to Los Angeles to help him.

It was after he had closed the suitcase and carried it into the living room that his attention was drawn to the TV he had left droning in the background after seeing the weather report so he would know what clothes to pack for the trip to L.A.

What he saw there caused him to collapse on his easy chair. It was a photo of a boy, a boy he had known. The boy from the meeting. The boy from the woods. The boy named Danny. Except the announcer was saying the boy's name was Daryl Walker, and he was the son of a Colorado state senator. His body had been found in the mountains. It had just been identified and police were asking for help solving the murder.

As the broadcast continued a few details were provided and Doug listened with a sickening feeling of dread. He'd heard about the body, of course. That had been reported over the weekend, but how was Doug to know it was the same kid? The initial reports sounded like the boy had died only recently. Now the anchorman was saying the boy was believed to have disappeared October sixteenth, and most likely had died the same day.

The day of Ryan's accident.

Nervously, he lit a cigarette and stared, unseeing, at the television while his mind raced. What if someone had seen him with the boy that morning? What if that same person could identify him as the man who was seen on TV that evening, giving details of Ryan's accident to those reporters in the hospital lobby? What if anyone found out where he had met the boy in the first place?

He exhaled a cloud of smoke at the television screen. What if Ryan learned the secret Doug had kept so carefully hidden all these years? It would devastate him.

And then he thought about Fred Dreyer, the private investigator who was a big part of Doug's life now. He and Fred had been working with the boy on that investigation just before Ryan's accident – just before the boy died. What would Fred do when he found out the boy had stopped coming to the meetings, not because he had gotten scared, but because he was dead? He drew another long drag on the cigarette.

Fred would recognize that date immediately and know that Doug had been there at the same time.

Fred used to be a policeman. Would he tell the police what he knew, or would he realize there was nothing they could have done anyway, that there was nothing to be gained now by coming forward?

He exhaled sharply, then crushed out the cigarette. There was nothing he could do now. The boy was dead. Nothing would change that. And he had a plane to catch. Ryan needed him.

* * *

Doug spent his first morning in L.A. making sure Ryan's horse had been settled into his new quarters near the park and talking to the trainer who had already started working with him. If he'd had his say in the matter, he would have sold the horse, but Ryan was fond of the young gelding and Ryan usually got what Ryan wanted, so Doug had to settle for making sure he was being ridden regularly by an experienced trainer.

Ryan hadn't been on a horse since the accident, and Doug knew it wouldn't be long after the horse's arrival before Ryan would be on his back again.

He bought a riding helmet and left it hanging on the bridle hook in the tack room. Maybe Ryan would take the hint.

After seeing to the horse, he drove to the studio where the special was being made to meet Ryan and his manager during the lunch break.

Although the place was nearly empty when they arrived, Ryan and his manager, Tony DiMartino, had to wait for a table to be cleared before they could sit down with their food in the studio's cafeteria. The busboy laboriously moved on to an adjacent table, clearing dishes and glasses with a noisy racket before giving the table a cursory wipe with a wet rag. A sharp word from Tony sent him and his bin of dirty dishes to the far corner of the cafeteria, leaving Ryan and Tony in relative quiet so they could talk.

Tony DiMartino was a short man in his late forties, with a round face and a slight paunch to match. His thinning black hair had already grayed considerably. For nearly three years, he had been Ryan's manager and currently was producing the television special. Tony had been in charge of everything but Ryan's finances, which Ryan handled himself with the guidance of Fritz, his CPA. For nearly three years, Ryan had relied on Tony to hire and fire, plan his tours, make his reservations, handle the various needs of his fan club, issue press releases and coordinate interviews, and keep Ryan generally informed of what the world thought of him.

And Ryan didn't trust him.

Doug arrived a few minutes after they sat down.

"Over here, Doug," Tony called, waving, when he saw Doug enter.

Ryan, sitting with his back to the door, twisted around to greet his brother and was rewarded with an instant headache for the effort. He rubbed his temples as Doug sat down opposite him after greeting Tony with a handshake.

"You okay?" Doug asked.

"Yeah, fine," Ryan replied. "Just a twinge all of a sudden. You're not eating?" He took a bite of his sandwich, grimaced, then opened it up and pulled out a jalapeño pepper.

"Ate on the way back from the stable. Looks like I'm not missing much," he added, watching Ryan pick through his sandwich looking for other unwanted surprises.

"You missed a good rehearsal," Tony said. "That skit will have them rolling in the aisles." He picked a wilted leaf from his salad.

"I'm sure it will," Doug replied. "Ryan told me about it on the phone last night after I got in."

"We should be ready to start taping Monday or Tuesday," Tony added. "So, Doug," he continued, "how long are you staying in town? Just through the show?"

Ryan and Doug exchanged glances, then Doug answered, "Not sure yet. Maybe indefinitely."

Tony waved at a heavyset man with red hair and a full beard who entered the room. "Hi, Biff. Want to join us? There's room for one more here if you don't want to eat alone."

Doug looked up but this time Ryan decided not to risk another sharp pain by turning around so he waited until Biff arrived at the table to greet him, "Hi, Biff. How's the soap going?"

"Going just fine. Can't join you right now, though, thanks. I'm meeting someone in a few minutes. Some guy looking for work as usual. This one I may need to keep on file, though. He's a sound man and you know how scarce they are right now with the threat of a strike in a few weeks."

"Good luck," Tony said. Biff sat at the empty table that had just been cleared behind Ryan and summoned the bus boy to request coffee.

"Who's that?" Doug asked.

"Oh, heck, Doug, I'm sorry I didn't introduce you," Ryan answered. "That's Biff Greene. He's producing a soap opera in the next studio. We're going to be borrowing a couple of his people part time when we start shooting next week." He had eaten half the sandwich and was picking at lukewarm french fries.

"Actors?"

"No, crew members. He's got a new makeup artist that he only needs for a couple hours in the morning, so we're going to use him when they're done over there. We're also getting one of his lighting technicians."

"Nice of him to share." Doug glanced up again and stared as a long-haired, bearded blond man entered the room and walked over to Biff's table. He sat down with his back to Ryan's table and handed Biff a sheet of paper. While the blond man leaned back in his chair, hands interlaced behind his head, Biff started reading, making occasional notes in the margin.

"You know, Doug," Tony commented, "we could do better than this for chow while we're doing this show. I hear you play a pretty mean barbecue grill."

Doug gave Tony a side glance. "Might be fun," he replied, "but Ryan would never eat my cooking. You'd be better off to call out for pizzas."

"What do you mean? He's the one who told me what a good cook you are."

"Oh, really? Did he also tell you he hasn't eaten anything I made that he didn't personally watch me prepare since the day I fed him Ex-Lax brownies?"

Tony burst out laughing, drawing glances from the few other diners. "When was that?"

"When we were working together at an ad agency in Denver. Before he became rich and famous."

"It's true," Ryan agreed. "I'd forgotten about it, though. I let you feed me in the hospital."

"That was before you started getting your memory back," Doug reminded him. "And that was someone else's cooking."

"He's right, Tony. I don't trust him. He was always slipping something into my coffee, too. Sometimes No Doz, sometimes a sleeping aid. Luckily I always drank decaf, so at least I never overdosed on caffeine."

"Yeah, you did it to me, too. Let's not forget that."

"Once. I got you exactly once."

"So I was better at it than you were."

Tony watched the two brothers banter back and forth and realized that no matter how long he worked with Ryan, he would always feel like an outsider when Doug was around. Three years as manager couldn't compete with a lifetime of brotherhood.

"How's Badger?" Ryan asked.

"He's fine. I've got him at the equestrian center and the trainer has already started working with him."

"Good. Hopefully I'll have time to see him this weekend. Hey," Ryan said suddenly, "What ever happened to my gun, anyway? You told me you were bringing my horse back, but what happened to my rifle?"

"It's in Denver. A friend of mine has a gun safe and he offered to store it until I come back. Why? You planning to shoot me over that Ex-Lax thing? Or have you come to your senses and decided to shoot the horse?"

"No, of course not. I haven't thought to wonder about it until now," Ryan remarked. "I was so busy trying to remember what happened before the accident I never got around to finding out everything that happened afterward."

"Well, I'll tell you, Ryan," Tony said, "it sure shook me up when I talked to you after you came out of the coma and you didn't even remember things we talked about three weeks previously. You're really lucky you got it all back. Some accident victims never get back their lost memories."

"I didn't get quite all of it back, Tony. I remembered everything that was important, though. But I never remembered the accident itself plus some unknown period of time just prior to it. Probably just a minute or two, according to the doctors."

"Must be weird to have a gap in your memory like that."

"Not really. I don't think about it much anymore. It's like waking up from a dream. You know how you wake up from a dream that was really vivid or emotional and then two minutes later you can't even remember what it was about? All you remember is the way it made you feel? It's kind of like that. I know there was something that I can't remember, but I also know it doesn't really matter so I don't dwell on it."

"Sounds like you've adapted to it pretty well."

"Had to. Life goes on. I was more concerned with whether I'd ever remember how to play a piano again. Now, *that* was scary."

Doug said quietly, "I don't think I've ever seen you more scared, before or since, Ryan, than the day you sat down at that piano at the rehab center and realized you had no idea how to play it."

"I don't think I've ever *been* more scared, before or since, than I was that day," Ryan affirmed. "And let's talk about more pleasant topics, okay? That's a part of my life I wish I *didn't* have to remember. And I hope I never have to go through anything like that again as long as I live. I felt like I'd been told I couldn't be me anymore, that I had to be someone else the rest of my life. Someone I didn't know or even like very much." He shuddered. "No, thanks, I think I'd like to let that memory go into the same black hole where my memory of the accident went."

Ryan glanced around self-consciously, suddenly aware that the cafeteria had fallen nearly completely silent while he talked about a very painful personal experience.

"It wasn't such a fun part of my life, either," Doug said quietly. "What are you working on this afternoon?"

"The dance numbers."

"No reason for me to hang around, then," Doug remarked.

"Not if you have something else to do," Ryan answered, a little sharply. "I thought you were going to be here the rest of the day now that the horse was taken care of."

"Have a couple errands to run. Want to reactivate the car phone in the Corvette among other things. Don't worry, Ryan. I'm not going to bail out on you. I just want to get these things taken care of now, before you get to the parts where you might need me to be here."

"Oh, okay," Ryan replied, relieved. "See you tonight for dinner?"

"Sure, Ryan, sure. I'll be there." Doug stood up. "I need a cigarette, so I'll see you guys later." He patted Ryan on the shoulder as he walked by. "And no lectures, okay? I've heard it all already."

"I gave up on that a long time ago, Doug," Ryan replied. After Doug was gone, he said to Tony, "He doesn't really smoke all that much but I wish he'd quit. Our mom smoked and I think that's why she had her heart attack."

"Did you ever smoke?"

"No, I tried it once in college but it affected my voice and that shook me up a little. I'd already started singing in clubs at that point and was seeing that I had a shot at making a living at it. Never mattered with Doug, though, since he never performs." Ryan sighed. "He says it calms him down. I guess it's true. He used to be – I don't know how to describe it – more hyper? Hyper isn't the right word. Restless, maybe. Edgy. Not really nervous, just on edge all the time."

"How long has he smoked?"

"Couple years, I guess. Odd for someone to start smoking that late in life, too. Most people start as teens and spend their entire adult life regretting it and trying to quit."

"Lots of things we do as teenagers we spend the rest of our lives regretting. You never did drugs, did you."

"Never. I saw what it did to one of my brother Christopher's friends. Chris got into drugs for a while, just pot, but he hung out with some LSD users. One of them thought he could fly and jumped off a fourth floor balcony. Unfortunately, it didn't kill him. It just left him completely paralyzed and brain damaged for life. That was all I needed to know. I never went anywhere near the stuff, not even marijuana. I've never used anything stronger than aspirin unless a doctor prescribed it. The whole idea scares the hell out of me."

* * *

That evening, Doug drove over to Ryan's house after taking care of various errands. He let himself into the house, glanced around, and sighed. Ryan was not home yet, which meant he had worked at least ten hours that day.

It had been five months since he had left Ryan and returned to Denver with his friend, Fred Dreyer. Prior to that, he had been with Ryan almost constantly since the day of the accident, helping him with rehab, and helping him readjust to self-care in his own home after he was released from the center.

As long as Ryan needed him, it had been all Doug could think about. He had little thought for the life he had left behind in Denver, his job, the investigation he had been helping Fred with, and the battle he had been waging within himself, a battle Fred had been slowly helping him win.

But he had been scared of winning that battle. And had been almost glad to have the excuse of taking care of his brother to give him reason to back away, to tell Fred he was giving up, and to cut off all contact with him after the day Ryan entered the rehab center.

It was only after Ryan no longer needed him that Doug realized that he couldn't hide from the truth any longer. He had called Fred for the first time in over a month, and Fred had immediately gotten on a plane and come to Los Angeles, where he had been invited to the dinner party the world-famous singer, Ryan North, had thrown for his band and crew a few days after Christmas.

He hadn't even known that Doug knew Ryan North. He certainly did not expect to discover him living in the famous singer's house, co-hosting his dinner party.

After the party, Doug drove Fred over to Doug's vacant condo, where Fred was to spend the night. It was there that he told Fred for the first time that not only was he Ryan North's lyricist and business partner, but that he was also his brother, and that he had been at Ryan's side since the day of the hunting accident.

And then Fred had asked Doug what he was going to do. Was he going to stay with his brother, and remain in denial of who and what he was, or was he going to come back with Fred to Denver, and finish the investigation they had been doing, and continue to work on accepting himself?

Doug had gone back to Denver the next day.

Doug wandered around the house, waiting for Ryan to return. He noticed a small exhaust fan that had been built into the wall of the living room next to the chair Doug usually sat in, an ashtray strategically placed in front of the fan on the end table between the chair and the sofa. He smiled. Ryan had been bothered by Doug's smoking, but the fan was a sign that he had accepted Doug's choice but was going to assert some boundaries about it. If only everything could be that simple….

He sat in the chair and flipped on the fan. Then he lit a cigarette and watched as the smoke was drawn to the fan. Clever.

He drew on the cigarette and glanced at his watch, wondering when his brother would be home, wondering if he would immediately start pressuring Doug to make a commitment to stay permanently, to be a part of his life again, to give up everything he had back in Denver to be his manager.

Doug was torn, unsure if his destiny lay with his brother and their song writing career, or with the new life he was starting to make with the help of Fred.

It would soon be time to make a commitment to one course or the other. The special would only take a few weeks to make, and then he would have to decide.

But there was Fred to think about. Finally explaining Ryan to Fred at Christmas had been hard enough. How could he ever explain Fred to Ryan? Could Ryan ever understand that Doug had been essentially dead, and Fred had saved his life? Made him see that life was worth living? How could he ever tell his totally-in-control and usually perfect older brother how close he had come to blowing his brains out one night? How could he ever tell him that he had spent the last three years in therapy, trying ever since the death of their mother to come to terms with his internal demons?

Death would have been preferable to having to explain all that to Ryan.

Fred had convinced him otherwise.

Fred had been through the whole thing himself. A former police officer, he had once stared down the barrel of his own gun and wondered how big a mess it would make if he blew his brains out, and which of his bigoted co-workers would be the lucky one to get to investigate his death, the one to scrape bits of brain from the wall, the one to learn all of Fred's secrets, the one to break the news to Fred's ex-wife and ten-year-old son. It was thinking of his son that made him put the gun down that night.

Fred had understood only too well what Doug was going through. He understood the whole family thing, the self-loathing, the internal battle between being right in everyone else's eyes and being what he was, the trying to change, the realizing it was impossible. And he understood that only self-acceptance would make life livable, and that once that point was reached, the rest didn't matter anyway.

It had taken months of patience and understanding on Fred's part, but Doug was almost ready to accept himself. Almost.

He crushed out the cigarette with finality. Fred was lucky, he thought. He had come to terms with it. Doug had not. No, this was not the time to tell Ryan the truth. Not yet. Maybe not ever.

He heard a car door slam and realized the limo had pulled up in front of the door. A moment later, the door opened and Ryan came in.

"Ah, there you are," Ryan said. "I was hoping you'd come back by the studio after you ran your errands."

"Took me longer than I expected," Doug answered. "And I figured you would have been home long before this. I thought you were supposed to keep it to an eight-hour day."

Ryan strode over to the bar and poured a Scotch. "That's not always possible," he replied. "Drink?"

"Sure. Scotch is fine," he added.

Ryan poured a second drink for Doug and sat in his recliner. "I'm bushed," he admitted.

"You have only yourself to blame for that, you know," Doug said unsympathetically.

Ryan shot him a sour look. "It's not my fault. We've had some delays and I've had to make up for lost time. Trouble finding some crew members we needed, things like that."

"Is that why you wanted me to come back?"

"Well, not really. But this is the sort of thing that you'll be having to handle when you become my manager in August. I thought maybe you could kind of keep an eye on Tony for me. See what you'll be getting in to. And help make sure he doesn't drop the ball when I need him the most."

"I haven't agreed to be your manager, Ryan. I told you I'd think about it."

"Oh, come on, Doug. You know you'd like working with me again. I mean full-time. Not like we've been doing."

Doug sighed. He really didn't want to get into this whole thing right now. "We'll talk about that later," he said. "Have you had dinner?"

"No."

"Is there anything here to fix or have you been eating out since I left last December?"

"I've been cooking," Ryan said defensively. "But not since we started work last week. I don't know what's in there. But we could always get a pizza."

"Let's do that," Doug said. "It's getting kind of late to be cooking."

Ryan picked up the phone and speed-dialed the pizza parlor and ordered his "usual." Doug suspected Ryan had been eating pizza more often than he had been cooking, but he said nothing.

"Okay, that's handled," Ryan said. "We've got a lot of catching up to do," he said. "I've hardly heard from you since you left. What have you been doing?"

"Not much," Doug said evasively. "Working mostly."

Ryan sobered. "Working with that friend of yours, what was his name? The one I met at Christmas. The investigator with the gun."

Doug lit a cigarette before answering. "Fred Dreyer."

"Yes. Him. Have you been working with him? Or do I even want to know?"

"We finished up a job we had started before your accident. Finished it a few days after I got back."

Ryan studied him. "Doug, I tried to call you at the ad agency a couple weeks ago when I couldn't get you on that cell phone of yours. They told me you didn't work there anymore."

"I don't."

"You quit?"

"I never went back. I took a leave of absence when you had your accident and I just never went back."

"So what have you been doing if you're not at the ad agency? And why didn't you tell me you quit?"

"I can answer both those questions with the same answer," Doug said tersely. "It's none of your business."

Ryan looked stung. "Excuse me?"

Doug sighed. "I'm sorry. But it really isn't. As long as I deliver your lyrics when you need them, it's really none of your business what else I do with my time."

"It may not be any of my business," Ryan said slowly, "but I do care about you. Why all of a sudden are you shutting me out of your life?"

"Maybe just to see if I can," Doug answered defiantly. "Trying to see if I can set boundaries and actually have you respect them. Because you never have before."

"Look, if you don't want to be here, you're free to leave," Ryan said.

Doug sighed. "See? I knew you'd get this way. This isn't about my not wanting to be here. Making music with you is what I do. I have no problem being here and helping you with this special. It's my music too. But just because we work together doesn't mean we have to know ever minute detail of each other's life."

Ryan held his tongue, remembering how withdrawn and evasive Doug had been during the few weeks he had stayed with him after Ryan was released from the rehab center, and remembering that Doug really had started pulling away from him shortly after their mother died. And he had forgotten that it was right after Ryan had pressed Doug for details about his life in Denver that Doug's friend had shown up and Doug had returned with him to Colorado, leaving Ryan alone.

Apparently nothing had changed in the ensuing months, and Doug was determined to leave Ryan shut out of his life.

"I'm sorry," Ryan finally said. "I don't understand what's happened between us, but I won't ask any more questions."

"Thank you," Doug replied, proud of himself for standing his ground. Fred had been a good influence on him, he realized. He'd never stood up to his brother before.

"It's not that I think you owe me any explanations for your life, it's just that I missed you. I liked having you here with me again. I had hoped you would stay, and then all of a sudden you were gone."

"Ryan, I was gone before your accident. You didn't seem to mind then."

"I had Lisa then," Ryan answered.

Doug sighed. "You could still have her now if you weren't so stubborn. You think the sun rises and sets on you and never seem to think about what others need or want."

"Come on, Doug," Ryan argued. "You know what happened with my marriage. I couldn't do that to Lisa too. It wouldn't be right."

Doug finished his drink and stood up. "I probably know more about your marriage than you do, Ryan. I was the one who was there with Linda while you were out on tour all the time. I think I knew her better than you did. But Lisa was not Linda and you didn't give her a chance to prove it." He walked out of the room, leaving Ryan sitting there alone.

The pizza was delivered a short time later, and the two men managed to talk about the show without further conflict the rest of the evening. They had always been at their best with each other when working on their music and it took only a few minutes for them both to get totally focused on the project at hand and start working as the team that had made Ryan an international success in their chosen field.

Ryan gave Doug a copy of the schedule and they discussed the areas Ryan felt he needed Doug's help, and by the end of the evening the earlier discussion seemed to be forgotten by both of them.

Doug left around ten o'clock to go to his condo for the night, promising to return the next night for dinner, much to Ryan's relief. He hated eating alone.

Later that night, Ryan went to bed only to wake up in a fearful sweat two hours later. The recurring nightmare of the green unicorn that he hadn't had since shortly after Christmas was back again.

CHAPTER 23

RYAN SPENT MOST OF Saturday resting. He'd been having headaches again for a couple of nights and felt they were caused by the long hours that he had been working. So he had rested and relaxed and was feeling much better by the time Doug came over and cooked dinner for both of them.

But the headache returned after he ate, so he went to bed early and Doug returned to his condo. Once again, the nightmare returned, but Ryan merely crawled out of bed and took several aspirin to deal with the headache that always accompanied it.

He tried not to think about the fact that the return of the headaches and nightmare might mean he was not as healed from the head injury as he had thought he was. Surely it was just the stress from the show.

He awoke Sunday feeling pretty good and since he had nothing else to do, he decided it was time to deal with something that had been bothering him since his accident. It was time to get back on a horse. Badger had arrived and he was anxious to see him again. It was a clear, sunny day, slightly cool from an offshore breeze, perfect for his first ride in more than seven months.

After saddling and bridling his horse he put on the helmet Doug had left him and nervously swung up on the horse's back. He rode down the trail that ran alongside the Equestrian Center, then crossed a bridge and rode down to the first of three underpasses leading into the park. The young horse put up a bit of a fuss when Ryan asked him to enter the first tunnel, but with a little encouragement he finally entered then walked quickly to the other side with his head held low as if afraid he might hit it on the roof. As he rode under the freeway, the hollow clip-clop of the horse's hooves was a sharp contrast to the overhead hum of the traffic.

Badger flung his head back up and snorted loudly when he reached the other side, and Ryan laughed. His initial nervousness had left him after just a few minutes in the saddle and he quickly relaxed to the rhythm of the horse's stride. But he couldn't relax too much. The horse was just as frisky as he remembered.

He rode through two more tunnels, then reached an open section of the trail that ran parallel to the park road. Badger pulled insistently at the bit, and Ryan loosened the reins and allowed the horse to break into a gentle canter. The trail was shaded by trees growing along both sides, and he loped through patches of sunlight as he rode.

A few minutes later, he stopped at a fork in the trail. "That felt good," Ryan said to himself. He patted the horse's neck. "Good boy, Badger. I've really missed this."

He nudged the horse into a walk to go up a hill, keeping a firm hand on the reins. They continued along a ridge, Ryan enjoying the quiet and solitude of the park. Some joggers approached on the trail ahead and Ryan stopped Badger while two women passed by, giving him only the slightest glance.

Neither did a double take, and Ryan didn't know if he should be relieved he hadn't been recognized, or worried that he had been but the women didn't care. It had been a long time since he had found himself surrounded by a growing mob of fans. He realized he missed the attention.

He continued along the trail another half mile then stopped at a point overlooking the golf course and some other bridle trails. He watched a man and woman ride past the golf course, laughing, holding hands from the backs of their horses. Wistfully, he recalled a day about a year before, when he had been riding with Lisa, the only woman he had dated since his divorce. They, too, had held hands like teenagers despite their horses' failure to cooperate. He had nearly been pulled to the ground trying to hold Lisa's hand when her horse perversely decided it was time to return to the stable and doubled back on the trail without warning. He let go in time to keep his own balance and they had laughed about it most of the way back to the stable.

Sitting on Badger's back, he lost himself in memories of Lisa. He had felt he had no alternative but to break up with her when he realized he was falling in love with her. He hadn't been fair to his first wife, and he did not want to make the same mistake again. Lisa deserved a man who would be there for her, not out on the road all the time.

Lost in his thoughts, he didn't notice another horse approaching on the trail about a hundred yards away until it whinnied loudly. Badger alerted and started to gather himself to reply but before he could make a sound, Ryan snatched the reins in a panic and wheeled Badger back in a circle away from the other horse, kicking him hard without thinking.

Badger bolted in surprise, stumbling slightly as he started back up the slope.

Confused, Ryan pulled up his horse and looked back at the other horse who had whinnied. He stared at it for a moment, wondering why he had felt the flash of urgency to flee. Badger danced nervously and tossed his head, pulling the reins through Ryan's hands. "Sorry, Badger. Easy boy," he said softly, shortening the reins again. His head started to pound and he nudged Badger into a walk. He badly needed an aspirin and he hoped his driver, who was waiting at the stable with the car, would have some.

As he rode back toward the stable, Ryan puzzled over his reaction. Why should he be afraid of a horse's whinny? Then he remembered. He rolled his eyes. That stupid nightmare. That stupid nightmare with that stupid green unicorn. He'd been relieved when it finally stopped about a week after Christmas, but it had returned again, the same bizarre dream that always left him with a feeling of terror and dread – feelings that were associated with a screaming sound in the dream, a sound that was much like the shrill whinny that had precipitated his panic reaction a few minutes before.

He thought about the nightmare, the confusing images and sounds he'd grown accustomed to several months before that were now a part of his nighttime routine again. He wished he knew what it meant, but he also knew he would never talk to anyone about it.

How would a thirty-year-old world-famous singing star explain to anyone that he was dreaming about a talking green unicorn every night –

a unicorn who filled him with such dread that his reaction was to flee in fear? No, this was one to keep to himself. He had never even told Doug, never even told his doctor. In fact, he could barely stand to admit it to himself. It was too silly, too childish.

It had gone away by itself before. It would go away again. He was just working too hard, that was all. Once the show was finished, the nightmare would go away again.

* * *

Monday morning, Doug arrived at the studio about ten o'clock to find the place in an uproar. Over the weekend, someone had broken in, rifled Tony's office, broken several spotlights, and thrown trash around Ryan's dressing room.

Doug found Ryan in his dressing room, talking to a police officer. He gave the cop a disgusted look behind his back but sat down in a chair to hear what had happened.

"So you worked late Friday," the cop was saying, "and did not come back over the weekend?"

"That's correct," Ryan replied. "Nobody was here over the weekend. The other shows that use this building don't shoot on the weekend either."

"The guard didn't see anyone," the officer commented. "But there was only one guard on duty at a time all weekend and this is a pretty big lot to keep tabs on."

"I don't know why anyone would break in here," Ryan said. "There's nothing of any particular value here. Nothing was taken that we can tell, although some of the sound equipment was apparently gone through. Some of the button microphones were scattered around on the floor."

"Well, Mr. North," the policeman said, "my guess would be that it was teenagers with nothing better to do. Probably hoping to find someone's drug stash. Lots of people in the industry use, as I'm sure you know."

"Well I don't," Ryan retorted. "And anyone who knows anything about me would know that."

"That doesn't mean people on your staff don't. A couple of them have priors for drug possession, you know."

Ryan didn't answer.

"Well, I've taken the report but there's not too much we can do at this point. We don't normally take prints for something like this, especially when there are so many people who legitimately belong here. You've just taken possession of this studio a few days ago. Who knows who might have been here before and left prints all over the place." He snapped his clipboard shut and handed Ryan a business card. "If anything else happens, or if you discover anything missing after all, please give me a call." He turned and left the dressing room, nodding to Doug, who ignored the gesture with stony silence.

"Shit," Ryan said when he was gone. "I don't need this right now."

Doug stood up and started picking up some waste papers that had been strewn around the dressing room. He uncrumpled one of them and looked at it. It was a copy of the rehearsal schedule, listing what they were planning to work on each day. It had been crossed out and altered to reflect the delays in the early days of the project. He dropped it back in the trash can.

"Nothing was stolen?" Doug asked.

"Not that we can tell. Tony said the personnel files had been gone through, though. He's going to move them over to Wanda's office today. Hopefully there won't be any identity theft as a result of this. But they're all there, and there was no indication anyone used the copier. They did take fingerprints from that, and did a quick comparison to Tony, since he's the only one who normally uses it. The only prints on it were Tony's. If anyone else had used it, even with gloves, his prints would have been smudged. But they weren't."

"So this is just pointless vandalism?" Doug asked skeptically. "Did any of the other studios get vandalized too?"

"Nope, just ours."

"Doesn't make sense," Doug muttered. "If they were looking for drugs, why wouldn't they look in all the offices, not just Tony's?"

"Don't know," Ryan replied. "Well, they should have the stage swept up of that broken glass by now. Guess we should get to work." He walked out of the dressing room.

Doug finished picking up the trash and then followed Ryan out to the sound stage.

He stood off to the side with Tony, watching as the director set up the part they were scheduled to rehearse that day. After the band was settled in their places and the dancers took their positions, Ryan sat down at the piano and put his hands to the keyboard and then ... nothing happened.

For one alarming moment, Doug worried that Ryan had relapsed, and could not remember how to play again. And then he realized that keys had been depressed but no sound had come out. Ryan banged his hands repeatedly on the keys to no avail and then the director came over and helped him lift the lid.

Doug and Tony walked over, perplexed, and saw what Ryan was looking at with an angry look on his face.

Tar had been smeared all over the piano wires, sticking them to each other and preventing any sound.

"Damn," Ryan muttered. "Damned little bastards."

Two hours later, after the police had again come and gone and an insurance adjuster had come to photograph the damage, Ryan sent the band and crew home. It would be late the next morning before a replacement piano could be delivered.

The source of the tar was traced to a roofing job on the next building over. Buckets of tar had been in the alley between the two buildings, and one was found to have been opened and some of the gooey substance dipped out with a small piece of wood, which was used to spread the tar inside the piano. How the perpetrators had managed to do it without getting any tar on the outside of the piano was a mystery. Ryan ordered Tony to arrange for additional round-the-clock security for the studio for the remainder of the show, then he and Doug left in the Corvette Doug had driven to the studio.

* * *

"We've got another problem," Tony DiMartino said to Ryan in the privacy of his dressing room two days later. "Jason's been arrested."

"Arrested? For what?" Ryan stared down at his manager.

"Possession of narcotics." Tony straightened his shoulders and met Ryan's gaze. "He says he's being framed but the police don't believe him since he has priors. Anyway, looks like he won't be able to do the show."

Ryan felt the throbbing begin again as Doug walked into the dressing room. "What's going on?"

Ryan walked across the room and sat down on the couch, gazing back at the other two men, hoping they wouldn't notice that he was in pain again.

Tony answered Doug's question. "Jason Sloane, our sound mixer, can't do the show. He just got arrested early this morning. His wife called, pretty upset. She doesn't think she'll be able to make bail."

Ryan listened to him with little emotion. Hey, why not lose the sound mixer now? Not like anything else had been going right. Rehearsals were behind schedule, the studio had been vandalized, his headaches were back, and his sleep was disturbed with nightmares of a green unicorn every night. "But, Tony," he finally said, "can't we bail him out so he can do the show? How high could it be?"

"I don't think you're going to want to do that, Ryan. Bail hasn't been set yet, but his wife says it will be pretty high. I guess several years ago when he got into trouble, he tried to jump bail. You really don't need the publicity that would come with it if you bailed him out and he skipped," Tony explained. He looked at Ryan, then at Doug. "This may stop the show, you know. We were supposed to start taping tomorrow and losing a sound mixer now brings us to a complete halt. Jason finished setting up and testing all the equipment yesterday, but we need someone to run it. We were lucky to borrow him from Victory as it was. Even though they've got the recording contract for this project, it wasn't easy for them to lend him to us for a week. There's no way they can give us anyone else now. I already talked to them as soon as I heard."

"Ryan, why don't you give this up?" Doug asked, sitting down at the makeup table. He picked up the aspirin bottle, uncapped it, glanced inside, then recapped it and returned it to the table. "This isn't doing your health any good, you know."

Ryan's eyes followed Doug's inquisitive fingers. "There's nothing wrong with my health, damn it," he said unconvincingly. "We'll find a sound mixer somewhere. They can't all be busy."

"That won't be easy, Ryan," Tony interjected. "Of course, I haven't started looking yet," he amended with a quick glance at Doug. "I'm sure I'll find one somewhere. I always come through in a pinch, don't I?" He attempted a laugh. "You can count on me."

Ryan caught Tony's glance at Doug, and he also noted the anxiety in the man's voice as he essentially promised to pull a rabbit out of a hat for Ryan. The man's grandiose back-patting had annoyed Ryan more than once before, and was a large part of the reason Ryan wanted to replace him. But he grudgingly had to admit that Tony usually *did* come through in a pinch, so he let the remark pass.

Tony glanced at his watch. "You ready, Ryan? The crew will be expecting to start again soon."

"Be there in a minute. I want to talk to Doug." Ryan waited until Tony had left the room before speaking again. "Horses today, huh?" he said lightly, nodding at Doug's shirtfront, where a small embroidered black horse tossed its mane above the pocket. "Is that for my benefit?"

Doug glanced down at the front of his light blue pullover. "I didn't pay any attention." He looked back up at Ryan. "You didn't send Tony away so you could talk about my shirt."

"No, I sent Tony away so we could talk about Tony." Ryan stood and walked over to the chair Doug was seated on. He nudged him. "Move it." Doug moved to a different chair so Ryan could sit in front of the mirror, combing his hair carefully across his forehead to hide the scar that was the only visible remnant of his accident the year before. "Tony better find someone quick. I'm not giving this show up, Doug. You know why I have to do this."

"Ryan, you can't shoot without a sound mixer."

"Do you think I don't know that?" Ryan replied irritably. "That's why I want you to help Tony out any way you can. I think Tony knows his days with me are numbered and I'm afraid he may let the show drop just for spite."

"More likely, he'll dig in his heels and do the best job he's ever done, hoping you'll change your mind."

"Whatever. Just so we finish the show on time." Ryan looked over to see if Doug was watching before he picked up the aspirin bottle and slipped it into his shirt pocket.

Doug was glancing idly at a magazine he'd found on the table and didn't seem to notice.

Ryan stood up. "I've got to hit the can, then I'll be ready to go back to work." He walked confidently to the bathroom to take the aspirin, hiding his pain behind a jaunty gait.

"Try not to take more than two, Ryan," Doug called to him before he closed the door. "Too much aspirin isn't good for your stomach."

CHAPTER 24

THE AFTERNOON AFTER THE arrest of Jason Sloane, Ryan North and Doug Norton sat in his dressing room waiting for Tony to finish interviewing a possible replacement for the sound mixer.

"I talked to Jason this morning," Ryan now told him. "He swears he's being framed. He said that Tuesday he noticed his car door was unlocked when he left the studio but didn't think anything of it. He got arrested after an anonymous tip told police to search his car for drugs. He insists they were planted."

"They picked a fine time to do it," Doug remarked. "The day before you needed him the most."

"Well, call me paranoid, but I'm starting to wonder if someone is really trying to disrupt the production," Ryan said. "And if so, that explains the other things that have happened this week. I didn't think that much of them at the time, but it could be that the person who had Jason arrested is the same one who vandalized the studio. Security thought it was teenagers but the only damage done was to my stuff, no one else's. I don't think they're ever going to get that tar out of the piano, either. Luckily it was insured. I really like the new one we got to replace it."

"I don't know Ryan; it's a pretty big leap from petty vandalism to having someone arrested on false felony charges," Doug answered skeptically. "And who would have a motive for stopping the show?"

"I have no idea," Ryan replied. "I don't have any enemies, and Tony's had someone reading my fan mail all along. There haven't been any death threats or other crank letters since long before my accident."

"Have you thought about it being an inside job?"

"I've considered the possibility, but why would someone who makes his living off my career want to ruin it?" Ryan shrugged. "I suppose anything's possible. Anyway, we'll continue with the show and see if we can get the taping done on schedule. And," Ryan continued, "at least Tony got lucky with finding another sound mixer. If he hires him, we want him to start right away, so maybe we can get back to work in the morning." Since no taping could be done without a sound man, they had spent two days rehearsing songs that didn't need rehearsing, rearranging scenery that didn't need rearranging, and changing light filters that didn't need changing. Ryan was anxious to get back to some productive work.

"Well, that's good news. You're lucky to find a replacement that quickly, especially with the labor problems."

"Not as quickly as I'd like to. And we didn't find him – he found us. It's that guy who was around here Friday talking to Biff about a job. He contacted Tony yesterday. I guess word got around that we were in a spot."

"So you won't have to hold up production any longer. You can still meet the deadline if nothing else happens."

"I know." Ryan agreed. "All these disruptions have eaten into the cushion we started out with."

"Well," Doug said, "let's hope Tony hires this guy so you can get back to work."

"Even if he hires him, we won't be able to do anything until tomorrow. We won't be here much longer today. You coming home with me? I've got nothing to do and you know how I hate to be alone. I'll let you cook dinner for me if you behave yourself."

"Some deal. Actually, I have a guest. Fred is in town. The private investigator you met at Christmas," he reminded him. "He drove over here and will be staying at my condo with me. He got here about an hour ago."

"Bring him along. He may come in handy if we have any more problems with vandalism or something." Ryan stood up. "Come on, let's go see if Tony's through with that guy yet. I guess I should meet him, even though he'll be working with the director more than me. I leave the technical details to Tony and the others."

Doug stood up and followed him out of the dressing room. "Let's just hope this guy knows his stuff so you can get back to work."

After introducing Doug and Ryan to the new sound mixer, Walter Hussman, Tony gave Doug a folder with Hussman's references and resume. "Would you mind dropping this off with Wanda on your way home? We don't really have time to worry about checking references now," he commented quietly. "He's only going to be with us for a few days anyway. We'll know quick enough if he can do the job or not." Doug raised a questioning eyebrow, but said nothing as he took the folder.

Doug looked at the new man, trying to conceal his disgust. The man was almost as tall as Ryan, stocky and broad-shouldered, with scraggly long blond hair and a sparse beard. An earring glinted from his left ear. He appeared to be more than forty. He wore faded jeans and an oversized sweatshirt. "Have you been working in Hollywood long?" Doug asked him.

"No, I just arrived here last week. It was lucky for me I heard about this opening. I've been around looking for work, but no one was hiring."

Ryan had been silent since being introduced. Now he spoke up. "We start shooting tomorrow at seven o'clock. Spend the rest of today familiarizing yourself with the equipment and crew." Ryan abruptly turned to leave. Doug followed Ryan back to his dressing room.

"Well, what do you think?" Ryan demanded when he walked in.

"About what?"

"About Hussman. What do you think of him?"

"I think he looks like a bum. Why?"

Ryan paced restlessly back and forth. "I don't know. Maybe he reminds me of someone I don't like, but the instant I saw him, I had this urge to – to – " He gestured with his fist as he searched for the words to convey his feelings.

"To what? Hit him? You'll ruin your nice-guy image that way."

"No, I don't know. I just didn't like him. I've never had that kind of reaction to anyone before." He suddenly realized his fist was clenched and dropped his hand to his side.

"So tell Tony to find someone else."

"No, I can't do that. We're lucky we found him. I'm probably just being silly. Maybe I'm just reacting to his appearance. Call me square, but I'm not used to longhairs like that anymore. I guess that's what it was." He started to calm down.

"Well, I'm sure Tony wouldn't have hired him if he couldn't do the job."

"Yeah, you're probably right. Anyway, if you're coming home with me I need to go tell Leonard we won't need him any more today."

"I'll call him," Doug said, pulling his cell phone out of his pocket. He punched the number for Ryan's limo driver and conveyed the message. "Lot of static," he commented after hanging up. "Batteries must need charging."

They left the dressing room and walked out to where the Corvette was parked. Doug used his cell phone again to call his own condo to ask Fred to meet him at Ryan's house. "Must be something going out on this thing," he said, slipping the phone into the holster on his belt. "The static's gone now, so it must not be the battery after all. I'll have to get it checked out."

Ryan shook his head. "You and your silly gadgets. I don't even know why you had one put in the Corvette for me. I get enough phone calls as it is without them following me around."

"Well, Ryan, someday you might find yourself on the side of a road somewhere and be very glad I did."

Ryan snorted. "Not likely. I don't even know how the damn thing works."

"I made it easy for you. There's a big E button on it for emergencies. Just push that."

Ryan shook his head. "Don't bother trying to tell me, because I don't want to know. Besides, the doctor won't even let me drive for another six months anyway, so it's kind of a moot point, isn't it."

* * *

Fred Dreyer arrived at Ryan's home a few minutes after Doug parked the Corvette in Ryan's garage. "Glad to see you again, Mr.

North," he said. "You know, I didn't know you two were brothers until after we met last December."

"I didn't tell him until I took him over to my condo after the party," Doug explained sheepishly.

"I'm surprised he told you at all," Ryan answered with a grin. "I think he's embarrassed to admit he even knows me sometimes. And please call me Ryan."

"Well, he keeps a secret very well, believe me." Ryan and Fred were seated in the living room while Doug poured drinks. "Mind if I smoke?" Fred asked, noticing the ashtray on the coffee table.

"Go ahead," Ryan answered. "Just turn on the fan."

Fred turned on the exhaust fan and lit up, noticing the smoke drift immediately toward the fan. "Thanks for inviting me for dinner," Fred said. Doug came in with the drinks and sat on the sofa near Fred, within reach of the ashtray.

"Glad to have you. You here on business?"

Fred darted a glance at Doug before answering, "Sort of. Thinking of moving out here."

"Really? Doug said you're a PI. What do you do?"

"Security work mostly. Some domestic surveillance and insurance jobs."

"Must be interesting work. How long you been doing it?"

"Three years. I used to be a cop."

Ryan looked at Doug, then back at Fred. "Really. A cop, huh? Where at? Denver?"

"Yes."

"Really," he repeated. Doug remained silent. "I can't help being surprised. My little brother here never used to like cops. How'd you two ever get to be friends?"

"I wasn't a cop when I met him."

"How'd you meet?"

Doug spoke up, "What is this, Ryan? The Inquisition? We had this conversation before. Enough of the questions already. Someone I knew was thinking of killing himself. Fred talked him out of it."

"Okay, okay," Ryan said, "I won't ask any more questions."

"Thank you."

"Actually," Fred said, "As a PI, I'm more interested in how you've kept Doug's relationship to you a secret. I sure never would have guessed you were brothers. In addition to the last names being different, you don't look much alike at all, do you?"

"That's what makes it easy to keep it a secret," Doug injected. "My real name is Victor. I started using an alias when Ryan signed his first recording contract. After our mother died, I had it legally changed, then I quit my job at the ad agency where we had worked together and went to work somewhere else as Douglas Aaron Norton."

"Why did you wait until your mother died to make it legal?"

Doug gave a short laugh. "Didn't want to hurt her feelings. It's like this: When our brother Christopher was born, John Kennedy was running for President. So he was named Christopher John. Ryan is named after Ted Kennedy. His full name is Ryan Edward. I got Bobby."

"Victor Robert," Fred supplied, nodding with understanding.

"Right. Anyway, Mom was such a Kennedy fanatic, she would have been upset to have one of us dump the name while she was alive. When she wasn't angry with us, she called us by our middle names, or maybe I should say, our middle nicknames, Jack, Ted, and Bobby. I still answer to Bobby from force of habit." He drew on his cigarette before continuing, "At least Ryan's namesake is still alive. Chris and I are named after dead guys. Another good reason to dump the moniker."

"Where did you get Aaron?"

"I was a Presley fan. That's Elvis's middle name, except I use the conventional spelling with two A's."

"He's dead, too, Doug."

"No! Don't tell me that! I saw him at a Circle K buying beer just last week!"

The three men laughed together for a moment. Ryan said, "I didn't really want him to have to change his name, Fred, but he convinced me that if I took a stage name instead, people would still know what my real name was and it would be easy for them to continue bothering Doug. Since he changed his name instead, nobody's figured it out."

"I like it that way," Doug said. "Keeps me out of the limelight. I lead a fairly normal life most of the time, but as I'm sure you can understand, Ryan doesn't. Even in the hospital, they had to put him in a private area just to keep the tabloids away. And even with those precautions, someone got into his room and tried to drug him." He flicked his cigarette ash into the ashtray. "I never told you about that, did I?"

"No, but I read about it in the paper. Did they ever find out who did it?"

Doug gave him a sour look. "It seems I was the only suspect. The asshole who was investigating finally decided to blame it on a nurse. Saved him the trouble of finding out the truth once he figured out he couldn't hang it on me."

Ryan arched an eyebrow. "Asshole?"

"Sorry. Those cops in Lakewood and Denver are all a bunch of jerks."

"All of them?"

"Fred here is the only cop I ever met who wasn't a complete shithead and he wasn't a cop anymore when I met him. And he confirmed my opinion of the rest of them. They're a bunch of jerks. That's why he left the force."

"That true, Fred?" Ryan asked.

"To some extent," Fred affirmed. "There are some exceptions, of course, I know one in particular who wasn't an asshole, but a lot of the ones I worked with shouldn't be on the force. Calling them jerks is a compliment."

"It's none of my business, but what happened to make you think they're all jerks?"

Fred took a long drag from his cigarette then crushed it out in the ashtray before carefully blowing the smoke toward the fan. "It's a long story, Ryan, and I don't think I want to talk about it. I've been too long trying to forget."

CHAPTER 25

"GOD DAMN IT, MEL, I'm telling you that's enough!" Ryan angrily pushed the makeup man away from him. The man retreated quickly, glancing back in puzzlement as he left the dressing room. Ryan stood up and pulled on his shirt, tucking it into his pants, wondering why he had been so impatient with the man. "Shit, I guess I'll have to apologize to him later. I don't know what's got into me today."

He finished dressing and left the dressing room. He looked around for Mel but didn't see him anywhere. Doug came over. "Everything okay? They're ready for you on stage."

"Yeah, fine," he answered, distracted. He glanced up to the sound booth, and felt his ire returning as he caught sight of Walter, the new sound man, for the second time that morning. "Sure wish I knew what there was about that guy I don't like," he muttered, half to himself.

"Who?" Doug asked. "Walter Hussman?"

"Yeah. You sure he doesn't remind you of anyone we know? Someone I don't like?"

"Sometimes I think he looks vaguely familiar, but I can't place him at all, and the name means nothing to me."

"Wish I knew why he rubs me the wrong way. I guess maybe it's just because of his unkempt image."

"Well, you usually don't have forty-year-old hippies working with you. All your regulars know better than to show up with scraggly beards and hair down to their shoulders. I'm the only one who ever got away with that. But Tony didn't have any other options and I understand his references were impressive."

"Just keep him out of my way," Ryan muttered in reply, walking over to the piano.

That morning, they taped two songs following the dance number and proceeded to the comedic song *It's Hard to Say I Love You with a Gun in my Face.* Tired and irritable, Ryan struggled with the song, trying to give it the humorous treatment it needed. After five attempts, he called for a break and retreated to his dressing room with his usual headache.

He had already swallowed several tablets from the aspirin bottle, noting that it was emptier than he remembered, by the time Doug came in to check on him.

"Why don't you call it a day, Ryan?" Doug urged. "You're trying too hard."

"Gotta finish this up. We've got a deadline to meet, remember?" He studied himself in the mirror, decided he needed his makeup touched up, and picked up a phone to call Mel.

"You're just not with it today. Why don't you do this part another day?"

"I don't *have* another day," Ryan snapped. "We've got to finish taping this week. Don't worry, I'll get it right on the next take, at least I would if you'd quit pissing me off all the time." A tap at the door announced Mel's arrival and Doug let him in.

Doug and Ryan were silent while the makeup man worked, then resumed their conversation as soon as he left. "Ryan, you've got another of those headaches, don't you," Doug stated flatly. "Why don't you at least go see your doctor about them?"

"They're not that bad." It was the first time Ryan had openly admitted he even had a headache and he berated himself silently for doing so. "I took some aspirin."

Doug picked up the aspirin bottle and shook it. "I'll say you did. How many this time? Five? Six? Twelve?"

"Just two," Ryan lied. Well, it was half true, anyway.

"Sure."

"Ah, fuck it," Ryan exploded. "Just leave me alone, okay? When I need your help I'll ask for it."

"No, you won't," Doug replied evenly. "That's just the problem."

Ryan stood up, feeling suddenly light-headed. He grinned at Doug. "Don't you know when I'm kidding, squirt? Let's go make some music. I'm gonna sing a song of sixpence, pocket full of rhymes."

Doug looked at him strangely, but said nothing as he followed Ryan out the door and accompanied him back to the stage. "Remember, now," he said when they reached the piano, "this is comedy."

"Yeah, comedy, right!" Ryan started to laugh loudly.

Doug left him at the piano and took up his usual position at the side of the stage, out of camera range.

"Let's go, everyone," the director called hastily when Ryan sat on the piano bench and began playing "Chop Sticks," still laughing out loud. "Places!"

Ryan looked at the piano. He'd never seen anything so beautiful in his life. *His* piano. His white piano. He was going to play his white piano. Sing a song of sixpence, a pocket full of rhymes. He laughed again.

Play the piano, Ryan. Play the piano. He began to play. The song filled his head. Beethoven's Ninth Symphony. Or was that Braham's Lullaby? Hey, it was both!

He looked down at his fingers, strumming across the keys. His fingertips elongated as he lifted his hands away from the keyboard, the tips remaining on the keys while his hands stretched above them. He lifted his hands as high as his face, but his fingertips remained on the keys, his fingers stretched between keys and wrist like rubber cement. No, like mozzarella cheese on pizza, long and stringy. Yeah, that's what it was. Cheese fingers. He laughed again.

Then he saw them coming. Over the top of the piano, the snakes started to come for him, first one, then another, then one with three heads slithered into the open piano, across the wires, winding through the wires, past the hammers, to rise up in front of Ryan's face. He screamed and pushed away from the piano, stumbling across the stage. The piano bench became a huge dog, black and slavering, growling savagely, chasing Ryan across the stage.

The curtains surrounding the stage turned red, running with blood, pooling on the floor, forming a river of blood that flowed toward him.

He screamed again, then pushed away the snakes that were crawling all over his body, around his neck, into his shirt, down his pants, squeezing him around the arms and chest.

He crawled away, slapping the snakes away from him, but the snakes kept holding him, keeping him from moving. Then the headlights started toward him, headlights of a huge truck, a truck with a goat's head on the front of it. Trembling, he lay helplessly, constrained by the snakes, while the truck rumbled over him with a roar. He screamed again.

"No, no, no, no, no, no, no!" He sobbed, watching the black dog devouring a child, a child that was reaching both arms out to Ryan. Ryan reached for the child just as the dog turned into a snake and swallowed the child whole.

The snakes squeezed tighter, tighter, around Ryan's neck. He screamed again, choking, gasping, until he finally succumbed and slipped into a welcome blackness.

* * *

"Hallucinations? His head injury gave him hallucinations?" Doug asked the doctor. "His neurologist never cautioned us about hallucinations. Mood swings, depression, amnesia, personality changes, but not hallucinations."

"No, no, you're correct, Mr. Norton," the doctor replied hastily. "The hallucinations were not caused by his head injury. His head is fine. We did a scan. No tumors or other physical problems at all."

"Then why did he suddenly start to hallucinate?" Doug asked. They were seated in the doctor's private office, away from the curious crowd that had formed around the emergency room when word got out that there was a celebrity on the premises. Ryan had been moved to a private room after having his stomach pumped and a guard from the studio was posted outside his door to keep people out.

"Mr. Norton, how well do you know Ryan North?" the doctor asked gently. "Have you ever known him to use drugs before?"

Doug glared at the doctor. "Ryan does not use drugs," he declared emphatically, then qualified the statement, "except for a lot of aspirin. That couldn't do it, could it?"

"No, not by itself. Why has he been taking a lot of aspirin?"

"He's been having headaches every day since he started working on this show," Doug explained. "But if it's not aspirin, what could it be? I know he doesn't use drugs."

"Well, he used them today, Mr. Norton. We're doing tests to try to find out exactly what drug it was, but hopefully this incident will scare him off any further drug use. I know how prevalent drug use is in his industry. Don't look so shocked, a lot of them hide it very well from their friends and family." The doctor heard his name paged over the loudspeaker. "I'm sorry, but you'll have to excuse me. He's sleeping now, but you can go back in to see him again if you want. We'll keep him overnight for observation, but he should be able to go home in the morning. He's sedated right now. It will probably be a few hours until he awakes."

"Guess I'll go back to the studio and see what I can find out. I'll be back later."

A few hours later, Doug returned from the studio and sat in a chair by Ryan's bed trying to read a magazine until he heard Ryan stir. Looking up, he saw him open his eyes slowly, staring around the room as if wondering where he was. Then his eyes settled on Doug. "Hi," he said weakly.

Doug put down the magazine. "You gotta stop doing this to me, Ryan. I'm not all that fond of hospitals."

"What happened?"

"You had a bad dream, only you weren't asleep when you had it."

Ryan thought a minute. "Snakes. I dreamed there were snakes in the piano. At least it wasn't a unicorn this time," he muttered to himself. "But why am I here?" He tried to sit up and Doug pressed the button to raise the back of the bed for him.

"The doctor says you took some drugs that made you hallucinate."

"I've never taken drugs in my life, except on a doctor's instructions," Ryan answered. "You know that. God, I feel so strange! Like my head belongs to someone else."

"Does it hurt?"

"No, it just feels like it's detached from my body. I didn't feel this weird when I woke from that coma last year." He grinned weakly. "It *was* just last year, wasn't it? I haven't been doing a Rip Van Winkle, have I?"

Doug smiled. "No, buddy, it's only been a few hours." He sobered. "I know you've been taking a lot of aspirin. There must have been something other than aspirin in the bottle. But the bottle's gone now. I tried to go back and find it but it wasn't there." He scowled briefly. "I had to call the cops, but you know what good that will do."

Ryan groaned. "Doug, anyone could have gotten to that aspirin bottle; my dressing room is never locked." He sat up carefully. "How long do I have to stay here? What did they do to me?" He smacked his lips at the bitter taste in his mouth.

"They pumped your stomach and took blood for tests. They're also analyzing the contents of your stomach to find out what kind of drug it was. The doctor said you could go home tomorrow. I think he thinks you just had a bad trip. He didn't believe it when I told him you don't take drugs."

"I suppose he's heard all the excuses. No one wants to admit their friend or relative takes drugs. But it's really something I've never been into. Mr. Clean, that's me." He chuckled ruefully. "Guess someone wants to tarnish my image. Wonder how long it'll take the press to pick up on this incident. Hey, maybe the publicity will help the show."

"Don't joke about it, Ryan," Doug said sharply. "You could have been killed. Again. And that's not all – " he broke off at a knock on the door.

The door to the room swung open and a nurse came in, accompanied by a policeman. "Oh, good, you are awake," she said. "Mr. North, this officer needs to ask you some questions."

"I'm Sergeant Sandoval. Are you all right?" the officer asked.

"I think I'm all right," Ryan replied with a forced smile. "Feel pretty strange, though."

The policeman stepped into the room and stood by the foot of the bed, a clipboard propped against his stomach, preparing to take notes. "I just have a few questions, Mr. North," he began. "I went through your dressing room a couple hours ago with Mr. Norton here," he said, nodding toward Doug, "and we did not find the aspirin bottle. Did you take it from the dressing room when you went out on the stage?"

"No," Ryan replied slowly, "I left it right there on the makeup table."

"That's what Mr. Norton thought, but he said it was gone when he got back there. That's why he called us in. We did find something else, though. We found a hidden microphone. Any idea who might have reason to bug your dressing room?"

"A bug?" Ryan looked at Doug. "There was a bug?"

Doug nodded. "That's what I was about to tell you."

Ryan glanced back to the policeman. "I have no idea who would have planted a bug," he finally replied.

"Mr. Norton said the microphone is a common type used in television productions, the same kind of wireless mike you'd use on stage."

"Could have been anyone, then. Those things are probably lying around all over the place."

"I talked to everyone at the studio after we found it. Your manager, Tony DiMartino, said the mikes are easy to get, but the receivers aren't. Someone had to have at least some knowledge of recording equipment to use it."

"That lets out the janitors, but that's about it," Ryan responded. "Probably anyone on my crew would know how to use it, and where to get the equipment. I couldn't rule anyone out at this point. Doesn't even have to be someone on my crew. There are other productions going on in that studio all the time."

"Ryan," Doug started, "until we figure out who did this, you'd better start thinking hard about what you've said in that room."

Ryan snorted. "I doubt I'll be thinking of anything else for a long time, Doug. Most of those conversations were between you and me." He looked at the officer. "I'm not accusing anyone, understand that. But I'm planning to replace Tony DiMartino with Doug here as manager in a couple months. Tony's been my manager for three years. Doug will take over in August. Whoever planted that mike could have heard at least two conversations where we discussed that."

"You think your manager may have planted the bug?"

"I didn't say that. But whoever did plant it, may know what I'm planning. What he'll do with the information is anyone's guess."

"Is there anything else you remember talking about?"

"Fixing a song that wasn't working. Whether my old head injury would keep me from being able to finish the show."

"Anything in those conversations that might be damaging to you in some way?"

"It would give a listener some insight into my personal life and problems. Things I normally wouldn't talk about to anyone but Doug. Things I prefer to keep confidential." Ryan sighed. "God only knows what I might have let slip in there. I'm not one to be that critical of people, but you know how it is when you're under a lot of pressure. You spout off, feel better, then you're glad nobody heard you say what you did."

"I know what you mean," the policeman replied.

"Ryan," Doug started, "remember the day Tony hired the sound mixer? Later, in the dressing room, you told me you didn't like the way the guy looked."

"Yes. I remember. I thought he looked like a hippie. Still do, for that matter, but I hope that didn't get back to him. He's done good work."

"Who are you talking about?" the officer asked.

"Tony hired a guy as a replacement for our regular sound mixer. The first day he showed up with hair down to here, a scraggly beard, earring, the whole works. Right out of the sixties. Rubbed me the wrong way and I mentioned it to Doug. He still irritates me, but he's never done anything to deserve it."

"Anything else you can think of?"

"Doug's been ragging on me about the amount of aspirin I've been taking. That's probably how this guy got the idea to tamper with the aspirin." He paused a moment. "I wonder why he didn't use cyanide?"

"Jeez, Ryan, don't talk like that," Doug protested.

"No, I'm serious. He could have killed me, but he didn't. Why didn't he?"

"Why, indeed?" The officer closed his notebook. "Well, this is a bit more serious than tar in a piano, but it still appears to be a prank of some kind. If you think of anything else, anything that might give a clue to who's behind this, give me a call. It doesn't sound like there's any evidence pointing to any particular suspect at the moment."

"So you're going to do nothing?" Doug demanded.

"There's nothing I can do at the moment. We don't know when the pills were switched, so getting everyone's alibi isn't going to help. The bottle's gone, so we can't get any fingerprints, and even if there were any, Mr. North's would have obliterated them. We'll check the microphone for prints, but they won't prove anything. If those mikes are lying around all over the place, anyone could have touched it at any time. I'll file the report. If anything else happens, maybe we'll be able to do more. A motive would help point us in the right direction."

After the policeman left, Ryan repeated, "Why didn't he kill me?"

"Why don't you just be glad he didn't?" Doug asked. "He doesn't want you dead, apparently."

"Or he knows he'd be the only suspect if I did end up dead," Ryan pointed out. "You heard the cop. I've been bugged and drugged. Not a big deal. No suspects. Maybe if I ended up dead, the finger of suspicion would point in one direction. Pretty obvious that if I were in the morgue instead of the hospital, they'd have everyone who was at the studio today down at headquarters, asking them questions, running background checks, verifying alibis. At the moment, whoever did this is running around scot-free. No suspicion because the crime wasn't enough to justify investigating."

"Well," Doug said with a sigh, "let's just hope it stays that way. And if these idiot cops won't investigate, we'll have to do our own." He hesitated. "Good thing Fred's here right now. He'll help us, and keep his mouth shut about it, too."

CHAPTER 26

THE NEXT MORNING, AFTER Ryan was released from the hospital, Doug brought Fred Dreyer to the studio for the first time. Although it was Saturday, Ryan was determined to make up the lost time and had called in his band and crew. While Ryan tried to finish the taping on stage, Doug showed Fred around the studio and explained what had happened.

"This is where the microphone was?" Fred said when they reached Ryan's dressing room.

"Yes. Over there, near the phone. Hidden under the edge of the table."

"And the aspirin?"

"Ryan had left the bottle in the middle of the table there. It was gone when I got back from the hospital. A cop found the microphone. Tony made me call the cops when I got back and told him I thought someone had put something in the aspirin bottle. Fat lot of good it did. Since Ryan didn't die, he said he couldn't do anything."

"Okay, Doug," Fred said after glancing around the room. "Who are our suspects? Who had access to this room?"

"Hell, Fred, anyone could have gotten in here."

"Who could have gotten in here that if they were seen here nobody would have thought a thing about it?"

"Well, Ryan, me, Tony, and his makeup man, Mel, I suppose. Maybe his driver, Leo. He sometimes comes in here to wait for Ryan to finish up for the day or to use the restroom or phone."

"Who's Tony?"

"Tony DiMartino. Ryan's manager. He's the guy Ryan wants me to take over for this summer. His personal manager. He's also producing the show."

"Who knew Ryan was taking aspirin?"

"Only me and whoever was on the other end of that bug."

"Tony didn't know?"

"I don't think so. He may have suspected Ryan was having headaches, but Ryan wasn't even taking the aspirin when I was watching. I doubt he did it with Tony around. I figured it out by watching the level in the bottle go down."

"Do you think Tony would have any reason to harm Ryan?"

"That's the tough one, Fred. Normally, I'd say no. But if he's behind the bug, then he could have heard Ryan say some unkind things about Tony in here, and he could have found out Ryan's plans to dump him when his contract was up. I can't see Tony trying to hurt Ryan, though. They've been together for three years, and he'll continue to make money from Ryan long after his contract ends. But I don't know him that well, and Ryan's been uneasy about him for a long time, so anything could be possible."

"I'll need personnel records and financial information."

"I'll take you over to the office later on."

"The motive is going to be the key, you know. We need to figure out who would benefit from hurting your brother, or who might be wanting revenge against him for some reason."

"Don't refer to him as my brother, Fred. Only Tony knows."

"Sorry. I don't know how you've managed to keep it a secret this long."

"Hasn't been easy. I keep expecting to read it in the paper ever since that cop figured it out after that other drug incident at the hospital. He said he wouldn't put it in his report, but he also let me know he wasn't real happy that I didn't tell him myself. That deputy was the same way, gave me a hard time because he didn't know it until the other cop told him."

"Well, in their defense, I probably wouldn't have been too pleased either if I'd been the officer conducting the investigation and someone withheld that kind of information from me."

"Don't turn back into a cop on me now."

"Sorry. Just stating a fact."

Doug gave him a sour look. "I have a right to some privacy, you know."

Fred shrugged. "Cops don't see it that way. Not saying it's right or wrong, it's just the way it is."

Doug sighed. "Seen enough here?"

"Yes. I'd like to meet Tony now."

Later that afternoon, Doug called Wanda at home and asked her to meet them over at Ryan's business office so he could get the personnel records and a financial statement for Fred.

"Oh, Doug," Wanda said after giving Fred the information, "there's something else. I had a call the other day from Cindy Vincent, the girl who found Ryan when he had his accident."

"I remember her. What did she want?" Doug asked.

"She said he told her to call if she was ever going to be in the area, and she's going to be here next weekend, through Tuesday. I know with the show being so far behind and Ryan just being in the hospital again, he probably won't want a starry-eyed fan around, but I think she'll be terribly disappointed if she doesn't get to see him, at least for a few minutes. Can you see if he can fit her in somewhere and let me know?"

"I can ask."

"Here's her phone number if you want to call her yourself. I told her we'd let her know one way or the other by Thursday night."

"I don't know," Doug said. "I'd sure hate to disappoint her, but it's really not the best time. But maybe he'll see her for a few minutes, since she'll be in town. I'll call her after I talk to Ryan about it."

"Let me know what he says, okay?"

"Sure thing."

They returned to Ryan's house, where Fred spent some time inspecting the property for security weaknesses and checking the house with an electronic sensor, looking for listening devices. At Fred's recommendation, Doug called a security service and requested an around-the-clock guard to patrol the property and watch the gate.

Ryan arrived home about six-thirty, exhausted after finishing the taping that day. "Didn't think we'd ever get it finished," he said, slumping into a chair in the living room. Doug poured him a Scotch and brought it to him. "Thanks," Ryan said. "Figure anything out today?" He flicked a glance at Fred, who had settled into another chair with a martini.

"Not yet," Doug replied. "Why don't I let Fred tell you all about it while I go start some dinner?"

"Thanks," Ryan replied. "I'm so tired I was going to order a pizza, but if you'd like to fix something, that would be great."

"No problem. By the way," he said, suddenly remembering his conversation with Wanda that day. "Do you remember Cindy Vincent, the girl who found you when you had your accident?"

"I remember you telling me about her, that she came to see me in the hospital."

"Do you remember that we invited her to visit you if she ever made it over here?"

Ryan thought a moment. "I was barely out of the coma when I met her but it sounds like something we would have done. Why?"

"She called Wanda. She's coming to Disneyland next weekend and is hoping like mad that she'll be able to see you. I know this isn't the best time, but do you think you can squeeze her in somehow? You know how teenagers are. She'll probably kill herself if you say no."

Ryan laughed. "Can't have that, now, can we? I'd be delighted to see her. Set something up with her. She's only here for the weekend?"

"Through Tuesday. I thought maybe a studio tour Monday? We'll still be working on the editing then, but it should be a little less hectic than these last few days have been."

"Sure. We'll let her visit me in my dressing room. That'll really give her something to tell her friends at home. It'll be fun. We could use a little diversion around here."

Doug grinned. "I agree. I'll call her as soon as I get dinner started and put her out of her misery. She's probably been hanging by the phone ever since she called Wanda."

Doug turned to go to the kitchen, and Ryan turned back to talk to Fred. Fred was watching Doug leave the room, his eyes lingering on Doug's retreating back and he only looked back at Ryan after Doug disappeared into the kitchen. His face flushed slightly when he realized Ryan was looking at him curiously, but he lit a cigarette and said only, "That was nice of you to agree to see her."

Ryan sipped his drink and said, "It was the least I could do. So tell me, how are we going to solve this thing?"

* * *

"Hello?" Cindy had answered the phone on the first ring.

"Is this Cindy Vincent?"

"Yes, yes. Who is this?"

"Doug Norton. Ryan North's partner. We met at the hospital last year."

"I remember you. You were the one with the skunk on your shirt."

"You have a very good memory. One of the nurses gave me that shirt because they were tired of seeing me in the same shirt day after day. Anyway, Wanda gave me your message and I just talked to Ryan a few minutes ago. He said he'd be happy to see you again, and we wondered if you would like to come to the studio where he's working for a tour on Monday."

"Oh, yes, yes!" Cindy could hardly believe her ears. "How do I get to the studio? My dad will have to drive me."

"Have your dad call Wanda Monday morning and she'll tell him what to do. We don't take holidays off so we'll be at the studio all day, probably, so you can come any time you want to. Traffic shouldn't be too bad that day. And make sure you bring your camera, so we can get a picture of you with Ryan."

"Oh, I will. I will. Thank you so much. And tell Ryan North thank you. I can hardly wait."

Cindy hung up the phone. "Yippee!" she cried. "I get to see him again!" She hurried to the living room to tell her father the news.

"He wasn't just being polite," she announced triumphantly.

Howard Vincent looked up from the television show he was watching. "Who wasn't?"

"Ryan North. I get to go to the studio Monday for a tour. You promised to drive me up there if I arranged it. His partner just called and said he'd be *happy* to see me."

"Well, how about that?" Howard Vincent shook his head. "I was sure they'd tell you that he didn't have time. He must be a heck of a guy to take time out from his busy schedule to make a little girl happy. Okay, Cindy, I'll take you to see him."

"You need to call Wanda — that's his secretary, I think — Monday morning and she'll tell you how to get there. Oh, Daddy, I'm the luckiest girl in the world! Gloria is going to be *so* jealous. I wish she could come with me. I'm going to go call her right now!"

Howard Vincent chuckled as his daughter raced from the room. Good thing he wasn't expecting any important phone calls. He knew he wasn't going to get anywhere near the phone for the rest of the evening.

* * *

"I really appreciate your help with this," Ryan said after Fred told him what he had done so far, and what he planned to do next. "Be sure to bill me your usual rates. I don't expect any favors because you're Doug's friend."

"I'll work out the billing arrangements with Doug. He's done some favors for me in the past. I'm glad I could help. I understand how hard it must be for you to deal with security issues when you're in a fish bowl all the time. Everything you do gets reported in the paper."

"The press does get to be a bit intrusive at times, but sometimes publicity helps in ways you wouldn't expect. Take this little girl coming to visit me. Tony will issue a press release about it. Something like 'Ryan North's Rescuer Visits Star on Set.' She'll have a thrilling moment, seeing her name in the paper with mine, which is fine, but Tony will include enough information to plug the show as well. I end up looking like a really nice guy, and we profit financially as well. Tony loves that sort of stuff." He grimaced.

"Is that why you said she could come?"

"No, I said she could come because I really am a nice guy," Ryan said with a grin. "And I owe her an awful lot. If she hadn't seen me, I'd probably be dead. I'd be a real shithead if I couldn't take a couple hours for her." He sobered. "I remember why Doug said he let her come see me in the hospital. She was having nightmares that I'd died, and that everyone blamed her because she didn't keep the snow off me. Poor kid. No, this trip is for her, and I'll do everything I can to make sure it's perfect for her. If I get a little publicity about it, that's okay, but I'd do it even I didn't have a show to plug. The publicity is more for her benefit, so her friends will really believe her when she says she was here."

"I see why you're so popular. You must have earned that reputation of being a nice guy. But if you're such a nice guy, who's trying to hurt you?"

"I have no idea. How do you even start to figure something like that out?"

"Checking acquaintances. I'll be starting to check all your personnel tomorrow, Ryan, trying to find someone with a motive to harm you. Meantime, we'll surround you with personal security, bodyguard, et cetera, and take precautions when you're on the road. There will be a guard here on the premises twenty-four hours a day until we get this figured out. And you probably shouldn't be alone. Maybe Doug should stay here with you for a while." He looked up when Doug entered the room.

"I told her to call Wanda that Monday morning to get directions to the studio. Or do you think we should send a limo for her instead of having her father drive her up?"

"Now, that's a great idea, Doug. Let's do it. And get a complete set of all my CD's and a portable stereo for her, too. Can you handle the arrangements for me?"

"No problem. I think Wanda keeps some sets in the office."

"Good."

Fred interjected, "You're really going all out for her."

"I want this visit to exceed all her expectations, Fred. I don't want her to be disappointed about anything except the fact that she had to go home afterward."

"Dinner is almost ready, Ryan," Doug said. "You want to eat in here or the dining room? It's just spaghetti."

Ryan glanced at Fred, and found him staring at Doug again. "We have company tonight. Let's eat in the dining room, even if it is just spaghetti."

Part IV
May 23-29, 1994
The Clues

CHAPTER 27

THE MORNING JIM HARRISON flew to California to try to see Ryan North, Sheila Fernelli sat at her computer terminal in the newsroom and typed rapidly:

Head: Singer Ryan North Questioned in Walker Homicide

Clear Creek County moved one step closer to solving the murder of Daryl Walker, son of State senator Gene Walker, when Sheriff Harley Watson dispatched detective Jim Harrison to Los Angeles today to interrogate singer Ryan North. North was found unconscious less than a quarter-mile from the boy's body on the day Walker is believed to have died.

Sheriff Watson has denied that North is a suspect. Evidence about North's potential involvement with the case came forth when Wayne Elliot, the Alpine Rescue Team volunteer who had helped carry both North and Walker from the area, pointed out the proximity of the two scenes.

Later it was discovered that the boy's disappearance had taken place the day of North's accident, prompting Harrison's visit to Los Angeles.

No motive for the murder has yet been determined.

She paused, reread it, and decided it was enough. "Just enough to keep you on your toes, Harley Watson. And it's nothing but the truth."

Then she hesitated. How would Jim react when he read it? She read it again. No, it was all right. Nothing but the truth. Certainly no secret, either. Or was it? She'd heard it from her friend the dispatcher, not from Jim. Perhaps it wasn't meant to be public knowledge yet.

"You're still a journalist," she chided herself. "You agreed to tell Jim about any information you found before you printed it. You didn't agree to get his permission before printing what you learned about *his* investigation."

With just the slightest guilty conscience, she pressed the key on her computer terminal to send the story to typesetting.

$*\ *\ *$

Having convinced Ryan and Doug that Doug should stay at the house with Ryan, Fred had stayed alone in Doug's condo. He had spent all day Sunday working on the computer, checking various databases, searching for any hint of trouble in Ryan's past business and personal relationships. Not sure whom to trust, Ryan had agreed to use only Doug as his personal bodyguard, leaving strangers provided by a security service to protect the studio and his home. Fred had spent the day searching for motives among Ryan's current and former employees, but so far had found nothing.

It was appearing as if Tony DiMartino was the only person who could potentially be considered "disgruntled," and only if he were the one responsible for the listening device found in Ryan's dressing room. If he didn't know Ryan planned to dump him, then he had no motive either.

What bothered Fred was the nagging idea that the two drugging incidents, the attempted one in Denver, and the actual one in L.A., might be connected somehow. And Tony hadn't been anywhere near Denver while Ryan was in the hospital. Knowing that Ryan was planning to fire him, Doug had made some excuse to keep Tony from visiting and the manager had remained in Los Angeles after the tour was canceled. At the moment the drugs were being left in Ryan's room, Tony had just been wrapping up a late-afternoon meeting with lawyers in Los Angeles regarding the canceled shows. But adding the fact that the arrested sound mixer had been framed for drug possession, there remained a strong possibility that the incidents were all related.

Fred had set up a portable office in Doug's two-bedroom condo and spent most of the time either on the phone or working on his laptop computer. He would spend the next day at the studio, this time pressing hard to find out who might have been seen near the dressing room after Ryan was taken to the hospital. Someone had re-entered that room to dispose of the evidence, but so far nobody had volunteered any information.

He finally gave up the effort around five o'clock and called out for a pizza. He needed a break, badly. While waiting for the pizza, he drove to the corner convenience store and picked up a six-pack of beer to go with the pizza, renting a couple movies from a kiosk while he was there. He would spend a quiet, relaxing evening alone. Maybe he'd spend some time in the hot tub before going to bed.

He wished Doug were there. Maybe he'd call him later. It had been Fred's idea that Doug should be Ryan's bodyguard, but he was now regretting that decision.

Ryan and Doug had spent the day in the editing room, finally knocking off about six o'clock. They were halfway home when Doug's cell phone rang. He handed it to Ryan. "It's Tony."

"Ryan, there's a sheriff's deputy here needing to talk to you," Tony said. "He got to the studio right after you left. I guess he's been trying all day to find out where you were. The guard at your house told him you were here, but by the time he got here, you had just left."

"I'm whipped, Tony. I'm not coming back there now. What's it about, anyway? The drugs?"

"He says he just has to ask you some questions. What if I bring him by the house later, maybe after you've had time to eat?"

"Fine, do that. But not before seven-thirty." He handed the phone back to Doug to disconnect the call. He never had learned how to use the cell phone.

"What's up?"

"Some cop wants to ask me some more questions. Tony will bring him by after dinner."

"Probably that same idiot who didn't think it was worth investigating. Maybe they heard we hired a PI and decided to do something finally."

"Maybe." Ryan closed his eyes and leaned back against the headrest.

They ate quickly when they got home, finishing up the leftover spaghetti Doug had made the day before. Ryan stretched out on the couch to rest while Doug cleaned up the kitchen and loaded the dishwasher. He had no interest in talking to any cops.

When he heard two cars pull up outside, Ryan opened his eyes and looked at the clock. It was seven-thirty on the nose. "That must be Tony and the sheriff's deputy." He stood up and went to open the door.

"Hi, Tony, come on in," he said.

"Hi, Ryan," Tony answered. He gestured toward the broad-shouldered man that accompanied him. "This is Detective Jim Harrison, of the Clear Creek County Sheriff's department. Detective, this is Ryan North."

Ryan shook hands with the detective and said, "I remember you. You saw me in the hospital, didn't you?" He gestured Jim toward a chair.

Jim grinned and lowered his tall frame into the leather chair. "So you remembered after all. You thought you wouldn't."

"Sometimes I surprise even myself," Ryan said with a smile. He and Tony sat on the sofa.

"So how have you been?" Jim asked. "I lost track of your recovery after the news reports stopped."

"Well, it was pretty tough for a while, spent some time in a rehab facility, but once I learned to tie my shoes again it was all downhill after that."

"Did you ever get back on a horse again? Or have you given up riding?"

"Funny you should ask. My horse is back over here now and I rode for the first time just last Sunday."

"No fear?"

"Not at all. Felt good to get back on him. He's at the equestrian center by Griffith Park now. It's not the same as riding in the mountains, but it's a nice park."

Jim made a mental note about the location of the horse, then shifted his position slightly and looked down at his clipboard.

"What's this about?" Ryan asked. "Still wanting to know if I remembered the accident? Because I still don't know what happened. I could have told you that over the phone, you know."

Jim replied, "Ryan, I'm investigating a homicide. I asked Tony not to tell you that over the phone earlier."

Ryan sobered. "Homicide?" he repeated. "Someone I know? Not my ex?" Concern was evident in his face and voice.

"No, no, Mr. North," Jim Harrison hastened to explain. "Nothing like that at all. I'll start at the beginning. A couple weeks ago, a body was discovered on Mount Goliath in Colorado. You know where that is, don't you?"

"Yes, that's where I had my accident," Ryan replied.

"That's right. At the time of discovery, we couldn't tell how long the victim had been dead, and it took a few days to make a positive identification."

"Do you know who it is now?" Ryan asked.

"We know now that it was Senator Walker's son Daryl. We didn't make the connection right away because he didn't disappear in the mountains. There also was a mix-up with some photographs, but that was finally straightened out. He had been listed as a runaway. But now that we know it was Daryl, we have a pretty good idea of when he may have been killed." The detective looked at Ryan. "You see, he disappeared just about the time you had your own accident."

"That's an amazing coincidence, but what does that have to do with me? I spent most of that week in a coma."

"One of the rescue workers tipped us off. He pointed out that we had picked you up not far from where we later found the body. Then we discovered that your accident happened two days before the senator returned home from a three-day trip and reported Daryl missing." He handed Ryan a color photograph. "We're pretty certain he was killed and buried within hours of your own accident. He may have been riding a horse. Did you see him?"

Doug had glanced into the living room when the two men arrived. When he saw the Colorado sheriff's detective standing there, shaking hands with Ryan, he blanched. They knew. Somehow, they knew, and had tracked him down at Ryan's house. Shaken, he leaned against the refrigerator and listened while Detective Harrison explained to Ryan about the boy … the boy Doug had known.

Ryan studied the picture without recognition. "I didn't see anybody that day at all. I'm sorry, but I think you've come a long way for nothing. But maybe we should check with Doug. He wasn't with me most of the morning. He might have seen something."

"Doug?"

"Doug Norton," Ryan replied. "My partner. Well, you know he's really my brother, but remember we don't like the press to know that."

"I've been trying to find him. Do you know where he is?"

"Sure, he's in the kitchen. Hey, Doug!" he called. "Come here a minute."

Doug sighed, wiped his sweaty hands on his jeans, and reluctantly stepped into the living room. It was over. He knew it.

To his surprise, Detective Harrison merely shook his hand and said, "Glad I found you, Mr. Norton. I've been trying to find where you moved to so I could ask you some questions."

Doug sat woodenly in a chair, waiting to be read his rights. He listened while Jim Harrison repeated what he'd told Ryan about the discovery of the boy's body, then Jim handed him a photo of the boy. "Did you see him there that day?"

Sensing a trap, Doug decided to hedge. A flat out denial wouldn't do if someone had already told the detective he had been seen talking to the kid. He studied the picture carefully, then said slowly, "Not that I can recall." He handed the photo back. "Things were pretty hectic that day," he added. "I was worrying about Ryan." Well, that part was certainly the truth.

"What about anyone else who might have seen him? Do you remember seeing anyone else that day? Any other vehicles? Other hunters?"

"There were no other cars in the parking lot when we got there. And I imagine you already talked to the man and girl who found Ryan," Doug supplied, struggling not to show relief when he realized he was not being arrested. His instincts had been right. Better not to volunteer anything. "When I rode out after you all came, there was a reporter there trying to question me, and the sheriff was there."

"We talked to Mr. Vincent, yes. He couldn't help us either, I'm afraid." Jim Harrison stood up. "I'm sorry to have bothered you, Mr. North. I was really hoping you might have seen something. You see, I visited the spot where they found you under that tree, and the place we found the body can be clearly seen from there, with binoculars." He gathered up his clipboard and walked to the door, followed by Tony. "I knew it was a long shot, but I could only hope you had caught sight of some activity and could give us a clue about a horse or vehicle or anything that would have started us in the right direction. We have very few clues, and no motive, no idea at all why someone would kill a sixteen-year-old kid and dump his body in the woods."

"Probably drugs," Ryan suggested. "Isn't that what most kids are killed over?"

Jim declined to confirm that they were investigating that possibility, saying merely, "We may never know the whole story. Thank you for your time. Good evening." He handed Ryan his card. "If you happen to think of anything that might be helpful, please give me a call," he said, and walked out the door with Tony.

Ryan sat in silence for a minute after the door closed, while Doug quickly returned into the kitchen to finish up the dishes. Suddenly Ryan jumped up and ran outside to where the detective sat in his car, putting his clipboard into a briefcase before leaving. Tony's car was already disappearing out the gate.

Ryan tapped on the car window. Startled, Jim turned and rolled the window down. "Yes, Mr. North?"

"I was just wondering," Ryan said awkwardly, "do you know what the kid was wearing?"

"Blue jeans. White shirt with a red jacket over it. White high-tops. He may have been wearing a red cap from the grocery store he worked at. He worked there as a stock boy in the meat department. His parents say the cap is missing, but we didn't find it with the body."

"Thanks. If I recall anything later on, I'll let you know. It has been more than seven months, and I still have a gap in my memory, you know."

Ryan walked back into the house, thinking about the bizarre nightmares he'd had after the accident, and had been having again ever since a few days after he started working on the special. Come to think of it, he realized, that was just about the time the detective said the body was found.

He didn't really believe in ESP, but how else to explain the image of the red cap in that dream? He locked the door behind him. Coincidence? Not likely.

CHAPTER 28

SHEILA WALKED NERVOUSLY into the lobby of the Marvin Bryce Ad Agency Monday morning and hoped fervently that she would not encounter anyone as perceptive as Evelyn Moore there. "Hello," she said to the receptionist. "I'm here to see Mr. Overholt. I'm Mary McDaniels."

"Have a seat, Ms McDaniels, and I'll let him know you're here," the woman answered, punching a button on her intercom.

Sheila sat in one of the plush armchairs in the lobby and hoped she could pull off the charade she had planned. She intended to try to find some clue to Ryan North's past that might explain his connection to Daryl Walker or his reluctance to come forth with evidence. It was her hope that by the time Jim Harrison returned from Los Angeles with the results of his interrogation of Ryan North, she would already have discovered the motive behind North's actions.

She knew Jerry Overholt had been a friend of Ryan's for years; she could only hope he wouldn't realize what she was doing before she had the information she sought.

"Ms McDaniels?" Sheila almost didn't respond to the name she had chosen. "You can go back now. It's the last office on the right through those doors."

Taking a deep breath, Sheila marched determinedly to the indicated office, slipping a hand into her pocket to activate her tape recorder before she reached the door. Jerry Overholt stood up to shake her hand when she entered. "Nice to meet you, Miss McDaniels," he said warmly, making her feel even more like a heel for the deception she was practicing. "I'm Jerry Overholt."

"Thank you for seeing me, Mr. Overholt," she replied nervously. "I know you must be pretty busy."

"Call me Jerry," he responded. "May I call you Mary?"

"Please do."

"Coffee?"

"No, thanks."

Jerry sat back behind his desk after Sheila had been seated. "How can I help you with your project?" he asked. "You're doing a piece on the prior careers of the rich and famous? Sounds interesting. I've always been fascinated by rags-to-riches stories, myself."

"That's what the people at *Lifestyles Magazine* are counting on, Jerry," she said carefully, hoping desperately that *Lifestyles* was the same magazine she had said she worked for when she called. She had debated between three magazines before choosing the one she hoped was the most obscure.

If she had made a mistake, Jerry gave no indication. She started to relax a little. "Jerry, one of the subjects of the article is a former Denver resident who I understand used to work here."

Jerry nodded knowingly. "You must be talking about Ryan North. He's the only celebrity who ever worked for us. We're not that large an agency. He wrote a lot of music for jingles when he was here. He and his brother used to work on them together."

Sheila's heart gave a leap. The *brother* had worked here too? "Victor?" she responded, hoping to sound knowledgeable.

"Yes," Jerry replied. "His name was Victor. He wrote the words to the jingles."

"Does Victor still work here?" she asked, trying to appear casual in her interest.

"No, they both quit at the same time when Ryan had his first hit. They were both out of here like a shot." Jerry replied. "I don't know where or even if he's working now. But we all know what happened to Ryan. So what sort of information do you need from me?"

Disappointed that she hadn't found Ryan's brother yet, Sheila continued with her ploy. "We're looking for a brief summary of the kind of work Ryan did here, but mostly we're looking for anecdotes about him. Any little story about him, maybe something mildly embarrassing, but harmless. Something that would show the human side of Ryan

North, so people will identify with him as a human being, not as some awesome celebrity."

"Embarrassing, huh?" Jerry chuckled. "He and Victor were always playing practical jokes on each other, and everybody else, as I recall. Little things, like replacing all the felt markers in the main conference room with disappearing ink markers. God knows where they got them. Victor was the one who put the goldfish in the water cooler one day. Turned out it wasn't a real goldfish, just plastic, but one of the secretaries switched to bringing her own bottled water from home after that."

"Practical jokes? Ryan North?" Sheila asked incredulously. "He never struck me as the type."

"Oh, have you met him?" Jerry asked, then answered his own question before Sheila had to make up another lie. "I suppose you must have if you're doing an article on him. He probably told you to make sure he got a copy of the whole magazine after it's published, not just the article itself."

Sheila looked puzzled, so he explained further, "He doesn't keep a scrap book like normal people. He has what he calls the scrap heap. Says it helps him keep his perspective, you know? So he doesn't get too bigheaded about his career. I try to watch the papers around here and send him any articles with his name in them. In fact I have a few papers I'm getting ready to send him today. You probably saw those articles about the murder investigation where that reporter Sheila Fernelli keeps trying to link him to the murder of a teenage boy last year?"

Panicked, Sheila just nodded mutely. He was sending Ryan the articles? *Oh, my God*, she thought to herself. What would the sheriff do if this guy tipped Ryan off before Jim Harrison got to question him? Out loud she replied, "I saw them." Nervously she asked, "What does Ryan think about what's been said about that?"

"Oh, I haven't sent them yet so I doubt he even knows about it. It's just a local paper. I don't think any of this has made the national wire services yet. I'm going to send them this afternoon. I haven't talked to him in a long time, but if you want, I could call him and let you know what he says about it. Might make an interesting slant to your article to describe how as soon as someone achieves fame and fortune, he becomes fodder for the rumor mills, no matter what the topic – sex, drugs, murder."

Sheila suddenly realized why Harley Watson had been so reluctant to pursue the Ryan North angle. "No, that won't be necessary. I'll mention it to him next time I talk to him," she said, hoping desperately that Jerry wouldn't tip Ryan off before Jim Harrison got to him.

"Well, you wanted anecdotes, so let's see if I can remember anything useful. One thing you might mention is Ryan's corny tie collection. Try to get him to show it to you. You wouldn't believe what they'll print on a necktie these days. Some of it is mildly X-rated, so you may not be able to print pictures of the best ones. Of course, he never wears those in public," Jerry added quickly. "Might affect his image. You'd think Victor would be the one with the X-rated apparel, but he leans more toward polo shirts with little animals over the pocket."

Sheila jotted a few brief notes. She was relying on her tape recorder for the details.

"They were always kidding around, sometimes slipping each other some harmless stimulant or other. Nothing illegal, you understand," he explained hastily, "just playing around with over-the-counter remedies like caffeine tablets and sleep remedies. Just sophomoric pranks. They were both careful not to do anything really dangerous." He laughed. "Victor's the one who baked the laxative brownies one day."

Sheila smiled. "I suppose Ryan never forgave him for that."

Jerry gave a short laugh. "Oh, yes," he said wryly, "Ryan always forgave Victor. It's almost uncanny how close those two are, considering that in many ways, they're as different as night and day."

"How do you mean?"

"Well, Ryan, as I'm sure you well know, is pretty straight about everything. I don't think he has any vices, drinks only in moderation, doesn't smoke, gamble or chase wild women. I don't think he's ever had a parking ticket, and if he did, I'm sure he paid it promptly. Mr. Responsibility."

"But Victor is different?"

"Let's just say Victor tends to walk on the wild side, okay?" Jerry replied with a smile.

"How wild are we talking about here?" Sheila asked. Maybe if she knew what Victor was like, it would help her locate him.

"Well, he drives red sports cars and drives them too fast. He bought Ryan a red Corvette once but I think he drives it more than Ryan does. He doesn't care much for cops and doesn't mind taking shortcuts if the end justifies the means. He does things his way, and in his own good time. And while I don't think he'd ever start one, he's certainly not afraid to end a fight. Since he works out several times a week, believe me, you do not want to get into a fight with him. He's pretty strong. He did some bodyguard work for Ryan during his first tour, but I don't think he does that any more."

"Is he bad-tempered?"

"No, no, nothing like that. It's more a matter of standing up for himself. But around here, he'd get bored pretty quickly if he and Ryan didn't have a really big campaign to work on. We started sending him out doing PR work just to get him out of here. You've heard 'the devil finds work for idle hands to do'?"

"Yes."

"Well, if Victor North wasn't busy, he'd be up to some mischief or other. Sending him out to high schools to give talks about careers in advertising was one way to keep him from driving us all nuts with his pranks when work was slow. He enjoyed that, and the kids seemed to like him. Ryan did it too, once or twice. You could mention that. Maybe if you check with our PR department, you could learn which schools he visited and get some stories from the teachers, too."

"There's a good idea," Sheila remarked, pretending to jot another note. She already knew from Evelyn Moore about Ryan's visit to the high school. "So basically, they were both into practical jokes, but Victor more so than Ryan."

"Victor was pretty much nonstop, at least while he worked here. He's changed since then, I understand. I hear from Ryan that he's settled down somewhat, gotten more serious. Someone even said darker. I think he changed after their mother died, about three years ago. Sobered him up. I heard he also took up smoking."

"But when he was here he had a good sense of humor unless he was backed into a corner."

"That's a pretty good description. He was usually a lot of fun to be around, but give him too much hassle and he'd find some way to take you down. Ryan, on the other hand, rolls with the punches and generally avoids confrontations. For instance, he has dozens of people in his employ most of the time, but I don't think he could fire someone if his life depended on it. He's not a marshmallow, though. He just doesn't care to deal with unpleasantness himself. He lets his manager do the dirty work for him. He does things by the book, the correct way, always on time. He's a perfectionist with strong respect for deadlines. But as I recall, his desk was always a complete mess and Victor's was always tidy. Go figure."

Sheila made another note, shaking her head. "You're right, it sounds like they're nothing alike. Yet you say they're close?"

"Very close. There's nothing Ryan wouldn't do for Victor, and I suspect the reverse is equally true. You know the rest of their family is dead or gone, don't you?"

"Yes. I guess Ryan hasn't seen his father since he was about ten or eleven, according to the background I read. The mother and older brother both died."

"That's right. If anything happened to either Ryan or Victor, the other would be alone in the world."

"Jerry, if they're so close, why has nothing been written about Victor in years? I checked some news databases, and there is no trace of him, not even a DMV record. I began to suspect he had died, too, but I couldn't find an obituary either."

"Simple. He changed his name so his wild lifestyle wouldn't reflect on his brother's altar boy image."

"Where is he now? I'd really like to interview him, too," Sheila pressed. "What's his new name?"

"Uh-uh. I've probably already said more about Victor than I should have," Jerry said. "Victor also changed his name to avoid the publicity that surrounds Ryan. He won't appreciate it if something I said gets him a reporter on his doorstep looking for an interview. Please just forget about him. He doesn't want the attention."

"It's not important," Sheila shrugged. "This has been interesting but the story's about Ryan. Is there anything else you can tell our readers about him? What work did he do for you? How was he to work with? Did he get along with everyone pretty well?"

"Ryan's one of a kind, Mary. He's a total perfectionist about his work. When he takes on a task, he throws himself into it one hundred percent, and won't let up until it's finished to *his* satisfaction. He mostly wrote jingles for us, and they were always appropriate for the client, professionally arranged, and delivered on time. He worked well with the artists in coming up with complete advertising concepts for a client."

"Sounds like a very purposeful person," Sheila commented. "He must be tough to work for."

Jerry laughed. "I think I gave you a wrong impression. Ryan drives himself, and hard, but he doesn't step on others to get what he wants. Ryan North is one of the nicest guys I've ever known. He'll give anyone the shirt off his back if he thought they needed it. He also does a lot of charity work, or at least he did before his accident, and he used to answer a lot of his own fan mail. He's popular with fans from age ten to sixty, and everyone who works here liked him immensely."

"Surely he has a skeleton in a closet somewhere," Sheila goaded him. "Nobody's that perfect."

"If Ryan North has a blind spot, I'd have to say it's his brother," Jerry admitted, "which is probably why I said so much about Victor. To understand Ryan, you have to understand his relationship with Victor. Those two were a great team, and very supportive of each other. I think they have a strong sense of each of them being the only family they have left. Ryan told me once they were both devastated when their older brother died and it brought them closer together. I think it was fear that Ryan was going to die that made Victor stay with Ryan day and night when Ryan was in the coma last year." He suddenly looked at her sharply. "But that's off the record. Ryan would have a fit if he found out I told a reporter anything personal about his brother. I hope you'll respect that."

"Don't worry. I told you the story's about Ryan."

"Well, always glad to help Ryan get a little publicity. Since his accident he's been out of the limelight and he probably misses it."

"I think I'll go now and let you get back to your work. Thanks for your time."

Sheila glanced around the office as she stood up and took in the many posters on the wall of ads for various products and businesses. A low table held a few trophies that had been won by the agency in professional competitions. A drafting table occupied a spot near the window and held a partially completed drawing for a pet store ad. This was Ryan North's old life. And the elusive brother's.

Three framed pictures were on another table near the door. She peered at one of them, recognizing Jerry Overholt and Ryan North as two of the people in the picture. Could the stocky, grinning, blond man with them holding an award plaque be Ryan's brother? He looked vaguely familiar, but she couldn't place him.

As she walked out of the building, something nagging at the back of her mind told her she had just been handed a major clue. Something that contradicted something she thought she knew.

Surreptitiously, she slipped a hand in her jacket pocket and clicked off the tape recorder. She would go through every word back at the office and wouldn't rest until she figured it out.

There was something there … something important … something about Ryan and his brother ….

CHAPTER 29

ONDAY FRED JOINED Ryan and Doug at the studio where they continued editing the show while Fred spent the day chatting with several of the crew members. Later the three returned to Ryan's house and discussed security issues. Fred felt that it would be safer if Ryan moved to Doug's condo temporarily, somewhere nobody would expect him to be. "There's too much risk here," Fred explained. "Your property backs up to a hillside. Even with the guard out here, it's too risky. It's been bothering me all along. I'd feel better if you were somewhere else."

"If this place is being watched, they'd know right away if it was suddenly abandoned, wouldn't they?"

"I could stay here," Doug said. "Keep up appearances. If Fred stayed with me, they'd see two people coming and going."

"Could work," Ryan agreed. "Shall we try it tonight?"

Fred nodded. "Let's do it. I keep feeling like something else should be happening soon. You're almost done at the studio, so if someone wants you dead, they're going to have to get at you here."

"You know, Fred, I have no intention of letting you or Doug fill my coffin for me. Who's going to keep you two safe while you're protecting me?"

"My good friends, Smith and Wesson," Fred replied, patting his left side where his gun was concealed. "Doug has a gun, too, and knows how to use it."

"I don't want to know about it," Ryan said abruptly. "I'll just worry."

They left in two cars later on, Ryan and Doug in the Corvette, and Fred following in his Volvo. After Fred gathered what he needed from Doug's condo, he returned with Doug in the Corvette, leaving Ryan and the Volvo at the condo. To help with the masquerade, Ryan left wearing a bright yellow windbreaker that Fred put on for the return trip. If the guard or anyone else was watching, they would assume it was Ryan returning with Doug and that Fred had simply gone home alone.

Fred sat back on the couch at Ryan's house later that night and sipped the martini Doug had made for him. "Thanks, Doug," he said. "Glad we got a chance to be alone tonight. I was afraid you were going to change your mind and want to stay with him. But he'll be safe there. Nobody but us knows where he is." He took out a pack of cigarettes and lit one. Doug sat next to him on the couch, sipping his own drink thoughtfully.

Fred stretched an arm across the back of the sofa behind Doug and idly rubbed Doug's neck. Doug tensed momentarily, then relaxed, saying, "I don't know if I'm ever going to get used to that, much as I want to."

"You'll get used to it once you accept yourself. I've told you that before."

The two men were silent for several minutes while Fred gradually moved the massage to Doug's shoulders. "Boy, you're really tense tonight," he commented.

"I know," Doug agreed. "I almost died when that detective showed up asking questions yesterday. I didn't know what to say."

"Good thing you didn't say anything," Fred answered. "You've been so worried about how much Ryan might already know, that would have really opened a can of worms."

"I know, but I don't know what to do about that cop. I think I've smoked two whole packs of cigarettes today, worrying about what he might know. I don't think he was really here to ask Ryan anything. Everyone knows Ryan has amnesia. I think it was me he was after. And maybe you, if he had known you were here."

"Calm down. You're getting your back knotted up again," Fred replied. "We used aliases. If that cop knew the whole story, he would have asked you a lot more than a couple of vague questions. He wouldn't have left if he'd known you were lying to him."

"You think so?"

"Don't sweat it. He obviously doesn't know anything or he wouldn't have left so quickly. You said he didn't even know you were here until you came out of the kitchen."

"I hope you're right," Doug said, reaching for his martini again. He sighed. "Fred, there's something I haven't told you."

"About what?"

"The boy. Danny. Daryl."

"What about him?"

Doug took a long drag from the cigarette, replaced it in the ashtray, and exhaled sharply before answering. He finally turned to look Fred in the eyes and said, "I saw him in the woods."

"You saw him? The day he died? Are you sure it was him?"

"We talked."

"Why was he there?" Fred asked. "Was he hunting?"

"No, he didn't have a gun, although his horse was decked out in the same orange ribbon Griffith gave us for our horses. He wouldn't say why he was there, but he got a little flustered when I asked him how long he'd owned the horse. I don't think it was his."

"Doug, this could be serious. Sounds like you might have been the last person to see him alive, other than his killer."

"Think I don't know that? But what could I say about it? I have no idea why he was there. They already know he was in the woods that day. What good will it do to tell them I saw him? Then they'll want to know how I knew him, so why bring it up?"

Fred sighed. "You're sure you have no idea why he was there? Was he meeting someone? Was anyone with him?"

"No, he was alone. Fred, if anyone finds out I saw him, especially once they find out how I knew him, I'm the prime suspect. You know how cops think."

"I know." He sighed again. "This isn't being investigated by Denver P.D., but we have no way of knowing if this detective is any more open minded."

"It's the same one who investigated Ryan's accident. He gave me a hard time then, too. Acted like he thought I'd tried to kill my own brother."

Fred took his hands off Doug's back and frowned. "He gave you a hard time while your brother was lying there unconscious?"

"Well, not really then, but later, in the hospital. He was asking questions like he thought I had something to do with Ryan's accident. This was after that drugging incident."

Fred hesitated. "Doug, I don't want you to get mad at me, but is it possible he was just asking normal questions and you only thought he was suspicious of you? I mean, he had no way of knowing you were gay, did he?"

"He's a cop, Fred. He probably figured it out somehow."

"I doubt that, and despite things I've said before, they're really not all bad, you know. Asking questions is their job. Remember when I told you what happened to me, why I left?"

"Of course."

"Well, one of the detectives tried to stop it."

"You said the whole squad was in on it."

"Might as well have been the whole squad. But this one detective told them to knock it off, leave me alone. I forget his name. John something, I think. A couple of them went for him, shoved him bodily out of the restroom."

"But they still did … what they did to you."

"He was outmanned and outgunned. The only way he could have stopped them would have been to shoot a few of the ringleaders. He tried going up the chain of command, reported what he'd seen."

"What happened?"

"The captain said he didn't want any fucking fags on his squad and told him to mind his own damn business if he knew what was good for him. Tore up the report he wrote."

"How do you know all this?"

"He came to see me in the hospital the next day. I was still half out of it then, from the pain medication, which is why I don't remember his name anymore. He told me what he did, and what the captain said. He also told me he was going to put in for a transfer to the west side. He didn't think he could keep working at that snake pit after what happened. There's an unwritten code that cops don't rat on other cops, and he violated it when he went upstairs with that report. He knew he had to leave. I asked him to take in my resignation when he went. He did." He took another pull on the cigarette. "He wanted me to go with him to the FBI about it. They have jurisdiction over corrupt police departments, you know. I couldn't do it. I was afraid they'd kill me if I did. But it meant a lot to me that he was willing to stick his neck out like that for me."

"So there was one decent cop in the whole precinct," Doug said with a shrug. "He was probably gay, too."

"He wasn't, but all that doesn't matter here. I just brought it up as an example that they're not all bad. But whether this one is bigoted or not, it doesn't sound like you know anything helpful, so let's leave it alone for now."

"I'm glad you feel that way, Fred. I hated keeping this from you, but I was afraid you'd think I should turn myself in. Once a cop, always a cop, that sort of thing."

"If I thought you were withholding vital evidence, it would be different. But as you said, they already know he was killed in the woods. Having you confirm it isn't going to put them any closer to a solution." Fred turned around and lifted Doug's hand to the back of his neck. "Come on. Your turn to do me. I've been on my feet all day and my back is killing me. Don't be so shy," he added when Doug hesitated. "You do it for Ryan all the time."

"Ryan hasn't been trying to seduce me for the last nine months," Doug retorted, putting his other hand on the other side of Fred's neck and massaging firmly.

"Neither have I, Doug."

"I know. Sorry."

They didn't speak for a long time while Doug concentrated on working the soreness out of Fred's shoulders. Finally, Fred picked up the smoldering cigarette and took a final drag from it before crushing it out in the ashtray. "So," he said, "where do we go from here on this drugging thing? Is there anyone on the crew that you don't know fairly well?"

"Ryan's makeup artist, Mel, Sam in Lighting, Walter the sound mixer. They're not his regulars and I don't know anything about any of them." Doug stopped and turned to face Fred again. "Maybe we should get to know Hussman the hippie better. Mel and Sam came from Biff's crew, but Hussman is a complete unknown." He paused, yawning. "I'm beat, Fred. I think I'm going to hit the sack." Fred stood and held out a helping hand and Doug let himself be pulled to his feet. "Thanks."

"You're sure you're okay with these arrangements?"

"Yes. Ryan will be safe at my condo alone, but if anyone does break in here, I'd feel better with you and your gun here with me." He led the way down the hall, pushing open the door to a room at the far end of the hall.

Fred paused at the door. "I'll work on Hussman and the lighting technician starting tomorrow. I already checked out Mel, but didn't find out much about him. Except that he used to date one of my old boyfriends."

"Small world," Doug grunted, switching on the light. "You can sleep in here tonight. There's a bathroom through that door with everything you might need in it. I'll be down the hall."

"Good night, Doug," Fred said, pulling him into an embrace without thinking.

For the briefest moment, Doug returned the hug, then shoved away from the other man, fighting fear and nausea. "I – can't – " he gasped.

Fred looked at his friend sadly. "Damn that therapist anyway, Doug. I'm sorry. I just forgot. I wasn't trying to push you. You okay?"

Doug leaned against the wall with his eyes closed, trembling, fighting the conditioned response he'd been battling for several months. "It's all right," he said tensely. "I know you weren't." He finally got control of himself and looked back at Fred. He reached out a hand, which Fred gently took. "I don't know why you hang in here, Fred. Will I ever get over this?"

"I don't know, but you've been making progress. And I hang in here because I want to." He gave Doug's hand a squeeze, then released it and turned away. "Good night, my friend. Sleep well."

CHAPTER 30

"SO HE HADN'T SEEN anything after all, huh?" Somehow, Harley Watson wasn't surprised. Jim had just gotten back from the airport after coming back on a noon flight and had stepped into Harley's office to brief him.

"No," Jim Harrison replied, "and his partner, Doug Norton, who was up there at the same time, said he didn't remember seeing anyone either. Well, we knew it was a long shot, but I'm glad I checked it out anyway. I left my card in case he remembered something later on. You know how it is when you're put on the spot to recall something without having time to really think about it. I did find the horse," he added. "I'll send some hairs to the lab so we can try to rule him out."

"I certainly hope you can." Harley tossed a folded newspaper to Jim. "Read what Sheila Fernelli wrote."

Jim Harrison read the short article. "You've got to be kidding. She as good as says that North is our prime suspect. How the hell does she think she's going to get away with that?" Silently, he fumed, wondering what the hell she was playing at.

"Oh, she's clever. Nothing she wrote is an actual lie. It's what's between the lines that smacks of libel, but you can't sue someone over what's between the lines. I just hope Ryan North doesn't get wind of this. At least the wire services haven't picked up any of her stories yet."

"Well, there's nothing to be done about it now," Jim said aloud. He would deal with Sheila Fernelli later. "I suppose we need to keep working the case from the boy's angle."

"From what you told me before, it certainly sounds like he had at least one enemy," Harley agreed. He took another sip of coffee, grimaced, and set it aside. "The thing that bothers me is that I can't imagine that he was investigating a drug ring. That's pretty heavy stuff for a high school news reporter."

"But he was investigating something. That much we do know. What could he have been investigating that could have gotten him killed?"

"Jim, it could have been anything or nothing," Harley replied, shaking his head as he flipped through Jim's report on the investigation so far. "He probably wasn't blackmailing anyone – that doesn't fit in with the profile of a young journalist. Journalists don't want to be paid to keep quiet; they want to be famous for spilling the beans." He grunted. "Like Sheila Fernelli. When she gets some beans she just can't wait to spill them."

Jim laughed. "You know, she never discovered the hospital connection." He sobered. "I've got some good leads if I could just put them together."

"Let's go over what you have so far. Maybe if we talk it back and forth we'll think of an angle we haven't tried yet."

"Okay," Jim agreed, rocking back in his chair with his hands interlaced behind his head. "Sixteen-year-old Lakewood High School student. A 'B' student the previous year, some teachers said his grades had slipped a little that year. Too early in the school year to judge, though. He disappeared before midterms. General opinion is that he was preoccupied with something."

"Preoccupied."

"That's the term they all used. He did not confide in his friends, other than to tell them he was working on a case, and his father would be proud of him when he was done. His case may have involved one of several clubs that met on Tuesday nights. I have met with members of all the campus clubs that met on Tuesday night. He was a member of the chess club, but had not attended their meeting for three weeks before he disappeared. Nobody in the Biology, French, or Astronomy clubs had seen him that month. He had reported on the Astronomy club's activities in his regular column the week before he disappeared."

"Anything noteworthy about his article?" Harley inquired.

"They had spotted a comet. Three members were mentioned by name, nothing unfavorable. Just a routine report of an interesting incident."

"Must have been a slow news week," Harley commented dryly. "What else do we know?"

"The only other Tuesday club on the campus listing was not a school-sponsored club. According to the principal of the high school, they agreed to post meeting notices for the Lesbian and Gay Society that meets over at the college after a faculty member made a pitch to the school board. The principal himself was opposed to it but gave in to pressure from the school board. I have not been able to contact members of that organization, mostly because they don't have a membership list, and apparently most of them don't use their real names at the meetings anyway."

"Not likely that Daryl's school reporting would have taken him to that organization anyway. What would he be able to report?"

Jim contemplated that for a moment. "Perhaps an AIDS benefit? But I don't see how that could be considered a 'case' that needed to be 'broken'."

Harley sighed. "No, not really. Probably his big mystery had nothing to do with the clubs. Maybe your witness misunderstood him, or he was deliberately trying to mislead her about the nature of his case."

"Then there's the mugging victim he visited in the hospital. Who happens to be a member of that L and G group."

"I thought all four of them denied knowing him."

"I talked to all four boys and they all said they never met Daryl Walker. I found out from another source that Richard Farrell was lying to me, though. But they all refused to discuss the circumstances of their attacks." He wisely refrained from identifying Sheila Fernelli as the source who had tipped him to Farrell's lack of candor.

"The Tuesday Night Marauder."

"Yes. And I discovered that none of them filed a police report."

Harley leaned back and stroked his chin thoughtfully. "Jim, why would an assault victim not report an assault?"

"Because he knew the attacker and feared another attack? Because he lacked faith in the police?"

"And why would he lack faith in the police?"

"Racism?"

"Are any of these boys of a minority group?"

"Two are Hispanic. They seemed to have nothing in common." Jim hesitated. "Except …."

"Except what?"

"Well, all of them struck me as extremely nervous, almost paranoid. Like they were afraid to talk to me at all."

"After being assaulted badly enough to land in the hospital, you'd be nervous and paranoid, too. Anything else?"

"Well, I told you Ricky Farrell is gay."

"Oh, he's the fag?"

"Yes. But one was built like a jock. I wondered how many people had jumped him. He was a pretty big guy."

"Two Hispanics, a fag, and a jock," Harley mused. "And one of the Tuesday clubs was the Lesbian and Gay club and all these assaults took place on Tuesday night."

"Could be a coincidence. Ten percent of the male population is gay."

Harley grunted. "Thank God for the other ninety. Jim, we're getting an awful lot of coincidences here. Go find out if the Hispanics and the jock were also fags. I can't think of a better reason for a boy not to report a beating than if the reason for it was because he's a gay jock and he's not out of the closet yet. It may have nothing to do with Daryl's murder, but it strikes me as a loose end that needs to be tied up before we can proceed. On the other hand, Jim," he continued with a disgusted look on his face, "this just might explain the pantyhose."

* * *

"The deal's off, Sheila," Jim snapped over the phone as soon as he left Harley. "I thought we had an agreement, then you go and run a story like that." He had called her on his cell phone from a parking lot after leaving the office, having no desire to have Harley overhear him talking to the reporter.

"I'm sorry, Jim. But what was I supposed to do? Wait until I read it in the *Post*, then try to explain to my editor why I didn't know you had gone?" Sheila shifted the phone to her other ear. "I promised not to print anything I learned on my own, but I can't agree to sit on information I get from other sources."

"What other sources, Sheila? I didn't tell you I was going to Los Angeles. We didn't issue a press release, either. How did you find out?"

"You know I can't reveal my sources, Jim. I never said I got the information from you."

"I can't operate like this, Sheila," Jim warned. "Harley's mad enough. In fact, if he ever gets wind of that conversation we had, it just might mean my job. I've been having to play along with his Sheila Fernelli bashing for quite awhile now." He sighed heavily. "If he thinks I'm giving you information I don't know what he'll do."

"I'll take care of that, Jim," Sheila assured him. "I'll go in and do a little Jim Harrison bashing this afternoon. He won't suspect a thing."

"See that you do. Talk to you later." He started to hang up.

"Wait, Jim," Sheila said quickly, "I was going to call you anyway about something I found out while you were gone."

"What's this about?"

"Ryan North. I found something out."

Jim repressed an exasperated sigh. "Okay, I promised to listen if you came up with something. What about him?"

"When he was in the hospital over here last October, do you remember hearing about someone giving him the wrong medication? It was in the paper."

"I remember. The detective in charge called me about it. They decided it was accidental."

"I talked to someone who knew Ryan North before he was famous. Ryan and his brother used to work together at the same place. This friend of theirs told me that the brother made a habit of playing practical jokes on Ryan, slipping things in his coffee or food, things like laxatives and caffeine pills."

"Meaning what?"

"This friend also mentioned that Ryan's brother never left his side the whole time he was in the hospital. I checked with the reporter we had on the case at the time. According to him, Ryan's business partner,

Doug Norton, was the only visitor Ryan had at the hospital while he was in the coma. The partner must be the brother."

"Okay, I can confirm that he is, but don't use me as a source," Jim warned. "If he's trying to conceal that fact, it's not my place to out him. He changed his name to protect his privacy and I hope you'll respect that. He's not under suspicion for anything."

"Maybe he should be."

"Why do you say that?"

"The *L.A. Times* had a story the other day that Ryan North was admitted to the hospital with hallucinations caused by someone substituting acid for the aspirin he kept in his dressing room."

"I know about that, too."

"Jim, his brother was at the scene of both of those incidents. And he has a history of doing similar things for a joke."

Jim smiled to himself, relieved that Sheila's investigation of Ryan North had led her somewhere other than his homicide case. He was silent for a minute, thinking, then said, "Well, if I had any jurisdiction over either incident, I might make an inquiry or two." He heard Sheila exhale a sharp sigh of relief over the phone and he smiled.

"Thanks, Jim," she said. "I was afraid you'd blow me off the way Harley always does. Should I call the detectives in charge of those cases?"

"I'm not sure the Denver incident is considered open, and there was no harm done anyway since he didn't take the pills," Jim replied, thinking out loud. "Knowing their standard procedures as I do, they're not going to expend any more resources on a case they couldn't prosecute even if they did prove he did it." He paused doubtfully for a moment but decided he was correct. Since North had not taken the pills, and Norton had not asked him to take them, a case of attempted murder or even assault would never stick. Satisfied with his analysis, he continued, "The other incident is still under investigation. LAPD is handling it."

"Then maybe I'll call them."

"Well, don't be surprised if they don't pay any more attention to you than Harley does. The idea of his brother trying to hurt him sounds pretty far-fetched. He clearly had opportunity, but where is the motive? Besides, if he really wanted Ryan North dead, he surely could have figured out a more effective way of doing it."

"Maybe he's not trying to kill him, just mess with his head a little."

"Why would he do that?"

"Maybe Ryan knows something about his brother that his brother wants him to forget."

"What would that be?"

"Think about it, Jim. Who was in the woods the day of the murder? How many suspects do you have?"

Jim couldn't answer for a minute. So this was where she was leading – right back to his homicide after all. Finally, he spoke. "Sheila, I know you're trying to help but you are simply way out in left field now. You're forgetting one little thing. We need a motive for the murder. I think you're suggesting Mr. Norton killed Daryl Walker, Ryan North saw him do it, so now Norton is drugging his brother to make him forget? Why would Doug Norton have killed the boy in the first place? There's no indication they knew each other. And don't you think if North remembered anything he would have said something by now? And if he isn't talking because he was in on it with him, why would Norton be trying to mess with his head now?" He shook his head. Maybe Harley was right. Maybe Billy Williams had been right. Maybe Jim Harrison was completely losing his ability to read people. "And seven months have gone by in the meantime. If he was so worried about what Ryan North might have seen, why hasn't he done something before now?"

There was silence on the line, causing Jim to fear he'd hurt her feelings. She was trying to help, but where did she come up with these ideas?

Finally, Sheila spoke. "Sorry I bothered you, Jim. I'll let you go now."

"Wait, Sheila. I didn't mean that the way it sounded. I'm sorry. Please don't go away mad."

"Just go away? Is that it?" she replied coldly.

"No. That's not what I mean at all."

"Then what do you mean?"

"I mean I'm sorry. You've apparently given this a lot of thought in the last few days. I don't think there's any evidence to support your theory, but I don't have a whole lot of support for my own theory, either, and my job is to look at all possibilities. Tell you what. See if you can find out if Norton ever met the boy. If you can establish any connection between them, no matter how slim, I'll put him on my suspect list. Fair enough?"

He could almost hear her smiling through the phone, and wished he were there to see it in person. "Thanks, Jim. I'll let you know as soon as I come up with anything."

True to her word, Sheila Fernelli marched into the office later that afternoon and faced Sheriff Harley Watson across his desk that afternoon. "Why are you so willing to ignore me, Sheriff? Your lousy investigator didn't even find out the truth about Ricky, let alone this Peter person."

"So what would you have me do, Miss Fernelli? Start hauling in every Peter in the phone book? I've made a note of what you said. If our investigation turns up anyone named Peter, we will contact your Ricky to see if he recognizes him. But with no more than that to go on, there's not a hell of a lot I can do."

"I talked to the coroner, Sheriff. He found horse hair on Daryl's clothing. Haven't you tried to find the horse yet?"

"We've asked at the stables and ranches in the area. It was hunting season. Most of the rental horses had been rented by hunters, and none of the records showed Daryl Walker as a customer. But there are dozens of privately owned horses within riding distance of where the body was found, Miss Fernelli, and without probable cause and a search warrant we can't exactly interrogate all their owners."

"Ryan North was on a horse."

"So?"

"Have you checked to see if the horse hair you found on the body matches his horse?"

Harley Watson glared across the desk at the reporter. "Miss Fernelli," he began curtly, "I have heard just about enough of your Ryan

North theory. I know you used to work for some tabloid, and you're trained to make mountains out of nonexistent molehills, but this is a homicide investigation! This is not a story about a five-year-old boy who gave birth to an alien baby or any of those other stupid fabrications you're used to writing. I'm sure the *Chronicle* is not interested in being sued by Ryan North, and I am not going to dignify your ridiculous theories with a response." He wasn't about to tell her that Jim had learned the location of North's horse and gathered a few hairs from the animal while he was in Los Angeles.

He paused to regain control. "Now, Miss Fernelli, you can rest assured that if new information is uncovered that the public needs to know about, we will issue a press release and you can write whatever *factual* story you like. But if I see this nonsense about Ryan North in the paper again, I will personally mail him a copy and suggest he show it to his attorney. Now, good day!"

He looked down at his desk and began to read a report. Sheila slowly got to her feet. "You're going to feel like a fool, Harley, when I figure out what the connection is." The sheriff didn't look up, and Sheila turned and walked out of the office. Walking past Jim Harrison's office on the way out, she gave him a surreptitious wink and a grin. He shook his head, chuckling, having heard the whole conversation through the thin wall.

After Sheila Fernelli left, Harley Watson reread the report on his desk. Harrison had checked out the helicopter sighting several days before, but the rest of the lab results had just come in that morning. Fingerprints on the pop can had been inconclusive, but Daryl's mother had confirmed his preference for Dr Pepper and Baby Ruth candy bars. Tests on the manure samples confirmed that it had come from the same horse whose manure was also found behind a bush near where the body had been found. While the horse had been confirmed at both locations, there still was no definite proof that Daryl Walker had been. His mother said the boy had once taken riding lessons, but she had no idea why he would have been riding, nor where he would have obtained the horse.

Harley leaned back in his chair and thought about what Sheila Fernelli had said. *Daryl told Ricky he had to go ride for Peter that weekend.* The horsehair on his clothing and traces of horse sweat indicated that he had probably been riding the day he died.

Daryl might have been a "mule," someone who carried drugs for someone else. But who had killed him, and why? Had someone surprised him in the woods, stolen the drugs from him? But who? A hunter? Had he been followed? Had the people he worked for killed him? This man, Peter, perhaps? Or was this what he had been investigating? Perhaps he had hidden in the woods to spy on the drug operation?

Harley read the part of the report that described the cache Jim discovered, a camouflaged box that turned out to have traces of cocaine inside. Apparently the drugs were to have been dropped off by helicopter and picked up later by someone on horseback. That made sense; they certainly would not have wanted the chopper to wait around for the horse to arrive.

He also realized that a landing helicopter would have terrified most horses. No, if the boy was a "mule," he was not supposed to meet the chopper directly. Yet the candy wrapper and pop can indicated that perhaps he had arrived early. Had he been killed because he saw the helicopter pilot's face? Or had he been killed by someone else, someone he encountered in the woods on his way back?

He picked up another report Jim Harrison had dropped on his desk a few minutes before Sheila's arrival. He had checked on the four assault victims. His suspicion that all the boys were gay had been confirmed, but they were still at a dead end as far as finding a connection to Daryl Walker's homicide, despite Sheila Fernelli's interview with Ricky Farrell.

Sheila had told Jim that Ricky hadn't been sure Daryl was gay, and Daryl's parents were unequivocal when they affirmed that Daryl positively had not been gay. So the only reason they could come up with why he might have been attending Lesbian and Gay Society meetings was that he was investigating something.

Or had he been dealing drugs there? Ricky hadn't said anything to Sheila about drugs, but that didn't mean Daryl hadn't been selling them. Harley straightened the papers and put them back in their folder. Perhaps that's all it was. He was holding out from the drug dealers he worked for, selling on the side, and they found out and killed him, probably as an example to others who were working for them.

In fact, Harley realized suddenly, maybe there was a whole string of "mules" in that L and G group. Maybe the assaults were warnings.

He pressed his intercom. "Jim, come in here a minute. I have an idea I want you to check out."

CHAPTER 31

TUESDAY RYAN RECALLED his band and crew to re-shoot a dance number he had not been happy with. Fred stayed at the condo when he and Doug went to pick up Ryan and tried new searches based on things he had learned in conversations with the crew the day before.

The complicated dance routine required five takes, and it was late afternoon before everyone was satisfied with the performance. Ryan sent Doug to review the tapes with Tony and walked, exhausted, into his dressing room and sat down on the makeup stool to remove the makeup from his face.

He finished removing his makeup, then stripped and stepped into the shower in the bathroom that adjoined the dressing room.

As he turned off the shower and stepped out of the stall a few minutes later, he heard the outer door to the dressing room close. "Doug? Is that you?" he called, alarmed. Getting no answer, he quickly dried himself and wrapped the towel around his waist. He looked through the bathroom door into the main part of the dressing room and glanced around. The room was empty. "Must be imagining things," he muttered to himself.

He crossed the room to the couch where his clothes lay, and began to dress. He was just buttoning his shirt when he heard a knock on the door. "Ryan? You still in there?"

"Come on in, Doug," he answered. The door opened and Doug stepped into the room.

"Tapes look fine, Ryan," Doug said. "We'll be ready to resume editing tomorrow."

"Good, good," Ryan said, smiling. "Maybe we can get this thing finished after all."

"Well, the special-effects guys will be here tomorrow, and if we stay on schedule, we should be done in a week. After that the network will own it and you'll be home free."

"I can hardly wait. Let's get out of here, Doug." He glanced at the clock on his dressing table to see how late it was, and suddenly stiffened. "Shit!" he exclaimed.

"What's the matter?" Doug asked. His eyes followed Ryan's gaze and he saw what Ryan had seen. "How did that get there?"

"Must have been while I was in the shower. I thought I heard the door close just as I was getting out, but then I figured it was my imagination when I didn't see anybody."

Doug walked over to the table and read aloud the message that had been scrawled on the mirror with a red felt pen. "'*Next time you're going to die.*' Better not touch anything over here until the police get here. I've already touched the doorknob, so any prints there would be destroyed." He looked down at the dressing table. "Did you see this?" he asked, pointing.

Lying on the table was the photograph of Ryan that his stylist used to make sure Ryan's hair was combed identically in all the scenes even though they were shot on different days. In the same red felt pen, the intruder had drawn a dagger, pointing into Ryan's heart.

Ryan stared wordlessly, then picked up the phone and called security. Then he sat down on the couch and held his head in his hands, his elbows on his knees.

"You all right?" Doug asked, coming to rest a hand on Ryan's shoulder, rubbing it gently, feeling the tension.

"Well I guess there's no question this is personal now," Ryan replied bitterly. "Up till now we couldn't be certain if I was the target or just a random victim. Anyone with a headache could have gotten that acid from my aspirin bottle, and there was always a chance that bug was planted before we took the studio. But what does he get out of scaring me? Why doesn't he say what the hell he wants? He keeps threatening me, and harassing me, but hasn't really tried to kill me, Doug. All he's doing is driving me nuts."

"I don't know, Ryan," Doug replied. "We've been all over that topic."

"But he's proven that he can get to me. I guess it's my own fault. I'm supposed to have someone with me at all times, and I sent you over to review that tape without me. If I hadn't been here alone, this wouldn't have happened."

"It's as much my fault as yours," Doug argued. "I shouldn't have left you alone. Fred won't be happy about this. He told me to stay with you at all times." He sighed.

They were interrupted by a knock on the door, and the security guard entered with Tony. Ryan pointed wordlessly at the mirror and the picture, then said, "The doorknob on this side needs to be dusted for prints. We haven't touched it, or the dressing table."

"The police are on the way. When did this happen, Mr. North?" the guard asked.

"Maybe twenty minutes ago. I was in the shower."

"Any chance it was here before you came into the room?"

"No, I was sitting at that table removing my makeup before I took the shower. I heard the outer door here close just as I stepped out of the shower. That must have been when he left."

"So you didn't hear him enter, or know if he knocked or said anything before he came in?"

Ryan shook his head. "I was in the shower. I didn't hear a thing."

"Mr. North, I don't get it," the guard said, scratching his head. "This entire section has been buttoned up since that drug incident. Only your own crew and our security people have been allowed in or out. We'll see if we can find anything here, but I doubt we will. The police didn't find any prints at the other scenes that didn't belong there. You need to consider the possibility that the person who is doing these things is part of your crew."

Ryan didn't answer, and the guard walked to the door. "Don't touch anything until the police come. I'll see if I can find anyone who saw someone come in here." He left the dressing room.

"Part of the crew," Ryan echoed after the guard left. "That's what I've suspected all along." He stood up. "I'm going to leave," he said tiredly. "Tony, stay here and wait for the police. You can tell them what I said. I've got to get out of here. Come on, Doug." He led the way out to the parking lot where the Corvette waited.

* * *

It was with some trepidation that Sheila arrived at the meeting of the Lesbian and Gay Society that night. She had spoken briefly with the coordinator, a woman named Christy Benham. The woman gave her an idea what to expect and promised to give her a few minutes to address the group. The meetings were very informal, primarily social events, although they tried to have a speaker occasionally on topics of interest to the members.

Sheila knew she was attractive, but it was a little unnerving to walk into a room full of strangers and realize it was the eyes of other women who followed her as she walked across the room, rather than the eyes of men.

She found Christy, introduced herself, and sat in a chair near the podium. Christy called the meeting to order. She introduced Sheila and explained why she was there, then turned the microphone over to Sheila and sat down.

Sheila nervously looked out over the group of about thirty people, ranging in age from mid-teens to mid-forties, then realized they were all looking at her with interest and curiosity, not hostility or suspicion. She began to relax. "Hi," she said. "I hope some of you may be able to help me with something, and I promise complete anonymity if any of you can give me the information I need."

A twitter of laughter moved through the group, and Sheila remembered that Ricky said most of them didn't use their real names anyway.

"I'm looking into the death of Daryl Walker. I recently spoke to one of your members who told me that Daryl Walker, using the name Danny, attended these meetings for several weeks before he died. He was in disguise, so you probably didn't know it was him. I believe he was investigating something and got in over his head and that may have been the reason he was killed. I also know that about the same time, you had a private investigator working for you, trying to find out who was ambushing your members after the meetings. My source said that Daryl spent a lot of time talking to this investigator." She paused and looked around the room for reactions. A few people were nodding slightly, as if they remembered the boy and his interest in the investigation.

She plunged ahead. She had been warned to be very brief. "So what I'd like to know is, did any of you know what Daryl was investigating? And do any of you know how I can get in touch with the investigator Jeff or have any idea what his last name is? We believe that Daryl may have taken Jeff into his confidence about what he was working on, maybe getting tips from him on how to investigate whatever it was he was interested in. Or he might have been helping Jeff with his own investigation. I'll be here for a while after the meeting, and I will also leave my business cards on the table in case you want to talk to me privately." She hesitated a moment. "And just so there is no confusion, I am straight. I hope that doesn't matter to any of you."

The room erupted with laughter at that comment. Sheila smiled nervously and sat down. Christy chuckled as she retook the podium. "Sorry, Sheila. We can't help finding it amusing that every straight person who comes to talk to us feels they have to explain that. We can usually tell within two minutes that someone is straight, unless they for some reason want us to think they're gay. We get a few of those every year."

"Sorry," Sheila said, blushing.

"Don't worry about it, honey." She turned back to her audience. "Okay, I'm sure some of you may be able to help Sheila, so even though she's not one of us, please make her feel welcome and help her if you can. I remember the boy, and I'm sure some of you do too. He's the one who wore a bad disguise and did a pretty poor job of trying to convince us he was gay last fall. But he may have been trying to help Jeff help us, so let's do what we can to help solve his murder, okay? That's all I had on the agenda tonight, so let's start the party."

Sheila mingled with the members for over an hour, pleased that she was accepted so quickly. She wondered how much acceptance any of them would have felt to walk into a room full of heterosexuals and announce that they were gay. She suspected it would have been a very different scenario indeed.

One man approached her. "I don't know if this will help you any, Sheila," he said, "but I happened to be sitting next to the boy the first night the investigator showed up. Did you know Jeff brought a friend with him? When Danny saw them, he said, 'I think I know him.' I asked him which one he meant, and he meant the friend. Later, when he overheard Jeff introduce the friend as 'Bobby,' Danny told me that wasn't his real name. I told him to shut up about it, that if he wanted it known who he was, he'd use his real name, and if he didn't, it wasn't up to Danny to tell anyone."

"What did he say to that?"

"He said I was right. That was all he said about it. Later I saw Danny go up to the friend and introduce himself. Next thing I knew, they were off in a corner together, heads together, talking real earnestly."

"Did he ever say anything about them again?"

"Not to me, but they always got here early and talked in the parking lot for quite awhile before coming inside. Both Jeff and his friend smoked, so they'd stand outside talking before the meetings since we can't smoke in here. Danny was always with them. The last time I saw them together was the night Jeff said they were getting close, had a plan, but he would be out of town for a couple weeks but in the meantime his friend would continue the investigation and everyone should continue being careful leaving the meetings. But the next week, none of them came. We never saw Danny again, and it was a couple months before Jeff and Bobby returned. Jeff said an arrest had been made and we shouldn't have any trouble anymore. That was the last we saw of them."

"Funny that they would fade out the same time Daryl did."

"I'm sure they had nothing to do with his murder, if that's what you're getting at. They seemed to really like the kid, and, no, I'm not talking about physically. They asked about him that time they came back, but nobody knew where he was. We didn't even know he was the senator's kid until Ricky told us last week so we didn't know at the time he was missing. I assume they knew he wasn't gay. Most of us figured it out right away just watching him interact with the other boys."

"How can you tell?"

"It's easy. He never checked anyone out. You know, how you look someone over when you're interested in getting to know them better? You heteros do the same thing. I've seen it. Well, Danny never once checked any of the men out. He didn't seem embarrassed when someone looked him over, or maybe he didn't even realize it was happening, but he never did it to anyone. Except once," the man said with a chuckle, "I caught him checking out one of the girls. He probably didn't even realize he was doing it."

Sheila heard a couple other similar stories before deciding that whatever Daryl was working on, he did not confide it to anyone still in the group, but he probably had confided in Jeff and Bobby. Could it be that he was trying to investigate the gay bashing incidents all along? Was he working with Jeff or just getting advice from him to help with his own investigation, whatever it was? Or was he really there, as Ricky had suggested, because he was having trouble with girls and wondered if he might be gay?

She asked about former members, but everyone was very vague. There had never been a membership list and Ricky had been correct about the extensive use of aliases.

Ricky was not there that night. She suspected he had not told her everything he knew, but she also knew it was too soon to try to contact him again for more information. She left somewhat frustrated. She had some new information, but none of it seemed to be leading anywhere. The only thing she had managed to accomplish was to confirm that Daryl's investigative efforts had been connected with the L and G group.

As she left the parking lot, she didn't notice Jim Harrison sitting in his old white Chevy pickup truck near the door to the meeting room. He had already recorded the license numbers of most of the cars in the parking lot and was waiting for some of the members to leave the meeting so he could talk to them quietly about drug activity in the area.

He'd noticed her car in the parking lot while he was writing down the license numbers. Now he watched her drive out, wondering why she was there. Could she be working the drug angle, too, despite her prior agreement to leave that part of the investigation alone?

Or was she there every Tuesday night, perhaps as a member, not as a reporter? He found himself hoping not, suddenly realizing that it mattered to him. Her taillights disappeared from sight while he kicked himself for not stopping her before she left. He could have asked her out for coffee, found out what she was doing, maybe delivered another warning about getting involved in a police matter. Maybe she would have told him why she was there without him having to come out point blank and ask her.

He sighed. Maybe it was just as well. A cop and a reporter? That was one relationship that would never work out. And Harley Watson would never stand for one of his people socializing with any reporter – but especially not Sheila Fernelli.

* * *

Later that night, Fred arrived at Ryan's house in the Volvo to discuss the latest incident. The three men sat in the living room, Ryan in his recliner and Doug and Fred sitting together on the couch near the exhaust fan.

"I think I should start coming to the studio with you every day, Ryan," Fred said soberly after he was filled in. "I can do the research at night. And we won't even get into why you were alone in the first place," he added with a wry glance in Doug's direction, "but it's not going to happen again." He took a sip of a beer.

"I still don't think he wants me dead," Ryan argued. "He's had two clear chances to kill me if he wanted to, with the drugs last week and then today, when I was alone in the shower."

"Doesn't matter if he wants you dead or not. Until we find out what's going on, Ryan, I don't even want you going to the bathroom alone at that studio. You understand? He's getting bolder, coming into that dressing room when you were in it. You don't know what he'll do next." His face was stern and professional. This was his area of expertise and he was not backing down on this point.

Ryan glanced at Doug, who was fidgeting uncomfortably, and said, "You're the boss on this, Fred. And I'm really sorry I sent Doug away like that. You two are trying to protect me and I'm not doing much to help."

"I'm sorry too," Doug said. "I shouldn't have gone." He lit a cigarette and blew smoke toward the exhaust fan.

"Don't apologize, Doug," Ryan said. "You know darn well that if you'd tried to argue the point I would have made you go anyway."

"True."

"Okay," Fred said, satisfied with Ryan's quick acquiescence. "That's agreed. Now, the question is, do we still want you staying at the condo alone. I'm not sure what to do about that."

"Fred," Ryan replied, "everything that has happened has happened at the studio, not here. There's nothing to connect me to Doug's condo at all. I think it will be okay for me to be there. It's gated and has security."

"I'd sure like to bait this guy over here where I could get him," Fred mused. "And I'd rather I was the bait than you. Well, let's keep to that plan for now. I'd like Doug to go stay with you, but that would leave me here alone and I think it's more likely if something was going to happen it would be here not there."

"Fred," Ryan said, "you've been digging into this for four days now. Do you have any theories at all about what motive anyone could have for trying to hurt me? I mean, even if you don't have a suspect, what's your thoughts on why anyone would do this?"

Fred lit a cigarette before answering. "Usually something like this is going to be motivated by greed, jealousy, or revenge."

"How do you mean?" Doug asked, moving the ashtray to his knee where Fred could reach it. "Nobody could profit from this."

"Well, the big unknown is what this person's intentions are. If he's playing with Ryan before he kills him, that's a different situation than if he's just trying to mess with his head and scare him."

"You think this could actually lead to a real attempt on my life?" Ryan asked. "Not just a series of pranks?"

"It's possible. So let's look at that scenario. Someone really is planning to kill you and is testing the waters a bit beforehand either to torment you or to try to see what is the best approach to do it and get away with it. So the question is, why would they do that? Well, who could possibly profit financially if you died?"

"Nobody," Ryan said. "Well, Doug, I guess," he added. "He's the sole beneficiary on my will. If I died, he would get everything."

"Your ex-wife wouldn't get anything?"

"Nope. She doesn't even get alimony. And that was her decision. The divorce was amicable and she received a large settlement at the time."

"No kids?"

"No."

"So it's only Doug who would get anything if you died. Not Tony or anyone in your group?"

"No. Tony will get a percentage of my royalty income forever on everything I've done since he became my manager, but that's whether I'm dead or alive."

Fred turned to Doug. "You want him dead for some reason?" he asked with a wink.

"Only some of the time," Doug replied with a smile, flicking ashes into the ashtray.

"Okay, the other possibilities are that someone wants revenge for something or is jealous of you."

"Fred, a lot of people could be jealous of my success, but I have no idea who would want revenge for anything. I have never knowingly hurt anyone, never had any affairs with married women, haven't even broken any hearts lately. Hell, I've been recovering from a head injury for the past seven months. I haven't had any opportunity to piss anyone off."

"Ryan, there's one other possibility that has been bothering me."

"What's that?"

"That detective that was here the other day, asking about the murder."

"What about him?"

"He wanted to know if you'd seen anything before your accident."

"Yes, but I hadn't."

"What if the killer doesn't know that?"

"Huh?"

"If the detective connected that you were there when the kid was buried," Fred explained, "maybe the killer did too. If he thinks you saw him and can identify him, there's another motive for murdering you."

Ryan thought about the green unicorn of his nightmare but said nothing about it. "Wouldn't he assume if I'd seen him that I would have already told the police?"

"I don't know," Fred admitted. "It was just a thought. Tell me about what happened back then. I didn't pay much attention to the news reports at the time because I didn't find out until two months later that you were Doug's brother."

"Maybe Doug should tell you," Ryan said. "Mostly I was unconscious that day. All I know is that after we decided to hunt separately, I rode around looking for deer with the binoculars. I was heading down a hill when I had to duck a tree branch and that's the last thing I remember about that day. But I never saw anyone other than Doug up till that point, although I know there were other people out there. You want to fill in the rest of it, Doug?"

Doug took a sip of his martini before answering. "That was the longest day of my life. I had left Ryan with an agreement to meet back at the trail crossing at noon. I rode off down one trail and he took another. I hunted for about three hours, I guess, but only saw one deer, and it wasn't a buck, so I turned back to meet Ryan as we'd arranged. I was a little late getting to the crossing and Ryan wasn't there, so I rode back to the trailer. I found his horse there and rode back down the trail to look for Ryan. Ran into Howard Vincent, the hunter who had found Ryan, and used the cell phone to call the sheriff to send a helicopter." He omitted mentioning seeing Daryl Walker since Fred already knew it and he didn't want Ryan to know.

"There was a little girl there, too, wasn't there?" Fred asked. "That girl you called the other night?"

"Yes," Doug continued. "Howard led me back to where his daughter and Ryan were. Ryan was unconscious, had a big gash on his forehead. It wasn't until the next day that I heard the cop figured out the horse had run him under a tree branch. The helicopter came awhile later with rescue workers and that detective. He wouldn't let me in the helicopter with him, so I had to ride out. I called the ranch to come get the horses and drove the truck to Denver. By the time I got to the hospital, he was already in surgery. I managed to find the operating theater and watched part of the operation before someone made me leave. But I watched them drilling into his skull to put in a drain." He shuddered. "I still think of that every time I shave. The buzzing sound that drill made was the same pitch as my electric razor."

Ryan startled slightly. "Buzzing sound?" he asked, remembering the buzzing sound in his nightmare.

"Yes," Doug replied, "like I said, the exact same pitch as my razor." He continued the story, "A few hours later, the doctor told me he'd come through the surgery just fine, but wasn't coming out of the anesthetic. I had to deal with the press that evening. My cell phone battery had died with all the calls I made to Tony that afternoon and I went to the lobby to find a pay phone so I could check my voice mail and there was a whole herd of reporters there."

Ryan smiled. "And I know how much you love reporters."

"You got that right. But I told them what I knew, mostly to get rid of them. Anyway, the next morning, he was still in a coma. I was basically a basket case at that point. I called Tony and asked him to handle the press and refused all phone calls at the hospital. Told the hospital to refer all inquiries to Tony. I stayed with Ryan even though he didn't know I was there. All I could think of was that if he were going to die, he wasn't going to do it with only strangers around. They set up a cot in his room for me once they saw I wasn't going to leave."

"It must have been quite an ordeal for you," Fred said quietly. "He was in the coma for five days?"

"Yes. By the third day, doctors said he was improving and I began to take heart. I started talking to him almost nonstop, trying to talk him into waking up. I worked on songs there. I tried joking with him. It sounds slightly lunatic now, but I was alone with him in a private room the whole time, and the hospital staff only came in about once an hour or so to check his vitals."

"I've heard doctors encourage family members to talk to coma victims," Fred said. "They say hearing is the first sense to return."

"Well, it's probably true. The fifth day I was writing a song I was going to call *When Your Horse Yells 'Duck,' Do It.* I guess it finally got through to him, because I was saying the lyrics out loud and all of a sudden I heard him say, 'I think it sucks.' I almost jumped out of my skin. It was the first thing he'd said since the morning of the accident. I wasn't sure if I should hug him because he was out of the coma or knock him back into it for being rude." He smiled over at Ryan.

Ryan, however, was lost in his own thoughts, realizing that here was another clue to the bizarre recurring nightmare he was still having nearly every night. He had not had it the previous night, he realized, when he had slept alone in Doug's condo and wondered why.

"How long was he in the hospital after he woke up?" Fred asked.

"About another week. We let Vincent and his daughter come see him the second day. She was a big fan of his, and her father said she was having trouble sleeping, and when she did sleep, she'd have nightmares about Ryan dying. She had stayed with him for two hours trying to keep the snow off him until her dad and I got back there, and she was afraid he was going to die because she didn't keep him warm enough. Neither of them were getting any sleep, she was that upset."

"Poor kid," Fred said.

"That's why we felt it best that she be able to see for herself that he was okay. Anyway, Ryan was released a week later, after that other attempted drugging incident I told you about, and then spent a month in the rehab center. We came back to Los Angeles after that. I stayed with him for the first month after he got home, then went back to Denver with you after Christmas."

"You know," Fred said, "if the drugging incident in the hospital is related to what's been going on here, my theory may well be correct — that this is related to the murder of that boy."

"The police thought that drug mix-up was an accident," Ryan said, looking at Fred uneasily. "If you're right, that would suggest there is a murderer on my crew, who somehow got access to me in the hospital last year," he said flatly. "How could that be?"

"More importantly, who could that be?" Doug countered.

"I don't know," Fred said. "If the boy was killed in Colorado, then the killer had to have been there last October. I haven't found any indication any of them were. Just the two of you."

"Well, that's a dead end," Ryan said with a sigh.

"Well, I wasn't specifically looking for that so I've got some more digging to do. Of course, another possibility is that the killer isn't on your crew but is using someone on your crew to get to you. And if that's what's going on, it could be anyone." Fred crushed out his cigarette. "I guess all we can really do is keep you as safe as we can while you finish up the editing."

CHAPTER 32

"WELL, HARLEY, YOU were partly right," Jim Harrison said Wednesday morning.

"Right about what? The mugging victims were all mules?"

"No, but I managed to find another boy from that L and G group who was approached by a man about transporting drugs."

"He wasn't a mugging victim?"

"Nope. His name is Fernando Garcia, and he said a man followed him home one night and said he had a job for him. Garcia was looking for a job at the time, so he talked to the man."

"He have a name?"

"No. He said the man was about five-eleven, dark hair, slender. Full beard and mustache. Wore a black ball cap, pulled down over his forehead. Garcia thinks the beard may have been fake."

"So what was the job?"

"The man asked if Garcia could ride a horse. Garcia said he could. The man asked if he wanted to make some money picking up some stuff on horseback and delivering it somewhere. Garcia asked if it was drugs. The man said he would find out the details only if he agreed to do it, that it wasn't anything dangerous. He said Garcia would earn two hundred dollars, cash, and could do that every weekend if he wanted to."

"What did Garcia say?"

"He told the man he wasn't going to do anything illegal. That's when the man asked how Garcia would like it if everyone found out he was a flaming queer." Jim looked at Harley. "And Garcia told him he'd rather be known as a flaming queer than a patsy for a drug operation. At that point, Garcia turned and ran to his house and called the police."

Harley stroked his chin thoughtfully. "Naturally, the man was long gone by the time the cops got there."

"Worse than that, Harley. The cops never showed up at all."

Harley shook his head. "No wonder those people don't trust us. Damn it, Jim, I don't like fags any better than any other red-blooded American male, but refusing to take reports on drug activity from queers isn't the way to combat moral turpitude."

"Harley," Jim said tersely. "Will you listen to yourself?"

"What?"

"Queers. Moral turpitude. You don't like fags. What was it you said the other day? Thank God for the other ninety percent? Damn it, Harley, I may be totally out of line here, but sometimes your attitude is no better than the city cops!"

Harley stared at his detective. "You are out of line," he said coldly. "But don't let that stop you. Say what's on your mind."

Jim shifted uncomfortably. "They're human beings, Harley. They have rights. Sometimes they need help. And it's pretty disgusting that you're willing to use them to get evidence of drug crimes, but deep down you really wish they didn't exist. Same with women. You've got a chauvinistic attitude about women. You think they're inferior, and shouldn't be taken seriously. You make it very hard for me to do my job with an open mind, Harley. I'm tired of pretending I agree with you." He paused a moment for breath. "Anyway, that's what's on my mind. If you want to fire me, go ahead."

Harley resisted the impulse to take the suggestion. Instead he asked, "How long have you felt this way, Jim?"

"I guess ever since I realized that Sheila Fernelli was beating me to potential sources because she didn't have to check with you first."

"Sheila Fernelli."

"Yes, Sheila Fernelli. She's made some pretty good guesses here, because she's willing to look at this thing from angles you'd rather I didn't pursue."

"Ryan North."

"Yes, Ryan North. I didn't want to tell you this, Harley, but I have a feeling there's more to that story than meets the eye."

"You do."

"Yes, I do."

"I can't agree."

"You weren't there, Harley."

"And you were."

"And so was Sheila Fernelli."

There was silence in the room while Harley struggled to maintain his control. Jim Harrison had never stood up to him like this before, and Harley wasn't quite sure what to do about it. "I have a lot of respect for you, Harrison. I thought it was mutual. Is there anything else you want to say to me?"

Jim swallowed hard. "No. I'm sorry I had to say what I did, Harley, but that's how I feel. Now that you know how I feel, do you want me to stay or leave?"

Harley Watson looked at his star investigator. Jim was thirty-five, experienced, highly trained, and, Harley recalled, fair. It was one of the qualities Harley liked to brag about when talking about Jim to other sheriffs at law enforcement gatherings. He had always felt lucky Jim had wanted to work for him instead of staying in the big city where he could have made more money and worked nine to five instead of being on call twenty-four hours a day. He had even hoped Jim might succeed him as sheriff someday. Could it be that Jim was already a better lawman than Harley?

He pulled away from Jim's unwavering gaze, shifted some papers on his desk, then looked back. "Am I really that bad?" he asked finally.

"I'm sure you don't mean anything by it, Harley," Jim replied. "But there is a recurring theme running through a lot of our conversations. Sort of like people who don't think they have prejudices but they enjoy a good Polish joke. I don't think you realize how your comments sound sometimes."

"Old habits die hard, Jim. Much as I'd like to boot you the hell out of here right now, I suppose you're right. I guess it's a good thing you're the one doing the investigating, not me." He paused a moment. "Is this why you left Denver P.D.?"

Jim nodded, mutely.

"Arlo's another sexist pig like me?"

"Far worse. Racist and sexist. Openly discriminates. He makes you look like a boy scout." He hesitated. "I had to leave, Harley. It wasn't just him. It was even worse at my first precinct. We had a gay-bashing incident perpetrated by cops that got pushed under the rug by my own captain. I couldn't be a part of it any more. Made me sick. The whole chain of command was the same way."

Harley nodded. "Here it's just me. You've got guts, Jim. Your old man would be proud." He shoved the file across the desk. "This is your baby. Handle it your way." Harley pushed back from the desk, picked up his hat and coat, and walked out the door.

CHAPTER 33

DETERMINED TO PROVE to Jim Harrison that she was right about Ryan North's brother, Sheila drove to the hospital, hoping to find someone who would remember something about him that might be helpful.

She knew from Jerry Overholt's unguarded comment that Doug Norton had been at the hospital day and night while Ryan was recovering from the accident. Surely someone had gotten to know him during that time.

She started with the ICU nurses, but was told that Ryan had been in their area for less than twenty-four hours before being moved to a secured area to cut down on reporters trying to see him. There was something about the way that information was given to her that made Sheila beat a hasty retreat lest the nurse decide she was being entirely too intrusive and call security to escort her out, as they had done with three tabloid photographers seven months previously.

The nurses had mentioned the fifth floor, though, and Sheila went there next. The isolation ward, where Ryan North had spent five days in a coma and a week asking why he was there, was empty. She located the nearest nurses' station and asked if they knew the names of any of the nurses who cared for Ryan North. "I'm trying to find Doug Norton," she explained. "His business partner. I understand he spent some time here while Ryan was in the hospital and I need to interview him for a follow-up story we're doing on North's recovery."

This time she hit pay dirt. "If it's Doug Norton you're interested in, you should talk to Rita McConnell," she was told. "Rita probably knew him better than anyone else. She might know where to reach him."

"Where can I find her?" she asked, trying not to appear too eager.

The nurse glanced at her watch. "Probably out on the fire escape, sneaking a smoke. She's on break and that's where she usually goes." She pointed down the hall to the exit door.

"An alarm isn't going to go off if I don't use a key, is it?"

"If she's out there, the door will be blocked open. It doesn't open from the outside, so don't let it shut behind you or you'll have to walk downstairs to get back into the building."

"Thanks for your help," Sheila said, then walked quickly to the indicated door. She found it blocked open with a brick and pushed it open. A blonde woman, who appeared to be a little younger than Sheila, stood on the balcony smoking a cigarette. "Rita?" she said tentatively. "Can I talk to you for a minute?"

The woman turned around and gave her a questioning glance. "About what?"

Sheila stepped through the door and closed it against the brick. "I'm Sheila Fernelli," she said. "I'm a reporter for the *Rocky Mountain Chronicle*. We're doing a follow-up on Ryan North's accident and recovery and I was hoping you could help me locate a friend of his, Doug Norton."

Rita blushed, then tried to cover it up by turning away and pulling on her cigarette. "I don't know where he is. Why would you think I knew where he was?"

"One of the nurses told me you knew him best. She didn't explain why. I'm sorry if I stepped into something here. Was there a problem between you?" Not having a clue what was going on, Sheila wasn't sure how to respond to Rita's sudden evasiveness.

Rita didn't answer for a moment, then laughed and said, "I don't know why I'm being so silly. The whole thing was all in my head anyway."

"What was?"

Rita turned back to face her, the awkwardness gone. "Doug and I spent a lot of time out here, smoking cigarettes, every day for two weeks. Sometimes I'd join him for coffee in the cafeteria, too. He seemed lonely. Sometimes we'd talk and sometimes we'd just look at the lights and smoke. I'm not supposed to smoke out here, but I'm the only smoker on the floor so they put up with it. And nobody wanted to tell

Doug he had to go downstairs to do it. So we became buddies, I guess. Except I thought it might be more than buddies. I used to flirt with him, and he was always sweet about it, never gave me a hint he wasn't interested or that I was stepping out of line. I thought he liked me, too. Except he never flirted back. I was too dense to realize that at the time."

"So what happened?"

"I made a fool of myself. I came onto him a little, the night before Ryan was supposed to move to rehab. Again, he was very sweet about it. Told me he was flattered but he wasn't looking for a relationship."

"Do you think he had a girlfriend already?"

"I'm almost certain he didn't. He never called anyone, and nobody came to see him. Even the few times his cell phone rang, he never took a call. I saw him check his voice mail a few times but he never returned a call, except when the Vincents wanted to visit Ryan, and they're the only visitors he had the whole time he was here. You know, the people who found him in the woods. If Doug Norton had a girlfriend, they must have a pretty unusual relationship to go two weeks without speaking."

"Maybe they'd broken up."

"I don't think so. I don't think there was anybody else. I finally decided I wasn't his type, or he thought I was too young or something. Looking back on it, he treated me more like a sister than like an available member of the opposite sex."

"How old is he?"

"He said he was twenty-nine. I'm twenty-five. Maybe he goes for older women, although from what I heard around here, it doesn't sound like he ever gave anybody else a second glance either. But he was probably too worried about Ryan." She sighed. "I know we're not supposed to get involved with patients, but this was a nice, good-looking single man living here for two weeks who wasn't a patient. I guess I got carried away with some fantasies."

"You said Ryan North left for rehab the next day. Did you ever see Doug after that day?"

Rita's face clouded over. "Ryan didn't leave the next day. He didn't go for two more days, not until after the investigation."

Sheila decided to play dumb. "Investigation?"

"A few minutes after I made a fool of myself, someone tried to kill Ryan. I think Doug knew who it was, too, but wasn't talking. He lied about going into Ryan's room, but I saw him. I hated having to tell the police that, but it was true. When I first said it, I didn't know he'd already told them he hadn't been there. Then I didn't know what to do."

Sheila's heart was pounding. Could the police be wrong? "What happened then? Didn't the police believe you?"

"The problem was that I didn't see his face, I only saw him from the back. Then I went into the restroom, the one near the elevator. When I came out, I got a glimpse of him getting onto the elevator. I didn't want to ride down with him right after I made a pass at him, so I waited for the next one. About twenty minutes later, Ryan found the pills in his room and called the nurse to see what they were. Luckily he was smart enough to realize they weren't the same pills he'd had before. I guess he really hates taking any kind of drugs. The medication nurse said she had to argue with him to get him to take the antibiotics and anti-convulsives after they took the drain out of his head. You know, after he was out of the coma. Before that, he got his meds through the IV."

"Why did Doug deny being in the room? Especially once he knew you'd seen him?"

"I don't know. As I said, I think he may have seen who did it but didn't want to say. Maybe he was afraid."

"Or maybe he put the pills there himself."

Rita looked down at her cigarette that had burned itself down to the filter while she talked. She pushed it into the coffee can full of sand and turned to glare at Sheila. "I can't believe he did that. I can believe he went in and out of the room and either did or didn't see who put them there, but I can't believe he did it himself. If he could try to kill his own bro – " she broke off with a stricken look on her face. "Oh, shit, you're a reporter. He'll have a fit if he finds out I said anything."

"It's okay, Rita. I already knew they were brothers. What were you going to say?"

"If he could try to kill his own brother after holding that vigil next to his bedside all those days, he must have been on drugs himself. And I'm no judge of character at all."

"Could he have been on drugs?"

"Not without my knowing it. I used to work in a detox ward. I know all the symptoms, and he had none of them."

"You're sure you weren't blinded by your feelings for him?"

"No," Rita snapped. "No way. I may have made a fool of myself, but I'm still a professional. That was part of what attracted me to him, that I knew he was clean."

Sheila sighed. "Well, I still need to talk to him. Do you know any way I could get his address or phone number?"

"Not from anyone here. It's probably in Ryan's file, as next of kin, you know, but you'll never see that without a court order." Abruptly, she turned. "I gotta go. My break was over five minutes ago."

"Thanks, Rita."

"You'd better not print anything I said."

"I won't. The story's about Ryan North, not his brother."

CHAPTER 34

S HEILA FERNELLI'S PHONE rang at 8:05, just after she had arrived at her desk at the *Rocky Mountain Chronicle*. "This is Sheila," she said into the receiver.

"Hello, are you the reporter who's been writing about the Daryl Walker killing?" a male voice inquired.

"Yes. Who is this?"

"I – I'd rather not say. I was wondering if you could tell me what the latest news is. I don't live in Colorado, so I haven't heard anything other than that the body was discovered and identified."

"Well, yesterday's paper carried an interview I did with an anonymous source. I found out that Daryl had been attending Lesbian and Gay meetings, and had been doing something for a man identified only as Peter. My source said he really wasn't sure if Daryl was gay, or just going through one of those adolescent sexual identity crises." She explained what Ricky had said about boys who would panic when another man actually tried to seduce them.

"Was he molested before he was killed?"

"The coroner says no. The sheriff put out a story yesterday that says that Daryl may have been involved with transporting drugs from a rendezvous point on the mountain, but he hasn't talked to my sources, and I personally think he's grasping at straws."

"You think the sheriff is wrong?" the still-unidentified voice asked.

"I think my source was on to something. If Daryl found himself in a sexual situation and panicked, the other man, maybe this Peter, may have had to kill him to keep from being charged with attempted rape or something. I'm not sure what the law is, but Daryl was a minor and Peter may have been a grown man. And remember, Daryl was the senator's son. No way would Peter have gotten off without going to jail." She hesitated a moment, then continued, "Daryl also was a reporter for the school paper. He told a number of people that he knew something damaging about some public figure, or a relative of a public figure. He never told anyone who it was, though, or what damaging information he had."

"Do the police have any suspects? I heard that Ryan North was … questioned. What can you tell me about that?"

Sheila was reluctant to discuss that, having been thoroughly admonished by her editor to keep North's name out of things unless the sheriff proved a connection. "Uh, he denied any knowledge of the murder," she began slowly. "There's no proof of his involvement."

"But what is being alleged?" the voice persisted.

Sheila glanced around to see if anyone was listening to the conversation. Her training told her to be cautious of giving information to an anonymous caller, but she couldn't help feeling flattered by the fact that someone seemed to be genuinely interested in Sheila Fernelli's opinion for a change. In a conspiratorial whisper, she said, "It just seems to be one hell of a coincidence that he could have been so close to the scene, able to see it for sure, and possibly able to hear something, yet he says he knows nothing. It's like he's covering up for someone, you know? How could he not at least have seen someone? He was looking for deer and he had binoculars. He should have been glassing the entire area."

The caller was silent for so long that Sheila wondered if he had hung up. "Hello?"

"I'm sorry, I'm still here. Can you tell me if the sheriff thinks – uh, Mr. North – is involved?"

"No, the chauvinistic pig doesn't listen to women. Every time I bring up the subject, he speaks to me in the most condescending way and tells me I'd better not print what I know, and I – " Sheila broke off suddenly, realizing she had said far more than she should have. "I'm sorry. I'm a bit touchy this morning. Is there anything else you wanted?"

"No-o-o," the voice said slowly. "Thank you very much." The caller hung up.

Sheila replaced the phone in the cradle and stared at it thoughtfully, wondering what non-Colorado resident had such an interest in the case. Or was it Ryan North the caller really was concerned about?

Harley Watson picked up the telephone receiver and pressed line two to take the incoming call on Jim's line. Jim was expecting the lab to call with the results of the test on the horse hairs and had asked Harley to cover the phone for a few minutes while he walked over to the courthouse to get a warrant signed. "Watson," he answered gruffly without thinking.

"Sheriff? Uh, I'm sorry, this is Sheila Fernelli. I was trying to reach Jim … Detective Harrison. Did they transfer me to the wrong line?"

"No, Miss Fernelli," he replied, bristling at the sound of her voice. "He's out right now. What is it this time? Have you found evidence that Elvis Presley was involved, too?" *Oh, hell, I'm doing it again*, he thought, remembering his conversation with Jim Harrison. He picked up a copy of *Police Procedure* Magazine and thumbed through it distractedly, pausing at an ad showing a well-built policewoman modeling the latest in uniforms.

"Look," Sheila said, "I'm just trying to be a good citizen, Sheriff. I got an anonymous phone call first thing this morning about the Daryl Walker case. I had the call checked through a source at the phone company, and it came from Los Angeles – from an unlisted number billed to North Star Productions. The man who called was very concerned about Ryan North's possible involvement in the murder."

"Was he, now?" He turned a few more pages and studied a picture of a new 10mm pistol some departments were testing. "And why did this man think Ryan North was involved?"

Sheila hesitated. "He knew Detective Harrison questioned him the other day."

"Well, since Detective Harrison hasn't told anybody about that visit, maybe he read all about it in the *Rocky Mountain Chronicle*." He turned a few more pages. "Is that all?"

"Yes." Deflated, Sheila sighed, then asked, "Will you please tell Detective Harrison I called?"

"The minute I see him. Have a nice day, Miss Fernelli." He knew she hated being called "Miss." He hung up the phone.

"I just hope North doesn't sue the pants off the *Chronicle* over this," he muttered, leaning back in his chair to read the article titled, "How to Keep the Press from Prosecuting your Case."

* * *

Jim Harrison returned alone to the location where the helicopter had been seen the previous fall. Having already hiked in and out of this area once before, he decided to give his horse the exercise this time. He tied Patch well back from the yellow "Police Line" barricade that he had strung earlier to mark the area while he and Clayton had gathered evidence from the possible crime scene.

Watching the ground closely, he walked slowly into the middle of the small clearing. He needed to find evidence – evidence that would lead to the identity of the boy's killer.

The previous search of the immediate area had turned up very little. But Jim was a tracker, and he had come out today to try to put together what might have happened. Assuming the horse manure and pop can had been left the day the boy died, there had to be a trail from the helicopter clearing to the uprooted tree where the body was found.

He pulled out a map of the area and oriented himself. "Now," he said to himself, "if you were a sixteen-year-old boy, expected to pick up the drugs, and for some reason, you wanted to see or talk to someone in the helicopter, what would you do?"

He pictured the boy on a horse while the helicopter landed. The horse would be upset. The boy would have to stay on the horse to control it, otherwise, the horse would have broken loose and run away. Or the kid would have had to stay well back until the chopper landed and shut off the rotor so the horse wouldn't be frightened. That would be more likely. According to his parents, Daryl had only had a few months' worth of riding lessons. The chances of him being able to control a frightened horse were pretty remote. But would he have known that?

"Okay. The kid stays with the horse until the chopper lands. Then he sees the person on the ground, the one who is going to put the drugs in the box." He looked from the place where the horse had been to the place where the box had been found, about fifty yards away, on the other side of the clearing.

He studied the relationship of the location where the horse had waited to the landing site. The horse had been behind some trees. He walked over to Patch and untied him, leading him to where the manure had been found. He tied him up and walked back into the clearing and looked toward the horse. He realized that he could not see the horse from the ground. But he looked up to the sky above and projected the sight lines from a descending helicopter and realized that the horse would have been easy to see from the sky. The trees that concealed the horse from a man on the ground were not tall enough to block the view from the helicopter.

Poor kid, he thought. *He hid here to spy on the drug drop and they saw him anyway.*

He was getting a picture of the scenario. Boy hiding in the bushes, thinking he was going to get a story for his paper, bad guys seeing him from the helicopter, realizing they were going to have to silence him. They probably landed, killed the engine because of the commotion the horse was making, and one of them walked over and hauled him out of the bushes before he could get on the horse and escape. But the horse would have been frightened, and would have been trying to get away from the helicopter. Daryl would have had to turn his back on the helicopter to deal with the frightened horse, to try to hang on to him, or try to mount the animal to get away if he realized he'd been seen. It would have been easy for the bad guys to grab him from behind while he was distracted with the horse.

So where was he killed? Scuff marks which would have indicated the scene of a struggle had been obliterated by the passage of time. And where had the horse been while its rider was being strangled? Jim remembered the coroner's report, which had noted a reddened area on the boy's left wrist. A rope burn? Had the reins been looped over the boy's wrist, leaving a burn mark when the horse pulled back in fright?

274

"Okay, let's pretend the boy was killed near here," he said to himself, surveying the area behind the bushes where the manure was found. "You're a drug dealer. You've suddenly got a stiff on your hands that might be connected to you and your operation. You don't want to leave the body here, and have it be obvious he was killed in connection with your drug activity. You're going to take the body far away from here to dispose of it. Fortunately, you've got a horse to carry it."

Okay, he thought, the killer puts the body on the horse, probably covers it so anyone who might see him from the distance would assume it was a dead deer, and now he's going to ride or lead the horse somewhere. The helicopter is going to leave. The reason they don't just take the body in the helicopter and drop it somewhere into the woods is because of the horse. If they leave a horse running around in the woods, someone's going to start a search for its rider. So someone stays behind to dispose of the body and get rid of the horse ... which meant there were two people involved in the boy's death: the one who disposed of the body and the horse, and the helicopter pilot. And unless there was a second horse somewhere, they had both come in the helicopter. And either of them could be the actual killer.

Jim walked over to the probable site of the homicide and consulted his map. The body had been found over a mile due west of the clearing. He began to walk slowly in a long arc west of the clearing, examining the ground closely. He turned back, moved further west, and walked back the way he had come. Then he turned back, moved still further west, and walked the arc again. He continued this slow, serpentine pattern until he was fifty yards from the clearing. There he spotted a lone hoofprint, frozen in the dried mud in a slight depression in the ground.

He stared at the print for a long time. It was pointed in the right direction. Following an imaginary line to the west, Jim spotted one more track about ten feet away. He turned and walked straight back to his horse, untied him, and walked back to follow the hoof prints, leading his horse by the reins. Somewhere along this old, cold trail, there would be a clue. He just had to keep his eyes open to find it.

He had been leading the horse down a hill and was only about a half mile from the landing site when he stopped at a small ravine. "Oh, heck!" he exclaimed on noting that the hoof prints he followed led straight to the edge of the narrow chasm. "They must have jumped!" He could see that the opposite bank, just three feet away, held the tracks he sought. He looked up and down the gully, trying to find a more passable spot, but heavy fallen timber made the passage on either side of this crossing just as difficult.

"Hope you're part rabbit, Patch," he muttered as he mounted his horse and turned him back the way he had come so he could get a running start.

Patch cleared the gully with ease, but stumbled slightly on landing, throwing Jim to the ground.

Muttering an oath, Jim stood up, unhurt, and brushed dirt off his pants and shirt while Patch stood by, unconcernedly chomping at the grass he was suddenly able to reach.

"Come on, glutton," Jim said affectionately. "And stay on your feet from now on." He bent to pick up his hat from the ground and froze.

There on the ground, glinting in the late afternoon sunlight, was a shiny medallion on a chain. Even a season's snow and rain hadn't dulled the gold plating on the medal depicting the zodiac's Taurus, the bull. Jim studied it carefully, trying to remember his astrology. He had a cousin who was a Taurus. When was his birthday? Oh, yes. It was April 27. So Taurus must run from mid-April to mid-May. He consulted his pocket notebook. Daryl Walker's birthday was May 2. Given that this was not a regular trail, it was unlikely that anyone other than Daryl and his killer had ever had to jump that particular ravine before.

Jim extracted a camera from his saddlebag and snapped pictures of the ravine and surrounding area, showing the location of the necklace, then he pulled out his map and marked the spot. He took a small paper bag and a pen from his pocket, labeled the bag as to date, time, and location, then carefully used the pen to lift the unbroken chain, medallion attached, and slip it into the bag.

Satisfied, he spent a few minutes searching the ground for other items, but found nothing.

"Come on, Patch," he said finally. "At least this hasn't been a total waste of time. Let's see if anything else turns up."

He led the horse slowly down the hill, his eyes never leaving the ground, his ears deaf to the sounds of the forest.

It was much later that day when Jim and Harley examined the medallion under a microscope. A clear thumb print was on the back of the gleaming disk and they grinned at each other triumphantly.

"Well done, Jim," Harley said, clapping him on the shoulder. "That must have been like finding a needle in a haystack."

"I probably would have missed it if Patch hadn't thrown me," Jim admitted. "And that's probably how it got dislodged from the boy's neck. If the other horse was packing double, he probably went to his knees when he landed."

"Probably. Well, the bull on this medal matches the one in that picture Senator Walker provided, and that fingerprint isn't Daryl's so it's a fair bet we've got our killer there."

"Now we just need a suspect, Harley. We know when he was killed, how, probably why and where. We just don't know who did it."

"Too bad the gay community has to hide behind aliases so often," Harley mused. "I have a feeling the solution to all this lies in that organization, but without knowing who else might have been members last year, we'll never find anyone else who might have known anything."

Jim noted the shift in Harley's attitude but refrained from embarrassing Harley by commenting on it. "I'll keep looking, Harley," he said. "Someone out there knew Daryl was working undercover. Someone knows Bobby and Jeff by their real names. Daryl said he had met one of them once before and knew his real name."

"Keep at it, Jim. At least we're off that crazy Ryan North angle. Finally, we're getting some facts."

CHAPTER 35

AFTER TALKING TO THE REPORTER in Colorado, Ryan North decided it was time to do something about the nightmare, find out what it meant once and for all. He called his neurologist on the phone, and the neurologist referred Ryan to see his psychiatrist, explaining that recurring nightmares were more often caused by psychological traumas rather than physical traumas. On hearing who it was who needed the appointment, the psychiatrist, Albert Miller, agreed to see Ryan that afternoon, canceling one additional appointment so there would be no other patients waiting in the lobby when Ryan arrived.

Reluctant to tell Doug the truth, Ryan told his brother only that his doctor wanted him to see his psychiatrist to make sure there were no lingering effects from the LSD. Doug accepted the explanation without comment or question and asked Fred to drive Ryan to the appointment in the Volvo so Doug could continue working with the special effects experts on the editing of the show. He said he would meet them at the house later on.

"Hello, Ryan," the doctor said when Ryan walked into the office, leaving Fred in the waiting room. "It's about time you kept that appointment you made last summer."

"Hello, Dr. Miller," Ryan replied with an embarrassed grin. "I guess I did stand you up last time, didn't I. Sorry. Heck, that was almost a year ago."

"That's okay. I billed you for the appointment anyway. Have a seat. Or would you prefer the couch again?"

Ryan sat in one of the comfortable easy chairs opposite the couch in the corner of the office. The doctor sat to his right in another chair.

"So, Ryan, how have you been since I saw you last?"

"Did you hear about my accident?"

"Your neurologist told me about it this morning. At least the medical facts. I understand there was some amnesia."

"Well, not much. I just don't remember being knocked off the horse. They said I hit a tree branch, but I don't remember it. But I'm afraid I may have seen something important before I hit it. I've been having recurring nightmares. I think the nightmares might have something to do with my missing memory."

"Tell me about it. How long have you been having these nightmares?"

"It started after the accident. I had this recurring nightmare for about a month after I got out of rehab. Then I didn't have it for months. Now it's back again."

"Have you seen a doctor about it before?"

"No. I didn't think it was that big a deal at the time."

The doctor sighed. "Ryan, a recurring nightmare can be a symptom of other problems. You had a head injury. Why didn't you tell your neurologist about it?"

"It just never came up. People have nightmares all the time."

"This started when you were in rehab? Tell me about your recuperation. You were in a coma?"

"Yes. Five days."

"Then what happened?"

"I didn't remember a lot of things right away. I didn't even know I was in Colorado. They kept me in the hospital for another week, and I gradually got my memory back, except for the accident itself. After that, they sent me to a rehab center, where I had to relearn how to eat and dress and all."

"I understand. When did you start having the nightmares?"

"I'm not sure because of the amnesia, but I remember having it once or twice in rehab. I think it took me awhile to realize it was the same nightmare, over and over again. I remember it mostly after I came home to Los Angeles. Doug came to stay with me for another month. I think I was having the nightmare almost every night."

"And you never told your doctor."

"No. The whole thing was so silly. I never even told Doug about it. I woke him up once or twice with it, you know, calling out in my sleep?"

"Yes."

"But I let him think it was just the headaches. Actually, it wasn't really a lie. I always woke up with a headache afterwards."

"And you're having headaches now."

"Yes, but I think it's from stress of working. They said I'd have headaches for up to a year or more after the accident."

"Let's start with the accident, Ryan, so I can put this in a context. When and how did it happen?"

Ryan proceeded to tell him about the interrupted concert tour, his visit to Colorado to see his brother, the hunting trip, separating from Doug and hunting alone, and then waking up in the hospital after being in the coma for five days. "And I've never remembered the accident itself," he concluded. "And nobody saw it happen." He grinned wryly, "And my horse isn't talking."

The doctor chuckled slightly at the last comment. He had been jotting notes throughout Ryan's narration. "Now, tell me about the nightmare, Ryan," he said, turning to a fresh page in his notebook.

"It starts out like I'm hunting, riding through the woods. Then I see a green unicorn throwing branches in a hole, and he also picks up a red beret and throws that in the hole too. I hear a scream and turn to flee, and feel like I'm falling. I tell someone not to go over there, but I don't know who I'm talking to or where I'm talking about. I hear a buzzing sound. Next thing I know the unicorn is talking to me, talking nonsense. Says 'duck,' and the words 'Do it.' I reply that I think it sucks. Then the unicorn gallops off and I beg it not to leave me. That's when I wake up, terrified, sweating, and with a headache."

"And you have no idea what any of this means?"

"I've recently learned that Doug was working on a song while I was in the coma called *When Your Horse Says 'Duck,' Do It* and that I came out of the coma when he was reciting the lyrics to me and the first words I spoke were 'I think it sucks.' So that part of it I understand. The buzzing sound in the dream may have been a memory of them drilling into my skull in surgery, and the screaming sound that may have been a horse's whinny. But I don't understand about the unicorn."

The doctor was thoughtful for a minute, then asked, "Ryan, do you get up after the nightmare or go back to sleep?"

"I usually get up and take a pain pill then go back to bed. It usually happens about an hour after I go to sleep."

The doctor's brow furrowed. "You're sure?"

"Yes. It always does. Why?"

The doctor ignored his question. "When you go back to sleep, does the nightmare come back?"

"No, not that I know of."

"What did your doctor tell you about the amnesia?"

"He said I may never remember the accident. That the memory might not even exist in my brain. Or I could remember all of a sudden some day. Or something might trigger it to come back. I've never been that concerned about it, until now."

"A talking green unicorn throwing branches into a hole," the doctor repeated.

"I told you it was silly."

It was silly, but it had all the markings of a post-traumatic nightmare, and the doctor was puzzled. Post-traumatic nightmares were usually based in some sort of terrifying reality, not in mythical green creatures.

What had happened that was so traumatic Ryan had chosen to bury it in a dream?

"So what do you think, doc? How can I find out what it means?"

"Ryan, you know the brain is very complex. There are no easy answers here. But my best guess is that something very traumatic happened that day, before you were knocked out. Something frightened you badly. I don't think you really have amnesia, I think you're repressing something. Something you don't want to know, don't want to remember. And I don't think the nightmares will stop until you know what it was. What could you have seen?"

Ryan sighed. "That's what I was afraid of. I was hoping you'd tell me it was nothing but hallucinations." He looked at the doctor and finally admitted what he suspected. "I believe I saw a murder, Doctor Miller. There was a body found in that area, and the kid may have been wearing a red cap at the time. Because of the red cap in the dream, I think I may have seen him, and maybe his killer too. But how in the world am I ever going to know who I saw? All I see is a unicorn."

"Have you thought about hypnosis?"

"I tried it once. I can't be hypnotized."

"We'll see about that. I can give you a tranquilizer. That often works with people who resist. Do you want to try?"

"Let me think about it. This could get very embarrassing if it turns out all that happened was my horse and I were frightened by a bear. The business with the red cap could be a coincidence."

The doctor sensed Ryan's retreat. "Ryan, call me tomorrow, okay? No excuses. This is only going to get worse the longer you keep the truth from yourself. There's no reason for you to feel embarrassed. Nobody's going to hold a press conference about it. If you decide you've seen something, it will be up to you what you do with the information. In the meantime, I'll talk to another doctor I know who is a hypnotist. See what he thinks. But I really think you need to do this, Ryan. The nightmare won't go away until you know what it means."

"I'll think about it, doc. I'll call you tomorrow."

He walked into the waiting room and nodded to Fred, who escorted him out to the Volvo. "Everything okay?" Fred asked after they were seated in the car.

"For the moment," Ryan said evasively. "I may need some more tests," he added. He had not yet decided if he was going to go through with the hypnosis or just forget the whole thing.

Fred pulled out into traffic and headed for Ryan's house.

"So, Fred," Ryan started, "how long have you known my little brother?"

Fred gave Ryan a quick, curious glance. "Almost a year," he finally said. "We met last summer." And then he forestalled any further questioning by saying, "He already told you about that. And if he didn't want to give you any more details than what he said the other day, I don't think I should talk about it."

Ryan sighed. "I don't mean to pry, Fred. I'm just worried about him. He's gotten so withdrawn and secretive and we used to be so close."

"For what it's worth, Ryan," Fred said as he merged onto the 405 freeway, "Doug is just fine. You don't need to worry about him. He's just dealing with some personal issues. When he's ready to talk to you about it, he will."

They drove the rest of the way in silence.

The guard handed Ryan a FedEx package through the window of the car when they arrived at his house. Ryan stayed in the car until Fred entered and checked the house, where he found Doug already waiting for them. Ryan had started reading the enclosed letter when Doug came to the front door and called to him to come on in the house.

"What's that?" Doug asked when Ryan came through the door with the opened letter in his hand and the FedEx box full of newspapers under his arm.

"Letter from Jerry."

"Overholt?"

"Yes. Haven't heard from him for quite awhile. He sent a bunch of papers for the scrap heap."

"Papers? Why would your name be in the paper now? He already sent you all the articles about your accident last year."

"I don't know." He sat in his usual chair with the package from his former boss and pulled out the stack of newspapers. "Humph," he snorted. "It's about that boy's murder."

"What?" Doug asked, trying to mask his alarm. "What does that have to do with you?" He sat on the sofa, glancing nervously first at the pile of newspapers that Ryan had dropped on the coffee table, then over at Fred, who walked over and sat next to him and touched him reassuringly on the arm.

Ryan did not notice the gesture. "I don't know. Let me read it." He picked up the oldest paper and read the article Jerry had circled with a yellow highlighter. "It's nothing," Ryan said. "An article about the rescue team. The same people who carried me to the helicopter must have carried out the boy's body, that's all. They mentioned some of their previous rescues, and my name is there."

"So what are all the other articles about?"

Ryan glanced through them one by one. "Mostly more of the same, just pointing out that my accident happened in the same area." His brow furrowed. "This one almost sounds like they think I had something to do with it. Wonder what that's all about. That detective sure didn't give me any hint he thought I was a suspect."

Doug pulled out a cigarette and lit up, relaxing slightly. "Fucking cops never play straight."

"Stop bad-mouthing cops, Doug. I don't know what your problem is, but I wish you'd stop making out like every cop in the world is the enemy."

Doug gave him a sour look but said nothing. He reached over and switched on the exhaust fan for the cigarette smoke.

"I need to go to the condo and get my computer," Fred said. "I have some things to look up and it would be easier if I just moved it over here since I'm at the studio all day and here at night."

"I'll go with you," Doug said quickly.

"No, you won't," Fred countered. "You need to stay with Ryan while I'm gone. I won't be long."

"Sorry," Doug said. "I forgot again. I guess I'll get something together for dinner while you're gone."

Fred stood up and walked to the front door. Ryan looked up from his perusal of the papers in time to see Doug's gaze follow Fred as he left. Ryan glanced at Fred, then back at Doug, and his brow creased slightly with puzzlement. Then Fred was gone and Doug crushed out his cigarette and stood up.

"I'll go put this stuff away," Ryan said. He picked up the pile of newspapers and took them into his study. Curious about the murder investigation, he decided to read through the full articles before adding them to the growing pile of newspapers and magazines on the shelves in the study. He picked up the first story and started reading.

He never got past that story. By the time he read the description of how the boy had been hidden under a pile of branches, he knew without a doubt that he had seen the person who hid him. Ryan's nightmare held the solution to a murder.

The problem was that according to Ryan's nightmare the guilty person was a green unicorn.

CHAPTER 36

JIM HARRISON AND SHEILA Fernelli drove up to Ricky Farrell's home together. Jim knew Sheila had probably been stunned when he called asking for her help in getting some answers from Ricky. She had eagerly agreed, knowing she would have an exclusive when the murder was solved if she helped him with the previously uncooperative boy.

Jim had gotten nothing but lies from Ricky the last time he had spoken to him. While he would have a hard time explaining to Harley later on, Jim knew the clock was ticking and he couldn't waste time trying to beg, threaten, or cajole a scared young man into talking. He needed Sheila's help.

"Ricky," Sheila started after they were seated in the tiny living room of Ricky's shared one-bedroom apartment, "we need to know about Bobby and Jeff, the men who worked on the gay-bashing investigation. I think you know more than you've told us. You mentioned Jeff to me before. Did you also know Bobby?"

Ricky looked nervously at Jim Harrison, then sighed with resignation. "A little," he answered after a brief pause. "Jeff was asked to investigate the beatings. We had a meeting about it and everything to take a vote to pay for a detective. Jeff was the detective. I think Bobby was his lover, but they worked together."

"Who hired Jeff? Someone must know his real name, Ricky. What about your leader? Christy? Did she hire him?"

"The leader back then was Ben Voorhees, but he died two months ago from AIDS."

"I'm sorry to hear that," Sheila said awkwardly. "Was he the one who hired Jeff?"

"Yes. He said he had a friend who might do the work for expenses only. When Jeff came to the meeting for the first time, Ben introduced him as Jeff Stevens, and it was pretty much understood that it wasn't his real name. He promised to try to find out who was ambushing the teenagers and report anonymously to the police. If that didn't get action, he said he would come forth publicly and testify if necessary. He said he'd rather work incognito – is that the right word? – but he was more concerned that whoever was doing it be stopped."

"When did you meet Bobby?" Sheila continued. They had agreed Jim would let her ask most of the questions since Ricky trusted her. So far, he was keeping his promise.

"The same night, but Ben didn't introduce him to us right away. He was just there with Jeff, and as Jeff came around asking us questions about whether we'd been beaten up, he introduced Bobby. He never used a last name but Danny knew Bobby's real name. He told me once that Bobby had visited his school and gave a talk but he never called him anything but Bobby when I was around."

"Did Bobby ask questions, too?"

"Yes, he was asking questions and taking notes too. After a few weeks, they said they were pretty sure they knew who the guy was, but they were trying to get more evidence."

"How were they going to do that?"

Ricky looked at Jim before answering. "I think they were trying to set Danny – uh, Daryl – up as a victim, then follow from a distance and see if anyone took the bait."

Jim spoke up then. "Let me get this straight, Ricky. This private investigator, Jeff Stevens or whatever his name was, planned to use a sixteen-year-old civilian as bait for a mugger? What did he plan to do when the bait was taken, sit back and take pictures?"

"No, Bobby was going to do that, with a video camera. Jeff was going to run the guy off as soon as they had some footage. You see, this guy who was doing this didn't just jump on a guy and start beating. He taunted us first, calling us faggot, asking if we'd like him to ...." His voice trailed off and he flushed before continuing, "That's why they knew they'd have time to get some film before they ran him off."

"How were they going to do that?"

"Oh, you should have seen those two. They were both big, broad-shouldered, stocky guys. And Jeff had a gun. Danny wouldn't have been hurt," Ricky stated positively. "They had it all planned out. Danny told me about it the day I drove him to work. They were going to try it the next Tuesday after the meeting."

Jim spoke again. "Ricky, would you know them again if you saw them? Can you describe them to me?"

"I think so. Jeff was about six feet tall, they both were, actually. And Bobby had blond hair and a beard … not much of a beard, actually. I think he had just started growing it. Jeff had brown hair and was clean-shaven. I don't remember what color eyes either of them had. But they both looked strong, like football players maybe, only not muscle-bound."

"How old were they, Ricky?" Sheila asked.

"Bobby was maybe thirty, I'm not sure. It's hard to say because of the beard, you know? Jeff was a little older, I think. Maybe thirty-five or so."

"What about their vehicles? Did you see what kind of car they drove?"

"Once it was a Corvette and the other times it was a Volvo sedan. Bobby drove the Corvette. Oh – and it had California license plates on it, but the Volvo had Colorado plates."

"I suppose we'd be pushing our luck to ask if you remembered the license plates," Jim said dryly.

"The Corvette had one of those special plates on it. I forgot about that until now," Ricky replied eagerly. "It was something about music." He thought a moment, then exclaimed, "I remember! It was 'SING IT.' I remember now I asked him if he was a musician and he said, no, he had borrowed the car. He did seem kind of flustered that I noticed the plate. And he never drove the Corvette to the meetings after that, they were always in the Volvo."

Jim shook his head, disbelieving. He had seen that Corvette, at Ryan North's home, the evening he had visited there to ask Ryan about the homicide.

"Ricky, when was the last time you saw Jeff or Bobby?" Sheila asked.

"That's the funny thing, Sheila," Ricky answered. "They were around for about three, four weeks then Bobby, Jeff, and Danny stopped coming around at the same time, right after I got out of the hospital. No explanation. They just weren't there. We all figured they'd decided what they were doing was too risky. Ben got sick with pneumonia about that time, so nobody wanted to ask him to call Jeff. But that must have been when Danny — Daryl — got killed. I don't know why Bobby and Jeff stopped coming around. We ended up changing the meeting location and that stopped the beatings for a while, but a couple months later we went back to the college and right away someone else got beat up. It was the week after that when suddenly Jeff and Bobby were back and told us the guy who had been beating us up had been arrested. Turned out it was the brother of the Lakewood High School principal. I haven't seen them since. That was in January."

"Ricky," Jim said, "do you know if Daryl was involved with selling drugs?" He looked straight at Ricky, watching for his reaction.

Ricky looked perplexed. "Daryl? Drugs? I seriously doubt it." After a brief pause, he added, "And I'm telling you the truth this time. If he was selling drugs, he wasn't doing it at the meetings."

"Would you necessarily have known if he were?" Sheila asked, giving Jim a curious glance.

"I would have known." A trace of defiance crept back into his voice. "I don't think I want to answer any more questions about drugs, okay?"

"Okay, no problem," Jim said hastily. "That's not why we're here. There's just one more thing, Ricky. Something we've been wondering about for a long time. Ricky, everyone who knew Daryl swears there's no way he was gay. But I know that men who cross-dress often aren't gay. We haven't released this information, because we thought it would embarrass his family, but Daryl was wearing pantyhose when we found his body. Any idea why?"

Ricky laughed. "So he took my suggestion after all."

"You put him up to wearing pantyhose?" Sheila asked, surprised.

"No, no," he shook his head emphatically, then admitted, "well, maybe yes, I guess you could say so. But not the way you think. The last time I saw him, he was sore from riding a horse that weekend. I told him he should have worn pantyhose under his jeans to keep them from rubbing him raw."

"You're kidding, right?" Jim said.

"Heck, no. I rode a mule down into the Grand Canyon when I was about thirteen and we were told to wear pantyhose under our jeans or bring plenty of salve. Of course, I thought it was just a joke so I didn't do it but my cousin did. Sure enough, I was practically blistered when we got to the bottom and he wasn't sore at all, except muscle soreness. Daryl laughed when I told him that. But he did admit it sounded like a good idea. Sounds like he took my advice."

Jim Harrison stood up. "Well, I guess that solves that little mystery. Sheila, we have all the information we need. Ricky, thank you for your time. I know this wasn't easy for you to do. I appreciate your help. Sheila?" He held the door open for her and they left the apartment.

"Well, Jim," Sheila said, "I helped you with Ricky. Now, what's going on? Harley has been absolutely adamant that I was *persona non gratis* at that sheriff's office. So tell me, why the sudden change of heart? Did you find some evidence about Ryan North, or are you fishing for something else? I know his brother's middle name is Robert; I've known it for a long time. Is he the Bobby Daryl Walker knew?"

Jim's eyes never left the road. "Sheila, you are not to print any of this until after an arrest is made, is that understood?"

"I agreed to that earlier. I'll hold my story and you give me an exclusive upon arrest."

"Okay. Victor North, a.k.a. Doug Norton, is the Bobby Daryl knew. The license plate was the clincher. I saw that car at Ryan's house when I was there."

"What's his connection to the homicide?" Sheila had her notebook open, pencil poised to write something she didn't already suspect.

"I frankly don't know. I don't know what to believe." Jim stopped for a red light and turned to face Sheila. "I don't know what the motive could be. We know there were drugs involved. What we don't know is if Doug Norton was involved with the drugs, or just with Daryl Walker. Sounds like he and Daryl were friends. Why would he kill him?"

"What if he came on to Daryl and Daryl didn't like it? Remember, Daryl wasn't really gay, but did Norton know that?"

Jim turned back to the intersection and saw that the light was green. He pressed the accelerator. "I don't know, Sheila. When I showed Doug Norton Daryl's picture a few days ago, he didn't even flinch. And he didn't admit that he knew the boy. There was no shock or surprise on his face. If he knew the boy as Danny, like Ricky did, wouldn't he show some surprise at being shown the picture and hearing that the boy was the dead son of the senator?"

"He must have seen the picture when the boy was first reported missing, Jim. He probably knew all along it was the senator's kid. But you think he killed him, right? Did he know it was the senator's kid when he killed him, or only afterward?"

"I don't know, Sheila. I still don't see a motive here. Say, I'm going to go by the school now. Ricky said Norton gave a talk at Daryl's school. We'd better find out about that. I assume you'd like to come with me."

"You assume correctly," Sheila replied, relieved to be openly working with him for once, instead of against him.

Jim continued as he turned left onto the road in front of the high school, "I wish we had enough evidence to arrest Norton now, but it's going to take more than this. I can have him picked up for questioning, now that I know he lied to me, but without more evidence, I won't be able to hold him for long. There's obviously *something* going on with him, but all our other evidence points to something else entirely."

One thing he did know was that Harley Watson was not going to be amused when he learned that Jim's quest to discover the identities of Jeff and Bobby had led right back to Ryan North's doorstep – literally.

* * *

After leaving the school, Jim dropped Sheila off and returned to his office to tell Harley what he had learned. Harley's jaw clenched briefly when Jim told him about Sheila's assistance but to the older man's credit, he said nothing. Jim told Harley that Ricky Farrell had identified Doug Norton as "Bobby," and that Evelyn Moore had confirmed it by identifying Doug Norton as the advertising agency representative who had visited Daryl's journalism class the month before he disappeared.

"I think I need to go back to L.A., Harley. Doug Norton obviously is lying through his teeth to me, and now I have a connection between him and the boy. I can't say he's the killer, but there's certainly enough suspicion to question him."

"Christ, Jim," Harley said with exasperation, "I can't believe we're back on Ryan North again. The press is going to have a field day with this."

"Not Ryan, his brother, and we don't need to release that fact anyway. Sheila's the only one who knows, and she's agreed to hold her story until after an arrest. As far as anyone else needs to know for now, Norton works for an ad agency. I have no reason to think Ryan North was involved."

"Unless he's covering up for his brother."

"Good point, but if he is, he's in the wrong profession. He should be an actor."

"Maybe he is, Jim. Maybe he is." Harley was quiet for a minute, debating what to do. "I guess you're going to have to talk to Norton," he said finally.

"I guess I'm going to have to talk to Ryan North again, too. Even if he wasn't involved directly, if he has been covering up, that's obstruction. I'm going to have to find out what he knows. He hinted when I was over there that he might remember something. Maybe he wanted to tell me then but decided to pretend he didn't remember."

The intercom buzzed and Harley pressed the button. "Yes?"

"Sheriff, there's a call for Jim Harrison. Is he with you?"

"Yes, he is. Who's on the line?"

"He says he's Ryan North. Caller ID is blocked so I can't confirm."

Harley looked at Jim. "You want to take this in your office?"

"Yes." He stood and left the room.

"Put it through to Jim's office. He's headed there now."

Back in his own office, Jim picked up the phone and said, "Hello, Mr. North. What can I do for you today?"

"Detective Harrison, I have a problem," Ryan said slowly. "And I don't know what to do about it."

"What's the problem, Mr. North?" Jim asked, leaning back in his chair.

"I think I've been having nightmares about that murder."

"I'm not sure what you mean, Mr. North. I'm not a psychiatrist."

"Oh, I know that. I've already seen my psychiatrist, actually, just yesterday and I talked to him on the phone again a few minutes ago. He thinks I'm repressing something terrifying. The problem is, these nightmares are making me think I actually saw your murderer, and I'm repressing it because it was too awful for me to face."

Jim sat up straight. "Excuse me?"

"I think I saw your murderer."

"Maybe you'd better tell me about it."

"It's insane, Detective. Or maybe I am. In the dream, I'm on a horse, riding through the woods, like I was when I was hunting. I look through binoculars like I did when I was hunting. I see something move, try to look closer, and I see a green unicorn some distance away, throwing branches in a hole. It also picks up a red cap from the ground. Then I hear a scream that might be a horse's whinny and the unicorn's head comes up, like it's startled. I'm afraid it will see me, so I turn my horse around fast, and have a sensation of falling. Then the unicorn turns away and I beg it not to leave me. Throughout the whole thing, I feel sick and scared, like I've seen something terrible and horrifying. Was the body badly mutilated? Could that be what was so horrifying?"

"I shouldn't discuss any details with you at this point, Mr. North."

"Oh, of course, I understand. I need to remember on my own, don't I?"

"Yes." Once Ryan mentioned the branches, Jim didn't need a dream analyst to tell him why Ryan North thought his nightmare was important to the investigation, but he didn't like the timing. "When did you have this nightmare? After I talked to you?"

"No, Detective. This is a recurring nightmare. I had it for the first time a couple weeks after my accident. I had it a few times when I was in rehab, and nearly every night for over a month after I came home. Then

I didn't have it for months. It started again about the time you found the body. I never had a clue what it could mean until the night you came to see me. Since then, I've read some articles about the murder. When I saw that the body had been covered with branches, I knew then that I must have seen something. And you mentioned the boy might have been wearing a red cap. Based on the dream, I'd guess that's why I hit the branch that knocked me off my horse. I was fleeing in shock, afraid I'd be seen."

"You've been having this nightmare for a long time. Have you talked to a doctor about this before now?"

"No. I haven't told anyone, not even Doug. I almost didn't tell you at all, but I've talked to your local reporter and it sounds like I may be under some suspicion in this case. It's pretty clear to me, Detective Harrison, that if I saw branches being thrown into a hole, I must have seen who was throwing them. But I can't remember, and I have no idea where I got a unicorn from, let alone a green one. I know this is no good as testimony, but what should I do?"

"You never consciously remembered anything after you ducked a branch, right?"

"Right."

"So this may be your missing memory. After you ducked the branch, you saw something that frightened you, spun your horse around, or maybe something scared your horse, too, in any event, you hit the branch and never remembered that you'd seen anything."

"That's what I'm thinking. My shrink seems to think so, too. He thinks I'm repressing it. He wants to try hypnosis. I'm not sure what to do."

"That's probably your best bet at this point. For now, while it seems clear to me you probably saw something important, I can't do anything because there aren't any unicorns around here to arrest, you know what I mean?"

"I know. I'm glad you aren't laughing about this, frankly."

"You took too big a risk telling me at all for me not to take this seriously. Try to set up a hypnosis session. I'd like to be present. If you remember under hypnosis who you saw, who that unicorn represents, I want to be the first to hear it."

"Sure thing. I'll call right now and try to set up an appointment. I'll call you back later."

"Thanks, Mr. North. And thanks for calling about this."

Jim walked back into Harley's office. "This is too weird," he said, shaking his head. He flopped down in a chair in front of Harley's desk.

"What happened?"

"Sounds like Sheila's theory was right."

"Jeez, not her again. Which theory is that?"

"Ryan North may be an eyewitness after all. He's been having a nightmare that sounds as if he saw whoever hid that body. I think I told you he never remembered his accident. It may be that the missing part of his memory is coming out in a dream."

"So who buried the body?"

"A green unicorn."

Harley snorted. "Come on, Harrison. What is this, a joke?"

"No joke, Harley. Whoever he saw has been substituted by a green unicorn in this nightmare."

"So his testimony is worthless."

"It is unless we can get him to fill in the blanks under hypnosis. He's going to call his therapist and see if he can get referred to a hypnotist. I'm going to try to be there for the session. If this works, he may be able to give us a description. I don't know what else to do. As soon as I hear when the hypnosis appointment will be, I'll call the airlines and get a reservation back to L.A. right away. And, whether the hypnosis works or not, I still need to have a chat with his lying brother." He stood to leave.

"Fine. And Jim?"

"Yes, Harley?"

Harley looked Jim in the eyes and slightly arched one eyebrow. "Try not to tell your girlfriend where you're going this time, okay? I don't want to read about it in the paper tomorrow."

Blushing furiously, Jim turned without a word and left the office.

* * *

After committing himself to the hypnosis session, Ryan decided to take the weekend off from working and rest up as much as he could. The editing was going well, everything was on schedule, and nothing else had happened at the studio.

His psychiatrist had given him a prescription for a tranquilizer and told him to take one each day so he would be familiar with its effects before the hypnosis session. Ryan had no trouble complying, and spent most of the weekend napping at home, but returning to Doug's condo under cover of darkness each night. He had wanted to ride his horse again, but Fred and Doug overrode his wishes, fearing that the public stable and park would be too hard to secure. "You can ride all you want after we find out who's doing this," Doug insisted. So Ryan gave in and spent the weekend napping and watching old movies on television in his room.

Fred was continuing his search for any hint of a motive for any of Ryan's crew to want to harm or harass him, fearing that as the production wound down, the stalker might make one last desperate attempt to cause real damage to Ryan.

Sunday evening after dinner Ryan finally asked Fred, "Have you had any luck in your research yet? Any thoughts on who's been stalking me?" They had lingered in the dining room drinking coffee while Doug tidied the kitchen.

"One dead end after another," Fred replied. "I'll keep talking to people tomorrow while you're working. We know someone on your crew is our man. But I'm afraid whoever it is has been on their guard around me. I need someone to slip."

"No sign that anyone's been messing around here though?"

"No, and I really wish they would," Fred replied with a sigh.

"Well I don't," Ryan came back. "I told you I don't want either of you filling my coffin. I'd rather this guy just lost interest and went away."

"It's not that simple, Ryan. He goes away now, you let your guard down, and then he's back to finish the job when you least expect it. Far

296

better to flush him out now while we're ready for him." Fred patted his side, where Ryan knew his gun was.

Ryan glanced through the doorway to where Doug was finishing wiping the counters, but knew he wasn't carrying. He was wearing a blue polo shirt with a parrot embroidered on the front. He knew Doug had a gun in his room, but he had never seen him wear it.

"I just hate having you both over here at risk. I know you used to be a cop, Fred, but that doesn't mean you're invincible. And if he comes in here with a gun some night, what is Doug going to do for you?"

"His job is to call nine-one-one," Fred replied. "With the guard out front we should have some warning that there's an intruder on the property. He's carrying a pushbutton alarm that will sound a warning on this receiver here." He showed Ryan a device similar to a pager that he carried clipped to his belt. "Doug has one too."

Doug came into the dining room and joined the conversation. "Fred's a security expert, Ryan. You wouldn't believe the stuff he carries in that Volvo, surveillance equipment, electronic ears, stuff like that." He sat at the table with his own cup of coffee.

"I don't want that guard out there filling my coffin either," Ryan said.

Doug changed the subject. "I talked to Wanda while you were napping. She's been in touch with Cindy Vincent and her father. She'll go with Leo to pick Cindy up tomorrow in the limo like we talked about. She's got all the stuff you wanted her to get. The father decided to let her come by herself. She wouldn't have as much time if he brought her since he has a meeting in the afternoon."

Ryan smiled. "I'm looking forward to seeing her. I've been a bit down lately with all the problems and everything that's happened, but it always makes me feel good to meet my fans, and there's no fan quite like a thirteen-year-old."

"Ryan is a little unusual," Doug explained to Fred. "He actually likes meeting fans, and often answers some of the fan mail personally."

"Probably why he's so popular," Fred said. "In addition to investigating everyone on your crew, Ryan, I've also read a lot about you, which is why I'm so uneasy about what's been happening. I have not found one single negative thing in your past. Everything I've read indicates you are seen as kind, unselfish, and charitable. No disgruntled former employees. No sexual scandals. Clean credit report. Taxes all paid according to your CPA. I just cannot imagine anyone having a grudge against you. Which brings me back to the murder."

"Well, maybe we can put out a news story saying I don't remember anything that happened that day. I don't think my amnesia about the accident itself every got reported in the papers. If the killer is the one doing this, maybe he'll just go away if he knows I can't finger him."

"I'd rather find out who it is and catch him, Ryan," Fred said, "than see him get away with murder."

"Let the cops catch him," Ryan said. "I'm afraid one of us is going to get hurt trying to track this guy down."

"This is what I do, Ryan," Fred reassured him. "I'm staying in touch with your local police. One word from me and a half dozen of LA's finest will be here in minutes. Your local police are very interested in keeping you alive, despite the casual attitude of the ones over at the studio."

"Just be careful," Ryan muttered. "You two want to escort me back to the condo now? We need to get back to work tomorrow, and I have another appointment in the afternoon."

Part V
May 30 – June 1, 1994
The Witness

CHAPTER 37

JIM WAS A LITTLE LATER GETTING to the gate Monday morning than he'd planned to be. Traffic had been bad getting to the airport and he had to wait in line to check his bags. Finally, he was given his claim checks and directed to the gate for the early morning flight to Los Angeles. He got to the gate just ten minutes before boarding time and glanced around the waiting area, debating where to sit. It was his practice to position himself where he could see anyone approaching him, but there was no seating against any of the walls. There were only about a dozen people waiting for the plane, though, and while he debated between a couple of less-advantageous spots, his eye was caught by a familiar head of curly red hair, bent over a paperback book in a seat facing the window. She was alone.

Frowning, he walked over and stood in front of her, saying nothing until she noticed him and looked up. "Jim," Sheila Fernelli said, flustered. "What are you doing here?"

"I was about to ask you the same thing. Nobody but Harley knew I was coming this time. He made a point of ordering me not to tell you where I was going. How did you find out this time?"

"What are you talking about? I didn't know you were going to be here."

"Right. You just happen to be flying to Los Angeles this morning, and for what purpose, may I ask?"

"Actually, I have an interview in Los Angeles this afternoon."

"With whom? Ryan North? His brother? I thought we agreed you were going to leave the homicide investigation to me."

Sheila glared at him with annoyance. "It's not with them, it's with Cindy Vincent. The girl who found Ryan North last year is going to visit him. We got a press release late yesterday afternoon, and I talked my editor into letting me cover it for a human-interest story. Sorry I forgot to copy you on the memo," she added pointedly.

"Isn't this convenient. So you're going to be seeing Ryan North today, and you didn't think you ought to mention it to me, knowing full well, and confidentially I might add, that his brother is a person of interest in my investigation. I thought we had an understanding about this."

"First off, Detective Harrison," Sheila started tersely, getting to her feet so she could glare at him better, "I don't need your permission to do my job. Second, I am not interviewing Ryan North or his brother. Not that it's any of your damn business, but I will go to the restaurant where Cindy is lunching with Mr. North, and I will take a few pictures with their permission, that's all. Then I will meet Cindy later on, at her hotel room, where she will tell me all about it. I will fly home tonight on the red eye. I think she will go back tomorrow. Do you have a problem with any of that? Would you like me to write it down so you can stick it in a report, or maybe you'd like to shove it somewhere else that might be convenient?"

She glared unwavering into his eyes. Jim was aware that a couple of people had glanced their way, but they both had instinctively kept their voices too low for anyone to overhear the conversation. Nevertheless, it was clear from the look on Sheila's face that she was very, very angry, and Jim was suddenly ashamed of having caused it. She was right. She didn't need his permission to do her job. He swallowed. "I'm sorry," he said. "I had no right to question you like that. Truce?" He held out his hand.

Taken aback by his quick acquiescence, Sheila's face softened. She looked at his hand for a moment, then shook it. "Truce." She sat back in her chair.

"Here I've been lecturing Harley about his attitude, then I do something like that," he mused, sitting in the seat next to her.

"You lectured Harley about his attitude?"

"Shouldn't have said that either, should I?" Jim said with a wry grin. "And I better not read it in the paper."

"You won't." She paused. "I suppose after that tirade I just delivered, I'd be completely out of line to ask you why you're going to Los Angeles."

"Yes, you would. And I'd be more out of line to tell you. I told you Harley specifically ordered me not to tell you where I was going."

"Why would he do that? I mean, I understand why he wouldn't want me to know, but why did he feel he had to order you not to tell me?"

"He thinks I told you the last time, and he didn't appreciate that article you wrote. Then I had to tell him you helped me with Ricky, and he jumped to some conclusions. He didn't actually order me not to tell you where I was going. What he actually said was for me not to tell my girlfriend where I was going."

"I didn't know you had a girlfriend," she started naively, then, "Oh. I get it." She glanced sideways at the detective. "He thinks I'm your girlfriend?"

"Looks like it."

"So did you set him straight on that point?"

Jim turned away from her gaze. "No." He glanced back and found her smiling slightly. His hand found hers and held it lightly. "Should I have?"

She felt the warmth of his hand on hers and looked down at it. "I — didn't know. I always thought you thought I was a royal pain in the ass."

"I do … I did, I mean," Jim replied, blushing. "Maybe I changed my mind." He squeezed her hand, then released it. "Sometimes you're okay. For a girl," he added.

Sheila smiled. "Sometimes you're okay for a boy, too. And sometimes," she added firmly, "you're a chauvinist pig like your boss."

"I know. I'm trying."

"Trying to be a pig?"

"No, trying not to be like Harley." They heard an announcement for boarding and stood up. "Looks like the plane isn't full. You want to try to sit together? Or are you flying first class?"

"Hah. Not on our budget. I was lucky they didn't make me take the bus." She reached for her carry-on bag but Jim grabbed it for her.

"Thanks," she said demurely, remembering in time not to insist she could do it herself. "So," she said as they walked down the jet way together, "if I'm supposed to be your girlfriend, does that mean you can tell me off the record what you're doing in Los Angeles?"

"No, it doesn't. It's not that I don't trust you not to report it, it's that I don't want to violate a confidence. The witness I'm seeing could be embarrassed if anyone knew why I was here. It's a bizarre situation, and I can't talk about it until after an arrest has been made."

"But you'll tell me someday?"

"If it turns out the testimony becomes relevant to the case. Otherwise, I have to respect this witness's privacy. I hope you will, too, Sheila. Regardless of whether Harley was right or wrong about us, I'm still investigating a homicide, and you're still a reporter." They walked together onto the airplane and found two seats together near the front. "But there's no reason we can't have dinner together tonight, is there?"

"No reason at all," Sheila replied with a smile. "I'll look forward to it."

* * *

Ryan's secretary, Wanda, had arrived at the studio early Monday morning bringing the set of CD's and other items for Cindy Vincent before leaving in the limo to go pick her up. Doug had asked her to escort Cindy on a studio tour, then bring her to Ryan's dressing room around noon.

She dropped off the gifts in the dressing room and confirmed the lunch reservation at a nearby restaurant when Tony came by and told her the limousine had arrived and was waiting for her outside the studio.

"Thanks. I'll bring her by to see Ryan after I show her around the studio a little."

"Oh, and I have some paperwork in my office for you. Remind me to give it to you before you leave this afternoon."

"Sure thing, Tony."

Cindy was every bit as excited as Wanda expected her to be, and they quickly became friends. They arrived back at the studio around ten-thirty. Accompanied by a studio security guard, Wanda showed her the studio, including the prop room, makeup room, dressing rooms, and she even got permission to take her into the studio where Biff's soap opera was being taped.

After they emerged from the studio during a break, Wanda led Cindy around to the editing room to look for Ryan. Ryan and Doug had already returned to Ryan's dressing room, so Wanda introduced Cindy to Tony DiMartino and they met Walter Hussman, who was still working on the tapes.

"Is he somebody famous?" Cindy asked excitedly as they walked toward Ryan's dressing room.

"Who? Tony? I suppose so. He's been Ryan's manager for the last three years. You might have heard of him."

"Not him, the other one. The blond one."

"The sound mixer?" Wanda replied. "I don't think so. He adjusts all the sounds on the tapes so they sound right on the finished product. You know, so the drums don't end up drowning out the singing, or something like that. He's only been here for about a week or two, I think."

"Oh." Cindy sounded deflated. "He looked familiar. I thought maybe he was somebody famous like Ryan."

Wanda laughed. "Sorry to disappoint you. But you're going to meet Ryan again in a minute. Hopefully that will make up for it. There aren't very many famous stars here today, just the ones shooting that soap opera."

She knocked on the door to Ryan's dressing room, where she knew Doug would be waiting with a camera to take pictures of Cindy with Ryan. Doug opened the door and Wanda led Cindy inside. Ryan was sitting at the table, and he smiled when he saw Cindy. "Hello, Cindy," he said. "Glad you could make it."

Cindy was tongue-tied for a minute until Doug said, "Why don't you go stand by Ryan, Cindy, and I'll take a picture of the two of you together."

"You're Doug, right?" she asked, finally finding her voice. "I met you at the hospital." Her eyes fell on the duck on his shirt. "You're the one who has animals on his shirts all the time."

"Right." He held up the camera as Cindy shyly stepped next to Ryan, who stood up and put his arm around her for the picture. She came just up to his shoulder.

"So, Cindy," Ryan said after Doug had snapped several pictures, "how have you been?"

"Fine," she replied. "Are you all better now?"

"Yes, thanks to you and your dad. I never really thanked you properly at the time. I was still pretty confused for a long time after I woke up. I hope it didn't upset you too much to see me in the hospital with my head all wrapped in bandages, but your dad said you were so worried about me you couldn't sleep."

"I couldn't, Mr. North," she admitted, blushing. "But I felt better after I saw you, even if you were in bandages. I was so afraid you might die because I didn't keep you warm enough in the snow."

"Call me Ryan, Cindy. And you did just fine that day. I'm sure it wasn't easy for you." He smiled warmly at her. "Do you have some friends back home who don't believe you know me?"

"Oh, they believe it because it was in the papers how my dad and I found you, but they're really jealous." She giggled. "Especially Gloria. She's just green with envy. I wish she could have come with me. She's my best friend."

"Well, I'll be coming back some day, and I'll make sure I come by Golden and see you and meet her too. In the meantime, you can share these with her if you want to," Ryan said, pointing to the pile of pictures he had been autographing before her arrival. He picked up the pen and wrote a special one for Gloria.

Cindy's eyes widened as he put the stack of photographs into an envelope. "Oh, Ryan, this is too much. There are enough pictures here for everyone I know. Thank you." She took the envelope.

"You saved my life. This is nothing compared to that. We also have a complete collection of my CD's for you, and Wanda even picked up a new portable CD player with headphones for you, in case you didn't have one already. Your dad will probably appreciate that," he added with a chuckle.

Cindy laughed. "You're probably right."

Wanda smiled as she watched Ryan put the young fan at ease. She knew Cindy would never forget this day as long as she lived. "Ryan," Wanda said, "the reporter who's doing the story on Cindy for the local paper over there will be at the restaurant to take a picture for the paper."

"Fine. You told him I wouldn't do an interview, right?"

"It's a woman, and yes, I told her that. She plans to interview Cindy at her hotel later. She'll take a couple pictures, then leave."

"Okay with me." He smiled at Cindy. "You're going to be famous again." She smiled back, her eyes sparkling with excitement.

A little later, Ryan, Wanda, and Doug took Cindy to lunch before the limo took her back to her father. Doug's camera assured Cindy that she would have plenty of memories to share with her friends in Denver, and Ryan promised to autograph some of the pictures after they were printed and mail them to her. The reporter, Sheila Fernelli, did as promised, taking a couple of pictures of Cindy at the restaurant with Ryan, then reluctantly retreating, promising to see Cindy later.

By the time Cindy Vincent left the studio, she was more in love with Ryan North than she had ever been, and she knew he would come visit her when he got a chance. Reluctantly, she said goodbye to all of them at the studio door, then turned and followed the uniformed driver to the limousine, her arms full of gifts from her idol.

Wanda started to leave the studio by a side door after Cindy left in the limo to meet the reporter for the interview. She was halfway to her car when she remembered that she had forgotten to pick up the paperwork Tony had for her. She walked back and headed for the editing room. She saw a man walking away from her and called out, "Doug, is Tony in there?"

The figure turned around and she realized it was not Doug, but Walter Hussman. "Are you talking to me?" he asked.

"Oh, sorry, I thought you were Doug. He was here a minute ago." She smiled at him. "That young lady we had here thought you were somebody famous. She said you looked familiar."

"Oh, really?" he asked with interest. "Who was she, anyway? One of Ryan's fans?"

"You could say that. She's the girl who found Ryan unconscious the day of his accident."

Walter's brow furrowed. "I thought he was found by a deer hunter."

"She was with her father, Howard Vincent. He was hunting but she was with him."

"Was she now?" Walter looked down the hallway. "She live in Denver?"

"Yes, well somewhere near there, anyway. Town of Golden. I think this was her first time in Hollywood. It was fun taking her around the studio, but I think she expected to see a bunch of movie stars around here. You must have reminded her of one."

"Well," he replied with a chuckle, "If I'd known pretty little girls would mistake me for a movie star maybe I would have trimmed my beard and cut my hair sooner."

"It sure makes you look different," Wanda agreed.

"I thought it was a good idea. Everyone else around here is so conservative, I felt a little self-conscious. Anyway, Tony's in there with Ryan," Walter replied, pointing to the editing room. "We've got a problem with one headset," he explained. "I'm going to the booth to get my other one." He turned to walk down the hall.

Tony directed her to his office, where he had left the papers on his desk. She was reading through them to see if she had any questions for Tony before she left when she heard a voice through the wall. She wasn't that familiar with the studio layout, but didn't remember there being a sound stage on the other side of the back wall. It sounded like someone was rehearsing lines for a show. Curious, she listened for a few minutes, wondering why the actor didn't have anyone to read the lines for the other character in the scene, or read them himself.

"I can't do it," the voice said. There was a pause, then, "I know nobody saw you … It was your hands around his neck, not mine … Is that a threat? … I'm in enough trouble because of that other thing, there's extra security all over the place now … You take care of your end … No … No … Yes … I'm not killing anyone for you … I may have a record, but it's not for murder … She's just a kid, for Pete's sake … I

know he was … Damn it, I said no! … Shit, someone's coming …"
There was a long pause of silence, then, "They're gone now. What? …
Don't do this to me … Damn you … Shit. You'd do it, too, wouldn't
you? … Don't you realize that … All right. You do what you think you
have to do over there. I'll take care of him even though nobody would
believe him anyway now … I'll get back to you." The voice stopped.

Must be some kind of cop show, Wanda decided. She'd just heard
the bad guy rehearsing his lines. She'd have to ask Tony later what show
it might be.

She walked out of the office a few moments later and walked
around the corner through a door. Puzzled, she looked over at the back
wall of Tony's office, surprised to realize it backed onto an open
courtyard, not another office or studio.

On the wall was a pay phone. She puzzled about it for a moment,
trying to remember what she'd actually heard, then shrugged it off. She
didn't know whom she'd heard, and whoever it was, he had said he
wasn't going to kill anybody anyway. She had to get back to the office
for now. Maybe she'd mention it to Tony later.

* * *

Jim arrived at the office of Ryan's doctor at two o'clock that
afternoon so he could brief him on the details of the murder and
hopefully help the doctor and the hypnotist steer Ryan in the right
direction when he was hypnotized the next day. Due to the seriousness
of the situation they were dealing with, and Ryan's need for privacy, the
doctor had opened his office on the Memorial Day holiday so he
wouldn't have to rearrange his other patients any more than was
necessary.

The doctor was about forty, and had a trace of gray at the edge of
otherwise jet-black hair. For some reason, Jim had half-expected the
psychiatrist to sport a goatee like Freud's, but he was clean-shaven.
"Good morning, Detective Harrison. I'm Doctor Albert Miller."

Jim shook his hand and said, "Please call me Jim."

"All right, Jim, Ryan wanted me to bring you in here first because he
thinks you can help me understand some things that have happened.

Ryan has told me that he's pretty sure he may have seen something related to a murder just prior to his accident, and that you are investigating it."

"That's correct."

"I know we don't want you to reveal anything you know to Ryan, but I'd like you to give me some information if you can, information that might help me understand what he might have seen, what might come out under the hypnosis. My first responsibility is to Ryan's mental health, you understand, and I'd like to gauge the degree of possible trauma he might experience by going through this hypnosis."

"I understand, but you need to know that my first responsibility is to solving a homicide."

"Hopefully we can both accomplish what we need to, Jim. Ryan has given permission for me to speak freely to you as I feel is necessary, so we won't be violating any confidences here." The doctor settled back in his chair and picked up his notebook. "Now tell me about this murder …."

Forty minutes later, Jim said, "And that's all we know so far."

The doctor studied the notes he had made with a troubled look on his face. "I've only met his brother briefly before," he said. "I really don't know him at all, other than what Ryan has mentioned in therapy. I do know they have always been very close, and he is the only family Ryan has left now. Very disturbing," he added, shaking his head.

"Well, it's my expectation that he's going to tell us his brother buried that boy," Jim said with a sigh. "I didn't really understand the implications of his memory loss last year when I talked to him, but at the time we didn't know there was a body out there. But we've turned up the connection to his brother and now it makes sense that he might have repressed the memory because he couldn't deal with his brother being a murderer."

"Well, your analysis is certainly valid on that point. The thought of his brother going to prison is probably one of the worst fears he would ever have to face. Do you know much about Ryan's family background?" he asked.

"Nothing at all," Jim said. "He's never been a suspect so I haven't looked into his past at all. I only know a little of what's been on news here and there."

"Well, he's had a series of losses that have affected him badly and left him somewhat unable to cope with relationships. First his father left the family when he was around ten. The three boys were raised by just their mother after that, and the father never contacted the family after he left, although I understand he kept up his child support obligations without fail. Then his older brother was killed at the age of twenty-one. Ryan was still in high school then. He and Chris had been best friends and the death devastated him. He and Doug became very close after that, and that's about when he started his singing career, with Doug as his partner. He married a few years later, and his wife miscarried a much-wanted pregnancy. Then she left him for another man because she couldn't deal with his career and his long absences when he was touring. Then their mother died shortly after that, about three years ago. And last year Ryan broke up with the only woman he ever dated after his divorce, a woman I am sure he was in love with. He was afraid she would end up leaving him too, and he has not dated anyone since. Ryan has been abandoned by so many people he cared about that he has a serious problem forming relationships now. Doug is all Ryan has left, so you can imagine how hard he would resist believing anything that would mean he would have to lose Doug too. To make matters worse, in the last few years even Doug has drifted away from him and Ryan doesn't know why."

"Wow," Jim said. "No wonder the poor guy had to repress what he saw."

"So I hope you can appreciate why I needed to fully understand what was going on here, so I can help protect Ryan from whatever wrenching changes are about to occur as a result of the hypnosis. He's really in a very fragile state, especially considering the head injury he suffered last year. I'm worried this may bring on a severe depression if he does in fact recover the memory and it turns out that his brother is indeed implicated."

"Well, I hope we can get to the truth without causing too much damage to Mr. North," Jim said. "I've only talked to him a couple of times, but I really liked him. He seems to be a genuinely nice person, rare in someone who is such a big celebrity."

"I am only going to push him so far, Jim," the doctor warned. "I cannot destroy my patient to help you. If he had seen nothing at all, you would have to make your case with other evidence. So understand that if recovering the memory would damage him, I will not press the matter."

"Doctor, I can appreciate your concern, but a boy has been murdered. If Ryan North is an eyewitness, I need his testimony. Surely whatever happens can be dealt with in therapy, or with medication?"

"I will be meeting with Ryan in an hour, to prepare him for the hypnosis tomorrow morning. I will do everything I can to help him cope with this. But understand, if I need to halt the session tomorrow, I will do so. It is possible the entire memory may not come out in the first session. It may take more than one attempt. But I will be watching Ryan closely and I will not let him be destroyed by this."

Jim stood up and shook the doctor's hand. "I appreciate your help in this. Hopefully we can both achieve what we need tomorrow."

"I will see you then. Good day."

Jim called Sheila from his cell phone in the parking lot of Ryan's doctor's office. "Are we still on for dinner tonight?" he asked, half afraid she might have changed her mind about seeing him that night. "Or will that be cutting it too close for your flight?"

"Yes," she replied. "I ... uh ... I don't have to leave tonight after all."

"Why is that?"

"Well, Jim," she said hesitantly. "My editor knows you're here. I didn't tell him," she said hurriedly. "Someone saw you talking to me at the airport and called him to find out if something had happened. He asked me why you were there."

"And what did you tell him?"

"All I told him was that you were questioning someone here but I didn't know who."

"So why aren't you going home when you were supposed to?"

She sighed. "He told me to stick around until I found out who it was and why. I'm sorry," she added. "It really wasn't my idea at all. But since you were here before on the Walker murder, he assumes that's why you're here now. So he told me to stay. Are you mad at me?" she asked nervously.

"No," he replied. "You're just doing your job. But I absolutely cannot talk about why I'm here and I may have to be here for a few days. You understand that?"

"Of course." She paused. "Do you still want to see me tonight? I promise not to try to trick you into saying anything."

Jim could hear the anxiety in her voice and he smiled a little. He did want to see her, and they were unlikely to encounter anyone here who would be telling her editor about it. "Yes, Sheila. I'd like that." He started his car and backed out of the space. "It'll take me awhile to get back to my hotel. Let me go there and change and check in with Harley and I'll pick you up about six-thirty. Okay?" He waited at the driveway to finish the call before pulling out.

"I'll be ready," she replied. "There's a nice restaurant just down the street. Would you like me to try to get a reservation?"

"Thanks, that would be nice," he said. "See you soon." He hung up and pulled out into traffic.

* * *

Ryan North arrived at the doctor's office later that afternoon after Cindy Vincent left in the limousine. Fred had already left the studio shortly before noon, so Doug drove Ryan to the appointment in the Corvette since the limo hadn't returned yet from taking Cindy back to her hotel.

He didn't care if Doug knew he was seeing a doctor but he hadn't wanted him to know he was seeing his shrink again, and certainly didn't want Doug to know about the nightmare, or what he suspected it might mean. He knew Doug would try to talk him out of the hypnosis, afraid of the publicity if Ryan got involved in the murder investigation. But

Doug didn't comment at all when he escorted Ryan to the office labeled Dr. Albert Miller, Psychiatry. He glanced into the waiting area to be sure it was empty, then left Ryan with the explanation that he was going to wait in the building lobby, which would give him a better opportunity to intercept anyone who might have followed them.

The doctor invited Ryan into the office. Ryan closed the door behind him and said, "Well, doc? Did the detective tell you what you need to know?"

"Yes. Please sit down, Ryan," he requested quietly.

Ryan sat down in the chair facing the desk. "So we're going to do it tomorrow afternoon, right?"

"Yes. I have it arranged with Dr. Andrews. Detective Harrison has given me some excellent information that will help us work in the right areas." The doctor still wasn't quite sure how to prepare Ryan for what might happen the next day under hypnosis. "Now, Ryan, I'd like to leave the subject of your nightmare and what you might be repressing and talk about your feelings in general."

"What do you mean? My feelings about what?"

"Ryan, this hypnosis may be somewhat traumatic for you, depending on what you get out of it. I need to explore where your major anxieties lie, so I can help you deal with your emotions after the hypnosis."

"Sounds like a couch session to me," Ryan commented, getting up and walking to the couch.

The doctor followed and sat in his usual chair, behind Ryan and to his left. "Ryan, how old were you when your father left?"

"Oh, you want to really get into some old stuff now, huh? I guess I was about ten. Doug was nine. Christopher was thirteen."

"What were you told about why he left?"

"Mom told us that sometimes people love each other for a long time, but then they change and they find they aren't happy living together anymore. And it may be better if they never see each other again."

"Did you accept that?"

"Christopher was upset, but Doug and I were glad he left. We could see that Mom was unhappy, and the fighting and arguing were really taking a toll on everyone. Dad never had much time for us anyway. Christopher felt different because Dad used to spend some time with him fishing and such while Doug and I were too little."

"You never felt any sense of loss?"

"Maybe a sadness for what never was, but no sense of having lost anything I ever had. Doug and I were always real close, almost like twins, I guess, because Christopher was older and didn't have much use for us, like Dad."

"I thought you and Christopher were pretty close before he died."

"Oh, we were. I was just talking about how things were when Dad left. Christopher and I were buddies when I was in high school. My first year of high school was his last year, so he was driving me to school while Doug was still in Junior high. Chris used to give me advice about high school, how to pick up girls, who to hang out with, which teachers could be conned." Ryan smiled wistfully as he remembered the camaraderie that had developed between them that year.

"And you remained close after that?"

"Pretty close. He went to college the next year, but he was still living at home. He always wanted to know how things were at high school, and if I had any problems he gave me advice. I guess during that time he was the closest thing I had to a father. He gave me my first condom." Ryan paused, remembering how he had chickened out in the back seat of the car that weekend and hadn't been able to admit to Christopher for nearly a month that he really hadn't lost his virginity that night.

"What was your relationship with Doug during this time?"

"Oh, we were still buddies. We always did consider ourselves to be more like friends than brothers. We never did fight much, like most siblings do. It was in high school that we began to dabble in song writing. Doug was always a poet, and I started to learn the piano right after Dad left. Mom thought it would be good to have a hobby. I found I loved it, and started to write a few melodies. Then one day, Doug and I got the idea to put one of his poems to music. The rest, as they say, is history."

"How did you feel when Christopher died?"

"How do you think I felt?"

"I wouldn't ask if I thought I knew, Ryan."

"I felt lousy. What do you expect? He was only twenty-one! I hadn't seen my dad in eight years, and now my brother was dead! Mom was a wreck. We were all devastated. Chris had always been the stabilizer of the family."

"Were you angry?"

"About what?"

"That he died. That he left you."

"Why should I be angry?" Ryan snapped. "I felt awful. It was such a tragic waste."

"Did you feel abandoned?"

"No! Why would you say that? The guy died! He didn't go off and leave me on purpose. He got killed by a fucking drunk driver!"

"But you felt a great void in your life, didn't you?"

"Of course I did! He was my big brother. He was the only 'grown-up' who gave a damn about me all through high school, even though he was really only a teenager himself. I loved him, okay? Is that what you wanted to hear?"

The doctor tried another topic. "Your mother died when?"

"Now we're onto my mother. Aren't you going to ask about Skippy?"

"Who's Skippy?"

"My Cocker Spaniel that died when I was seven."

"Let's stick with your mother. When did she die?"

Ryan sighed explosively. "Three years ago, okay?"

"How did you feel about that?"

"How do you think I felt? Never mind, I know. You wouldn't ask if you thought you knew," he said in a tone that mimicked the doctor's voice. "I felt like shit, okay? I hadn't even seen her for months when she died. I felt guilty as hell. She spent her whole life, almost, alone, raising the three of us, and just when we're out on our own – well, the two of us that were left, anyway – and making her proud, she dies of a heart attack. She never got to have a life of her own. She never got to have a grandchild to hold." Ryan's voice choked off in a sob, as he remembered his ex-wife's only pregnancy. Had Linda not lost the baby, his mother would have seen it before she died.

"Ryan, there's a reason I'm taking you back through all this," the doctor said gently.

"Yeah, because you like to see me break down and cry," Ryan answered tightly. "Well, you happy now?" He reached for the tissue box.

"Ryan, you've been through a lot. Your father left you at ten, your brother died when you were eighteen, and your mother died nine years later. How do you feel about that?"

"I'm just glad I have Doug. He's the only family I have left."

"Let's talk about Doug. You were roommates in college. How did that go?"

Ryan paused for a moment to let the emotions about his mother subside a bit before answering, "It was probably the best time of my life."

"Why was that?"

"Doug's the only one who ever really understood me. When we were in college, we really started to do a lot of song writing and started performing. He was performing with me then, although he refuses to now. But he plays guitar and we did some gigs together."

"You liked living with him?"

"Yes. We got along well as roommates, never argued about who would do what. He did most of the cooking but we shared the housekeeping chores. We're both night owls, so that worked out well. Didn't have any classes together, though, since I was a year ahead of him. But we did pretty much everything together. Neither of us really had any other close friends."

"What about dating? Did you double date?"

"No, not really. Doug was always a bit shy with girls. I went out now and then, and that was how I met Linda. Sometimes Doug would come with us if we went to movies, but mostly he would stay home and read if I went out."

"After your marriage, you remained close?"

"He lived nearby and was at my house for dinner most nights. He was friendly with Linda, and the three of us got along well. I was touring a lot by then, sometimes he'd come with me, most of the time he stayed home and kept Linda company."

"What happened after your divorce?"

Ryan hesitated. "Something changed then. I don't know what, but he started pulling away from me about then. And then mom died. After she died, I decided to move to Los Angeles, but Doug wouldn't come with me." His face clouded. "We had a bit of a fight about it. He said something about it being time he got on with his own life, as if I was holding him back somehow. He did buy a condo over here and I thought maybe some day he would move over here with me, but he stayed at the ad agency in Denver and wouldn't come with me. Said he wanted the condo as an investment. He would stay in it when he came for a visit once in awhile."

"That's when you started seeing Lisa, shortly after you moved over here without Doug."

"Yes."

"And you broke up with her just a few months before your accident."

"Yes."

"And then Doug came back to your side and is now living and working with you again."

"Yes." Ryan smiled. "Things are good again, although I don't know if I can get him to stay this time."

"Ryan, is Doug allowed to be Doug?"

"What are you talking about? Of course he is."

"Ryan, Doug has been your best friend since you were children. Is he Doug Norton, or is he just Ryan North's brother?"

"He's – I – I don't know what you're getting at," Ryan replied. "To me, he's my brother. To the rest of the world, he's Doug Norton. What is this doubletalk of yours, anyway?"

"Ryan, why is Doug over here with you now?"

"He's just keeping an eye on things for me. Sort of as a bodyguard."

"Ryan, a bodyguard is expected to die to protect the person he's guarding if necessary."

Ryan sat up and turned to face the doctor. "What are you talking about? I don't want Doug to die. Are you trying to say I want Doug to die? What the hell are you getting at anyway?"

"Ryan, I want you to think about your relationship with Doug, and try to find where the boundary is. You are Ryan, and he is Doug. He is not a part of you. You are not a part of him. You don't need to protect each other. Neither of you will be free until you realize that."

Ryan stared at the doctor with his mouth hanging open. The doctor didn't seem to notice. He stood up. "Our time is up, Ryan. I'll see you at Dr. Andrews' office at three tomorrow. You have the address?"

Ryan snapped his mouth closed and nodded mutely. What the hell was going on? What had the doctor meant? Why had he been so concerned about Doug? Did he think Doug was having a breakdown, too? "Doc, I don't understand," he started.

"Ryan, our time is up," the doctor repeated firmly. "I told you what I want you to think about before I see you again. You are to think about your relationship with your brother. That's all. I'll see you tomorrow."

CHAPTER 38

L ATER THAT EVENING, Jim called Sheila from her hotel lobby and she came down in the elevator to meet him. "Hi, Jim," she said with a smile.

His pulse had quickened when she stepped out of the elevator. It was one thing to spar with her as a reporter; it was quite another to see her as a woman he was about to dine with. She had exchanged her usual wardrobe of jeans and hiking boots for a simple green dress that brought out the green in her eyes. "Hi," he replied, staring at her awkwardly. "Nice dress," he added.

"Didn't know I had legs, did you," she teased.

"I ... uh ..." he stammered.

She took his hand. "It's okay. I feel a little funny too. Let's go. The reservation is for fifteen minutes from now."

Jim felt as awkward as a teenager. He had been attracted to Sheila from the first time he had seen her, but seeing her in a different context than as adversaries chasing clues in a murder case made him wonder if he knew what he was getting himself into. He had counted on being in control of the situation, him being the tough cop, her being the somewhat bumbling reporter but he had not reckoned on the effect it would have on him to see her when the subject wasn't the murder of a young boy – and when she was looking the way she was looking now.

He had not dated since his divorce. Now he worried about what to say, how to act, should he open her doors, would she try to pay the check, what should he do if she did. And he wondered what was going through her mind right then.

And she had taken his hand ....

As they walked through the lobby to the door, he marveled at the confidence he felt coming through in her grip. She didn't seem nervous at all.

He took a longer stride as they approached the door and reached quickly to push it open for her. To his relief, she simply said, "Thank you," and he relaxed a little. Maybe everything wasn't going to turn into a battle of the sexes struggle for political correctness.

He led her to his rental car, which he had left at the curb, and stepped forward again to open it for her. Again she thanked him and stepped into the car. He closed the door and walked around to his side and got in.

He relaxed once he was behind the wheel. Maybe it would be okay. So far, she was allowing him to exercise the manners his mother had drilled into him, but which many modern women shunned as sexist.

"The restaurant is just down there on the right," she said. "It's a steakhouse. I didn't figure you'd want to go anywhere too … trendy," she added.

"Thanks. I appreciate that. I'm not into tofu." He pulled out of the parking lot and drove the few blocks to the restaurant she had chosen.

They didn't speak on the short ride, and when he got to the restaurant and parked, he turned off the engine and turned to face her. "Sheila," he started, "I have to tell you something."

"What's that, Jim?" she asked. "Is something wrong?"

"Not really, except that I'm nervous as hell about this," he admitted.

She released a huge sigh of relief. "So am I."

Their eyes met. And then they both laughed. And then suddenly it was all right.

"I haven't been on a date since my divorce," he confessed. "I feel like I don't know the rules anymore."

"I haven't been on a date since I moved to Colorado," she replied. "And I've never dated a cop before," she added. "So I don't know the rules either."

"Well, I've never dated a reporter, so I guess we're even," he said with a smile. He picked up her hand.

"And this is a date, right? Not just two travelers having dinner together?"

"Well," he replied slowly, "if Harley asks, we were just two travelers having dinner together. But for me … I think it's a date. I've wanted to ask you out for a long time, but just didn't think it would ever work out. Does it feel like a date to you?"

She smiled nervously. "I've wanted you to ask me out for a long time, but I didn't even know if you might already be seeing someone or not. Nobody seemed to know anything about your personal life, or if they knew, they wouldn't tell me. But yeah, it feels like a date."

"Okay, then it's a date. And no talking about the case. Let's go eat."

While enjoying a good meal and a glass of wine, they talked about everything except Daryl Walker's murder. He asked about the interview with Cindy, and she told him how excited the girl had been to see Ryan again, and how jealous her friends would be, and how she was looking forward to his next concert in Denver since he had promised her front row seats for her and her friends.

"He's really a nice guy," she finished. "I didn't realize that before."

"That's the impression I got when I talked to him in the hospital last year," Jim agreed.

"So, Jim, Harley refused to tell me anything about you last year when you joined the department. Can I ask how you ended up working in Clear Creek?"

"Sure, but understand that I'm going to expect you to tell me how you ended up at the *Chronicle*."

"Fair enough."

"It's a bit of an ugly story, actually," he started. "And I'll try to give you the short version. I started out as a cop like any other cop. Graduated the academy pretty high in my class so I didn't have any trouble getting hired by Denver P.D. Married and divorced, I'll spare you those details. About the time of my divorce I made detective." He paused and took a sip of wine.

She interrupted the story. "Were there any kids?"

"No, and the ex moved out of state shortly after we split up. Anyway, it was after I made detective that I found out what kind of precinct I was in," he said darkly. "Again, I'll spare the details, but I discovered there was a corporate climate that was not exactly politically correct."

"Racism?" Sheila asked.

"Not exactly. There was a gay patrol officer on the squad at the time. Nobody had known he was gay. Then somehow, he got outed. I had heard about it, wondered why he had kept it a secret for so long, then I found out why." He stopped.

"What happened?"

Jim avoided her eyes. "Let's just say he ended up in the hospital. He was brutally attacked by his own squad. Probably half a dozen of them. I witnessed it."

He looked up at her. "The captain refused to take action. Seemed almost glad it had happened. The next day I put in for a transfer and brought him the victim's resignation."

"He refused to take action? How can that be?"

"Denver is not the most gay-tolerant place in the world, Sheila. What we learned from Ricky really wasn't any surprise to me, except I naively thought the rampant homophobia was confined to the east side. I was wrong."

"Couldn't you report the captain?"

Jim gave a short laugh. "Sheila, there are a lot more of them than there are of me. It would have been my word against the entire squad. And the cop that was attacked refused to go up against them. I tried to get him to go to the FBI with me and report what happened, but he figured if he did they would just kill him. So he quit; I took a transfer. I'm not proud of the fact that I didn't do more, but at the time I didn't see anything else I could do. I couldn't exactly arrest my own superior officer."

"Where did you transfer to?"

"Over on the west side, near Lakewood, actually. I wanted to be closer to my dad, since he was getting pretty sick and needed some help.

Once I got transferred, I was able to move in with him again. He died about a year later."

"I'm sorry to hear that."

"Anyway, I was there for a couple years, then something happened there too."

"Another gay officer attacked?"

"No, nothing so blatant. This was a subtle form of racial discrimination that happened to affect my black female partner. So that time I simply quit. I'd had it. I was a good cop but I was surrounded by bigots wherever I went. And I just couldn't seem to stand up to the brass when I needed to. But I hated the thought of moving, leaving my parents' home. Harley had been a good friend of my father. He'd told me when I graduated the academy that if I ever needed a job to let him know. So I did."

"And that's why you're in Clear Creek," she concluded for him. "I wondered about it, because I knew you must have been making more money in Denver than in Clear Creek."

"Some things are worth more than money, and I really love being in the mountains instead of the city anyway, so that was a real bonus. Harley's a bit of a sexist at times, but he's not a bad guy. And while he doesn't have much use for gays, he doesn't actually hate them or want them hurt. And when I confronted him about his attitude toward you, he admitted I was right and he's been trying to change his ways. Makes me wonder what would have happened if I'd tried telling Arlo how I felt, but it's too late for that now." He shrugged. "With Harley, I think he was just in such a habit of thinking women should be in the kitchen that it never occurred to him that he might be wrong until I pointed a few things out to him. And now it's your turn," he said. "Tell me how you left your tabloid background behind and decided to torment me by being an investigative reporter."

They left the restaurant an hour later and drove up into the Hollywood Hills and spent a couple of hours looking at the city lights and talking about everything except the Daryl Walker murder. By the time they decided it was time to head back, Sheila was nestled into Jim's side, his arm around her and her hand resting lightly on his thigh, and any lingering awkwardness about their relationship had long since evaporated.

But he remained the gentleman when he took her back to her hotel, making no suggestions about coming up for a nightcap, and leaving her with only a hug at the elevator door.

He drove back to his hotel with mixed emotions. It had felt so right, so comfortable to be with her, but he worried about what would happen when they could no longer pretend he wasn't a cop and she wasn't a reporter and they resumed being adversaries on a murder case. And he particularly worried what Harley would say if he found out his detective was actually dating the reporter whom he despised so much.

But he had to focus on his case now, and the next day he would witness the hypnotism of Ryan North, and hopefully confirm the identity of Daryl Walker's killer. And hope that Sheila did not figure out what he was doing before he had his case built.

* * *

That night, Ryan lay in his bed, staring at the shadows on his wall, thinking about his nightmare and the things the psychiatrist had said to him about his brother. He still didn't understand why his doctor was so concerned about Ryan's relationship with Doug. What did that have to do with the nightmare and his accident?

The hypnotism attempt was set for three o'clock the next afternoon, and Jim Harrison would meet him there. He hoped the hypnotism would work, and that once he knew for sure what he had seen, maybe the nightmares would finally stop and he could start getting some sleep at night.

He was starting to grow drowsy, and his mind drifted back to the unicorn. A green unicorn. Why a green unicorn? Obviously, he had not actually seen any such creature in the woods that day. He tried to think if he had ever seen a statue of a green unicorn, or a stuffed toy, or even a cartoon character.

He yawned, and his mind turned lazily to the horse's tail he had seen in the dream. He imagined he saw it switching back and forth, back and forth, back and forth, until, finally, he fell into a restless sleep ….

The unicorn turned away from the hole and faced Ryan for only a moment before Ryan turned quickly away and ran up the hill. He could feel the horse beneath him gather himself repeatedly to lunge up the hill, but he got nowhere. Then the unicorn was beside him, saying, "Duck. Do it."

Ryan answered, "I think it sucks!"

Suddenly he was in his bathroom, shaving, and the unicorn was beside him. "Where's Doug?" he asked.

"I'm here," it answered.

"Not you – Doug," he corrected. Then he looked over and saw that Doug was next to him, shaving. "You're the unicorn," he said.

"There is no unicorn," Doug answered.

Ryan closed his eyes and when he opened them, Doug and the unicorn were gone, and he felt himself falling into the hole. He saw the red cap falling on top of him, and he reached up to stop it, but it kept falling with him. He started to scream, "No! Don't leave me!" He jerked to a stop just before he hit the bottom, and awoke in a sweat ….

CHAPTER 39

"**M**r. North, can you hear me?"

Eyes closed, Ryan nodded. The tranquilizer had worked, and Ryan had readily submitted to the hypnotism this time. Jim looked on, taking notes. A tape recorder was running.

"Mr. North, hold up your right arm." Ryan extended his right arm. "Mr. North, put your arm down and open your eyes." Ryan obeyed. "Mr. North, we're going to go back in time, to the day of your accident, to October sixteenth of last year. It is now October sixteenth. Where are you, Mr. North?"

In a faraway voice, Ryan replied, "In Colorado."

"Are you alone?"

"No, Doug is with me. We're riding horses into the mountains to hunt deer."

"Do you stay together the whole time?"

"No, we get in an argument and he takes off by himself. I tell him I'll meet him at the trail crossing at noon."

"Now you're riding alone. What do you see?"

"I see trees mostly. Trees are dense. Can't see far off the trail in some spots. The ground is rocky, hard on Badger's feet. I ride a long time, then stop him at the top of a rise and use the binoculars."

"Do you see anything through the binoculars?"

"Too many trees. I turn him off the trail again and we ride down the side of the hill."

"What do you see now?"

"More trees. I have to keep dodging branches. Badger's rooting at the bit. He wants to go faster. Whoa, Badger." Ryan raised his hand slightly, pulling back on invisible reins. "Good boy." He lowered his hand.

"Go on," the doctor encouraged. "What do you see now?"

"I'm looking through the binoculars. See something move – across the gully. Go further down the side. It's a little clearer up ahead, more open in places. Trying to get to a clearing so I can see across the gully. I have to duck – " Ryan's voice broke off.

"Take it easy now, Mr. North. You ducked under a branch?"

"Branch – yes. Big, bare white branch."

"Close your eyes, Mr. North." The hypnotist had been told that this was the extent of Ryan's conscious memory. "Now, look past the branch. Do you see past the branch?"

"I – I – " Ryan squeezed his eyes tight as he tried to remember. Then he said, "I duck under the branch and stop. I straighten up in the saddle and look through the binoculars again." His right hand came up to his face as if holding binoculars while his left hand was suspended in the air over an invisible saddle horn, holding invisible reins.

"Good, Mr. North," the doctor encouraged. "What do you see through the binoculars?"

"I'm looking through the trees. I can't find what I saw before."

"Are you still looking through the binoculars?"

"Trying to. Horse dancing around. Trying to hold him still." Unconsciously, his left hand made a fist and moved back and forth, as if he were pulling the reins again. His right hand continued to hold imaginary field glasses to his eyes. "I – " Ryan's voice broke off again and he grimaced in pain.

"Mr. North, breathe slowly. The pain is going away now. When I count to three the pain will be gone. One. Two. Three. Is the pain gone?"

"Yes."

"Mr. North, look through the binoculars again. The pain will not come back. What do you see?"

"I – I – I see the green unicorn."

Startled, the hypnotist looked at Dr. Miller, who mouthed the word "Nightmare." The hypnotist nodded. "Mr. North, the unicorn is not in the woods. The unicorn was in your dream. It's October sixteenth of last year. You're in the woods. Look through the binoculars again. What do you see?"

"The unicorn is throwing branches into the hole."

"Mr. North, look again. What else do you see?"

"There's a horse over there. I see its tail. The horse is behind some bushes. All I see is the tail. A black tail. Switching back and forth. There's an orange ribbon hanging from it, like the one on my horse."

"What else?"

"There's a fallen tree, all uprooted. The roots are sticking up in the air, like fingers. The hole is at the base of the tree, where the roots were."

"What is in the hole, Mr. North?"

"A hand."

The doctor glanced at Jim, then continued. "Whose hand is it, Mr. North?"

"Don't know. Dead body. Unicorn is covering up a dead body." His voice was detached, emotionless.

"Do you know how the body died?"

"No. It's dead, though. Hand sticking up out of the hole. Unicorn pushes the hand down and throws in the red cap."

"Red cap?"

"Yes. Like a beret. Into the hole. Then he takes it back. Then throws more branches."

"Who is the unicorn, Mr. North?"

"It's a green unicorn!" Ryan shouted. "Don't ask me that!"

"All right, Mr. North, I won't ask you that. What happened next?"

Ryan's face twisted with anxiety. "The other horse whinnies. Badger starts to answer. Gotta get out of there. Turn the horse around." His right hand released the "binoculars" and dropped to his side. He jerked his "rein" hand to the left. "Kick him hard – " Ryan stopped again.

"What happened next, Mr. North?"

"Falling in hole. Fall for long time. Hear people talking to me. Tell them not to go over there."

"Mr. North, stop. Mr. North, go back. When you turned the horse around, did you see a tree limb?"

"Falling."

"The tree limb was falling?"

"No. I was falling."

"Did you see a limb, Mr. North? Before you fell?"

Panic was reflected on Ryan's face. Breathlessly, he continued, "Got to get away from the unicorn. Falling."

The hypnotist glanced at the psychiatrist, then at Jim, who shrugged. Dr. Miller drew his hand across his throat, indicating to the hypnotist to end the session.

"Mr. North, in a minute, I want you to wake up. I'm going to count to five. When I reach five, you will wake up, feeling fine, and you will remember everything you told me today. One. Two. Three. Open your eyes. Four. Five. Wake up, Mr. North."

Ryan blinked, then looked anxiously at the hypnotist, then Jim, then Dr. Miller. "How'd I do?"

"What do you remember, Ryan?" Dr. Miller asked.

Ryan was silent for a minute. "I think I remember everything up to where I must have hit that limb I had ducked on the way in. Is that what came out?"

"Do you remember seeing a body?"

"Yes, I do. A hand, anyway."

"Who covered up the body?"

Ryan stared at him. "That damned unicorn? I don't understand. I thought you were going to ask me about my accident, not my nightmare."

"Ryan, I think we've made a lot of progress here today, but I think we should try this again tomorrow."

Ryan looked at Jim, who nodded agreement. "I think you should."

"Okay. If you all think I need to."

"Mr. North, can you come back tomorrow morning?" the hypnotist asked. "I can see you at nine, and I'll cancel the appointment after that so nobody will be here to see you when you're leaving."

"Yes. I'll be here."

"I suggest you go home and relax now. Don't talk about what happened here, and don't try to remember anything that doesn't come to you easily."

Jim Harrison lingered after Ryan left the office.

"Do you think he'll remember tomorrow?" he asked the psychiatrist.

"What do you think?" Dr. Miller asked Dr. Andrews.

The hypnotist shrugged. "I think he remembers already. But he's not ready to face it."

"That's the impression I got," Dr. Miller agreed. "He got too angry when you pushed him."

"So what does this mean?" Jim said. "Is he going to continue fighting?"

"I think he needs to accept this consciously before his subconscious will let him admit it," Dr. Miller replied. "He'll be thinking about this tonight, and about what I discussed with him yesterday. I think tomorrow we will have a different result. I think he'll either tell us what he saw or refuse to cooperate at all. As long as he actually remembers, my work is done, whether he admits it to us or not. But I know that doesn't help you any. Let's hope for the best."

Jim saw Sheila again for dinner that night, but was not good company. He was a little disturbed by the hypnosis session, concerned that Ryan might actually be covering up deliberately, but realized that made no sense, since it would have been the easiest thing in the world for Ryan to simply have said he saw nothing. But Ryan had come to Jim. Ryan had suspected he knew something about the murder and wanted to find out what it was.

Jim had no idea what Ryan's reaction would be if he had, indeed, seen his own brother with Daryl Walker's body and was only just now realizing it. Would he back away? Would he lie? Or would he actually admit what he had seen, regardless of what it would mean to him and the only family he had left?

"Jim?" Sheila's voice finally brought him back to the present. "I asked if you were feeling all right. Do you want to call it a night?"

"I'm sorry, Sheila. This witness I'm dealing with is presenting a bigger challenge than I expected. I'm afraid my mind is working overtime tonight."

"You want to talk about it?" she asked tentatively.

"I can't. I can't violate his trust." Jim looked into her troubled green eyes. "Sheila, this is not about you. Please don't take it personally."

"I'm not," she said. "Is there anything I can do? Do you want to go back to your hotel and work, or do you want to do something to take your mind off it? I don't know what to do for you."

Jim reached across the table and took her hand and smiled. "Honey, I'd like nothing better than for you to take my mind off it," he said with a wink. "But I think you're right, I probably should call it a night. I'd rather spend time with you when I can pay better attention to you. And right now I just have too much on my mind."

"My editor keeps asking me if I've found out what you're doing yet. I think he's finally figuring out that I'm not going to know until you're ready to tell me, and I've assured him that you will tell me as soon as you can. But so far he hasn't asked me to come back yet."

"Well, it may be selfish of me but I hope he doesn't. I wish I could throw you a few crumbs to make him happy," Jim said. "But I just can't. But I think tomorrow will be a critical day for my investigation. I'll either find out what I need to know or I'll find out that my witness can't help me. So if you're still here tomorrow, I'd still like to see you again." He took out his wallet and extracted the appropriate bills to pay the check and laid them on the table.

"Well, I expect to still be here, and I'd like to see you too."

"Kind of a strange relationship we have," Jim said with a wry smile, standing up. "I hope once I'm done over here, we can spend some time getting to know each other the way normal people do."

Sheila laughed, and stood up from the table. "I'm not sure I know what normal people do, Jim. But I hope we can manage to keep our personal and professional lives separate enough not to get in the way." She walked with him to the parking lot.

* * *

Fred's Volvo was parked in the driveway when the limo pulled up in front of Ryan's house. Doug had been watching out the window after the car came through the gate, and he opened the door for Ryan. He had been worried about his brother ever since he had insisted on going to a doctor's appointment by himself in the limo, insisting that it would be better if Doug and Fred both stayed at the studio and kept an eye on things there.

Ryan walked in to find Fred sitting in one of the leather chairs, smoking a cigarette. "So, how did things go at the studio? Did anything happen?"

"Not sure what good it is," Fred replied, "but I learned that Walter Hussman is not Walter Hussman."

"How do you figure? I thought we had already checked him out."

"Well," Fred explained, "I got in a conversation with Walter yesterday. I've been trying to chat casually with as many members of the crew as I could, and yesterday was Walter's turn. I noticed he was wearing a jacket yesterday morning, and I commented on it, mostly because it looked a lot like one Doug wears sometimes. He said, 'I can't take this fickle weather. I thought it was warm in L.A. and instead I freeze every other morning.' Well, it *has* been cooler than usual, but hardly freezing lately. But when I checked his references, I was told Hussman left his job in New Mexico to go to Wyoming because he preferred the cold country. It made me wonder. So I called KCHY and asked someone to describe Walter Hussman to me. Nobody who had known him was there yesterday, but his former boss finally called me back about an hour ago and said he was skinny, and had dark brown hair, not blond, and a beard and that he was almost six feet tall and had brown eyes. So I described our Walter Hussman, and they said he sounded like a man who had worked with Hussman as his assistant for a few months one summer, a guy named Peter Hayward. Nobody knew what had become of him. In fact, nobody knows where the real Walter Hussman is right now, either."

"There's something else, Ryan," Doug injected.

"What's that?"

"Remember when you asked if he reminded me of anyone we knew, maybe looked like someone you didn't like?"

"I remember."

"Do you remember that I said he looked familiar but I couldn't place him?"

"Yes. Why? Did you remember where you'd seen him before?"

"I think I saw him at the hospital, Ryan. The day after you came out of the coma. He talked to me in the cafeteria. I thought he was a reporter. I didn't really recognize him when he showed up at the studio seven months later because I didn't really look at him that well at the hospital. I was hoping if I showed no interest in what he was saying he would go away without my having to come right out and ask him to get lost."

"You're sure it's the same guy?"

"No. I'm not certain. But it could be him. But if it is, there's something else, too. He mentioned at the time that he'd met you before. He was working in a Denver TV studio when you gave an interview. Said he ran into you in the hall and you'd said hello to him. Maybe that's why he seemed familiar to you, too."

Ryan looked puzzled. "In Denver?"

"Yes."

"Doug, I've never given a TV interview in Denver. Not in a studio, anyway. I've done some of those camera-in-your-face interviews backstage at concerts, and I've been on a couple of radio talk shows in Denver, very early in my career, but I've never done one on TV there. I've been asked a number of times, but you know how much I hate those things. The only studio interviews I've done have been in Los Angeles, late night talk shows. I won't even do daytime TV shows."

"Well, that was one of the lies he used to try to get me to talk to him. That's why I thought he was a reporter. Now I wonder what he really wanted."

"And he turns up here using false credentials to get a job with us. You suppose he's some kind of groupie? Someone who wants to be a part of my career and found a way to make it happen?"

"I have no idea," Fred answered. "It could be this guy just wanted a job and didn't have very good references himself, so he used Hussman's, knowing those references would check out. They did work together. He obviously knows what he's doing with the equipment."

"He took a heck of a risk. What if we'd asked for a description when we checked his references?"

"Well, how often do you suppose a prospective employer asks for a physical description of the applicant when checking a reference? If you want to make sure you're dealing with the person you think you are, you check ID or have him investigated."

"And I'm sure Tony didn't take time for any of that. He just needed a sound mixer, fast," Doug reminded them. "You were scheduled to start taping the day after Jason was arrested."

"And this guy probably knew we were desperate. So, Fred," Ryan said, "what did Tony say when you told him?"

"I haven't told Tony yet. Thought I should wait and see what you all wanted to do. I know this is the eleventh hour on this show. If his work has been okay, you may want to just keep an eye on him, but let him finish the job. I did run a check on Peter Hayward. Nothing came up on him in Wyoming, but of course, I have no idea where he may have been before that, and I can't get anything from the FBI unless a crime has been committed."

"Shit," Ryan muttered. "Why do these crazy things keep happening? Now we have to decide if we fire him for lying, or keep him because we can't meet our deadline without him. We've got, what, two more days to go before we finish up, Doug?"

"With any luck," Doug agreed, nodding. "Tough to have a setback now, but do you dare keep him on with all that's happened? Even though he is pretty good with the equipment," he admitted. "I wonder why he never mentioned to me that we'd met that day? He never gave me his name that day, so he would have known he was safe there. Of course, I was pretty rude to him. Maybe he was hoping I wouldn't remember him."

"You and your charming personality. Well, if he's been doing these things – the vandalism, drugging me – firing him won't make him stop, and then we lose our chance to keep an eye on him. If he hasn't, firing him just leaves us without a sound mixer at a time when we need one the most," Ryan muttered, almost to himself. "What do you think we should do, Doug?"

"I think we should get Tony in on this. He hired him. You want me to ask him to come over tonight?"

"No. Talk to him in the morning. I think I want to rest tonight. I know it's early but I think I want to eat soon and then get back to the condo and relax. I've got another appointment tomorrow."

Fred glanced at Doug. "I think I'll dash out and get some cigarettes if you don't mind. I'll be back in a little bit."

"I'll walk you out," Doug said.

Ryan watched them walk out together, wondering why Doug had done so, then smiling as understanding came to him. Doug came back in the house a few minutes later. "So what is for dinner, Doug? Have you made any plans yet?"

"There are some steaks in the freezer to thaw if you want. Or we can call out for something. I didn't know how long you'd be gone, so I didn't plan anything. If you want steaks, I'll fix them so you can stay there and relax. I promise not to put Ex-Lax in anything."

"That sounds good to me," Ryan replied, grateful to be able to take it easy. Doug went into the kitchen and Ryan and lay back on his recliner. A few minutes later, he decided to get up and get a drink.

He walked to the doorway, from where he could see Doug pulling the husks off ears of corn while the steaks thawed in the microwave. He wore a red checked apron over his blue jeans. It went nicely with his gray shirt with a red fox on the pocket.

"My, isn't this a domestic scene," Ryan said. "Every man's dream. Will you marry me, Doug?"

"Sorry, sweetie," Doug replied without looking up. "You're not my type." He rinsed the corn under the faucet and set a pan of water on the stove.

"Yeah, I know," Ryan said. He hesitated a moment, then continued, "But apparently Fred is."

Doug froze, then slowly turned to face him. "What did you say?"

Ryan arched an eyebrow and said simply, "You heard me."

"You're nuts," Doug said, turning back to the counter. "You better not let him hear you say that."

"Doug," Ryan said, "this is really silly, you know."

"What's silly?"

"I think Chris and I knew before you did."

Doug spun back around and glared at his brother. "Knew what? What is it that you think you know, Ryan?"

"How shall I put this? I know why you don't date women, Doug. Did you think I never noticed? I knew you were gay before you were in high school."

Doug turned pale.

"Well? Am I right?"

Doug sighed. "Yes," he said finally. "You're right. Hell of a time to bring it up, though."

"Blame my psychiatrist."

"And here Fred's always telling me I have no mannerisms to worry about. What gave me away?"

"I don't even know what Chris and I picked up on," Ryan said. "We were talking one day a year or two after Dad left. Chris asked if Dad had told me the facts of life before he left and I said he had. Then he said what about Victor? Does Victor know? And I said I doubted it would matter anyway. He said, 'Oh, yeah. You're right.' Then we talked about it a little. Somehow we both had recognized that you weren't interested in girls. It wasn't anything you were saying or doing. I think it was more a matter of little things you weren't saying or doing. Like showing no interest in Chris's porno stash. You never said anything negative about it, you just showed no interest at all."

"Why didn't you ever say anything to me?"

"Chris ordered me not to, and I felt he was right. If we were wrong, it could have devastated you to know we thought you were gay. And if we were right, well, we thought it should be your decision to tell us. When you got older and started dating girls once in awhile, I thought maybe we'd been mistaken after all and I was really glad we hadn't said anything. After Fred showed up here, I started putting a few things together. I noticed the way he looks at you. Wasn't too hard to figure out he was interested in you, but one day I caught you looking at him the same way and wondered about it. Then tonight when you walked him out, you sort of brushed up against him when you went through the door ... and I suddenly remembered the conversation I had with Chris." He shrugged. "I haven't had reason to think about your sexual orientation for years. I guess I've been so wrapped up in myself I never gave it much thought. But why didn't you ever tell me?"

Doug walked to the table and collapsed into a chair, burying his face in his hands, shaking his head. "I fought it for fifteen years. I tried to ignore it. I tried dating women. I tried therapy. I even tried aversion therapy last year. That really screwed me up. I didn't want women or men after that. I didn't want to be gay. I thought maybe that was why Dad left — that he'd guessed and was ashamed of me. I tried so hard to change. I was afraid of what you would think and I didn't want to hurt Mom after all she'd been through. I guess I didn't feel free to be myself while she was alive. I kept trying to be what she thought I was."

"Mom knew too."

Doug took his hands away from his face and looked at his brother. "No way."

"Sorry, Doug. But she knew. Trust me, she knew. Dad probably knew too, but that's not why he left."

"You mean I put myself through this hell trying to keep this from everyone and you're telling me everyone already knew?"

"Why were you so worried about keeping it from us? Did you think we'd turn on you or something? That we'd stop loving you? Kick you out?"

"It often happens. You wouldn't believe some of the horror stories I heard in some of the support groups I joined. I couldn't take the chance. Especially after Mom died, I couldn't take the chance of losing you, too." He sighed again. "Fred was right. He kept saying I should tell you and get it over with."

"I wondered why you seemed like you were hiding something, avoiding me," Ryan replied. "The way you booked out of here after

Christmas hurt but I thought it was because I kept nagging you about smoking."

"No. I guess I was back in denial when I was helping you. Once you were better, I realized I had to go back to my own life. So I left. I still couldn't tell you because mostly I wasn't ready to be out yet. I'm still not ready. But I guess I shouldn't fight it anymore." He stood up abruptly and walked back to the counter. He picked up another ear of corn and started to pull back the husk, then he dropped it on the counter. His shoulders started to shake as all the fear and relief he felt mixed together and came out in a sob.

Ryan walked over to his brother and placed a hand on his shoulder. "It will take a lot more than this to come between us," he said quietly. "You're my brother and always will be. No matter what your name happens to be. Or who you're dating."

Doug turned around, tears running down his face, and the two men hugged each other for a long moment. "Thanks, Ryan. That means a lot. I've been so afraid to tell you, afraid to tell anyone." He looked up at his brother and saw tears on Ryan's face too. "Hey, knock that off," he said with a wry smile. "Straight guys aren't supposed to cry."

"It's just such a relief to know why you were being so secretive and distant, Doug. I thought it was something I'd done." He wiped his face with the back of his hand.

"I'm sorry. I'm sorry I couldn't tell you. I know I've been pushing you away, but I had to prepare myself for the day when I finally told you, in case you rejected me like I've been expecting. I just couldn't bear to tell anyone, just couldn't bring myself to come out of the closet."

"Well," Ryan said, "I did hear a rumor about you and Fred down at the studio. If it's true, you may be further out of the closet than you think you are."

Doug pulled out his handkerchief, wiped his eyes, and blew his nose before saying with disgust, "I'll bet Walter Hussman was the source of that rumor. That was something else he said to me that day in the hospital. He said he'd seen me at a Gay and Lesbian meeting." He paused a moment. "But I never saw him there and I don't think Fred did, either. I wonder how that could be? Maybe he's not really the same guy I saw in the hospital after all." He shrugged. "Anyway, as for Fred, we're mostly just friends so far."

"He's the reason you went back to Denver, though, isn't he," Ryan said quietly.

Doug looked at his brother for a moment before answering. "Yes. Fred's been a big help to me going through this. He fought it for years, too. He even tried marriage for awhile. We met through my shrink. He put me in a therapy group of men who, like me, were in their late twenties or older and still in denial. Fred was a former patient. He came to one session to talk to the group, and asked me to go out for a drink afterward. We talked until four in the morning, just sitting in his car in the parking lot after the bar closed. I was lucky I found him. I was planning suicide at the time. He talked me out of it."

"Jeez, Doug, I had no idea," Ryan said. "It was that bad?"

"You don't know what it's like. My first time in a gay bar some guy I didn't even know grabbed me in the men's room. Literally, I mean. He grabbed my crotch. It scared the shit out of me. I'd had three months of aversion therapy and the physical contact from another man made me literally sick to my stomach. That was the night I started planning to kill myself. I felt like I'd completely fucked myself up. I knew I wasn't straight and never would be, and now I felt I'd screwed myself up for being gay, too. I met Fred three days later. I'd really only gone to that therapy session to say good-bye to people. I was going to drive up in the mountains and kill myself the next day. Something he said that night got through to me. When he asked me out for a drink, I went."

"I didn't think aversion therapy worked."

"Tell me about it. It won't make a gay man straight, but it can condition him to avoid intimacy with another man. Fred was great. We spent the first month just talking. I couldn't even let him hold my hand for a long time. But in the long run, he did more for me than any psychiatrist. By the end of the second month, I'd gotten to the point where I wasn't flinching every time he touched me, but I can only handle fairly limited physical contact. He hugged me a few days ago and I almost threw up."

"I just hugged you, Doug."

"You're my brother. My conditioning is against physical arousal. I'm attracted to Fred, so I can't let him hold me. I'm not attracted to you, so I don't react when you hug me. A real catch twenty-two, you know what I mean? I can hug anyone except the one I want to hug."

"This has been going on for how long?"

"I ended the therapy last July, and met Fred the middle of August. I'd known him for two months when you had your accident. I didn't dare return his calls the whole time you were in the hospital, and broke it off with him the day you went into rehab. He didn't even know you were my brother then. I think I used you as an excuse not to get any closer. Later, after we got back to L. A., I realized I missed him terribly." He sighed. "Gay or straight, Ryan, men can be stubborn, childish, selfish damn fools sometimes." He took the thawed steaks out of the microwave, put in three potatoes and restarted the oven. "I'm going to go throw these things on the grill," he said.

Fred returned a few minutes later with a carton of cigarettes and immediately noticed that something was different about the way Doug smiled when he saw him step into the kitchen. He gave Doug an inquisitive glance. "What are you grinning about?" he asked. He glanced from Doug to Ryan, who was sitting at the table sipping a drink, then back to Doug.

"Ryan knows," Doug replied. "He's always known. And apparently he's okay with it. I told him everything, how we met, what I went through."

"Good," Fred said. "See? You've been worrying for nothing. Now if we could just get you okay with it, too, we'd be getting somewhere. What made you decide to tell him?"

Ryan spoke up. "He didn't. I told him."

"And you're really okay with it? It's not going to make you uncomfortable for me to be here now that you know?"

"I'm not going to say it doesn't feel a little strange finally getting confirmation of something I've suspected for years but was never quite sure about, but I want my baby brother to be happy. Sounds like he's gone through a bunch of crap with trying to stay in the closet. I'm not planning to add to it. If I get uncomfortable about anything, I'll deal with that in therapy, not lay it off onto you two. Doug has the right to live his life, and you seem to be a decent guy, Fred. Sounds like he's very lucky to have you in his life. I'm glad you were there for him when I wasn't."

Doug and Fred accompanied Ryan back to Doug's condo after dinner, Fred checking all the rooms for possible intruders before Ryan entered the dwelling with Doug. "You still okay staying here alone?" Doug asked.

"I'm fine. Nobody's tried to kill me for a couple days. Maybe they've changed their mind."

Doug rolled his eyes. "Maybe our precautions have been working."

"That, too," Ryan admitted.

"I need to get some clothes for tomorrow. I think I have one more clean shirt in my closet, but I'll have to do laundry tomorrow."

Doug disappeared into his own room to get the shirt, emerging a few minutes later with a green shirt and some underwear and socks. "I was right. This was my last shirt." He dropped the items on the dining table. "I might as well check the mail while I'm here. Back in a second," he said, walking outside.

Fred walked over to the table and started to fold the clothing neatly. "Doug and his critters," he said with a smile. "Has he always done that?"

Ryan walked over to the table. "What? Worn little animals on his shirts?"

"Yes. He must have twenty different shirts like this."

"He started doing that in college, about the time I started my tie collection. What's that one?" he asked, nodding at the shirt.

Fred turned the folded shirt over to show Ryan. "Looks like a horse with a pointy forelock." He looked closer. "No, I'll bet that's a unicorn."

Ryan startled. "Unicorn? Let me see."

Fred turned the green shirt so Ryan could see it. "Isn't that a unicorn? Or is it a horse after all?"

Ryan stared at the shirt, puzzled. "No, it's a unicorn. I wonder where he got it."

"I don't know where he gets any of them," Fred said with a shrug as Doug walked back in with a handful of junk mail that he promptly dropped in the trash. "Ready to go?"

"Yes."

Ryan looked from the shirt to his brother, started to say something, then changed his mind and remained silent.

"What time should we come get you in the morning?" Doug asked him.

"Uh, I have another doctor appointment in the morning. Why don't you pick me up about seven in the Corvette like we've been doing? I'll leave you at the studio and I'll go to my appointment from there in the limo."

"Alone?"

"I'll be all right. I was fine today. And you need to get with Tony on that Walter Hussman business. I'll leave it to you three to decide what to do about him."

"I'd rather you didn't go anywhere alone," Doug argued. "I worried about you all day today."

"I agree," Fred said. "We still don't know what we're dealing with."

"I'll be fine. I'd rather you went to the studio and kept working on that edit so we can get this thing done. We're almost through. Besides, whoever drugged me must work at the studio, right? If I'm not there, he can't get me, right?"

Doug shook his head and turned to the door. "No point in arguing with him, Fred. He always gets his way. Let's go."

CHAPTER 40

FRED REMAINED IN TONY'S office the next morning while he called Peter Hayward, alias Walter Hussman, to the office. Doug had gone to meet with the director about the nearly-finished show, and Ryan's driver had taken him to his appointment. They had discussed the matter with Tony and decided to give Hayward a chance to explain himself. If his explanation proved satisfactory, he would be retained.

Fred stood up when there was a knock on the door. "Come in," Tony called.

Walter Hussman walked in. "You wanted to see me?" he said to Tony. "Oh, hello, Fred. Didn't know you were here."

"Sit down, Walter." Tony indicated a chair opposite the desk. "Or should I say Peter?"

Fred watched the man's face. His mouth opened, then shut, then he said, "How did you find out?"

"You didn't exactly try to disguise your appearance, Mr. Hayward," Tony replied. "You know we've had a detective working with us." He indicated Fred with a wave of his hand. "He discovered the truth. Now, would you like to explain why you're impersonating Walter Hussman?"

Hayward glanced at Fred, then looked back at Tony. "Maybe I should just get my things and leave now. You're going to fire me anyway, aren't you?"

"Mr. Hayward, we're trying to finish a show. Your work has been satisfactory. But in order to retain you, we need to know the reason for the masquerade."

"You'll fire me anyway, but I guess I'll take a shot at it." He folded his arms across his chest before continuing, "Hussman's a friend of mine."

"So we heard."

"I was released from prison four months ago after serving time for a drug conviction and haven't been able to find much work since. When I heard about this opening, I decided to use his name instead. That way anyone checking my background wouldn't find out about the conviction. I knew this job was only for a few weeks, and I figured the job would be over and I'd be gone before anyone figured it out. I didn't plan to stay in this area long, and I just needed some money to tide me over for a while. I thought with that strike pending I wouldn't have much trouble getting on somewhere."

Fred spoke up. "I found no record of convictions on you."

"It was in Oklahoma."

Fred looked skeptical but was silent.

"Are you clean now?" Tony asked.

"Yes. I learned my lesson the hard way. I just couldn't find work in Oklahoma. That's why I came out here."

"Mr. Hayward, get back to work now. I'll let you know later what we decide. We'll continue to call and refer to you as Walter Hussman until we figure out what to do. No point getting the rest of the crew in an uproar over this."

"Yes, sir." Hayward/Hussman stood up. "You know where I'll be."

After he left, Tony turned to Fred. "What do you think? Is he telling the truth?"

"I should check with Oklahoma before you make a decision. I know you really can't afford to lose him right now, but I don't have a good feeling about this. His body language says he's lying through his teeth, and if he just got out of prison in Oklahoma four months ago he's probably still in the parole system and shouldn't have left the state. Keep a close watch on him, Tony. It's possible he may be our troublemaker, although we'd never be able to prove it." He stood up. "Tell Doug I'll see him tonight. I've got some things to check out on the computer."

"Will you be back to pick him up when we're done? I can give him a ride home if you want."

"He's got his own car here," Fred replied. "You know how he is about that Corvette."

* * *

Jim Harrison, Dr. Andrews and Dr. Miller were already waiting for Ryan in the office. "Good morning, Mr. North," the hypnotist said.

"Hello, Dr. Andrews," he answered. He nodded to Jim and Dr. Miller.

"Are you ready to get started?"

"I've got a headache," Ryan answered as they sat down in their respective chairs.

"We'll take care of that in a few minutes," the hypnotist replied.

"And I want to do this without drugs today, okay?"

"Whatever you say, Mr. North. Perhaps you will be more relaxed today, since you already know what we're about here."

Jim watched as the hypnotist skillfully brought Ryan slowly under his control, without the use of the tranquilizer this time. "Mr. North, can you hear me?" he asked, when it appeared Ryan was ready to proceed.

"Yes," Ryan replied softly.

"Let's think back to the day of your accident, October sixteenth. Do you remember that day?"

"Yes."

"Think about what happened after you and Doug split up on the mountain. Do you remember what happened?"

"Yes. I was on my horse."

"Yes, you were on your horse. Do you remember riding your horse off the trail?"

"Yes. I rode down the hill to look for deer."

"What happened next?"

"Ducked under the branch." He grimaced in pain.

"Mr. North, when I count to three, you will not feel any more pain. One. Two. Three. Do you feel better now?"

"Yes."

"Okay, you have just ducked under the branch. Tell me what you are doing now."

"Looking for the deer. Looking through the binoculars."

"What do you see through the binoculars?"

"Green unicorn," Ryan said firmly.

"What else do you see?"

"Horse's tail. Fallen tree. Tree roots sticking up. I told you this before," he said insistently.

"What else do you see? Tell me again."

Ryan sighed. "There's a hole at the base of the tree. Unicorn is throwing branches into the hole. Covering up the hand."

"What else does the unicorn do?"

"Throws the cap into the hole. The red cap. Then takes it back. Looks up when his horse whinnies."

"What does the unicorn look like? How tall is the unicorn?"

"Don't know. Not as tall as I am."

"What color is the unicorn's hair?"

"Blond. No! Green! I told you it was green!"

"Is the unicorn a male or female?"

"Male."

"How do you know that? Are you close enough to see?"

"Because I know it's a male, that's all."

"Does the unicorn have a beard?"

"Sometimes. Not now. Did before."

"Have you ever seen the unicorn before that day in the woods?"

"I – I'm not sure."

"Do you know who the unicorn is?"

"Yes."

"Who is the unicorn, Mr. North?"

"Don't ask me that!" he shouted angrily. "I told you before not to ask me that. You said you wouldn't!"

"I'm sorry, but it's important that you know who the unicorn is. If you tell me who the unicorn is, I won't have to ask you again."

"It's not him." Ryan began to tap his fingers nervously on his right thigh.

"It's not who, Mr. North?"

"It's not Doug. It can't be Doug. Don't say that it's Doug." His fingers tapped harder.

"Did someone say it was Doug? Did someone say that the unicorn is Doug?"

"Yes." Now Ryan was clenching and unclenching his left fist while he continued to tap the fingers of his right hand on his thigh.

"Who said that?"

"I did."

"You said that the unicorn was Doug?"

"Yes." His voice began to rise.

"Is the unicorn Doug?"

"Don't ask me that!" Ryan shouted.

"Mr. North, I want you to rest for a minute. Close your eyes and picture the ocean waves, crashing on the beach. Do you see the ocean waves?"

"Yes."

"Watch them until I tell you to stop."

The hypnotist looked at Dr. Miller. "Should I push him?"

"I think he needs to confront what he is hiding, Dr. Andrews. He's been repressing fear for seven months. He needs to deal with it." He glanced at Jim Harrison and sighed. "No matter what it means in the long run."

Dr. Andrews turned back to Ryan. "Mr. North, stop looking at the waves. Open your eyes now. You are back in the forest, looking through your binoculars. Tell me who you see."

"Doug's chasing the unicorn away. I knew he didn't do it." Ryan's hands were now resting calmly in his lap.

"Who didn't do what?"

"Doug didn't kill that kid. The unicorn did. Doug chased him away."

"Mr. North, are you telling me the truth?"

Ryan didn't answer.

"You must tell me the truth. Do you know what the truth is?"

"Yes."

"Tell me what you really see."

Ryan started to shake, and tears welled up in his eyes. He clenched both fists and whispered, "It's Doug. He's covering up a body in that hole. I see his horse there. His plaid jacket."

"Do you see his face?"

"No, I just see him from the back." Ryan was starting to sob. "I don't want it to be Doug! Let it be a unicorn! Why did you make me say this?"

"Mr. North, do you believe it is Doug?"

Ryan sniffled. The doctor put the tissue box in his hands. "Why does it have to be Doug? Why did he do it? I don't want him to do it. I don't have to tell anyone I saw him. I'll just forget I saw anything. Then he won't have to go away. Nobody has to know!"

"You have to know. You have to know so you can get better. Mr. North, you must remember the truth. Do you still think there is a unicorn?"

"No." Ryan looked down at his hands, where he was twisting a tissue around his fingers. "No unicorn."

"Who hid the body in the woods?"

"Doug." Ryan looked dejected. "I think it was Doug. Maybe I just dreamed it."

"Mr. North, I want you to wake up in a minute. When you wake up, you will remember everything you said here. You will not have headaches anymore when you think about your accident. I will count to three now. When I reach three, you will wake up. One. Two. Three."

Ryan blinked, then looked at Jim, then back at the hypnotist. Then he started to sob again. "It can't be Doug! I must be mistaken." He looked at the doctor through reddened eyes. "Maybe I'm having a breakdown. Maybe I imagined all that." He reached for a tissue and blew his nose.

The two doctors looked at each other. Dr. Miller spoke. "Ryan, if I understand what's been going on here, you think your brother committed a crime. Is your thinking confused?"

Ryan sighed. "No. I guess I just couldn't accept it until I saw that shirt last night and realized what my mind had done."

"Shirt?"

"Doug has a green shirt with a unicorn on it. Apparently he was wearing it while I was in the hospital and I must have seen it. I couldn't figure out what that unicorn meant. Then when I saw the shirt, and realized what I had done, I realized that Doug must have been the person I saw in the woods that day."

"You said you didn't see his face."

"No, he started to turn toward me and I panicked, thinking if I could see him, he could see me. When I wheeled the horse around, that branch was right there. I had amnesia after that. We never knew until now that I had seen anything at all. If it hadn't been for the nightmares, I might never have known." His voice lowered to a whisper. "It would have been better if I'd never remembered." He glared accusingly at Dr. Miller. "This was what you meant the other day. You were trying to make me see that I might have to let go of Doug, like I had to let go of the rest of my family."

Dr. Miller did not answer. There was no need to confirm it. Ryan knew the truth now.

* * *

"This makes no sense, Jim," Ryan said, shaking his head. "My brother couldn't have killed anyone." It was an hour later, and Jim Harrison had asked Ryan to meet him in his hotel room so they could talk in private. So nobody would worry about him, Ryan had asked his driver to call the studio and tell Tony that he had to go somewhere for an X-ray and would be delayed a few hours.

"He may have only disposed of the body, Ryan," Jim replied. "Someone else may have strangled him."

"Why would Doug be a part of it? What reason could he possibly have had for participating in the murder of a boy he didn't even know?"

Jim hesitated. Normally he didn't make a practice of revealing information about his investigations but in this case he needed his witness to understand that what he saw was plausible, not impossible. "He did know him," he said slowly.

"How did he know him?"

"The boy was attending meetings every Tuesday night at the college. Doug was there. According to several witnesses, they spent a lot of time talking."

"What meetings? Doug wasn't involved in any groups that I know of."

"I'd rather not identify the organization right now. The bottom line is that he knew the boy, for at least a month, and they spent some time together. Yet he didn't say anything that night at your house."

Ryan looked at Jim thoughtfully for a minute. "It was some kind of gay support group, wasn't it."

"Yes, it was. I assume you've known all along he was gay?"

Ryan sighed. "Would you believe he just admitted it to me for the first time last night? He never told me he was, but I suspected it since he was in grade school. I finally confronted him last night. We'd never talked about it before, and he's gone through the motions of trying to be straight. I figured as long as he was trying to be straight, I wasn't going to confront him on it. I mean, if I were wrong, what would that do for his ego to know his brother thought he was gay? But after he showed up with a male friend who seemed to be a little more than a friend, I finally thought I should let him know that I knew and it was okay. He didn't have to pretend any more."

"Why do you suppose he never told you?"

"Afraid of rejection. Ever since our mother died three years ago, he's been withdrawing from me more and more. We used to be inseparable, lived together in college and all that. Even when I was married, he was over for dinner several nights a week and we spent a lot of time together. He never did have anything resembling a social life. But our mother died right after my divorce, and I tried to get Doug to move to L.A. with me when I went. He wouldn't come. Since then, he took up smoking and started going inside himself more and more. I never knew what was going on, but whenever I'd visit, he felt more and more like a stranger to me. I kept trying to be a part of his life, get him to talk about what he was doing, his job, friends, whatever, but he never wanted to talk. Apparently at some point he almost killed himself, too."

"Yet he came back to Los Angeles with you after your accident."

"Something was different. While I was in rehab, it was like he came back to himself. The month he stayed with me after rehab was like old times again. Then right after Christmas, this male friend from Denver showed up and he decided to leave suddenly. Went back to Denver. Didn't see him again until he came to help with the show."

"But he's still in the closet."

"Pretty much. Maybe now that he's over the hurdle of letting me know he'll be able to be what he is. Although," he sighed, "it probably doesn't matter now."

"Ryan, you know I'm going to have to take him into custody. Not because of what you told me, though, although I feel more certain of his involvement now because of that. I was already planning to come talk to him when you called the other day. As soon as we confirmed he had a relationship with the boy, I knew something was wrong. He's lied to me on several occasions now, starting with not telling me he was your brother the day of your accident, and ending with not telling me he knew the boy when I showed him that picture in your living room."

Ryan swallowed hard. "You don't think he and the boy were – lovers? I have the impression he hasn't crossed that line yet. To physical intimacy, I mean," he added awkwardly.

"I have no evidence of anything between them other than that they did know each other. I certainly have no cause to suspect him of sexual misconduct at this time and the boy was not sexually assaulted the day he died. We're also nearly certain the boy was not gay. But I haven't started to investigate your brother yet. Right now I want to call him down on the lies I know he's told me and see what he has to say for himself. If he buried that body, he may have been coerced into doing it. He'll have a chance to tell me what he knows. I know this is all new to you, Ryan, but I've been a detective a long time. I know things aren't always as they seem. Believe me, I will be as fair to him as possible." He stood up. "Now, where can I find him?"

"Are you going to arrest him?"

"I'm going to send a couple of LAPD officers to ask him nicely to come in for questioning. If he refuses, they will arrest him for interfering with the investigation."

"He's at the studio. Can I go with you when you pick him up?"

"I'm sorry, but I'd rather you didn't. I'm not even going to go myself because I don't want to spook him and cause a scene there that might draw media attention unnecessarily. Why don't you go on home and wait? I'll call you after we have him in custody. I'd rather not reveal to him that you've placed him at the scene of the crime until I hear what he has to say. You won't be able to talk to him until after I've questioned him."

"Should I get him a lawyer?"

"That would probably be a good idea."

* * *

Within an hour and a half, Doug Norton had been picked up and had been fingerprinted and confined in a holding cell at the local police station. He had tried calling Ryan at the condo but there was no answer so he tried Fred's cell phone. It was answered by voice mail, so he left a message asking Fred to find Ryan and have him get a lawyer.

Doug by this point was scared. Jim Harrison knew Doug had lied to him. That and the fact that he had been giving the detective a hard time since the day they met would no doubt combine to work against Doug Norton. He was their best suspect and he knew it.

After being allowed to contemplate his transgressions alone in a small cell for more than two hours, he was led into the interrogation room by a uniformed officer and politely invited to sit in the chair at the end of the table. His handcuffs were removed and he immediately rubbed his wrists.

Resisting arrest probably hadn't helped either. What the heck was he thinking?

"Detective Harrison will be with you in a moment," the officer informed him. Then Doug Norton was left alone.

He glanced nervously around the room. The table was about eight feet long and three feet wide. He sat in one chair and there were three others in the room. There was a video camera mounted high in one corner, but it was the corner behind Doug. He supposed that he would be moved to another chair after the detective arrived, probably the chair at the opposite end of the table that was in full view of the camera. One wall was mirrored – one-way glass, no doubt. He wondered who would be on the other side, watching and listening. He wondered how long it would take Fred to contact Ryan, and how long it would take either or both of them to find an attorney.

He tried to relax, but his heart was pounding, his mouth was dry, and he was already feeling rivulets of sweat coursing down his side from his left armpit.

He jumped when the door opened. Jim Harrison entered the room, accompanied by a young black man in a Clear Creek County uniform. "Hello, Mr. Norton," Jim said, holding out his hand to Doug, who shook it mutely. "This is Deputy Clayton Burns, my associate. He flew out here this morning to help with this investigation. Deputy Burns, this is Doug Norton." He sat in the chair nearest the door, at Doug's left.

"Hello, Mr. Norton," Clayton said, also holding out his hand in greeting.

"Hello," Doug managed, shaking the young man's hand.

"Can we get you anything?" Jim asked. "Something to eat? Coffee? Water? A Coke? You need to use a restroom before we begin?"

"Some water would be good," Doug replied. "The restroom may come later."

"Fine. Clay, would you mind asking someone to bring Mr. Norton some water, and I could use some coffee myself. Black with sugar."

Clayton Burns slipped from the room, returning a few moments later. "They'll bring it in a few minutes."

"Thanks, Clay." Jim opened his notebook and took out a pen. Then he pulled a microphone from a drawer under the table, plugged it into a jack on the edge of the table and placed it between himself and Doug Norton. "I'll have to record this, Mr. Norton, and Deputy Burns and I will both be taking notes. We'll start after they bring in the drinks so we won't be interrupted. Have you been treated well since you were brought in?"

"Yes, sir," Doug replied warily, wondering why he was being treated with such consideration. He certainly hadn't expected it – nor deserved it, for that matter, he realized. It must be some kind of trap, he concluded. He'd have to be careful. They were probably trying to get him off his guard.

"Glad to hear it. You had lunch, too?" Doug nodded. He'd been given a sandwich, but hadn't wanted to eat more than a few bites. There was a knock on the door and Clayton opened it and took a tray. He handed a large cup of ice water to Doug, then gave Jim his coffee and took a Coke for himself.

"Okay," Jim said, switching on the tape recorder. "We'll begin." He announced for the record the names of all present and the case number under investigation before turning to Doug. "I believe you were read your rights when you were arrested," he stated, "but I'm going to read them again now, for the record." He read the standard Miranda warning from the card he carried in his pocket. "Do you understand these rights?"

"Yes."

"Do you wish to have an attorney present for questioning?"

"Not at the moment. I didn't do anything. I just want to get out of here." He'd given the matter some thought while he had been waiting, and decided that demanding the presence of a lawyer would make himself look guilty. He was going to try to cooperate, and hope Jim Harrison would be satisfied if he didn't do anything else to antagonize him. Already he was sorely regretting his feeble attempt to escape at the studio.

"Are you willing to answer questions about your relationship to Daryl Walker?"

"Yes." Doug's voice was barely a whisper.

"Please speak a little louder, Mr. Norton."

Doug cleared his throat. "Yes," he repeated.

"Thank you. Did you know the deceased, Daryl Eugene Walker?"

"Yes."

"When did you meet him?"

"I met him for the first time when I gave a talk about advertising to his journalism class. It was around the second week in September last year. A Friday afternoon. I don't recall the date."

"Did you talk to him personally at that time?"

"He may have been one of the students who raised a hand and asked a question. I didn't specifically notice him."

"When was the next time you saw him?"

Doug swallowed hard and replied nervously, "At a meeting of the Lesbian and Gay Society at Red Rock Community College about two weeks later. It was a Tuesday night."

"Did he recognize you, or did you recognize him?"

"He recognized me and came over to talk. He introduced himself as Danny. I didn't recognize him at all. He was wearing a fake mustache and a ball cap, trying to hide his identity."

"What did you talk about?"

"I was there with a friend of mine, a private investigator. He had been hired to investigate a series of gay-bashing incidents that had victimized several of the members of the group. He asked me to come along and see if we could help since the cops refused to investigate." A hard edge had crept into Doug's voice. "The cops refused to take reports from the first two victims, saying they asked for it, then the other victims refused to report it at all."

Jim frowned. "Where was this? What jurisdiction?"

"West side of Lakewood, near the college."

"And Daryl Walker already had some information about this? Is that what you talked about?"

"He told me he was already secretly investigating, trying to get a story for his school paper about it. One of the victims had been the older brother of Danny's lab partner. She came to school in tears one day because her brother was in the hospital. She told Danny all about it, including that the cop wouldn't take the report. He was one of the first victims. Danny wanted to be the one to solve it, find out who was doing it. He was really angry about the cop."

"You're saying the name Danny. You mean Daryl, is that correct?"

"Sorry, yes. I never knew him by that name, though. And he knew me as Bobby. Nobody there uses their real name."

"How far along in his investigation was he?"

"Not very. He'd talked to some of the victims, and had a rough description of the guy, that was all. He offered to help us. All he wanted was the story. Said it would make his dad proud of him." Doug took a sip of water.

"How did the investigation go? Did you learn who was doing it?"

"Eventually. We were pretty sure we knew who it was after a week or two. We came up with a plan, but my friend got called out of town unexpectedly and then Ryan had his accident that same weekend and it was more than two months before I could get back to help with the investigation. Meantime, the group changed their meeting place a couple times. It was January before Fred and I finally nailed the son of a bitch and got him arrested. It was the brother of the high school principal."

"Who is Fred?"

Doug flushed. "The investigator. My friend."

"Your lover."

"Not my lover," Doug snapped. "We were just friends. Still are."

"We're going to have to talk to him, Mr. Norton. May I have his full name, please?"

Doug glared at Jim Harrison. "Can't we leave him out of this? He doesn't need any more cops hassling him either."

"Sorry, but no, we can't. He had dealings with the boy just before his death, which makes him a material witness. His name, please?"

Doug sighed angrily. "Fred Dreyer," he snapped.

"Dreyer?" Jim asked, puzzled.

"Yes, Dreyer. D-R-E-Y-E-R. Like the ice cream. I wish you'd leave him out of this."

Jim persisted, "Did he used to be a police officer?"

"Yes."

"Left the force about three years ago? Worked east side?"

"Yes. What of it?"

"Never mind," Jim said, shaking his head. "I think I knew him once, when he was on the force. I worked east side for a while."

Doug looked at Jim sharply. "Same precinct?"

"Yes, if he's the Fred Dreyer I remember. Six foot, stocky, dark hair and eyes? Mid thirties?"

"If you worked at his precinct when he quit, then you must be one of the creeps who . . ." Doug spat out, then broke off. "I want a lawyer."

Jim switched off the tape recorder and laid down his pen. He gazed levelly at Doug Norton for a moment, then said, "Deputy Burns, please go see if Mr. Norton's attorney has arrived." As soon as Clayton had left the room, Jim said, "I was not one of the bastards who attacked him that day, Mr. Norton. In fact, I tried to stop it. The whole thing made me sick to my stomach. I went to see Fred in the hospital the next day, and I was the one who carried his letter of resignation to the captain, along with my own request for a transfer to the west side. Which, as you're aware, wasn't much better."

Doug stared at him dumbly. "You were the one," he finally whispered. "Fred didn't remember your name." He buried his face in his hands and sighed. "Shit." He said nothing for well over a minute, struggling with conflicting emotions while Jim looked on impassively. Finally he muttered, "Detective Harrison, I owe you an apology, and I hope you can find a way to accept it." He looked up and swallowed hard. "I was beaten up once myself, not long after the first meeting I went to. It wasn't in Lakewood, it was on the east side. Three guys jumped me. I really wasn't out of the closet yet. Well, I'm still not really out of the closet even now, but it was one of my first attempts to approach my own kind, shall we say? I didn't know enough to take any precautions when I left the meeting. I wound up in the hospital. Ryan doesn't even know about this."

"What happened?" Jim asked.

"Per usual, the fucking cop wouldn't even take the report in the emergency room," Doug said bitterly. "Said no point wasting resources trying to track down the guy who did it, unless it was to give him a medal for taking another ass-fucking fag off the streets. Direct quote. I'll never forget it."

Anger flared briefly in Jim's eyes and he shook his head. "I'm sorry," he said. "That was terrible."

"I hated cops from that moment on. Not that I'd been all that fond of them before," Doug explained wryly. "I tend to collect a lot of speeding tickets. But I loathed them after that. Then I met Fred through my therapist. I'd already known him a few weeks before he told me he used to be a cop. I probably never would have spoken to him if I'd known it up front, but by that point we'd gotten to be good friends. He told me what happened to him, why he left the force. He almost committed suicide after that attack, you know. He only recently told me about you, but he didn't remember your name."

"Would it have mattered if he'd told you sooner?"

"I probably wouldn't have given you such a hard time if I'd realized you were the one straight-shooter Fred ever met, if you'll pardon the expression. I would have trusted you more, maybe."

Jim smiled. "I'm not the only 'straight-shooter' out there. Not all cops are bigots, but I won't try to tell you there aren't an awful lot who are. Even one is too many. Some precincts seem to collect them though."

Doug looked up at Jim Harrison. "I remember something that happened when I was seven and wouldn't play with some black kids because one black kid punched me in the nose once. My mother told me I shouldn't judge anyone based on how someone like them had treated me. This is the same thing, though, isn't it? You've been nothing but respectful and polite to me, even now when you think I'm guilty of murder. And I've been treating you like shit, even when you were trying to help my brother last year, all because a cop treated me like shit once."

"I wondered what was going on last year," Jim said. "Your brother told me you were a nice guy but I'd never seen it. And off the record, which we're speaking right now, I haven't decided if I think you're guilty of murder or not. You're here today because you lied to me about knowing Daryl Walker, and I was able to turn up a connection between the two of you. That makes you a suspect but there's still a lot I don't know yet. I'm not ready to accuse anyone until I know a whole lot more than I know now."

"Well, I'm sorry I've given you such a hard time, and if you'll call Deputy Burns back in, we can go back on the record and I'll tell you anything I can, without a lawyer. I have to trust that if any cop in the world will listen to me with an open mind, it's you. Can we start over?" Doug held out his hand and Jim Harrison took it and shook it.

"You do understand, Mr. Norton, that you are still considered a suspect? Are you sure you don't want your lawyer here?"

"No lawyer. I liked the boy. He didn't deserve to die. And the sooner I tell you what I know, the sooner you'll know that I didn't kill him. And I guess I better tell you right now that I didn't just lie to you about knowing him. I saw him the day he died. In the woods."

Now the recorder was back on, and Clayton was taking notes while his mentor walked Doug Norton through his relationship with Daryl Walker until they arrived at the day of the boy's death.

"Now tell me everything that you remember after you left your brother at that trail crossing, Mr. Norton," Jim said.

"As I told you last year, my parting shot to him to go piss up a rope was treated as a joke. He said he'd meet me there at noon and for me to bring the rope. He waved good-bye and I flipped him off. The last thing I heard was him laughing. I was steamed for about five minutes, then I laughed myself. I was glad nobody had been around to see us bickering like that."

"Where did you go? Clayton, please spread out the trail map." Clayton unfolded a map he had tucked in the back of his notebook and spread it out on the table, pushing it over to Doug.

Doug bent over the map, frowning. "Can I mark on this?"

"If you want." Jim handed Doug a pencil.

"We rode here," he said tracing a line from the parking lot to the trail crossing. "Then Ryan went this way," he drew a short line with an arrow down one branch of the trail, "and I went this way." He drew a line along the twisting trail to an intersection with another trail. "This is where I saw Danny. I mean Daryl. Sorry, it's hard for me to think of him as Daryl," he apologized.

"Not a problem," Jim said. "What was he doing when you saw him? Did you talk?"

"He was on a horse, riding fast up the trail. They almost ran into Rocket. My horse."

"Describe his horse."

"It was a dun horse, kind of a medium buckskin in color, a little darker than Ryan's horse. Average size, probably a quarter horse. Black points. Uh, that's mane, tail, and legs," he clarified.

"I know."

"Not sure if it was a mare or gelding. Riding with a blue nylon bridle and reins, older leather western saddle, canvas saddlebags. Bags appeared to be empty. There was orange ribbon on the bridle, saddle, and the horse's tail, like the ribbon we got from the outfitter to put on our horses."

"How was the boy dressed?"

"Jeans, red jacket, red beret, gloves."

"What kind of gloves?"

"Knit gloves, black or dark blue, I don't remember. Like you'd wear skiing. They weren't the kind you'd normally use on a horse."

"Shoes?"

"I didn't notice his shoes."

"So what was he doing? Hunting?"

"No, he didn't have a gun. He had a camera hanging around his neck. Maybe a Nikon, I don't know. A good camera, but not a fancy one. There was a zoom lens on it."

"Did he say why he was there?"

"No, and he seemed upset that I'd seen him. I was a little upset, too, since I was out there with Ryan North and I certainly didn't want a teenage reporter getting wind that I was Ryan's brother, or even that I knew him. Fred didn't even know at that point, and I didn't want him to hear it from the kid."

"What did you say to each other?"

"I said, Hey, Danny, where are you going in such a hurry? And he said, Oh, hi, Bobby. Is Jeff with you? (He knew Fred as Jeff.) I said no, I'm by myself. Then I said, I didn't know you had a horse. How long have you had it? And he said, I'm really in a hurry. I don't have time to chat. He started to turn away and I said, Wait a minute. What are you doing out here with that camera? I hope you're not working on an anti-hunter piece."

"What did he say to that?"

"He repeated that he was in a hurry and if he didn't get going he'd be too late. Then he kicked his horse and cantered up a rocky trail. He's lucky he didn't cripple the horse riding him like that."

"For all we know, he may have," Jim remarked. "We haven't found the horse yet. Where did he go?"

Doug pointed on the map. "Up this way."

Jim mentally drew a line from where Doug pointed to where the helicopter had landed. It was about a half-mile away.

"What happened next? Did you follow him?"

"No, I think I muttered something about him being a flaky kid, and rode down the trail he had come up on."

"Did you see him again?"

"No. Never." Doug paused and took a sip of water. "I should have gone to his funeral, but the day I found out he was dead was the day I was flying back to L.A. to help Ryan with the show. I don't even know when the funeral was."

"It was the Saturday after we identified the body. Okay, what did you do next?"

"Rode down the trail, looking for deer. Was a little distracted, wondering what the boy was doing, but I forgot about him after awhile. I rode about twenty minutes after I saw the kid, then I heard this helicopter. Wondered about it, why it was there. Thought maybe someone had gotten hurt, then I thought maybe that's why the kid was rushing up there, to cover a story of some rescue, but the timing didn't seem very likely. How would he have known to be there in the first place? Then the sound stopped. I rode down here," he drew another line on the map, "and saw a couple of deer but they were does and I had a buck permit. I did hear a gunshot about then, wondered if maybe Ryan or someone else had just shot a deer. I continued on this trail until it looped back and met up with this trail," he continued the line, "and I turned on it, headed back in the general direction of where I'd left Ryan."

"How long after you left Ryan would you say you saw the boy?"

"Hour, maybe. No more than that."

"And how long until you got to this crossing and turned back?"

"Maybe another hour. I rode to here," he pointed, "and got off and tied Rocket to a tree. I spent about forty minutes walking around in that area but didn't see anything. Then I checked my watch and realized I better get going if I was going to meet Ryan at noon."

"Wait a minute. Did you hear the helicopter leave?"

Doug thought a moment. "I suppose I must have, but I don't remember where I was when I heard it again."

"What time did you get back to the crossing to meet Ryan?"

"I was late. It was about twelve-thirty. I remember being pissed that Ryan wasn't there, figured he decided to ride off and teach me a lesson since I was late. So I didn't wait around, I just rode on back to the trailer, found his horse, then went looking for him. On this trail," he added. "The one we started out on. He was here." He pointed at the bend in the trail where his brother had been found.

"Mark an X there, please," Jim instructed. "Then mark an X where you encountered the boy." Doug did as he was asked. Jim stood and leaned across the table. He marked another X on the map. "This is where the helicopter landed. And here," he said, adding another X, "is where the body was found."

Doug looked at the map. "See? I was nowhere near it."

"So you say," Jim answered, sitting back in his chair. He leaned back, interlacing his fingers behind his head.

Doug looked up at him. "You don't believe me?"

"Who was in the helicopter, Mr. Norton?"

"I have no idea. I never saw the helicopter, I only heard it."

"You passed within a half mile of it, by your own admission, at about the time it was landing."

"I still never saw it."

Jim leaned forward and looked Doug straight in the eyes. "You want to know what I think, Mr. Norton? I think you were the one hurrying to meet the helicopter and the kid was trying to get a story. Once you saw the kid and knew he was heading the same direction, you had to kill him to keep him quiet. You took his camera and gloves, probably because he fought back and got your hair or skin on them, sent them away in the helicopter, then dumped his body and got rid of the horse. That's why you were late getting back to the trail crossing. You had to take the horse into the back country and kill him. No problem.

You had a thirty-ought-six with you for deer hunting anyway. Easy to kill a horse, and plenty of places to do it where only the mountain lions would find it. Probably sent the saddle away in the chopper, too, and buried the bridle somewhere after the horse was dead."

Doug stared at him, stunned. "You're nuts. I told you what I did, and I told you the truth. I didn't kill him, and I don't know who did."

"I've got a witness who saw you with the body, Mr. Norton."

"Then your so-called witness must be the murderer, and he's trying to pin it on me. Everyone knows I was up there that day, shit, I was on the ten o'clock news that night. It would be easy to frame me."

"My witness didn't know you knew the boy. Nobody could effectively frame you without knowing that."

"How do you know he didn't know I knew him? Who is this witness anyway?"

Jim looked long and hard at Doug's face before he replied quietly, "Your brother. Ryan North."

CHAPTER 41

OUG'S FACE WENT completely ashen and his jaw sagged. "No," he said. "He can't have. I wasn't there. I didn't do it."

Jim shrugged. "We have physical evidence that either will or won't corroborate what he told me. Can you think of any reason why your own brother would try to frame you?"

"Of course not. This is preposterous. I think this interview is over, Detective Harrison, until I see a lawyer. Are you charging me with murder?"

"Not yet. Right now I'm holding you for obstruction of justice, withholding evidence in a homicide investigation, and resisting arrest today. You remain a suspect and in custody for now. Meantime, I'm going to talk to Fred Dreyer, see if he corroborates anything at all of what you've told me today. Will you tell me how to reach him or do I have to do this the hard way?"

"You won't have to look far. He's probably either here already or on his way."

A knock sounded at the door. Clayton Burns rose to answer it. He spoke to someone for a moment, then turned to Jim. "Harley needs to talk to you. Something's come up."

Jim stood. "Since Mr. Norton is finished for now, have him taken back to the holding area, Clay. Mr. Norton, I appreciate what you've told me and I will attempt to verify what you've said. I'll be speaking to your brother again later. In the meantime, you will understand that I can't allow you to speak to each other, nor can you speak to Mr. Dreyer. When your attorney arrives, you will be given a chance to talk to him as much as you like until I return. Then we will continue."

Doug didn't reply and Jim left the room.

Doug looked at Deputy Burns. "I didn't do it. Why would Ryan say I did? This makes no sense."

"I don't think I should discuss anything with you, Mr. Norton, without Detective Harrison and your attorney present." He hesitated. "For what it's worth, I think you're probably telling the truth. But I'm not in charge of the case. From what I know of Jim Harrison, though, he won't charge you unless he has the evidence to make it stick."

"Thanks," Doug replied. "I hope you're right about him. I've got to trust him. I've got to trust him to find the truth. I believe he'll honestly try, but I just hope he's good at his job."

Jim stepped out of the room and walked down the hall to take the phone call. "What's up?" he asked.

"We got a phone call from Daryl Walker's journalism teacher," Harley Watson replied. "I'm heading over to Walker's school. She found several tape recordings in his old desk in the back of a drawer. Apparently the drawer has been stuck and they didn't know anything was in it until now. School is out now, and she was tidying up the news office for the summer when she discovered the stuck drawer and found the tapes."

"What's on them?"

"With any luck, the solution to this thing. She wouldn't tell me over the phone but said it was important. I called the senator so someone can ID the voice. They'll be waiting for me in the journalism office."

"I guess I'd better hold any further questioning until I know what this is all about."

"I suppose I'll have to handle your girlfriend for you on this. Too many people know about this to think we can keep it from the press."

A thousand miles away, Jim blushed, then muttered, "Sheila Fernelli won't be a problem for you, Harley. She happens to be in Los Angeles at the moment."

There was silence on the line for several seconds, then Harley said, "I guess we'll talk about *that* when you get back. Stay at that number. I'll try to get a speaker phone set up when we hear the tape so you can listen to it, too."

* * *

Senator Gene Walker's eyes shone with tears when he heard his son's voice on the tape recorder. He had met the sheriff at the high school, and they were led into a small conference room by Evelyn Moore. Harley had gotten Jim Harrison back on the line, who was listening with Clayton Burns to the recording in another conference room in the Beverly Hills police headquarters. Harley had reluctantly allowed Evelyn Moore to be present, knowing full well she had already listened to the tape before calling him. He had not allowed the maintenance man who had pried the drawer open to be there, though. His testimony would be limited to knowledge of how the tape had been found. He didn't need to know Senator Walker's reaction to it.

Evelyn Moore had fast-forwarded the sixty-minute mini cassette tape to the relevant portion near the end.

"It's October seventh, Thursday. I'm about to do something that may be dangerous. I don't know what else to do. I started the investigation into the beatings three weeks ago. I've been working with two men who call themselves Bobby and Jeff, who are also investigating the beatings. They don't know my real name, and I know they're not using their real names either, because I met one of them once. But that doesn't matter. While I was working undercover, a man named Peter came to me one day and said he wanted to hire me. He said if I didn't go along with him, he'd see that everyone found out I was gay.

"I'm not gay! I'm just pretending to be so I can do this investigation. If I can crack this case, my dad will finally have something to be proud of me for. But if I don't go along with this guy, Peter, he'll blow my cover for sure. I mean, I can't have him going around and telling people I'm gay, because then I'd have to explain I'm just pretending, and there would be a lot of talk, and the truth would come out and I won't be able to finish my investigation."

Harley knit his brow as he tried to follow the boy's story. He tried to show no emotion, watching Senator Walker's face as he struggled to maintain his composure while he listened to the recording left by his son so many months before.

Daryl Walker's voice, speaking from beyond the grave, was having a profound effect on everyone in the room. Evelyn Moore occasionally dabbed her eyes with a tissue.

"Peter wants me to pick up something in the woods for him. He never said it outright but I know it's drugs. He'll get a horse and I'm supposed to ride the horse somewhere near Mount Evans, pick up the stuff that's being dropped by helicopter, and deliver it somewhere. He said he'll pay me $200 but I'm betting he won't give me a dime. And I won't know where to take it until I pick it up, so there's no way I can have the police there waiting for him." An audible sigh was heard on the tape. *"And I won't know where to meet the helicopter until I pick up the horse. I either go along with this, or risk the investigation Jeff and Bobby and I are working on. A rock and a hard place, is that what they call it? So I'm going to go along with Peter's scheme and hope I'll at least get another story out of it."*

This was followed by several minutes of random notes about homework assignments and one cryptic comment dated Tuesday, October the twelfth, that just said, "Jeff says we're going to try it next Tuesday. Make sure to get off work that night."

There were a few other comments about homework, then a brief period of silence, broken by Daryl's subdued voice.

"Today is Thursday, October fourteenth. I can't believe Peter expects me to do it again! He told me when he first met me that he wanted me to do only one pickup, but now he's found out who I really am and he's threatening to put the word out that the senator's son is a drug runner if I don't keep working for him." The voice broke off. Was he crying? *"I can't let him do that, and I can't tell anyone. It would kill my dad if he knew. Even Jeff and Bobby don't know about this. How can I tell them and have them know that their whole investigation is at risk? We're so close to the truth now."* Another sigh, then, *"I'm an investigator, damn it! I'll just have to find out who Peter is, then I can blackmail him right back. Either he leaves me alone or I'll blow the whistle on his whole operation. I'll just have to play along with him until I find out more about him — and that pilot. Someone has to be flying that*

helicopter. This time I'll take a shortcut and get there early with my camera and take a picture of the pilot. Once I have that, I can blackmail them into leaving me alone until we finish the other case. They won't mess with me once they know I can give their pictures to the police.

"Tomorrow after school, I'll go hide the camera near the trail so Peter won't see it when he picks me up Saturday morning. I'll have to hide it after I get the pictures and then go back for it Sunday. If they see the camera, I know they'll probably kill me." There was silence for several seconds, then, *"I sure hope this works out the way it's supposed to."*

The tape rolled silently for several revolutions before hitting the end.

Harley looked at Senator Walker, who had covered his face with both hands and was sobbing silently, his shoulders shaking as he vented his grief. "It's all my fault," he whispered in a choked gasp. "He was involved in that damned investigation because he was trying to get my attention. You heard him! He was trying to make me proud of him. Damn it, I *was* proud of him. Why didn't I ever let him know it? Why did it have to come to this?"

The two other occupants of the room looked at each other uncomfortably, not knowing if some kind of sympathy should be offered the grief-stricken man, or if he should be left alone.

Sheriff Watson finally broke the awkward silence by clearing his throat. "Senator, you understand we will have to keep this tape for a while. There are several clues on it and in the notes Daryl left in that drawer." He hesitated a minute, then continued, "I'm really very sorry you had to hear this among strangers, but you understand we needed you to verify that the voice on the tape was actually Daryl's."

Senator Walker nodded mutely, swallowing hard before speaking. "I know." He looked at Harley Watson through reddened eyes. "Just do one thing, okay?" he hissed through clenched teeth. "Find the bastard who killed him and put the son of a bitch away for the rest of his life!"

After Mrs. Moore led the senator out of the room, Harley picked up the phone. "Did you hear all that?"

"Yes. Loud and clear," Jim replied.

"Does it help you?"

"Unfortunately, it helps me mostly to know I've been barking up the wrong tree. But I suppose I have to count that as progress if it keeps me from focusing on the wrong guy."

"How'd it go with Ryan North?"

Jim snorted. "He fingered his brother under hypnosis. Unfortunately, Daryl Walker did not corroborate that opinion on that tape. We're back to Peter again. Who the hell is Peter? And why does Ryan North think he saw his brother with the body?"

"I don't know, but we did get Norton's prints and they do not match the print on the medallion. Maybe Peter killed the kid and Norton disposed of the body."

"I'll work on him some more. I've been playing nice with him so far, and he did talk quite a bit after I found out why he hates cops so much. We had a little rapport going for a while until I told him his brother could place him at the scene. Then he demanded a lawyer."

"So now you get to play bad cop for a while."

"Guess so. Clayton says he's learning a lot, by the way."

"Well, I thought it would be good for him to see you in action, and I'd rather not have to subpoena an LAPD officer as a witness to the interrogation. Cheaper to send Clay now than to have to put someone else's cop up in a hotel during a trial when Norton starts claiming you coerced a confession."

"Well, you may have wasted the airfare, Harley. So far, Norton isn't confessing to anything."

"Was anything he told you helpful?"

"Well, he admitted seeing the boy the morning he died. He told me the kid had a camera and was riding fast up the mountain, concerned about being too late for something, and that was certainly corroborated by that tape."

"Something else to think about, Jim," Harley said. "Did Ryan North ever corroborate Norton's story about when and how they came to separate that day?"

"No, I never asked him about it after that day in the hospital, and with the hypnosis, we didn't backtrack to the time before they split up. The first thing we asked him was what he did after Doug left. Maybe we should have gone back further."

"Didn't you tell me last night that Norton didn't know Ryan was going to undergo hypnosis? What if Norton has been feeding you a line of pure bull because he thought Ryan couldn't contradict his story? Remember, Ryan's being there with him that morning was unexpected. He was supposed to be on tour that week. What if Norton was there that day for the sole purpose of trailing Daryl Walker, and he had to ditch his brother so he could get to the helicopter site?"

"That's a possibility. Well, Harley, I thought that tape exonerated Doug Norton, but now I'm not so sure. I guess we'd better hold him awhile longer, at least until I talk to his brother again."

* * *

Doug's brother was waiting in the lobby of the jail with Fred Dreyer when Jim Harrison and Clayton Burns emerged from the conference room.

"Hello, Fred," Jim said, holding out his hand, "Jim Harrison. It's good to see you again."

Fred stood and shook hands with Jim Harrison. "It's good to see you, too. I didn't realize until a little while ago that you were the detective in charge. Ryan just mentioned your name and I remembered. I'd forgotten your name before this."

"I know."

Fred looked puzzled. "You knew I'd forgotten your name?"

"Doug Norton told me. I need to talk to you, Fred, and you, too, Mr. North. Do you mind waiting while I talk to Mr. Dreyer? And has Mr. Norton's attorney arrived?"

"Yes, she's with him now." Ryan stood up. "I really want to see Doug. If he'll see me. I want to understand this," he said quietly.

"I'm sorry, Mr. North, I can't let you see him just yet. I need some more information from you first. I shouldn't be too long with Fred. Please excuse us for now."

Ryan returned to his seat and Jim Harrison had Clayton check Fred for weapons before escorting him to the same interrogation room where he had spoken with Doug Norton a couple hours previously.

"So how have you been, Fred? Everything work out after you left the force?"

"Eventually," Fred replied. "Became a private investigator. Stayed the hell away from the east side, though. How did you end up working for the county?"

Jim sighed. "I transferred to the west side right after the ... incident ... and found myself in a nest of equal opportunity bigots. My captain hated gays, blacks, and women. Something else happened and I quit. Figured there was no point in putting in for a transfer. By then I suspected the cancer went all the way to the top, if I can borrow an expression from Watergate, all the way to the commissioner's office. So I quit. Sheriff Watson was an old friend of my dad's. He'd told me when I graduated from the academy that if I ever needed a job to come see him. So I did. Luckily, his detective of twenty-five years decided to retire last year, so Harley was able to hire me right away."

"Things better out here?"

Conscious of Clayton Burns' presence, Jim replied quickly, "Much," and changed the subject. "I need to ask you some questions, Fred, and I'll have to record this, you know."

"I know."

"Fred, based on your acquaintance with Doug Norton, and the fact that he is a prime suspect at the moment, I suggest you may want an attorney present."

"I don't need a lawyer. Turn on the recorder, Jim, and let's get started."

Jim turned on the recorder and again stated the case number and identities of those present. He then advised Fred of his rights and asked for the record if he wanted an attorney. After Fred reaffirmed that he did not desire a lawyer, Jim began with the same questions he had asked

Doug regarding when and under what circumstances he had known Daryl Walker.

An hour later, he shut off the recorder. "Well, Fred, that's it for now."

"What do you have on Doug?" Fred asked.

"Not as much as I thought I did a few hours ago," Jim replied. "I need to talk to Mr. North again. I'm sorry, but due to your relationship with Mr. Norton, I can't discuss any evidence with you. And I won't be able to let you talk to him for a while longer. I'm still trying to put some things together. I'll tell you this much. Nothing you said to me contradicts anything Doug Norton told me, so either you rehearsed really well or you're both telling the truth. Can I ask you something else, though, off the record?"

Fred glanced at Clayton. "Jim, I'd like to chat with you all you want about this, but I'm not sure how many witnesses I want there to be to anything I say off the record."

Jim nodded at Clayton. "Clay, you understand about admissibility of evidence. I may need you to corroborate what was said here, so if you don't mind, I'm going to take Mr. Dreyer somewhere more private so we can talk about some personal matters."

"No problem, Detective Harrison. You want me to take care of the tape?"

"That's a good idea. Set up a fresh one and bring Mr. North in here. You can keep him company for a few minutes. See if he needs anything to eat or drink. He probably missed lunch."

"Sure thing."

Jim led Fred into the conference room and closed the door.

"So what did you want to ask me, Jim?" Fred asked.

"How did you know Daryl Walker wasn't gay?"

"He told us, straight out, the night we met him at the meeting."

"There's a theory that Norton tried to seduce him and killed the boy when he resisted."

Fred laughed. "Whose theory is that?"

"Doesn't matter. Why did you laugh?"

"Doug Norton has never tried to seduce any male, ever. He fought being gay so hard he went through three months of aversion therapy. Do you know what that is?"

"Tell me."

"They hook a – patient isn't the right word, victim is more like it – up to electrodes and show him pictures of naked men. If he gets aroused, or even looks at the picture too long, he gets zapped. If he gets aroused at pictures of naked women, he doesn't get zapped. It's an arcane, ineffective process that some quacks still offer as a cure for homosexuality. The problem is, it doesn't work. It won't turn a gay man straight. But it can make him fear sexual arousal in any form."

"You're saying Doug Norton is not a practicing homosexual?"

Fred responded with a wry grin, "Oh, he's 'practicing' all right, but he hasn't gotten it right yet. That therapy damn near drove him to suicide, Jim. I met him a few days after the night he decided to kill himself. He was only out of that therapy a couple months when we met Daryl Walker. Believe me, there is no way Doug Norton came on to that boy or anyone else. Frankly, he wouldn't know how."

"Then you're not lovers."

"No, we're very good friends. Someday, if I'm patient enough, we might develop some intimacy, but Doug Norton right now is scared shitless of being gay, scared shitless of anyone finding out he's gay, and up until a couple days ago, he was particularly scared shitless of his brother finding out he's gay." He paused. "He didn't know that Ryan's known it for years. Ryan finally confronted him the other day."

"Why was he so worried about that?"

"He was afraid Ryan would reject him. He's also afraid that if anyone finds out Ryan's brother is gay, it will somehow reflect on Ryan." Fred looked searchingly at Jim. "Is this all going to come out now?"

"Not if it doesn't have to. And nothing you've said since the recorder was turned off is going into any reports."

"I appreciate that." Fred stood up. "I'm glad you're on this case, Jim. Did Doug tell you what happened to him, why he hates cops?"

"Yes, if you're talking about what happened when he was beaten up."

Fred nodded. "If he told you that, he must have some faith in you, too. Jim, I know he didn't hurt that kid. He liked him. So did I. Please, find out who really killed the boy. I'll help you any way I can."

"I'll find out who killed him, Fred. And I hope it's someone else. Right now, I'm afraid he's still my best suspect."

* * *

"Mr. North," Jim said, "I want you to go over everything you remember about your accident, starting with when and how you decided to go hunting that morning. Whose idea was it?"

"Doug's. We used to go hunting every year with our older brother when we were teenagers. Chris died when he was twenty-one and we've never gone again since. He wanted to do it, sort of for old time's sake, you know?"

"When did you make this plan?"

"I got to Denver Wednesday afternoon. I think it was the next evening Doug suggested it."

"Thursday?"

"Yes."

"Did you already have a license?"

"No, that's why we couldn't go until Saturday. We spent Friday getting hunting licenses and deer permits and arranging for the horses and gear."

"How did you get permits that late? Don't you have to put in for a drawing months in advance?"

"Not in that section. They had over-the-counter permits available, but only for deer, not elk. Guess not very many people care to hunt in the wilderness area."

Jim mentally compared the timing of the decision to go hunting with the timing of Daryl's tape recording. Coincidence? Or had Doug's presumed accomplice, Peter, given Daryl his marching orders Wednesday night leaving Doug to spend the next day trying to figure out how to get to the woods for the day to make sure the kid did what he was told while his brother was in town, unexpectedly?

"You rode your own horse."

"Yes. Doug tried to talk me out of it, but I guess I'm too stubborn for my own good."

"Tell me about Saturday. I want to hear everything you remember from the time you got up until you ducked under that branch."

Ryan told essentially the same story Doug had, including describing their parting gestures when they split up at the trail crossing. "I laughed at him. He's always flipping me off, and I always laugh at him. Of course, that pisses him off more, but he usually gets over it in a few minutes. It's almost a game with us, and we've been playing it for years."

"Mr. North, I heard the rest of the story when you were hypnotized yesterday. Have you recalled anything else?"

"No."

"You still believe it was your brother you saw with the body?"

"No, I don't believe it at all, but that's the way I remember it."

"Tell me again exactly what you saw through the binoculars."

"There was a tree on the ground, uprooted, and I was facing the bottom of the roots. There was a big hole where the roots used to be. In front of the hole, partially blocking my view of it, was a small pine tree. Behind the uprooted tree were a couple more small pines, close together. Behind those trees was a horse. All I could see was a black tail with orange ribbon on it, like the ribbon Doug and I tied on our horses. Between the tree roots and the small tree that was blocking my view, I saw movement. I saw there was a man there. Then I saw a body tumble into the hole. The arm flopped out. Mostly that's what I saw – the arm and hand, reaching toward me, almost. The man that dumped him there shoved the hand into the hole with his foot and started picking branches up from the ground and tossing them into the hole with the body. Then the hand flopped out again, and the man bent over and shoved the hand under a branch. That was the first time he stepped out from behind the small tree and I saw who it was."

"What did you see?"

"I saw blond hair, a beard, a red plaid jacket, and blue jeans. It looked like Doug. It looked like Doug's horse. But I still don't believe it was him."

"Did you see his face?"

"No. I only saw him from the back, and only for a second. I was horrified. Then his horse whinnied and I felt Badger draw a deep breath and go on alert, like he was going to answer. I panicked, snatched the reins and whirled him around. He took one lurch up the hill and I hit that branch that I'd ducked coming in. I remember nothing else until I was in the hospital."

"How much of what you remembered does Doug know you remembered?"

"While I was in rehab, I finally got to the branch. I remembered ducking the branch going in. He knows I remembered that much. I didn't know anything else until yesterday."

"Has he ever tried to stop you from remembering? Discouraged you from trying?"

"No, in fact he gave me a hard time constantly about the horse. I'd defend the horse and he'd say I had no idea what that 'crazy horse' might have done. I don't know how many times he told me he hoped someday I'd remember what the horse did, so I'd have to admit he was right about him."

"Did you ever tell him about your nightmares?"

Ryan fidgeted. "No."

"Why not?"

"I thought they were silly. I mean, I was dreaming about a green unicorn. How quick would you be to tell someone something that silly? Took me a week to call you after I figured out what it might mean."

"Had he worn that unicorn shirt since the day of the accident?"

"I know he had it on when I woke from the coma. He was wearing it when we went hunting, and never went home to get anything to change into. He wore it until one of the nurses gave him one with a skunk on it, but I hadn't seen it again until yesterday, at least, not that I remember. Maybe he wore it when I was in rehab, or when he stayed with me at my house after rehab, but I don't remember."

"The day in the hospital when you were given the wrong medicine, what were you given?"

"It was a fairly common pain killer, as I understand it. Tramadol? It wouldn't have been a problem except that they had me on a certain kind of anti-depressant at the time. The combination could have killed me if I'd taken it, or at least could have caused seizures or severe shock. There was another patient on the floor who was scheduled to receive some that night. They decided it was his medicine that I got. Since he was also sleeping, he couldn't say for sure whether the medication nurse ever came into his room."

"She never admitted making the mistake?"

"She swore she never came into the secured area where I was. She had no reason to. I had to take the anti-depressant with meals, so I'd already had it. I wasn't taking anything else."

"You have no idea who would have tried to kill you?"

"Not a clue."

"What if Doug figured out you'd seen him with the body?"

"How could he know that? I only saw him through binoculars. When he bent over the body, his binoculars weren't hanging around his neck. They must have still been on his horse. He couldn't have seen me."

"What about your horse? Couldn't he have heard your horse, and later figured out it was you when you were found?"

"My horse didn't make any noise. It was his horse that whinnied."

Jim flipped back through several pages of notes, wondering what else he could ask Ryan North that would help. He was stymied at this point. "I think that's all I need for now, Mr. North." He turned off the recorder.

"Can I see Doug now?"

Jim shook his head. "Not just yet. I want to talk to him some more, if his attorney will let me."

But the attorney made it clear she had advised Doug to exercise his right to remain silent until she had a chance to review the evidence against him. By then, it was nearly six o'clock in the evening and Jim knew he couldn't hold Norton past noon the next day without actually charging him with something. The evidence he had against Doug

Norton was circumstantial at best. It was not his thumb print on the medallion, and Clayton Burns had made a phone call and confirmed with Mike Griffith that the horse named Rocket was a dark bay, so the little bit of physical evidence they had did not tie Norton to the boy's death. Jim still had no motive, unless he could somehow tie Doug into the drug activity. All he had was means and opportunity, but absolutely no motive, and no evidence except Ryan North's eyewitness report, obtained under hypnosis eight months after a head injury. And all that indicated was that he disposed of the body, not that he killed the boy in the first place.

The rankest amateur of a defense attorney could make hash out of this case, Jim decided. He called Harley in his office to give him an update.

"I can't hold him, Harley," Jim started. "Much as I'd like to hold him until I find something to prove his innocence, our system doesn't work that way, and I don't have enough indicating he's guilty."

"What do you have that says he's guilty?"

"His brother, mostly, and it's hardly a positive ID. Norton had means and opportunity, but I haven't a shred of motive and no physical evidence."

"What do you have that says he's not guilty?"

"Everything he's told me has been backed up either by his brother, Fred Dreyer, or the boy himself on that recording. Once he started coming clean, I haven't caught him in a single lie, unless he's lying when he says he didn't do it. Everything else seems to check out."

Harley thought for a moment, then said, "Sleep on it, Jim. If you still feel this way in the morning, cut him loose."

"What do I tell the attorney?"

"Tell her you're going to question him again in the morning, with her present, and that if he does not cooperate, you will charge him with resisting arrest and obstruction of justice. Maybe a night in jail will loosen him up a little more."

"All right, Harley." Jim hung up the phone and returned to the lobby area where Doug's attorney was talking with Ryan North and Fred Dreyer.

"Well?" she demanded. "Are you going to charge him or not?"

"Ma'am, we're going to hold him until tomorrow morning. At that time I want to question him some more in your presence. I'm sorry, but he's going to have to stay here for the night."

"You'd better not be screwing with me, Detective Harrison," she snapped, "or I'll have a writ slapped on you so fast it will make your head spin. Don't think I won't."

"Ms Atkinson, may I remind you that we have other charges against your client for obstruction of justice, interfering with a police officer, and resisting arrest, which is all I need for a judge to deny bail right now. My inclination is to ignore all that, but if there is any interference by you, I'm more than happy to fill out some more paperwork and hold him on those charges. You decide. I'm trying to be as fair as I can but Mr. Norton does not have a good track record for cooperation. Don't make things worse and I'll try to show you the same courtesy."

Without a word, the attorney pivoted on her high heels and stalked out the door.

Jim shook his head and turned to Ryan and Fred. "I'll let you both see him for a few minutes if you like. Let me go have him brought out." He disappeared through the door to the jail area, returning a few minutes later. "He'd like to see Fred. Five minutes, Mr. Dreyer." A jail guard checked again for weapons before leading Fred into the jail area.

Jim sat with Ryan. "He doesn't want to see you. Maybe Fred will convince him otherwise."

"I doubt it. I've accused him of murder, Detective. I don't think he's going to put this in the same category as my telling Mom he broke the living room lamp."

"I know this is difficult."

"Do you have other evidence besides my word?"

"There's evidence. So far none of it is ironclad."

"Well, I hope you decide I've been hallucinating. I don't think I could live with myself if it turns out he had anything to do with that boy's death. I keep feeling that I'm missing something, but I know what I saw."

Jim nodded. "I know, Mr. North. This is a tough call to make. I'd feel better with a definite motive. Right now, I don't think we should discuss this any more. I'm tired and my judgment may not be the best. I don't want to say anything I shouldn't."

Fred came out a few minutes later and shook his head. "Sorry, Ryan. I tried."

"How is he?"

"Physically, fine. Emotionally, depressed. Mentally, he thinks everything will be okay and the attorney was fairly confident there's no case, but he doesn't have any faith in the system." Fred looked at Jim Harrison. "He's feeling a little betrayed by you right now. And he doesn't know what to think of what Ryan told you."

"I understand. I expect I'll see you both in the morning?"

"Yes," they both replied.

"Then I'll say goodnight."

CHAPTER 42

J IM HARRISON DROVE BACK to his hotel after dropping Clayton off at the home of a cousin where he planned to stay the night. He had made plans to see Sheila at seven-thirty for dinner, but was starting to have reservations about that. They had agreed not to talk shop at dinner, but Jim wondered if he dared see her at all now, especially now that Harley knew she was there.

He was trying to decide what to do when Sheila called him on the phone. "Are we still on for dinner?" she asked. "Or do we have a conflict of interest now that you've arrested Doug Norton?"

He lay back on the bed in the hotel room and grinned. "I was having second thoughts, but mostly because I was afraid I'd let that slip. How did you find out already?"

"I have my ways," she teased.

"What else do you know? And how soon will you be reporting?"

"Not until you charge him with something. Are you going to charge him?"

"No comment. What do you know?"

"I know he was picked up at the studio this morning, and that he made a feeble effort to resist arrest. I know his attorney's name is Atkinson and she thinks you're harassing him."

"Has she spoken to any other members of the press?"

"I don't think so."

"Did she tell you why I might be harassing him?"

"Well, she didn't say anything about him being gay, if that's what you're worried about."

"Good. What else do you know?"

"I know about the tape."

"Do you know what was on it?"

382

"I already have a transcript of it, but I promised my source not to print it without permission from either Sheriff Watson or the Senator."

"You've been a busy girl. What else?"

"That's it."

"In that case, let's have dinner," Jim said decisively. "Most of what I didn't want to let slip you already know. Pick you up in half an hour as planned?"

"I saved you a trip. I'm here in your lobby. Thought you might be tired. We could eat here in the restaurant."

"That sounds good. Put our names on the list. I'll be down in ten minutes."

She declined wine with dinner, saying she had to drive back to her hotel later. Jim bit his lip to keep from suggesting she didn't need to leave if she didn't want to, then decided it was too soon in their not-quite-a-relationship for him to suggest a sleep over.

They ate a leisurely dinner, avoiding discussion of Daryl Walker's murder altogether. At eight-thirty, they strolled outside and found some lounge chairs by the pool and spent an hour talking before deciding it was too cold to stay there any longer.

"Where should we go now?" Sheila asked when they got back to the lobby. "We could sit in the lounge."

"I'm not much for bar scenes," Jim replied. "We could go to my room," he said, "just to talk, I mean," he added, blushing, when she arched an eyebrow at him.

"Somehow I think talking may be the last thing on either of our minds right now," she said levelly. She smiled. "I think I probably should go back to my own hotel now. We still have to work together and I wouldn't want either of us to lose our objectivity."

He nodded. "Right. We're over here to work, aren't we." He escorted her to her rental car in the parking garage.

She unlocked the door and tossed in her purse, then turned to face him. "Thanks for dinner, Jim. Will you call me if you have anything you can tell me tomorrow?"

"If I can." He put his arms around her shoulders. "Thanks for joining me tonight, Sheila. Will you lose your objectivity if I kiss you goodnight?"

"Not if you do it badly," she replied with a playful wink.

"Sorry, I don't know how." He kissed her, a long, lingering kiss, then released her. "Good night, Sheila. Sleep well. Be careful driving out there, okay?"

"Good luck with your murder suspect, Jim. I'll talk to you tomorrow, I hope."

He returned alone to his room, partially relieved and partially regretting she hadn't stayed. He turned the TV set on for the background noise it provided in the silent room and read through his notes from the three interviews he had done that day, trying to figure out if there was anything he was overlooking.

He had been so sure Doug Norton was involved in the murder, but that conclusion had been based solely on his evasiveness and lies. His brother's belief that he'd seen Doug with the body had clinched things. But any semblance of a motive for murder was torpedoed by the victim's own accounting on that audio tape of what he was doing in the woods that day. And Doug had the best reason in the world for lying to Jim and failing to cooperate. His history had shown that any cop who learned he was gay would be just like the one who was sent to take his statement in the emergency room – a homophobic bigot. And there was no way he could have admitted knowing the boy without revealing how he knew him.

Sheila's proposed motive, that Doug had come on to the boy and been rejected, didn't work unless Fred Dreyer was lying about Doug's sexual history – or lack of it.

But Ryan North's eyewitness account made another of Sheila's theories more plausible – the one where she suspected Doug of trying to kill Ryan or "mess with his head" as she put it, to keep Ryan from testifying against him. In fact, given the hallucinations Ryan had experienced the week before, Jim couldn't even use Ryan's testimony in court. It would be immediately dismissed as a delusion.

Which may have been what Doug planned all along. Jim wondered if Fred Dreyer had counseled Doug regarding reliability of witnesses. Maybe he was in on this, too, although Fred had the exact opposite of a motive for killing the boy. Why would a gay former cop who had been victimized at the hands of a rogue police force harm the only child of a politician who had stood up against the bigoted police commissioner on more than one occasion, especially since it appeared the boy was following in his father's political footsteps?

The same could be said of Doug Norton – except that according to both him and Fred, they didn't know the boy was the senator's son until after the body was found.

Besides, it wasn't Doug's fingerprint on the medallion, so he couldn't have killed the boy. Could Fred have? No, they had run the fingerprint through the computer and it had come up dry. Fred's fingerprints would have been in the database because he had once been a cop. On the other hand, why would Ryan's brother think he saw Doug with the body if Doug wasn't there? It wasn't the first time Doug had denied being somewhere after an eyewitness placed him at the scene. The same thing had happened in the hospital when that nurse's aide saw him go into Ryan's room and Doug denied it and said he was in the cafeteria at the time.

Yawning, he set his notebook aside. He'd have to sort this out in the morning. Right now he was so tired nothing was making sense. Maybe it would in the morning.

* * *

Ryan had wanted to go back to his own house, but Fred had insisted it was not safe, so Ryan reluctantly agreed to return to Doug's condo and let Fred go back to Ryan's house alone. Fred said he would return in the morning and they could go back to the jail together.

Unable to sleep from the stress and confusion of the day, Ryan found himself lying awake at nearly one a.m., staring at the ceiling of the bedroom in Doug's condo. And that was when he realized what had been missing.

It was the orange vest. Doug had been wearing a daytime orange vest when they split up at the trail crossing. Ryan's memory of the moments before his accident was as crystal clear now as it had been totally absent two days before, and he was certain that the man he had seen bending over the boy's body had not been wearing any such vest.

That made two things missing: the binoculars and the vest. While it made sense that Doug would have draped the binoculars over the saddle horn while disposing of the body, it did not make sense that he would have removed his hunting vest – and cap, too, Ryan realized. He had not been wearing the orange cap either.

He remembered something else. The day of the medication mix-up at the hospital, the nurse's aide, Rita McConnell, had identified Doug by his red plaid jacket when she said she'd seen him go into Ryan's room. Like Ryan, she had not seen his face, and had identified him only by his clothing.

Ryan tried to remember if there was anything unique about Doug's jacket, anything that would help him know if it really had been Doug he saw that day with the body, but he hadn't seen the jacket since they left Denver when he got out of the rehab center.

But he had seen another red plaid jacket, similar to it, recently, at the studio. Try as he might, he could not remember who had been wearing it.

Relief at having remembered something to exonerate his brother mixed with exhaustion from the long day, and he finally drifted to sleep, determined to talk to Fred in the morning. Maybe Fred would remember who else had a jacket like Doug's.

He was too tired to carry his ideas through to their logical conclusion and realize that if the red-jacketed person at the studio were the same one he had seen with the body, it meant he had a killer on his production crew ... a killer who was not spending the night in the LAPD jail in Beverly Hills.

Part VI
June 2 - 3, 1994
The Killer

CHAPTER 43

WALTER HUSSMAN STRAIGHTENED up and walked over to turn off the hose, tossing the wet sponge into a bucket of sudsy water. He had just finished scrubbing all traces of blood and skin off the front bumper and fender of the pickup truck. He had already removed the broken headlight and disposed of it in a dumpster behind an auto parts store, and, after drying out the recess, he installed the replacement he had bought in an entirely different part of town.

There was nothing to connect the broken headlight in the dumpster with the new headlight he'd paid cash for at the busiest parts store he could find. No reason for anyone to remember him there; the cashier had barely glanced at him as she took his money.

One more loose end tied up, he thought. He'd taken the precaution of swapping out the license plates on the truck with ones he stole from a truck in the parking lot of a local hospital, figuring someone in the hospital wouldn't notice the plates were missing until they got out. He'd picked a vehicle with some cobwebs under it, suggesting the owner had been there awhile and likely would be there awhile longer. He'd returned to the parking lot in the middle of the night and replaced the plates. The other truck hadn't moved; the cobwebs were intact. He had given a quick swipe under the truck to clear them.

There was nothing he could do about the dent in the fender. But the truck was old and had other dents. Hayward had used this truck to haul the horse around to where they needed it. The only thing Hussman had left to do was go find a nice, dusty dirt road, lightly spray the front of the truck with water, then drive down the road and let the front of the truck get coated with the same layer of dirt that was on the rest of it.

He was pleased with his cleverness. Not that he would have minded hanging Hayward out to dry but you just never knew when the cops would cut a deal and give Hayward the chance to hang *him* out to dry. Better to do everything possible to keep them both out of trouble. For now.

He drove toward the mountains to find an appropriate dirt road. He noticed a farm road to his right, turned onto it, drove for a short distance to be sure an appropriate amount of dust would be thrown up, then stopped and got out of the truck with a spray bottle. He sprayed the truck, then got back in and put the truck in reverse and drove quickly for a short distance, slammed on the brakes, and watched with satisfaction as the dust settled and clung to the damp metal. He repeated the action twice, then turned around and drove back toward Boulder.

There was nothing more he could do now. He'd just been tying up another loose end, just as a precaution. Well, they'd never trace the truck back to him anyway. With the license plate swap, and the truck being Hayward's in the first place, there would be no reason for anyone to come knocking on his door about the hit and run.

He'd already shaved off his beard.

Oh, he was such a master at planning.

Hayward would be back in a few days. They would be getting a huge cash payout that night, more than enough to relocate both of them and enable them to lie low for a while, until the cops gave up on solving the murder of the boy. They'd both have new ID's within a week.

He glanced at his watch as he drove back toward the rented house he'd been using for the last month, debating if he had time to go trade the truck for his own car, then he turned onto the highway and headed to the airfield, deciding there wasn't enough time. He was to get the helicopter, make one more drop near Boulder, and when he returned the helicopter there would be the usual feed sack full of cash, only this time there were going to be hundred dollar bills instead of the usual twenties. He'd take the cash, wire enough to Hayward to fly him back to Denver after he took care of Ryan North, and then they would abandon Hayward's truck in an old barn he knew about and drive to Oregon.

Except Hayward would never get to see the Oregon coast. Hayward would die somewhere in the deserts of Utah.

Everything was so carefully planned. Just like he'd planned the boy's murder so that any suspicion would land on Hayward in the first place. But the cops were getting too close. Time to snip that last loose end. Hayward was the only person who could put Hussman with the boy.

Two hours later, Hussman settled the helicopter at the designated drop point, got out and hid wrapped packages of cocaine in the camouflaged box under the bush, and returned to the helicopter. "Bye-bye, Rocky Mountains," he muttered as the chopper lifted off. He flew to the place where he uncovered the aircraft numbers so he could fly back to the small airfield in an agricultural area north of Boulder without raising suspicion. By the time he returned, someone would have been there and left his sack of cash in a trash bin in the corner of the first hangar to the right of the landing pad.

He settled the helicopter and shut it down, got out, and walked over to the hangar and found the sack of cash. As he started to pick it up, he heard a sound behind him and turned around to see seven men pointing rifles at him.

One stepped forward and showed a badge. "DEA. You're under arrest for narcotics violations."

And that was not part of his plan.

* * *

Jim was still in bed that morning when the phone rang. "Jim?" he heard Sheila's voice. "Sorry, did I wake you?"

"Not quite. What's up?"

"Jim, my editor just called. We got a wire about Cindy Vincent. Someone tried to kill her yesterday."

"What?" Jim sat up, fully awake. "Who? How?"

"She was hit by a pickup truck. Hit and run. Deliberately run down in a crosswalk according to the witnesses. She's in the hospital. Do you want me to read it to you?"

"Yes."

Her voice breaking, Sheila read him the story. Probably the only reason the incident had come to the attention of the wire services was because of the victim's connection to Ryan North – the sort of thing that distinguished one thirteen-year-old girl from another.

Cindy Vincent had been struck down in the street while happily running to tell her best friend about the trip she had just made to visit Ryan North in Hollywood. Autographed photos and CD's, proof of Ryan North's appreciation for the little girl who had saved his life several months before, had gone flying in every direction when she was hit less than a block from her home. Golden police were looking for a dark-blue pickup truck with damage to the right front headlight and fender, driven by a white man with a beard and brown hair.

The story turned Jim's stomach. Cindy was one possible witness he had never interviewed, taking her father's word that she couldn't have seen anyone that day. Could he have been wrong? "I hope this is just a coincidence," he said when Sheila finished. "Her father said they didn't see anyone but Ryan that day."

"You didn't talk to her yourself?"

"No, he said they hadn't seen anyone else so I didn't talk to her. Oh, shit!" he exclaimed suddenly.

"What is it, Jim?"

"How could I have been so careless, Sheila? Cindy Vincent was alone with Ryan for almost two hours! She could have seen lots of things her father didn't know about! And now someone's tried to kill her the day after she visited Ryan North and his brother! Damn!"

"Jim?" Sheila said uncertainly.

"What?"

"It's not your fault. A hit and run. Ryan North and his brother are both here. This happened in Colorado. There can't be a connection. Just a miserable coincidence."

"Sheila, we've had too goddamned many coincidences in this case."

"What are you going to do?" she asked.

"Well, for one thing," Jim said with a sigh, "try to explain this to Harley."

Two hours after Harley Watson hung up from talking to Jim Harrison his phone rang again.

"Watson here," Harley said into the phone.

"Sheriff, this is Howard Vincent. I'm the man who found Ryan North last year in the woods. Your detective questioned me recently about the Daryl Walker homicide. They told me he's out of town right now so I asked for you."

"Oh, yes, Mr. Vincent. I'm sorry to hear about your daughter," Harley said awkwardly. "Is there some way we can help you?" He picked up a pencil.

"Sheriff, I'm going to tell you something quickly because I'm not sure how long I can control myself," Howard said huskily. "You understand?"

"Yes, sir, I do," Harley said with uncharacteristic empathy.

"Sheriff, my baby visited Ryan North the day before she was hit. On the way home, it was all she could talk about, all the things she saw at the studio and the people she met. Sheriff, I know you're still investigating that homicide, and I think she told me something on the plane that you would want to know."

"What is that, sir?"

"She told me that there was a man there, at the studio, that she thought she recognized at the time, but couldn't place him, you know?"

"Yes. Go on."

"Just as the plane was landing, she suddenly burst out, 'Oh, I remember now! He's the man I saw riding away on a horse while I was waiting for you to come back to Ryan North.' I asked her what she meant, and she said that she climbed on her horse several times after I left and looked around through Ryan's binoculars, trying to see if I was coming back yet. She told me that she saw Ryan North's sound mixer riding through the woods on a dun colored horse while she was waiting. It was before it started to snow and she had to unsaddle the horse to get the saddle blanket to put on Ryan."

Harley sat up, alert. "Ryan North's sound mixer? Don't you mean his partner, Doug Norton?"

"No, no, Cindy knows him, and he was on a bay horse. No, this was a man named Walter Hussman. Ryan's secretary introduced them at the studio. It wasn't Doug Norton. She wouldn't have made that mistake."

Harley was silent, his mind racing ahead. Not Doug Norton? Then how had so much evidence pointed to him? Unless he and this sound mixer were in this together ... somehow ....

"Sheriff? Do you get what I'm saying? She saw this guy from the studio there, sheriff. Don't you see? Don't you think that's a funny coincidence? Ryan and Cindy and this guy all in the woods on that day, the day that boy was killed. Then Cindy goes to visit Ryan, sees this same guy there, and gets run down the next day!" His voice broke off in a sob.

"I'm sorry, Mr. Vincent, I know this must be terribly painful for you."

There was silence for a minute while Howard Vincent composed himself. "Sheriff, this guy might be the one you're looking for. I was planning to call you yesterday, thinking your detective would want to find this guy and talk to him too ... then my little girl ... the accident ... ." The dial tone buzzed in Harley's ear as the connection was broken.

Harley buzzed the dispatch room. "I can't believe what I just heard. Run a make on a Walter Hussman. He's supposed to be working in Los Angeles for Ryan North. See what you come up with locally. And call the police in Golden and ask them to send an officer to guard Cindy Vincent's hospital room right away."

Ten minutes later the dispatcher appeared at Harley's door with a printout in his hand and a puzzled look on his face.

"Did you say Walter Hussman was *currently* working for Ryan North?"

"Yes, why?"

"According to this printout, a Walter Hussman was arrested late yesterday in a drug sting operation near Boulder. Police there are also looking for a Peter Hayward, whose truck Hussman was driving at the time. Hussman won't say where Hayward is or why he had his truck. They think Peter Hayward is part of the drug ring."

Harley stared at him, then grabbed the phone and dialed Jim's cell phone number, reaching him at the Beverly Hills police station where he and Clayton were trying to interview a suddenly uncooperative Doug Norton who was taking the fifth at every question per the advice of his attorney. "Jim, we may have just found Ricky Farrell's mysterious 'Peter.'" He told Jim about Howard Vincent's call, then took the printout from the dispatcher and read it to Jim.

"Harley," Jim said tersely, "your Walter Hussman could be the driver who hit Cindy Vincent. You'd better have that truck impounded and check to see if it's the same one that hit her. And I've got to find Ryan North ASAP. If his Walter Hussman is really Peter Hayward, North is in grave danger." He looked at Doug Norton, sitting across from him in the interrogation room. "And I'm talking to an innocent man."

He hung up the phone. "Where is your brother?" he asked Doug. "We've got to find him."

"I don't know. He's been staying at my condo, but he might have gone back to his own house last night with Fred. Can I use your phone?"

Jim handed Doug the cell phone and Doug called Ryan's house first, got no answer, then tried the condo. "Ryan, is Fred with you?" he asked. He listened a moment then said to Jim, "Fred never showed up to pick up Ryan this morning. Fred hasn't answered the house phone or the cell phone. Ryan's still waiting at the condo. He assumed Fred was on the way and just wasn't answering the cell phone but the condo is only a mile from Ryan's house so he should have been there long before now. He just tried the house again a few minutes ago and it just went to the machine like it did for me just now."

Jim stood up. "You're no longer under arrest. Come on, we've got to get your brother." Jim and Doug left the interrogation room, leaving Clayton to turn off the tape recorder and take care of the interview notes. The dumbstruck attorney followed them out, bewildered, to hear Jim talk to the dispatcher about sending officers to Ryan's house. A minute later another officer escorted Jim and Doug out to a patrol car and they sped off toward Doug's condo to pick up Ryan.

CHAPTER 44

A FTER TALKING TO JIM Harrison about Cindy Vincent, Sheila pulled herself together and decided that she was going to have to set aside her brief friendship with the girl and do her job. She was on the scene. The story was going to be big news in a matter of hours. She had to try to get a quote from Ryan North before anyone else did.

She already knew where Ryan North lived. She had learned that easily the first day she had been in the area, and had already driven by it a couple of times, wondering how she could get an interview with him, despite her agreement with Jim Harrison to leave Ryan alone. Now she had to put her knowledge to use. It was her job, and like it or not, Jim Harrison would have to get over it.

She arrived at ten o'clock and noticed that the gate was standing open. That was odd. It had been shut tight with a security guard standing by every time she had been there before. Without giving it another thought, she drove quickly through the gate and parked in the circular driveway behind a dark Volvo, noting that the garage door was standing open and a red Corvette was parked inside. She surmised this was the car Jerry Overholt had told her Doug had bought his brother for Christmas, and that Ricky Farrell had identified as the one Doug had driven to the meeting that one time. She got out and started to walk around the back of the car toward the front door when she glanced back at the gate, still curious why she had been allowed to approach the house unhindered, and felt a chill when she noticed a man's body under the bushes at the side of the gate.

She was fumbling her cell phone from her purse to call 911 when she heard a noise behind her and whirled around before having a chance to dial. There she saw the barrel of a gun pointed at her through the partially-opened front door. "Drop the phone and the purse and get in here," a man's voice said. "Quickly."

Terrified, she obeyed, dropping the phone back in her purse then dropping the purse on the ground before walking up the front walk to the door, her eyes never leaving the barrel of the gun pointed at her. The unseen man pulled the door open as she entered the house, blinking slightly as she stepped from bright sunlight into the dark gloom of the house. As her eyes struggled to focus, she looked from the barrel of the gun to the man who was holding it and had only one thought: Doug Norton. For a confused moment she wondered why Jim wouldn't have told her Doug had been released from jail. Then her vision adjusted and she saw that it was not Doug Norton at all, but another man of his height and coloring.

He motioned her into the living room where she saw a dark-haired man lying facedown on the floor with a bloody lump on the back of his head. It took her a moment to realize it was not Ryan North lying there; this man was stockier. She wondered who he was and whether he was alive.

Sheila swallowed hard. "Who are you?"

"Never mind who I am. I'm trying to figure why everyone's at Ryan North's house except fucking Ryan North. Where is he?"

"I don't know."

"Who are you, anyway?"

"Sheila Fernelli. A reporter. I came to interview him."

"Then he's expecting you. He'll be here then. Mister Punctuality would never miss an appointment. Sit down. You make a better hostage than pansy ass there, anyway. I may need you later."

Sheila stepped past the fallen man, wondering who he was and why he was at Ryan's house. Could he be another reporter? Then she remembered the car. It was a dark Volvo. She hadn't noticed if it had Colorado license plates or not, but as Jim Harrison had said just that morning, there had been too many coincidences already. She decided the man on the floor must be Jeff, the gay private investigator Ricky had told them about. She sat in the indicated chair, her heart pounding. If the man who was now holding a gun on her knew Jeff, and knew he was gay, he probably had known him in Colorado.

She quickly realized something else. In the dim light of Ryan's entryway, she had thought this man was Doug Norton. Jim Harrison had arrested Doug Norton yesterday. If Jim thought Doug Norton was the killer, not just a witness, quite likely he was wrong and the man sitting in Ryan North's living room was the real killer.

She glanced at him again and found him studying the dark-haired man with a frown. She'd seen Doug Norton two days before, lunching with Ryan North and Cindy Vincent and Ryan's secretary. This man looked enough like him to be easily mistaken for him, especially from a distance. This could be the person the nurse's aide, Rita McConnell, had seen slipping into Ryan's room. He may have been trying to silence Ryan North even then, before he even knew if Ryan could have seen him. And he probably had come here now to finish the job.

"Why'd you do it?" she asked.

The man glared at her. "Do what?"

"Kill him."

He glanced down at the man on the floor. "He's not dead."

"Not him. The kid. Daryl Walker."

"I didn't."

"You didn't kill him?"

"No."

"Then why are you doing this?"

"Because I'm the only one who can be traced to the kid. And if I don't take care of North, the guy who did kill him is going to take care of me, see? I got no choice."

"Why not turn in the real killer?"

"He has connections who would gladly kill me if he asked them to. I'm only safe if I do what he tells me to do."

"You killed anyone else?"

"Not yet."

"Then why don't you ask the police to protect you?"

"Shut the fuck up." He lurched to his feet and walked around to the man on the floor. He shoved his gun into his waistband. "Help me drag him into the hall. Don't want Ryan to see him when he gets here."

Sheila obeyed, taking one of the man's legs and helping drag him around a corner. The blond man felt around the other man's waist and produced a pair of handcuffs. He studied them for a minute, then cuffed one arm to the opposite ankle. "That'll keep him out of action," he said with a satisfied grunt. "He better stay asleep. I wouldn't want to have to shoot him before I was sure I had to." Sheila noticed the empty shoulder holster on the man and wondered if it was his gun that the blond man had.

"Who is he, anyway?" Sheila asked.

"Fucking PI. Name's Fred. He's another fag, like Norton and the kid. Get back to your seat."

Sheila returned to the chair, surprised to realize she was no longer frightened. "You have a name I should call you?" she tried again.

"Peter. You can call me Peter."

The phone started to ring and Sheila jumped. The portable handset was right at her elbow. She looked at Peter. "Should I answer it?"

"No."

The phone rang four times, then a machine clicked on in another room and Ryan's voice answered saying only, "I'm not here. Leave a message." The caller hung up before the beep.

They sat in silence for a few minutes, both jumping slightly when the phone rang again, and again the answering machine picked up. Again the caller hung up.

"Someone's playing games," Peter muttered. "Damn thing's been ringing ever since I got here."

"Well, he's not home. Maybe they don't like to leave messages."

"He's supposed to be home. He's supposed to be meeting with you. What time was your appointment?"

Sheila swallowed hard. She didn't dare tell this man that she had no appointment, that she stopped by hoping to catch the famous singer at home so she could tell him about Cindy's accident and get a reaction quote. "We didn't have a firm appointment," she replied. "He said he'd be here this morning and to drop by any time."

"Well, where the hell is he, then? This doesn't feel right." He stood up and stalked to the front window, looking out through the curtains. "He should be here."

Sheila suspected there was a door from the garage into the house, and while Peter's back was turned, she spotted one, a possible escape route if only she could get to it. She could see it on the other side of the dining room. She saw something else there – a key rack on the wall with a single set of car keys hanging on it. The red Corvette was the only car she'd seen in the open garage.

"Look, Peter," she said. "If we're going to be here awhile, do you mind if I look for something to drink?"

He glared back at her, then shrugged. "Let's go look. My mouth's a little dry anyway."

She stood and walked to where she suspected the kitchen was and found she was correct. She started to reach for the refrigerator door, but Peter stopped her. "No. I'll look. Get up against the counter there, where I can see you."

She complied, looking around the kitchen for weapons. The knife block was on the other side of the kitchen. Someone had left a can of cooking spray on the counter, though, and Sheila eyed it hopefully. *Maybe, just maybe.*

In the moment when Peter pulled open the refrigerator door and bent slightly to look inside, she grabbed the can and aimed. He turned at the movement and she pressed the button, spraying the stuff full into his eyes. Then she dropped the can and ran.

He clawed at his eyes, screaming in pain. "You fucking bitch!" he yelled as Sheila raced to the door leading to the garage.

She bolted through the door, grabbing the car keys from the hook on the wall as she went by. As she slid into the seat of the Corvette and fumbled to start the car, she was relieved to feel the first key she tried slide into the ignition and turn without resistance. The engine roared to life and she shifted into reverse and lurched backwards, straining to reach the gas pedal. She pressed the button on the power seat and felt her contact with the gas pedal grow more secure as the seat inched forward.

She knew the spray had not harmed the man. She would have, at best, a minute's head start.

In her rearview mirror, she saw that Peter had reached the Volvo and was already climbing in to come after her, still pawing at his eyes. Tires squealed as she turned onto the street, gas pedal pressed firmly to the floor. She drove down the winding road to Sunset Boulevard, grateful that she was in a car designed to maneuver such curves at high rates of speed.

But Peter was not to be denied. The Volvo was a powerful car and was rapidly closing the gap. Sheila leaned on the pedal and pulled away from him.

Her mind was racing as fast as the car. Desperately, she wished she had her purse and cell phone with her, then she noticed the phone cleverly built into the dash of the Corvette. She couldn't take her eyes off the road long enough to read any of the labels on the buttons. Tentatively, she pushed 9-1-1, not daring to hope. There was no response.

Sheila started to panic as she saw that traffic was backing up ahead of her. Quickly, she turned up a side street, trying to lose Hayward. She thought she had succeeded, but then he was in her mirror again, closer than before.

She prayed someone would see the two cars speeding through the exclusive neighborhood and call the police, but no flashing lights appeared in her rearview mirror, only the sight of the Volvo, growing closer with each curve of the road.

In desperation, she glanced back at the phone again, hoping to find a panic button that would dial the police automatically. She saw one with a large letter E on it. Emergency? She pressed it and was rewarded by the sound of ringing. "Nine-one-one," a voice said, "what is your emergency?"

"I need the police!" she screamed. "He's going to kill me!"

"What is your location?"

"I don't know. I'm in a car. I was at Ryan North's house. I turned right, then drove up in the hills. I don't know where I am." She whizzed past a sign. "The sign said 'Amhearst'."

"What are you driving?"

"A red Corvette. I'm being chased by a dark blue Volvo. It may have Colorado plates on it. I'm not sure."

"Just a moment." An eternity passed over the next few seconds, then the voice returned, "What is your name?"

"Sheila Fernelli."

"Just a moment." A moment later, Sheila nearly sobbed when she heard Jim Harrison's voice. "Sheila? This is Jim. We're on the way. Keep giving me landmarks."

Sheila called out the name of the next street she turned onto. "Where are you?"

"About a mile away. We were almost at North's gate when the dispatcher called us. We had just picked Ryan up from his brother's condo about a mile from there. I've got them both with me now."

Suddenly, she flew past a sign that read, "No Outlet" and her heart sank. A few moments later she rounded a corner and slammed on her brakes at the end of a cul-de-sac. "I'm at a dead end, Jim," she sobbed at the phone. "I have to leave the car. He's not far behind me. Hurry!"

She jumped out of the car and ran wildly up the driveway to the only house in sight. As she pounded furiously on the door, she heard the screech of tires as Peter brought Fred's car to a halt at the end of the driveway.

Sheila looked around desperately and only then noticed the "For Sale" sign on the lawn and the realtor's lockbox that was hanging on the doorknob. *An abandoned house.* Suddenly the world stood still. She was enveloped in total silence as she watched helplessly while Peter Hayward strode purposefully toward her with a look of determination on his face. The only sound she heard was the pounding of her heart.

"Thought you could get away, did you? Well, you've screwed everything up now, but this is a good a place as any to dump your body. It's not as good as a hole in the woods but it will do," Peter said to Sheila, who shook with fear as he approached. "I didn't really want to kill you, you know. I really don't want to kill anyone. But I have to do what I have to do. You understand. Nothing personal, of course." He waved the gun at her.

Sick with fear, Sheila couldn't move. She opened her mouth to plead with him. "Peter," she began, her voice shaking, "please don't do this. You haven't killed anybody yet. Nobody can prove anything. You don't have to do this. Just go away. I won't tell anyone. I promise."

"Sure, sure. You won't have to tell anyone," he spat. "It'll be all over your face. Except your face is going to be lying dead in the yard out back. Now move it!" He grabbed her arm and pulled, twisting it cruelly behind her back as he shoved her toward the driveway, the gun pressed into her side.

All she could do was play along and hope for a chance to escape, slim as those odds looked. Struggling would clearly be useless, especially with the gun against her ribs. She was vaguely conscious of the fact that it hurt. She forced her feet to move away from the door, dimly aware of a dog howling on the next block. Hayward shoved her toward the back yard, releasing his hold momentarily to reach for the gate latch. The dog howled louder and louder, joined by other dogs.

Numb with fear, Sheila imagined that the dogs could all jump their fences and run to her rescue, and she concentrated her irrational thoughts on trying to make her wishes heard by the unseen animals. Suddenly she realized that the howling had been joined by a rhythmic wail, a sound that reminded her of ....

"Shit! Cops!" he blurted. He shoved her aside and turned and ran for the car as Sheila watched in stunned silence. Before he could start the car, there was the scream of tires as the black and white patrol car roared into view, skidding to a halt across the entrance to the cul-de-sac. In the blink of an eye, two policemen crouched behind open car doors, guns leveled at Peter Hayward, who stepped reluctantly out of the car and put his hands in the air.

And just that fast, it was over. Shaking and crying, Sheila collapsed to the ground where she stood. A few moments later, a second police car arrived, and Jim Harrison jumped out of the front seat and rushed over to her, while the first two patrolmen handcuffed Hayward and read him his rights. She was barely aware of Ryan North and Doug Norton being released from the rear seat by the policeman driving the car.

"Thank God you're all right!" Jim cried.

"Oh, Jim," she sobbed. "It wasn't Doug! It was Peter! He looks like Doug Norton! He was going to kill me!" She started crying again.

Realizing she was on the verge of hysteria, Jim put his arms around her and held her tightly, smoothing her hair back with one hand. "There, there, don't cry. Everything will be all right."

"How did you get here so fast?" Sheila asked, looking at him with wonder through her tears. "I couldn't believe it when the police showed up. Jim, he was going to kill me! And, oh, God, he did something to the guard at Ryan's house, and Doug's friend is inside the house. I hope he didn't kill him before he came after me. But you thought it was Doug! I thought it was Doug! How did you ever figure out the truth in time?"

Doug's face turned ashen at the mention of Fred. Without saying a word, he ran to the Corvette and climbed in. A moment later he drove around the police cars, scraped over a curb, and roared back down the street.

Jim held her closely. "It's a long story. Come on. We need to get over to North's house and see what happened there. There should be other officers there by now. We sent four cars over when the phone wasn't answered a while ago."

* * *

The rest of the day was taken up with questions and police reports and getting Fred and the guard to the hospital. The guard had been hit hard enough to fracture his skull and was hospitalized but Fred escaped with a lump and a mild concussion and was released into Doug's care. Jim asked an LAPD policewoman to take Sheila's statement, knowing his feelings would interfere with his objectivity. With her safely on her way to give a statement at the police station, he remained at Ryan's house while crime scene investigators gathered evidence from the house and dusted for fingerprints.

He had taken a brief statement from Fred before he was taken in an ambulance to the hospital. LAPD detectives would get a more comprehensive one the next morning. Doug followed the ambulance to the hospital.

Hayward had been taken to jail. Jim would save questioning him until after he got him back to Colorado. He'd demanded an attorney the moment his rights were read to him.

Ryan, Doug, and Fred had returned together to Ryan's house after Fred was released from the hospital, Ryan having apologized to Doug repeatedly for identifying him as the man he saw with the body and Doug having largely ignored him due to his concern about Fred.

Clayton had flown back to Colorado leaving Jim to tie up loose ends and start the extradition process to bring Peter Hayward back to Colorado for prosecution on a growing list of charges starting with being an accessory to the murder of Daryl Walker. LAPD's charges of assault on Fred and the guard, the attempted kidnapping of Sheila, and minor charges pertaining to the vandalism of the studio would take a back seat to the capital murder charge.

Sheila had returned to her hotel room after giving her statement to the police, where she filed the preliminary story of the solving of Daryl Walker's murder. It would take a week's worth of follow-ups to tell the whole story after all the pieces came together.

It was a weary Jim Harrison who met her at her hotel room late in the evening as she prepared to leave for the airport. When she opened the door to him, he kissed her, then wrapped his arms around her and held her close while she clung to him tightly, murmuring, "I'm so sorry I didn't listen to you, Jim. You tried to warn me."

"Let's not go over that any more, Sheila," Jim replied, sitting in the chair by the desk while she finished packing. "You're safe and that's all that matters."

"There's one thing I never figured out, Jim," Sheila said as she unplugged the laptop and put it in its case. "How in the world did Peter get the best of that armed PI who was at Ryan's house? There was a guard at the gate and I know Peter somehow knocked him out. But how did he get the guard to open the gate in the first place? It was wide open when I got there. It's always been closed before."

"He was in Ryan's Corvette, which had a gate opener in it. According to Tony DiMartino, Ryan's manager, Hayward was there when Doug was taken into custody at the studio yesterday. After Doug was subdued, he asked the policeman who arrested him to give Tony his car keys and tell him to have Ryan or Fred take the car back home. Hayward saw Tony drop the keys on a table in the editing room after they took Doug out in handcuffs. Tony got busy with the editing and forgot about the car since neither Ryan nor Fred ever came back to the studio that day. When he came in the next day, the keys were gone and the car was gone so he didn't think anything about it, figured Doug had been released and had come back for the car. But we think Hayward swiped the keys and took the car when he left that evening. We think he hid the Corvette somewhere and came in his own car to case the place; the guard had noticed a car matching the description of Hayward's Jeep drive past a couple of times but didn't pay much attention to it. Hayward probably saw Fred come back, thought he was Ryan, didn't see Doug come back with him so figured he was still in jail. He couldn't try to get in that night, since obviously Ryan would have known that Doug hadn't been released yet."

"So ... let me guess ... the next morning he drove to Ryan's house in Doug's car."

"Yes. Used the gate clicker and drove in. The guard told us Hayward beckoned him over to the car as it came through and he went over because he didn't realize it wasn't Doug at the wheel until Hayward pulled the gun on him. The guard was a rent-a-cop Fred had hired and didn't know Doug that well – mostly he knew the vehicles. Hayward made him go over by the bushes, then cold-cocked him with the gun. The guard didn't have a chance to push the alarm button, which would have alerted Fred. Hayward left him where nobody would see him from the street, and drove up to the house. According to Fred, he heard a car and when he looked out and saw the Corvette driving into the garage, he assumed Doug had been released from jail and was home. His mistake was assuming any attack would come in the night, not broad daylight, so his guard was down, plus he was so relieved to think I'd let Doug go that he just wasn't thinking. Hayward parked the Corvette in the garage and Fred went to the connecting door and opened it. Hayward managed to overpower him before he could get to his gun. He tried to get Fred to tell him where Ryan was and knocked him out with his own gun when he just kept saying he didn't know. You arrived shortly after that."

"I hate to ask, but what did Harley say when you told him I was now involved in the situation?" Sheila asked as she gave one final glance around the room to be sure she had everything.

"Nothing printable in a family newspaper," Jim replied with a wry smile. "He was glad you weren't hurt but was not happy you'd put yourself in harm's way like that. Chewed me out a bit for not keeping you on a shorter leash. I didn't try to explain that I have no control over what you do."

"I'm sorry –," Sheila started.

"Don't," Jim interrupted. "Don't go there again. You had no reason to expect Hayward to be inside Ryan's house. I wouldn't have expected it before Harley told me what Vincent told him. Neither Ryan, Fred, nor Doug had bothered to mention to me that they had been taking extreme precautions to protect Ryan after that drugging incident. Nor did they mention that Fred discovered Hayward was using a false name since Fred was still trying to confirm his story. All our conversations had to do with the murder. I was aware that Ryan had been drugged, but wasn't privy to the information that they'd concluded the person who did it was on his crew, and while they'd talked about it once, they didn't really connect that person to the murder because Ryan only very recently realized he might actually be an eyewitness and all that stuff happened before that." He stood up and picked up Sheila's suitcase. "Ready to go?"

She nodded and slung her laptop case and purse straps over her shoulder. They left the room and walked to the elevator. "How long will you have to stay here?" she asked while they waited.

"Another day, maybe two. I'll have to go through all the statements everyone took today, and we still need to get more information from Fred and the guard. Then Harley will talk to the DA, both here and in

Clear Creek County, and most likely we'll try to get Hayward to waive extradition and go back voluntarily. If not there will be more paperwork to do. He's really damned if he does, damned if he doesn't because there are enough charges he'd face here if he doesn't cooperate to put him in prison for longer than he'll get in Colorado if he testifies against Hussman."

"Other than the attack on Fred and the guard, what do they have on him here?" she asked as the elevator arrived and they stepped in.

"Kidnapping you is a big one," Jim replied. "The moment he ordered you into the house he crossed that line. Attempted murder on Ryan for the drug thing, vandalism of the studio, lying in wait with intent to commit murder, grand theft auto for taking the Corvette, plus the two counts of assault and/or attempted murder of the guard and Fred. Put that all in a pile and you're talking pretty much life in prison, possible death penalty on the kidnapping charge, but that's pretty much a joke in this state. Then there's being an accessory to the attack on Cindy Vincent. Jurisdiction for that one is up for grabs. He was physically here when he told Hussman where she lived but the attack itself was in Colorado so probably we'll get that one. So if he goes back quietly, he's up for felony murder on Daryl Walker and accessory on Cindy Vincent, but I'd guess there's a good chance the DA will let him plead to accessory on both of those in exchange for him rolling over on Hussman. Probably part of the deal will be for California not to prosecute him. We want Hussman bad, Sheila. Everything Hayward has done is penny-ante stuff compared to Hussman. He's a nasty piece of work, attacking kids like that."

The elevator opened in the lobby. Sheila dropped her room key in the slot at the desk and they walked out to the parking lot and put her luggage in the trunk of her rental car.

Jim looked down at her and reached to pull her into his arms. She rested her head against his chest. "I'm glad this is over, Jim," she said with a sigh.

"Well, it's far from over for me," he replied, "but I know what you mean. Getting both of them into custody without anyone else being killed is a huge relief. Maybe I can stop worrying about you now." He turned her face up to him and kissed her.

"I learned a lesson," she admitted, "but don't you dare tell Harley that."

Jim laughed and released her. She opened her car door and slid inside. "Thanks for coming by before I left. I'll see you in a couple of days then. Call me tomorrow?"

"You bet. Have a safe flight."

She started the car, backed out, and drove out of the lot.

Jim got into his own rental car and drove back to his own hotel to face a mountain of paperwork and reports. It had been a long day and was going to be a longer night.

He looked forward to getting home and seeing Sheila again. He already missed her.

CHAPTER 45

*H*EADLINE: *WALKER HOMICIDE SUSPECTS ARRESTED*

Clear Creek County Sheriff Harley Watson announced that the murder of Daryl Walker, son of Colorado State Senator Gene Walker, was solved today with the arrest in Los Angeles, California, of Peter Thomas Hayward of Boulder, and the arrest yesterday of Walter Albert Hussman, address unknown, in a drug sting operation in Boulder.

The case was solved after unraveling a convoluted conspiracy between Hayward and Hussman to cover up the murder and attempt to discredit or kill two potential eyewitnesses. The murder itself was committed to avoid revelation of the details of a complex drug-delivery process involving helicopters, horses, and coerced couriers.

Hayward is suspected of disposing of the boy's body, which was discovered May 7 this year on Mount Goliath, but Walter Hussman is believed to be guilty of the murder itself. Sheriff Watson stated that they have physical evidence from the murder scene that confirms that Hussman was the actual killer but declined to say what that evidence was. Hussman initially denied involvement when asked about the Walker murder but when confronted with the physical evidence, he reportedly requested an attorney and refused to answer any other questions.

The Walker boy was reported missing in October of last year and was originally believed to have run away from home.

In an exclusive interview with a Chronicle reporter, Clear Creek Sheriff's Detective Jim Harrison stated that singer Ryan North was an eyewitness who saw Hayward hiding the body. North has had amnesia caused by a riding accident moments after he saw Hayward with the body. He has only recently regained his memory of the event with the help of hypnosis, and has cooperated with the police to determine the identity of the person he saw with the body.

Hayward also is charged with the attempted abduction of Rocky Mountain Chronicle reporter Sheila Fernelli, who arrived at North's house for an interview and found Hayward lying in wait for Ryan North. He is believed to have gained access to

North's house by knocking out both a security guard and a Denver private detective, Fred Dreyer, who had been engaged by Ryan North as a bodyguard after threats were made on his life by, police believe, Peter Hayward.

Sheriff Watson told the Chronicle that police had already been looking for Hayward in connection with the drug bust in Boulder when he was arrested in California on the assault and kidnapping charges.

Hussman is also charged with attempted murder in the hit and run attack Tuesday evening on Cindy Vincent, age 13, of Golden, who has stated that she saw Hayward near the scene of the crime shortly after he buried the Walker boy in the woods the day of Ryan North's accident. Vincent is credited with finding the unconscious Ryan North while she and her father were deer hunting in the Mount Goliath wilderness area.

She is currently in an undisclosed hospital, recovering from injuries she sustained in the attack.

Harrison explained that they believe Hayward and Hussman were running a drug operation, in which drugs were dropped by helicopter in remote wilderness areas, then picked up by young couriers on horseback. The couriers are believed to have been blackmailed into cooperation.

Evidence has been found suggesting that Daryl Walker was one of these couriers, and it is believed he was killed when he tried to learn the identity of the drug dealers who were blackmailing him.

Ryan set aside the faxed copy of the story that Jerry Overholt had sent him the morning after the arrest of Peter Hayward. He sighed, and looked up at Doug and Fred, who were sitting opposite him on the couch together. Fred's head was still bandaged. "What a story," Ryan said. "Hard to believe I got involved in something like that."

"I'd say we're all lucky to be alive," Fred responded. "After all we went through, all our precautions, I was stupid enough to just open that door, never thought for a moment that Doug would have called the moment he was released. I figured he hadn't wanted to wake me. Dumb, dumb, dumb," he said, shaking his head. "I'm supposed to be better than that."

"Hayward was pretty clever. Or Hussman, whichever one of them was actually figuring things out," Ryan said. "He was smart enough to recognize the opportunity that was handed to him when Doug left his keys with Tony. He couldn't have gotten in here otherwise, not without guns blazing."

"No, that's true," Fred admitted. "The one point I emphasized with the guard service was not to approach the gate or open it to anyone except one of us, and a photo and the license plate of each of our cars was given to all the guards we used so they wouldn't be fooled by a lookalike car. But I didn't do that with our own pictures because we wanted to fool even the guards into thinking I was you so nobody but the three of us would know you were staying somewhere else."

"We did succeed in keeping Ryan safe," Doug remarked. "Even if you did nearly fill his coffin for him." He was holding Fred's hand and gave it a squeeze. Fred patted his arm with his other hand.

"I figured if I told Hayward where Ryan was, he'd kill me anyway and go after him. But he told me Hussman was making him go after Ryan and that he himself hadn't killed anyone yet. I was just hoping that he wasn't ready to leave a trail of bodies in his wake until he knew he'd taken care of the only one who could link him to the boy – Ryan. I had a sense that as long as Ryan was still alive, he wouldn't risk putting himself on the hook for other murders. Luckily I was right. He seemed – I don't know – almost apologetic, like he didn't really want to do any of this but was stuck in a situation he couldn't get out of any other way. I have a hard time thinking he would have followed through with killing the reporter. My feeling is he would have knocked her out to buy time and then just run for it at that point. Otherwise I think he would have killed me before he went after her. And would have used cyanide instead of the hallucinogen on Ryan that day. I don't think he's a killer at heart. He never really felt evil to me at the studio. I think he was scared."

"I guess the courts will sort that all out," Ryan said. "I don't know if I'll need to testify or not since I obviously didn't know what I saw that day. I guess I knew it subconsciously, though, and that's why I had a negative reaction to him in the beginning. Consciously, I thought it was Doug and that's what I repressed, but subconsciously, I knew it was Hayward." He stood up. "I think when I go back over there in a couple of days, I'm going to see about going back to the scene of the accident. I have a feeling I won't get total closure on this until I do."

Part VII
June 5-7,1994
The Luck

CHAPTER 46

"HEY, CINDY," RYAN said, quietly stroking the young girl's cheek.

Her eyes fluttered open and she smiled weakly. "Hi," she whispered.

"Now it's my turn to visit you in the hospital," he said. "I'm sorry about your accident."

She swallowed. "Did they get him?" Her left arm and leg were in casts, and her head was still bandaged.

"Who?"

"The man who wanted to hurt you."

"Yes. And they got his partner, the man who hurt you and who killed Daryl Walker. But they can't hurt anyone else now. They're in jail."

"Good." She was silent for a minute. "Hospitals aren't fun, are they?" she said presently.

"No, they're not. Your doctor said you're going to be here a few more days."

"I know. I want to go home." She swallowed hard again. "The police were here. They asked me a lot of questions. Did they ask you questions when you were in the hospital, too?"

"Yes, they did. Jim Harrison did. Do you remember him?"

"Yes. He asked me questions yesterday, right after I woke up. Then there were two other cops. They asked about my accident. Am I going to have to go to court?"

"Well, Cindy, if you do, I'll be there, too. We're in this together now. But it looks like they'll probably plea bargain."

"Does that mean that man will get out of jail?"

"No. It just means he won't get the death penalty, even though he deserves it especially after what he did to you. But he'll never get out of jail, ever."

"I hope not. I don't want to see him again. Either of them. Walter Hussman, I mean, the sound mixer who was using his name, he told him where I lived and when I was coming home. That wasn't nice."

"No, he isn't a nice man, Cindy."

Cindy looked at Ryan, then said, "I think I want to go to sleep now. I'm really glad you came to see me."

"So am I. And I'll be back tomorrow, too. The reporter, Sheila Fernelli, who interviewed you after we had lunch last week, wants to talk to you again if you're up to it. I'll bring her with me if it's okay with you."

"It's okay. I like her. She's nice. But I don't think she likes you very much."

"She thought I knew who killed Daryl Walker and wouldn't tell. She didn't know I had amnesia. She apologized. We're friends now." He didn't tell Cindy that Hayward had tried to kill Sheila. Cindy had enough to deal with knowing she herself had nearly been killed. She didn't need to know how many other people nearly died at the sound mixer's hands before her father got word to the sheriff that Cindy had seen him in the woods that day.

He kissed the girl's forehead and left.

* * *

"I guess that wraps it up for now, Ryan," he said. "If we can't make a case now, we never will."

"Don't think I don't know that you only have a case because of that fingerprint, Jim," Ryan replied with a grin. "I know my testimony is worthless to you, and I'm sure the defense attorney knows it, too."

"Well, nobody should ever try to prosecute a case with only one piece of evidence. It's the whole thing together that makes it stick. What you saw, what Cindy saw, what Hayward said to Sheila before she got away from him, what he said to Fred before he knocked him out. I'm pretty sure we could make a case even without Hayward's turning state's evidence. Unfortunately the DA feels we're better off nailing Hussman to the wall and is willing to cut a deal with Hayward to get the ironclad case against him. The attack on Cindy Vincent was so shocking he wanted to be sure Hussman never sees the light of day again. But it does sound like Hayward was coerced to do the things he did and may deserve some leniency. He had a lot of motive and opportunity to kill a lot of people and couldn't bring himself to do it."

"You know what's really ironic, Jim? Doug turned out to be the one who knew the least."

"I know. Of course, he did ID Hayward's horse after we located it."

"It would never stand up in court, Jim, and you know it. He saw that horse with a winter coat last year. Winter coats are always lighter in color than summer coats. The horse had no distinguishing marks. All Doug knows is that the horse he picked out of that equine lineup was another dun. It was darker than the one he saw that day due to his summer coat. That's even flimsier than my identifying him, or Hayward, based on a red plaid jacket and blond hair."

Jim grinned. "You trying to convince me to let them go?"

"No, I'm just glad you've got some physical evidence to corroborate all this relatively worthless eyewitness testimony I've given you." Ryan grinned. "It was a sheer stroke of luck, your finding that medallion with Hussman's thumbprint on it."

"Luck is usually a critical element in solving any murder, Ryan. Usually it comes in the form of the perp making some mistake, usually due to his own arrogance, but sometimes … you just stumble over something. In this case," he said with a laugh, "my horse stumbled over it."

Ryan chuckled. "Funny how the various horses involved ended up being such key players in the whole thing. I rode up there yesterday, you know. That rescue worker, Wayne, loaned me a horse and took me to the accident scene and the moment I looked over to where the body was, everything came flooding back as if I were seeing it live all over again."

"No more nightmares about green unicorns?"

"Not since that second hypnosis session. No headaches either, for which I am very grateful," he said with a wry smile. "So how are things with you and Sheila?"

Jim blushed, as he always did when asked about the red-haired reporter. "We had our third real date last night. Harley's fit to be tied, but so far he hasn't ordered me not to see her. I don't think he will, either. We both got our jobs done, despite each other." He gave a grin and continued, "But I think it's going to be a long time before she sticks her nose into another of my investigations. I warned her she might run into the killer if she kept trying to solve the case, and she nearly got killed when my prediction came true. I was proud of myself. I didn't even say 'I told you so.' I was so relieved we got there in time and she was all right, I couldn't rub her nose in it."

"Smart move. Did you know Doug moved in with Fred? Looks like the whole thing knocked the aversion therapy right out of him. He climbed right out of the closet, in fact, he's going to change his name back to Victor North."

"Fred told me about it. He's lucky to be alive, too. If Hayward had been thinking clearly, he'd have taken the half-second to kill him when he grabbed his car keys out of his pocket, but he was so intent on catching Sheila he didn't think about it. Probably saved himself the death penalty as a result. He hadn't killed anybody himself at that point. He managed to leave himself something to bargain with. Maybe that's why he didn't kill him. Maybe he was smart enough to realize that, but then again, he said he was going to kill Sheila."

Ryan shuddered at the thought of how many people had been endangered by his loss of memory. "Fred told me he regained consciousness and had no idea where anybody was, he saw Sheila's car but didn't know whose it was or where the driver was, or if Hayward was still in the house or not. Luckily Hayward pulled out the handcuff key when he took the car keys out of Fred's pocket and left it lying there next to Fred. Fred said he was still in a daze when the cops got there, trying to load Doug's gun that he'd found in his closet after he came to. He was lucky they didn't shoot him."

"So what are you going to do now that this is all over, Ryan?"

"The show I made will air in about a month, then I'll probably start another tour as long as I don't start having headaches again. My doctor thinks that now that I've recovered the repressed memories, the headaches are gone for good. I fired Tony, especially after he was so careless about hiring Hussman in the first place. Doug has agreed to be my manager, but he'll stay here most of the time instead of moving to Los Angeles. Fred will be in charge of security for me. And I finally got up the nerve to call my old girlfriend, Lisa, the other day. We're going to give it another try. I was in love with her, Jim, and broke up for a lot of stupid reasons that somehow don't seem all that important anymore. Doug's told me for years that I thought the sun rose and set on me, and I never knew what he was talking about. After living through this last week, I finally got it. He's right, and now I know there are a lot of things in life that matter a whole lot more than I do. Maybe I can make it work this time. I'm sure going to try."

"Well, I hope it works out for you. Lord knows, I've got a challenge of my own trying to make it work with Sheila Fernelli." He shook his head with a smile. "She's one independent woman." He walked Ryan out through to the lobby and held the security door open. "Good luck to you, Ryan," Jim said, shaking his hand at the doorway. "And thanks for your help."

"Good luck to you, too, Jim. Let me know if this goes to court." He walked out and resolutely faced a small crowd of reporters gathered in the lobby of the sheriff's office. Solving a murder had been a strange way for him to make his comeback after the accident, but he was back now. And it was okay. Being in the public eye was his life, and he had missed it. He smiled and said firmly, "One question at a time, please ... No, I am not charged with anything ... I was only a witness ... Yes, he is my brother ... You'll have to ask him about that ... No, I did not know Daryl Walker ... You'll have to ask the detective in charge ... His name is Jim Harrison ...."

Jim Harrison had returned to his desk to work on his final report when Sheriff Watson paged him on the intercom. "Jim, Patrol has located an abandoned vehicle at the Echo Lake picnic area, said to be a big fancy motorcycle. Before you say anything, I'd like to see if we can get through this case without any Harley jokes, okay? You know how I feel about motorcycles, and I could kick my parents for naming me after one."

Jim grinned into the receiver. "Sure thing, Harley. Whose bike is it?"

"Burton Chambers, a truck driver from Phoenix. They called his wife. She says he's overdue from a motorcycle rally at Pike's Peak."

"Any sign of foul play?"

"Nothing obvious, but that's for you to decide. Better head over there and find out what you can. The guy probably went for a hike and got lost. According to the wife, he's overdue two days at this point. Rescue will meet you there to start a search."

Jim glanced at the pile of papers on his desk and shrugged. "I'm on my way." He picked up his hat and jacket and headed for the door, wondering briefly if Sheila would get there before him again.

He hoped this case would turn out to be something simple and safe, that the missing biker/hiker would be found waiting with a sprained ankle at the side of a trail somewhere. With luck, the case could be wrapped up by sundown.

Or his body would be found at the bottom of a cliff and by sundown Jim's work would just be beginning.

He climbed into the Blazer and pulled out of the parking lot, glancing up at the Rocky Mountains towering over him. Whatever the outcome of the case, he was glad to be working here, where he belonged.

THE END

ABOUT THE AUTHOR

KD Ryder wrote the very first draft of this book at the age of 12 and always knew that someday it would make a great novel. At the age of 35 the research was begun to turn that pre-teen idea into a "real book." It took two years to research and write *Sing a Song of Murder*, and another 20 years of edits and revisions before the fourth major revision was self-published as an Ebook, under the title *The Elements of a Murder*. "I had to publish it so I'd stop editing it," KD has been heard to say.

Along the way the second revision was a finalist in a contest at a national writer's conference in the early 1990's. The Ebook version attracted some good reviews and generated some sales, so it is finally being published in print with a new name. True to KD's determination to stop editing it, only four minor corrections were made from the *Elements* version. "I realized that some of the technology I referred to in a few places wasn't really common yet in the time period of the story," KD admits.

KD has one other completed manuscript that is slated for release in 2014.

KD Ryder lives in a small town in northern Arizona with a menagerie including horses, dogs, cats, one sheep and a lone chicken who lives on the porch with the dogs.

www.ingramcontent.com/pod-product-compliance
Lightning Source LLC
Chambersburg PA
CBHW061509020726
47502CB00006B/1992